LAWRENCE SCOTT was born in Trinidad. His previous novel, *Witchbroom*, also published by Allison & Busby, was shortlisted for the Commonwealth Writers' Prize in 1993 and read as a BBC Book At Bedtime. A collection of short stories, *Ballad for the New World*, followed in 1994, including 'The House of Funerals', winner of the 1986 Tom Gallon Award. He is a regular contributor to Radio 4's 'Short Story' programme and his work has been internationally anthologised. Combining writing with teaching English, he lives in London.

Aelred's Sin

Aelred's Sin

Lawrence Scott

First published in Great Britain in 1998 by
ALLISON & BUSBY Limited
114 New Cavendish Street
London W1M 7FD

A catalogue record for this book is available from the British Library

ISBN 0 74900 374 X

Design and cover illustration: PEPE MOLL

Edited by Alba Editorial, S. L.

Printed in Spain by Liberdúplex, S. L.
Constitución, 19, bloque 8, local 19
08014 Barcelona

For Jenny,
Caroline and Peter

A life is not 'how it was' but how it was interpreted and
reinterpreted, told and retold.

JEROME BRUNER

... and desire had entered this monastic, this boyhood bed.

JAMES BALDWIN

No other English monk of the twelfth century
so lingers in the memory ... he escapes
from his age, though most typical of it, and
speaks directly to us ... of his restless
search for One to whom he might give the
full strength of his love.

DAVID KNOWLES

Such atrocities were the talk of Bristol
... horrible facts about the trade were
in everybody's mouth.

PETER FRYER

But only those do we call friends to whom we can fearlessly entrust our
heart and all its secrets...

AELRED OF RIEVAULX

However closely the narrative may fit the facts the fictional process has
been at work.

BRUCE CHATWIN

Acknowledgements

I wish to acknowledge particular inspiration from John Boswell's *Christianity, Social Tolerance and Homosexuality* (the University of Chicago Press). I am grateful for the balance I received from Brian Patrick Mcguire's *Friendship and Community, The Monastic Experience 350-1250* (Cistercian Publications). It was with great excitement that I returned to Jean Leclercq's *The Love of Learning and the Desire for God*, New York, 1961; Aelred of Rievaulx's *Spiritual Friendship* (trans. Mary Eugenia Laker SSND) Cistercian Publications; *Aelred of Rievaulx's The Mirror of Charity* (trans. Elizabeth Connor OCSO), Cistercian Publications. My story of Jordan owes a debt to *The History of Mary Prince* (Pandora Press) and *The Life of Olaudah Equiano, or Gustavus Vassa the African* (Longman). I wish to acknowledge further Inspiration from Maud Ellman's *The Hunger Artists: Starving, Writing & Imprisonment* (Virago); Thom Gunn's *The Man with Night Sweats* (Faber & Faber); James Walvin's *Black Ivory* (Fontana Press); and David Dabydeen's *Hogarth's Blacks* (Manchester University Press).

I wish to acknowledge my use of quotes from the following: Jerome Bruner's *Actual Minds, Possible Worlds: Acts of Meaning* (Harvard Press); James Baldwin's *Another Country* (Penguin); David M. Knowles's *The Monastic Life in England* (Cambridge University Press); Peter Fryer's *Staying Power* (Pluto Press); Bruce Chatwin's *What Am I Doing Here?* (Picador); Gerard Manley Hopkins's *Collected Poems* (Penguin); Justin Mcann's *The Rule of Saint Benedict* (Sheed & Ward); Aelred of Rievaulx's *Spiritual Friendship and The Mirror of Charity* (Cistercian Pubications); Walter Daniel's *Life of Aelred* (Cistercian Publications); *The Jerusalem Bible* (Darton, Longman & Todd); also from the singers Bobby Darrin, Bob Dylan, the Beatles, Scott Mackenzie, and The Drifters; and from the calypsonians Arrow, Lord Invader, and The Roaring Lion.

I wish to thank in particular: Caroline Griffin, Margaret Busby, Ken Ramchand, Pam Kernaghan, Jill Wight who all read the manuscript, commented and encouraged. I am grateful to the monks of Mount Saint Bernard Abbey for their hospitality and use of the novitiate and monastic libraries; Bernie and Wendy Hewing for my stay at 'Pebbles' in Steyning; Mike Shannon for a visit to Rievaulx Abbey; Mike Green for Pop research; Astra Blaug; and Vanessa Unwin, Susan Herbert and David Shelley at Allison & Busby. Without the steadfast commitment of Elizabeth Fairbairn, my agent at John Johnson Ltd, Jenny Green's critical devotion and my editor Peter Day's faith, enthusiasm and understanding, I could not have completed this book. Thank you all three.

Contents

Prologue

for Joe and Miriam

High above the plains, sheer from the valleys, the forested mountains climbed to summits in the clouds.

This was a wild place.

The green enamel cracked into rock face and crumbled under the force of cataracts, waterfalls, cascades. The rivers surged around ancient stones, pulling at the roots of old trees; dragging at these mountains, at their might and wildness.

On one of those plateaux, which you come upon with astonishment and relief, wild grasses blowing in the breeze, trees called Immortelle, a small band of men built a cloister and a church in grass and mud; wattle, *tapia*, founded on stone.

Gardens flourished and workshops hummed with industry. Truly it could be said that they prayed and worked. *Ora et labora.*

Out of this wild and uninhabitable place, they harnessed the natural fertility of the ground for the provision of food and beauty. Bees within their own communities could cultivate the pollen, attended by butterflies; the monks extracted the honey. They cobbled shoes. They tended poultry and farmed a herd of cows which grazed in a highland savannah. They dammed the river for a reservoir.

Within this place of natural solitude, they fashioned spaces of light and shadow; shade from the heat, gardens with flowers and shrubs; oleander, pink like coral, white like first-communion clothes; climbing plants on arbours and trellises, bougainvillea and allamanda. At the centre of this perfected place, a fountain which small birds delighted in spilled its light. The birds darted to and fro. In this pool of light, goldfish swam.

Within these walls, this band of men became attached to higher qualities. They sought to detach themselves from mortals. They sought a Divine Wisdom. As one of their ancient writers wrote of them: ' ... as angels might be, they were clothed in undyed wool spun and woven from the pure fleece of the sheep. So named and garbed and gathered together like flocks of seagulls, they shine as they walk with the whiteness of snow.'

This was a paradise, a cloistered heaven.

Outside this cloister, they built a school for boys. They hoped that some of these young boys would join them.

The boy was twelve years old when he left the old wooden school, which smelt of coconut oil and which leant against the big stone church of Notre-Dame de Grace to go to the school in the mountains, following his best friend and the ideals of the monk, Dom Maurus.

Dom Maurus had white hands and beneath his pale skin the veins ran dark blue.

Blood, like Quink ink.

The boy saw the monk's blood written on the white pages of his copy book. When he lifted his eyes in church, he saw the same blood in the veins which ran in the white marble of the altar and along the arms and legs of the replica of Michelangelo's *Pietà*: the limp, naked, dead Christ in Mary's his mother's lap.

Dom Maurus's breath smelt of the white wafers of holy communion and the red wine which was blood and which the boy did not drink. It was not the custom then to commune under both kinds.

In the whirl of the school-yard play, the monk drew the boy and his best friend close to him, into the clouds of his white cotton habit, the wind taking his scapular. He hugged them. The monk's armpits smelt of incense.

Here, close to his friend, in the folds of the monk's habit, in the embrace of his cowl, the boy looked out at the world of other friends whose blood he could not see below the colour of their skin. In the heat, he saw rouge playing like a flame on their hard black cheeks. Red and black like a jumbie bead.

When, now, I look back at this boy, it is these things - blue veins, blood, holy communion wafers, the smell of wine and incense when caught up in the clouds of the monk's white cotton habit with his best friend - which made him leave his mother and father, his brother and sisters, to follow his best friend and the ideals of the monk, Dom Maurus.

When I look back, with him, I see his lost friends with skin the colour of cinnamon, eyes the green light of the sea. Others I see with skin the colour of black coral, eyes like tamarind seeds. Tamarind seeds in white shells. Still others, lost, with the skin that smelt of incense and sandalwood, black skin from Calcutta; eyes the colour of cumin powder and eyelashes which flicker in the breeze which blows in the sugar-cane fields.

So, the boy left the land of sugar-cane fields and the old

racatang town which tumbled down to the sea, and he climbed over the cocoa hills to the plains with the swamps, the rice fields and the oyster beds. He entered where the plains touched the entrance to the cool valleys.

The boy, with his best friend, ascended the mountain road to the monastery with its school.

They grew like Jonathan and David.

The boy became sick, homesick. He wouldn't eat. He entered the infirmary. His best friend was stronger and he lost him among the other boys. In the days afterwards, he kept looking for him. He hunted him, but did not find him.

On his first Sunday, very early in the morning, when it was still as dark as the night, the infirmarian, Dom Placid, woke him. After he had dressed, Dom Placid led him down the mountain path towards the abbey church. As they neared the church in the morning darkness, the boy could see a glimmer of the dawn growing behind the mountains. He heard the murmur of the pigeons. One pigeon's word, dou-dou. Then, like the waves he remembered hearing break repeatedly on the sands of his island, over and over again, he heard the antiphonal chant of the monks in choir, exchanging psalmodic couplets in the compositions of St Gregory which were to make him feel always that he had heard the angels singing in the interval between two waves.

He vowed to be one of those angels. He prayed: 'Had I but wings, I cry, as a dove has wings, to fly away, and find rest!'

The schoolboy visited the young monk in his cell. When he entered the young monk's cell and closed the heavy door behind him and sat himself on the low stool, Dom Placid, the young monk, said, What can I tell you about today?

The young boy answered, Tell me a story of one of your saints. Because what he sought was perfection and he delighted to hear of it in others, so that he might imitate them.

Dom Placid treasured the boy's ardour and cherished his young pupil's friendship, and on this day that is now remembered, he told him the story of Aelred. A young boy like yourself, who once sought perfection a long time ago, he told him. He was one of those Angles who would be an angel. Dom Placid smiled.

The young boy laughed at St Gregory's pun, remembering the story from the previous day.

Far away, in Northumbria, and a long time ago, a young boy called Aelred, whose beauty and manners were marvelled at, attracted the king of Scotland, and he asked the boy's father to let him come and be schooled with his own sons. They were called Simon and Waldef. Quite soon, Aelred became fond of his classmates. He grew in their favour and in their father's.

As time went on, Aelred became more than just a boy, but a fair youth. He himself tells us the story in his dialogue on friendship, which he wrote as an older man, remembering his youthful reading of Cicero's *De Amicitia*. Looking back on his youth, he tells us how he lost his heart to one boy and then to another during his schooldays. He was drawn by their charm and gave himself up to the affection which he felt. He tells us that he gave himself up to love in the way of youth. Then there was one whom he loved more than any other and who became dearer to him than anything else in life. This frightened him.

Why was he frightened, Dom Placid? the schoolboy asked.

He was frightened because now he was no longer a boy with the desires and feelings of a boy, but a man who knew that his feelings were a strong passion and that they could engulf him. He tells us so himself. The desire and passion which were awakened in him would never be satisfied. He would do some wrong, and he knew that the one whom he loved above all else would leave him. He loved him extravagantly.

He was burnt with a fire he could not put out. The sweetness of his love was mixed with pain.

Is love painful, then, father? the boy asked. Dom Placid nodded his agreement, but kept on with his story.

Poor Aelred was lifted up and then cast down. His blood raged and in his torment he felt driven towards the abyss of death. Then he whom he loved and delighted in more than anything else in life left the court and joined the religious life.

Aelred was desolate.

At this time, he took a journey south and learnt of a band of men who were building a monastery on the wide banks of the River Rye below a wild wood. Aelred went there with a young friend and was so struck by what he saw, a band of men living and working together for love, that he asked his young friend if he would like to visit again the next day. When the young friend said he would like to, Aelred led the way to the river bank and the new wooden building which served as a monastery in the wild place. Immediately, the two young men, Aelred and his young friend, asked for entrance into the monastery.

The sight of a band of men living for love drew Aelred from the court and his wandering love. Here he could confess his love without fear, as in the *Song of Songs*, 'Let him kiss me with the kisses of his mouth.' These men got his allegiance.

Do you want to hear more, little friend? Dom Placid asked the schoolboy at his feet on the low stool.

Oh, yes, Father, you can't leave it there, he answered.

We must, but you can return tomorrow.

The next day, the schoolboy came again to the young monk, Dom Placid's cell.

There the story of Aelred continued.

Aelred found at Rievaulx all that he had desired, which was to love and be loved. The monastic day, the Rule, the Scriptures and the love of his brothers set the boundaries for the love which men can have for each other.

In time, Aelred became novice master and then abbot and taught his monks, in one office and then another, that to live without love and friendship was to live like a beast. He loved his monks so much and taught them so well that it was said by one of his monks, so vehemently was this lover of us loved by us.

Aelred's young love was so caught up that his younger admiration for the beauty of his youthful friends did not lessen in intensity but was transformed, so that a young monk's face could speak to him, his listening, his silence. He loved them without fear, without guilt, without the fever heat within the blood. He wrote his treatise *Spiritual Friendship* and has left this for us, young monks like me, and schoolboys like you - Dom Placid smiled at his youthful pupil - so that we can read it and take example of how the love of one man for another may be embraced, how their hands may touch and how the kiss of love may be given.

The boy went back to school with his heart full of passion and his head filled with ideals.

And me - I follow where he tells me of that life and love, along lines written in blood, blue, like Quink ink. Allow me this hagiographic beginning, this preface to a brother's story. One story lies within another.

Robert de la Borde,
Malgretoute, Les Deux Isles, West Indies.
April 1988

The Clothing

Draw me in your footsteps, let us run.
Song of Songs

The Abbot sat on his throne with the prior and sub-prior, one on either side, one step down on the dais. In seniority, the other monks sat themselves around the chapter house. As the darkness of the early spring evening filled Ashton Park, those monks who sat facing the windows that overlooked the terrace could see the receding shadows of the day and the last smouldering light in the bare wood banked high above the fields.

They all waited in silence.

After the coughing had subsided and the arranging of the voluminous black cowls with their sleeves like the wings of archangels or enormous bats, depending on how you looked at them, had settled, the community waited, hooded, with heads bowed. The silence and then the swish of a cowl in the corridor outside still filled the older monks with anticipation. The soft, rapid footsteps which stopped at the door of the chapterhouse brought back longing to the older monks, and recent memories to the young professed monks and for the novices newly clothed who were sitting erect on the edge of their front benches. There was a firm knock on the chapter-house door.

'Enter,' the Abbot said, breaking the silence.

After another moment of anticipatory silence, Father Justin, the novice master, entered. He walked to the centre of the chapter house, lowered his hood and bowed to the Abbot. He spoke, facing the Abbot on his throne with his monks around him. 'Reverend Father, there is a young man at the door of the monastery who seeks admittance as a novice into our community.'

'Let him enter,' the Abbot answered solemnly.

'Amen,' the community recited in unison.

Father Justin bowed and left the chapter house.

The community waited. The early spring evening closed in. The shadows of the evergreens folded along the gravel path. Still, one last wood pigeon in the copse the other side of the park called to its mate.

Then Father Justin went to the front parlour of the monastery, where Brother Jean Marc de la Borde was waiting.

The young brother too heard the last wood pigeon of the declining evening: *dou-dou, dou-dou*, it sounded like to him. That a bird here should speak to him as he had been spoken to as a child moved him. Again, one last time, the wood pigeon sounded. It had flown to the apple orchard, to a branch sticky with new buds.

The young postulant was dressed in the brown suit, white cotton shirt and brown tie that he had worn the day he had entered the monastery three months before in that winter of winters in 1963. They had been kept in the mending room, where the old habits were repaired and the new cassocks, cowls and scapulars were cut and sewn by Brother Malachi.

His home clothes had been kept for this occasion. If he had decided not to ask for admittance to the monastery as a novice, but rather to abandon his vocation, he would have the clothes he came in to return home. Or it might have been still worse, if, as sometimes did happen, a novice had been asked to leave. Then he would have had his clothes to re-enter the world and the Abbot would return to him the money he had come with, so that he could get a train to Bristol or London, or wherever. What then?

And some, would run off suddenly into the night.

Dou-dou, dou-dou. A voice had come to live in the coo of a bird.

Brother Jean Marc de la Borde sat on the green leather upholstered chair in the small parlour. Leaded windows with yellow and red glass depicting scenes from the lives of monastic saints caught the last light. He did not recognise these saints, English saints. The furniture smelt of new polish. He sat and stared at his black boots which had been his friend's, Ted's, as if he had just this day come to St Aelred of Ashton Park from Les Deux Isles asking for admittance. He stared at Ted's black boots. But he did not think of him; no, not now, not at this moment.

He remembered the stories he had read when he was a schoolboy and first thought that he had a vocation. He remembered the stories of the young boys Maurus and Placid who had come to Subiaco to join the first monastery of St Benedict. He wanted to be like them, young boys giving up all for this ideal.

Then he thought of the story of the young Aelred of Rievaulx that Dom Placid had told him. And then, then he thought of Ted.

He had made a general confession of his life's sins in preparation for his clothing. He had confessed all again. He prayed for Ted. He was doing this for Ted. It seemed that way now.

This afternoon, after working on the farm, helping

Brother Stephen milk the cows, he had stood at the sink in the dairy and let the hot water scorch his hands and arms, washing off the sweet sticky smell of the fresh milk. 'You'd better go off now,' Brother Stephen said. 'It's *your* night.'

He walked slowly up to the abbey from the farm. Spring was in the air. Bulbs which had come before Easter in Lent crowded the grassy ground between the pollarded lime trees. How quickly time had gone since then. Lent with pussy willows for palms on Palm Sunday; then early Easter, with all the new flowers he had to learn. He pulled at the rosemary bush, rolled the leaves in his palms, lifted the crushed leaves and inhaled deeply a new smell, the smell of Ashton Park.

He entered the basement where the work boots were kept, wiping his hands on his denim blue smock. He washed again with soap, a rough detergent soap, yellow in the scoop of the old basin. The dimly lit place smelt of socks and leather boots, mud and silage. It smelt of the musty scent of sweat. He took off his wellingtons, peeling off his work stockings, sweaty like in the boarding-school changing-rooms after games.

They stood around him, the boys of then, the others. Even now he had to chase them from his mind.

He fetched down off the shoe rack Ted's black boots. He found his clean white stockings curled inside. No one in the community knew that these had been Ted's boots. The soles were thick and new, new leather. His mother had had them resoled before he left home.

In the mending room, he hung up for the last time the black serge cassock that he had been wearing as a postulant, and took down his brown suit, white cotton shirt and brown tie, which had been labelled and hung in the wardrobe marked 'Postulants'; *postulare*, to ask for, to ask for entry. He had been doing that for three months. He was now asking formally for that from the community. He was seeking God.

His brown suit and white cotton shirt and tie still smelt of his home far away. They smelt of his mother and father, his brother and sisters, whom he had left. They smelt of his country. They smelt of heat and sunshine and haze rising up to a blue sky above green cane fields and the shade of the cocoa hills. They smelt of wood smoke in the board-house villages of the poor rising from the dusty backyards and barrack rooms from where Toinette came. 'Morning, morning, *Dou-dou.*'

Toinette came to cook and clean, to wash and iron. Toinette came to mind children. He could still smell on his cotton shirt the suds of soap on whites in sunshine bleaching, the steam from the hot flat iron.

He heard Toinette. 'You get a lot of loving, *oui.*'

What was he doing here? A moment of doubt.

He smelt that smell of travelling in aeroplanes on the sleeve of his jacket. There was a musty smell of Ashton Park, then of his home Malgretoute: in spite of everything.

He put his hands into the pockets of his brown pants. He half expected to find something there. Something. He remembered a letter pressed in there for a week before he could give it. Another, received, which burnt his leg.

Brother Jean Marc de la Borde heard the swish of Father Justin's cowl in the corridor outside the parlour. He saw his hooded form through the glass door. His heart was beating fast.

Father Justin smiled as he entered the parlour. 'They're ready for you.'

Brother de la Borde smiled nervously and pushed back the heavy dark brown hair from his brow and drew back the loose strands of hair behind his ears with his fingers. He had wet his long hair in the washroom upstairs in the novitiate to keep it tidy. He followed Father Justin to the chapter house. He pressed his hair down again.

Ted's boots echoed through the cloister.

'It will be fine,' Father Justin smiled.

As they entered the chapter house, Brother de la Borde noticed his guardian angel, Dom Benedict, smile. Yes, his eyes had gone straight to where he knew Benedict would be sitting. Ever so quickly, a stolen glimpse, and then his eyes were lowered. He had learnt the rule of St Benedict, passed his test at the Abbot's Council, the Twelfth Degree of Humility: 'whether he is in the oratory, in the garden, on the road, in the fields, or anywhere else and whether sitting, walking, or standing', a monk 'should always have his head bowed and his eyes downcast, pondering always the guilt of his sins.'

Dom Benedict was a little amused at seeing his protégé dressed as he had been that first winter afternoon when he had arrived brown and bonny from a country far away. He was relieved that he had got through that terrible winter, that he had succeeded through his postulancy. His smile was one of encouragement, of congratulation, of admiration, and Brother de la Borde felt it.

Now he knelt in the centre of the chapter house with folded arms and lowered his eyes to the floor in front of him until the Abbot addressed him, asking him, 'What do you seek?'

Brother de la Borde raised his lowered eyes and gave the formal response to the Abbot, the representative of Christ on earth. 'I seek to serve God with Charity in this community.'

'Come forward,' the Abbot announced.

Father Justin led Brother de la Borde up to the Abbot's throne, where he knelt on the top step of the dais in front of the Abbot.

Then the ceremony of the clothing of a novice began.

The Abbot, assisted by Father Justin, took off the brown jacket. 'You must take off the old man.'

The community responded, 'Amen.'

The rubrics according to the ancient traditions of monasticism were once again followed. The brown jacket was folded and given to the acolyte of the clothing to be returned to the mending room. The Abbot unbuttoned his shirt at the top and removed his tie, reiterating, 'You shall take off the old man and put on the new,' this time intoning the exhortation.

Again, the community responded, 'Amen.'

The tie was folded and also given to Father Justin, who folded it once more and hung it neatly over his arm, from where the acolyte took it and laid it to rest with the brown jacket.

The young brother would not be stripped naked here. Later, he would remove his trousers and shirt when he returned to his cell.

. The Abbot then proceeded to clothe Brother de la Borde with the new man in the habit of a Benedictine novice. First the cassock: 'I clothe you with the new man who is Christ.' Then he unrolled the leather girdle: 'I gird you with the girdle of chastity.' He buckled it tightly around his waist. The scapular with the hood was placed over his head: 'With the scapular of peace.' Last of all, he shook out the cloak of the novice: 'And the cloak of our brotherhood.' After each admonition and gesture, the community responded with the response, 'Amen.'

Fully clothed in the ancient habit of the Benedictine novice, his novice's scapular reaching only to his knees and not full length to the floor, Brother de la Borde was marked out as a neophyte in this community of celibate men.

He was here to seek God according to the rule of the Holy Father St Benedict, who first wrote his Rule for Monks in the cave at Subiaco in the Italian hills near Rome in the fifth century: a young man, escaping the materialism of Roman society, his young passion tempted by the devil in the shape of a beautiful woman, so that he had to throw himself into a patch of brambles to stem that passion before moving to his monastery at Monte Casino. Brother de la Borde remembered his *Lives of the Saints*. They had been his fairy tales. His adventure stories had been the lives of the martyrs.

Jean Marc de la Borde forged this ideal out of what he saw when he was small: his parish priest, Father Maurus, with veins the blue of the blue in marble, blood like Quink ink, resplendently white like an angel in the white habit of monks on the missions because of the scorching heat, kneeling before the Blessed Sacrament, performing the liturgy of the Mass, intoning the Gregorian chant whose inflections moved him with their antiphonal intervals. He knelt in the shadow and light of these memories.

Later, when he went to his school, which was run by Benedictine monks, he came to love the measured order of their day, which he could observe closely, controlled by the tolling of bells: the angelus in the morning, at noon, at six o'clock in the evening and at sunset. He followed their call to the seven hours of the Divine Office: Matins and Lauds, Prime, Terce, Sext, None, Vespers and finally Compline, chanted in the darkness of the choir.

These monks, who seemed to float a few feet above the ground as if in permanent levitation, whose liturgy broke upon Jean Marc like the waves that broke upon the beach at Sans Souci on Les Deux Isles with the rhythm of the tides, became the heroes of his adolescence.

The ideal formed to enter their choir, clothed in their habit, reclining on the misericord, offering back to his brothers antiphonally the inspired chant of Saint Gregory: '*Dixit Dominus domino meo, sede a dexteris meus Gloria Patri et Filio et Spiritui Sancto... Secut erat in principio et nunc et semper, et in secula seculorum, Amen...*'

He convinced himself of all this. He saw Ted's face and renewed his commitment.

The moment of the naming arrived. 'Brother de la Borde, henceforth you shall be known among us as...' The Abbot paused for effect. The young novice held his breath. He could feel the community around him hold their breaths before the Abbot's secret was revealed: his name, his monastic name, always a point of excitement for the old monks, who had known many clothings, and for the younger monks, for whom it was relatively new, reminding them of their own clothing ceremony. The Abbot continued, 'Brother Aelred.'

Everyone sighed, smiling with approval, and the Abbot

looked around with almost a smirk of self-satisfaction that he had kept them all guessing. Would it be Chrysostom, who had just died? They didn't have a Leo. Everyone had had their own theory on the naming in the preceding weeks.

The new novice had an enviable name: the name of their monastery, St Aelred's of Ashton Park; the name of the great English Cistercian of the twelfth century, Aelred of Rievaulx.

The new Aelred remembered the story he had been told as a boy. He remembered his question then. Is love painful? He saw Dom Placid's answer in the nod of his head.

The Abbot drew him towards his embrace and gave him the kiss of peace on both cheeks.

Then the acolyte of the clothing came forward with a pair of scissors on a silver salver and offered it to the Abbot, who took the scissors and symbolically cut off a lock of the new Brother Aelred's hair.

Fully clothed and named, baptised anew, the old man stripped off and the new man put on, Brother Aelred was led by Father Justin to the opposite end of the chapter house, where he sat on a stool especially placed for him.

The chief cantor intoned the clothing sequence, '*Ubi caritas et amor, Deus ibi est*': 'Where there is love and charity, there is God.'

As each verse was in turn picked up by the choir of monks, antiphonally, the entire community, led by the Abbot, came to Brother Aelred where he sat on his stool clothed in the black habit of a young Benedictine novice. Beginning with the Abbot and followed by the prior and even the old men of the community, they knelt, each one, and, using the silver jug and basin offered by the acolyte of the clothing, they poured water over the naked feet of Brother Aelred, who had, immediately on sitting down, taken off his shoes and socks, his friend Ted's boots.

They washed his feet and dried them with the linen towel handed by the other acolyte of the clothing and then kissed his feet. All the while, the choir chanted the clothing sequence: '*Ubi caritas et amor, Deus ibi est.*' Each member of the community performed this act, as Christ had done to his disciples the night before he was betrayed and had said to them, 'Do unto each other as I have done to you.' It was on that night that the beloved John, he whom Jesus loved, had lain his head upon his chest.

Then it was the turn of the simple-professed monks, led by Dom Benedict. Brother Aelred kept his eyes lowered, but he noticed, in the solemnity, the encouraging smile of Benedict, as he liked to call him when he thought of him, remembering how kind he had been over the last three months helping him to settle in; Benedict, his guardian angel.

Aelred returned the smile of encouragement, lifted up by this wonderful expression of love and initiation into the community. His smile flickered over his lips as Benedict knelt in front of him and washed and dried his feet and then bent to kiss them. His lips on his bare foot. After kissing his feet he looked up and smiled again.

'*Ubi caritas et amor, Deus ibi est.*'

Brother Aelred was so overcome by these acts, and by the chant of love and charity, that he was thankful for Brother Stephen tickling his feet in jest, bringing a small irreverence to bear upon the solemnity of the moment. Brother Stephen had whispered earlier in the day while they were working on the farm, 'Make sure you wash your feet well before tonight.' Brother Stephen was well known for these little pranks and Brother Aelred already hoped he would get to work on the farm again with the old brother whose way with the animals was almost as inspired as St Francis of Assisi's.

As the community filed out of the chapter house to process along the cloister to the church for Compline, the last office of the day, they each, starting with Father Abbot, stopped to give the new Brother Aelred the kiss of peace, the monastic kiss offered on each cheek with their hands firmly placed on his shoulders. By now he was again properly shod in his friend Ted's black boots. The young monk, thus embraced, felt at one with his brothers.

Then it was Benedict's turn, and, quite spontaneously, they broke the formal embrace and hugged each other. Aelred's heart grew as big as his chest. They held on to each other and their cheeks brushed against each other, first the right and then the left. Benedict squeezed his hand and filed by as he made way for the next brother. The monks coming after smiled, knowing that Benedict was Aelred's guardian angel.

The chant continued. '*Ubi caritas et amor, Deus ibi est...*': 'Where there is love and charity there is God.' The refrain was picked up by the whole choir processing out of the chapter house into the monastic church for Compline.

In the dark church, with only the single candles on either side of the altar flickering, the acolyte of the door closed the doors quietly and stood inside the entrance, before proceeding to his place in the choir, to allow the acolyte of the choir to implore the Abbot's blessing upon the whole community and upon himself, before he should read the opening lesson for Compline. '*Jube, Domne, bene-dicere*': 'Pray, Father, a blessing.' The hooded monks with bowed heads received their Father's blessing, and then listened to the admonitions of the lesson: 'Fratres...': 'Brothers, be sober and watch, because your adversary the devil, like a roaring lion, goes about seeking whom he may devour. Resist him...'

The Confiteor was then intoned: '*Mea culpa, mea culpa, mea maxima culpa.*' The monks knelt to examine their consciences. They beat their breasts. The psalms were intoned and sung reclining upon the misericords. Brother Aelred was one of these in the church militant who joined their voices with the church suffering and the church triumphant with the hosts of angels, archangels, cherubim and seraphim, transcending themselves and being the mystical body of Christ.

The new Brother Aelred left for bed exalted by the tones of the 'Salve Regina' still in his ears. His fellow monks paid their visits to the altars of the saints, the Lady Chapel and the Chapel of the Blessed Sacrament.

The following morning, after Prime, Brother Aelred sat with a white sheet thrown about him, as Brother Walter shaved off his thick brown curls with an electric shaver. 'You'll soon get to like it, brother, and your hood will keep you warm.' Brother Walter tidied up the back and sides and mowed over the top once more, giving Aelred the monastic tonsure. He was like a sheep being shorn. He was now like a sheep led to the slaughter, a sacrifice for Christ, shorn of the adornment of the world, the sensuality of the flesh. His thick dark curls lay on the tiled floor of the sacristy.

Aelred stood fully clothed as a novice. He had removed his brown pants and wore only the customary vest and underpants beneath his habit. He stood in Ted's boots.

The Guest House, Ashton Park:
23 September 1984

Scattering sleep from our minds
Now before dawn...

I keep his breviary open at the appropriate hour, the ribbon in the crease where he marked his pages. I learn my hours and enter my brother Jean Marc's life, Aelred's. J. M. we always called him at home.

It was Chantal's, my sister's, idea. Call him J. M., Mummy.

This is a kind of waking sleep. What am I waking up to? What is it that I don't want to stir? Even now, having come all this way.

Robert, the guest master called my name, knocking me up for Matins. I sit here in my small room, my cell, neat and straight. A narrow bed is in the corner on the right as I enter from the dim and silent corridor. There is a wash basin in the other corner by the window seat, below a window in two stone arches. There is a narrow desk against the other wall and a crucifix on the wall above me. A cell like the one he had: I'm here for him. This is a younger brother's pilgrimage. Will there be a conversion for me in this? Me so different, our lives taking such different paths.

Cocoa planter! I say to myself, What you doing here, boy?

I sit with my prologue, the way I remember the *Lives of the Saints* told. We had the same book, read by our mother. Is this a fiction like those, a way of telling of a younger time in another place? Was his wish to be a saint? His life can now seem like a hagiographic tale itself. One part of

me writes it that way. To write it out is to understand it.
That was his method. Without his journals, I would be
nowhere. But then I'm also out of my depth.

I speak of him as another, Aelred. That was the custom,
named for a saint, clothed. It helps too with the distance
which time has wrought. I've made a character of him. To
think of him as not my brother, as someone else who did
those things, is perhaps easier. But there is too the brother
I always loved, for sure; the one who went away, the one I
lost.

As I say, I have his words, and words are everything:
journals, letters and my own words, enraptured by his
ideas. I was inspired by his youth, yes, but startled and
shocked. There is a sense of occasion, vocation. But can I
face up to what in some ways I don't want to know? I let
words stand on their own. Do they ever, those words? I
find myself hardly able to utter them. Our mother would
use that expression.

Unutterable, she would say, something that should not
have happened, something that should not be said, a
story which should not be told.

I know a secret history of Ashton Park. I know that this
will not be a pious story. The monastic life? Not the one I
imagined he had left all of us for.

I have come to see Benedict, his friend. I am confronted with my own memories as well as his. Things I don't
like to think about myself. It's a strange feeling, because
it's as if I'm the older brother now as I resurrect that
young man in the first year of his monastic life.

What can Benedict tell me? Will he? Can I really expect
him to talk to me of things I have read in the journals,
explain them to me, perhaps?

In front of me, the monastic day:

Sunday	Weekdays
3.30 Matins and Lauds	
7.00 Prime	
8.00 Breakfast	Conventual Mass and Terce
9.00 Conventual Mass	8.50 Breakfast
and Terce	10.30 Coffee
(coffee after Mass)	
12.15 Sext	
12.30 Dinner	
2.15 None	
3.30 Tea	
5.15 Vespers	5.30 Vespers
6.00 Supper	
7.30 Compline	

His day. This was how he spent his days.

Because he went away, and I was the one son among a family of sisters, I had to grow into our father's shoes and take on the management of the cocoa estate at Malgretoute. Life has fashioned me differently; from the same mother and father, the same home; loved and admired by the same sisters, by Toinette, the same nurse. How is that possible?

Now, I'm coming here, leaving the world I know, to try to say how it happened, tell it to myself, tell it all. Will that be possible, to tell it all? How do I remember it, now? Can I bear to? Ted? Ted and the others, they, the others, who still stand around me. They, those boys, who stood around him, him and Ted. This is in another place, in a younger time. That's what comes back on top of everything else. Is that why I'm here?

I am following the ritual. I get to know this life, this liturgy. The bells are so unashamedly, so scandalously, I think, ringing out, like loud gonging prayers themselves, waking up the neighbourhood. It is the voice that calls us to prayer, pealing out over fields, the distant town, over the stone enclosure wall and the sheep like stones as the world sleeps. '*Domine, labia mea aperies et os meum annutiabit laudem tuam...*': 'Lord, open my lips, and my mouth shall announce your praise.' I hear them in choir.

Open my lips. I need to tell his story. I owe it to him, owe it to myself.

The city hums at the edge of the fields, a horizon, an amber hum. There is the silence and my scratching pen, as when I'm up late at night at Malgretoute having to do the accounts. The rain drips in the cocoa. I miss home. I've been here longer than I first planned. I think of Krishna looking after the estate. I'm lucky to have such an expert to leave things to. I thought I would come and settle these affairs and return quickly. But it's taken much longer.

The affairs of the heart take much longer.

Keep an open mind, Joe said to me as he drove me down from Bristol. We had got drunk the night before, in the flat with all of J. M.'s things scattered on the floor, all those red notebooks with black spines, photographs of our parents, one of me.

Joe, out of the blue, had written, 'I have some things which belong to you.' I'm surprised how easily I get on with Joe. He's like any other guy really. Looks like a monk with his crew cut, not the earring though. I don't know of anything we have in common, except my brother, of course, and his desire to drink rum, a love of the sun and cricket. I go everywhere with my cuatro, so I strummed and sang him an old-time calypso that first night when he and his sister Miriam welcomed me to the flat in Bristol. I taught them the refrain: '*Sans humanité.*' A kind of wake!

Sing, 'Rum and Coca-Cola', Joe said.

They all want that tune.

In the clubs, he said, it's the popular calypso, Arrow's 'Hot Hot Hot', that they enjoy.

Yesterday afternoon, I took the road alongside the farm towards the fields. There I found a path, a forest trail pointed with yellow arrows, painted at intervals on fences and posts. I followed assiduously as if the place would yield something. I wanted it to. But always there is this double thing. I don't want to know.

I was circling the enclosure of the abbey, keeping the stock bell tower in view, the rest of the enclosure hidden. The landscaping of the natural woods encloses the cloister. I left the fields, and over a stile, made through some gorse scrub. I learn the words: gorse, scrub. I would say 'bush' back home. I learn that from J. M. He's provided me with a miscellany of English flora and fauna. Still I was being pointed onwards.

I surveyed this English park the way I do my cocoa estate. Just beyond the gorse bushes, through a little wood of oaks, I came into a clearing. The phrases are becoming almost natural, like 'Down by the mango tree, take a left for the pasture'.

If I could only bring him back!

Then I came upon it. At first, I hadn't taken in this other noise. I was attuned to the fields, the silence and the sheep like stones, the abbey getting smaller. But then, more than the silence, the hum drew me to the very brink of the escarpment. It horrified me, as it fell sheer in well excavated layers, like giant steps: a vast quarry of Bath stone, the guest master Father Dominic told me it's called. In the centre there was a large oval pool of water glinting on its floor like a mirror, or, a mass grave. Just a fancy.

Long ago, there had been fields here, the monks tell me. Here they had climbed. And even a longer time ago, I learnt, from J. M.'s journal, that dogs hunted their masters' prey in the nearby fields. I had thought that was a dream, but it was true. I once thought that it was a myth. The terrible trade! We were forced to confront it, my generation, in 1970 with Black Power! What do the dreams tell of that time? To dream a time past - is that possible? They stand around your bed in the light which is filtered through mosquito nets, like those of a waking child in another place, shadowy behind a scrim. Power! Power! So, he had found the beginnings of our history here?

Chunky lorries, almost like toys, those dinky cars we played with as boys, the ones of his I still have in a box somewhere at Malgretoute, were descending the terraced excavation, being loaded and then making the ascent. Huge arc lamps were harnessed to very tall pylons and girders for night work. Their metal glinted in the afternoon sun. My horror turned to awe and then fascination at the work. A notice told me that blasting took place between 11.00 a.m. and 2.00 p.m. I was safe. It was 2.45 p.m. I hadn't heard any blasting earlier. I circled the escarpment and then descended the other bank into a wood of silver birches, losing myself before finding my yellow trail again. I was lost among the silver birches.

They're holding hands. Look at them now. Phrases and conversations with myself, with him, his words. He's become word to me.

Dreams still haunt. Dogs - the cry of dogs still sounds where the water trembles over small blue stones the colour of blue blood, tongues lapping at the blood, flowing into the lake in the spinney. I see another running. Then, he turns, and throws a stone.

My memory haemorrhages with his words, phrases, metaphors.

In another river, in another place, a boy dives like a shaft of light into a bronze rock pool. Like an angel, scarlet like the petals of the flamboyante.

I make his poetry mine.

Both of them, angels? Athletes, angels! No, hardly angels.

The Feast Day

*In his longed-for shade I am seated
and his fruit is sweet to my taste...*
Song of Songs

The polished oak staircase ascended from the sacristy through three floors to where it tapered and became a smaller winding stair to the attic. It was Brother Aelred's daily chore to sweep these stairs, dust the banisters and polish both the stairs and the banisters after Prime, before going to his cell for Lectio Divina, his daily spiritual reading. It was divine reading. *Legere et audire,* to read and to hear, was the injunction. For these chores, he changed into a simple, cotton, denim smock with a hood, tied at the waist with his leather girdle: the girdle of chastity which the abbot had wound around his waist at his clothing.

The impressive staircase ascended in tiers. At the third landing was a mezzanine floor which housed the monastic library. Then the staircase continued up to the first, second and third floors on which were the cells of the senior monks. Those corridors were out of bounds for the novices. This was different to what the Rule of St Benedict instructed: 'The younger brethren shall not have their beds by themselves, but shall be mixed with the seniors.' Now, they were forbidden to go to a senior monk's cell.

It was now seven thirty in the morning. Prime had been at seven o'clock, and the community had been up since three thirty for the singing of Matins and Lauds, after which there were the Low Masses of the priests of the community. Brother Aelred had served the prior's Mass this morning.

Aelred had already had his breakfast of toast, honey and coffee. His enthusiasm for his new life was evident in his prompt rising for Matins, and his preparation for and participation in the liturgy. He took his daily chores seriously. If Father Justin, the novice master, had anything to correct in his charge, it was a tendency to rush from one thing to the other. 'All things in moderation, brother.' His enthusiasm would eventually have to be checked.

Before he had taken up his official chore of sweeping and dusting the oak staircase, he had already been out to the garden in the cloister and picked fresh flowers for the Lady Altar in the novitiate corridor. There were daffodils and pussy willow, which he liked. Before those, there had been a carpet of snowdrops and crocuses. He learnt their names. After fixing the flowers, he replaced the burnt-out candles before the icon of St Benedict in the common room.

Earlier, he had watered Father Justin's hyacinths, whose scent reminded him of the smell of pomme aracs. He inhaled them deeply. Home came on the breeze of the smell; from the big tree behind the house at Malgretoute. He and Ted had climbed that tree. One holiday, they gorged themselves on the red fruit. The perfume was on their breaths, the juice on their chins and fingers.

The hyacinths grew in the warmth on the sill above the radiator in the common room. Words came with a world: warmth, radiator. They named a world.

Aelred performed all these chores with regularity and enthusiasm. The young novice was an inspiration to all.

Old men smiled, looking at him. He aided the infirm up the stairs. He picked up Dom Michael's walking stick. 'Let me help you, father. Here, take my hand.'

The older monks were glad at his fervour. They knew it could not last and that the monastic boredom would eventually enter. They knew the disillusionment which could beset the fathers of the desert. The few knew the joy, once that desert was journeyed through, but they exulted at the young novice's first flush of fervour. They had all known it. It encouraged them, reminding them of their youth. Dom Leonard pinched Brother Aelred's cheeks with his bony fingers. 'Brother, young brother, young, young brother.' Aelred delighted him.

'Yes, father, let me help you with those books to the library.'

Brother Aelred had made strides since those first days as a postulant, racked by homesickness and doubt, writing home: 'Dear Mum and Dad, I am settling in fine... Love to Robert and all the girls. And a special hello for Toinette.' His grief remained between the lines for maybe a mother to notice.

He had never been quite sure if it had been the spring that had begun to appear before St Aelred's Day which had taken away that awful desolation of missing his home, and stopped him crying every time he received a letter from his dearest mother: 'My darling, I keep calling Robert by your name, which makes Giselle and the other girls giggle and tease me.' Or was it the feeling which he had that Dom Benedict, his guardian angel, was different and special? He wasn't sure that it wasn't the excitement and comfort of that which had got rid of the homesickness.

He still remembered that special hug on the night of his clothing. He remembered that he looked for Benedict where he knew he sat in the chapter house. He did that in the choir and in the refectory. He liked his official meeting with Benedict, when he was given advice or instructed in a new custom. Best of all, he loved it when they were put to work together and they would relax the rule of silence so they could chat. As when they were washing up, when Aelred said, 'So, you are ten years older than I am.'

And Benedict had answered, 'But that should not matter between brothers.'

Then there were moments when Benedict was different, with his hands under his scapular. There was a formality when he spoke, not cold, but formal. Then Benedict was his guardian angel: 'Brother, let's go over the lesson for tomorrow's Matins.'

It was at the celebration on the night of St Aelred's Day, his own feast day. After they had had a day full of the liturgy of the patron saint with the pomp of the Abbot's pontifical Mass, they were allowed a relaxation of the rules. The order of the day was like a Sunday, with a long siesta and a walk in the afternoon, followed by fruit cake and tea. In the evening they had a film, *The Song of Bernadette*, and were allowed to smoke cigarettes and were offered a glass of wine.

All during the afternoon walk he had been in Benedict's presence, but they did not talk. They were aware of each other, a guardian angel and his protégé. Till finally, when they had dropped behind the others, 'How is my boy from the tropics doing?' Benedict's arm was around his shoulder. 'Come on, we must catch up.'

It had been a walk of physical endurance. Father Justin liked to test the new novices. 'Coats on - it's just a bit nippy.' There was a driving wind, sleet and flurries of snow. 'It looks like we've not got rid of the winter.' The young novice savoured each new sensation. He heard the word 'flurry'. He forgot the meaning of heat on the skin. It was wind, not breeze. But he looked forward to the roaring fire in the common room. He thought of jolly Christmas cards. The world looked like a Christmas scene on a Christmas card: holly, laurel, ivy. England was a carol. Earth stood as hard as iron, water like a stone. He learnt the feel of 'bleak'.

Spring was in the air, but still the winter had not gone. There was snow among the daffodils.

Aelred stared out of the misted-up glass window of the chapter house, which had been arranged for the party. He rubbed away the condensation with his hand. He wiped away the wetness by putting his hands into the deep pockets of his woollen habit. In the glass against the darkness, and in the reflection of the orange lights of the chapter house, he had a smudged image of his face reflected back at him. Behind his face, one face on top of another, the face of Benedict merged with his. Benedict was smoking a cigarette.

'The late fall of snow has begun to melt. It'll be spring again,' Benedict said.

'It's spring, and then suddenly snow again. I'm not used to this change of seasons.'

'What do you have?'

'Dry season, wet season. Hot. It's very hot. I love it.'

'But you've left it. Given it up? Yes?'

'Yes,' the novice said, thinking it again, and saying it to himself and Benedict. 'I've left it all. Yes, I've given it up.'

'Look out on to the fields tomorrow and you'll see that the snow has begun to melt where there're no trees. The bright sun we've been having in the morning melts the snow. Stand in the sun, and you'll find that it's warm. Stand in the shade, and it's chilly. Cold.'

Aelred listened to the words used in a particular way: warm, chilly. There was always talk of the weather, each subtle change. And in the pantry on blind Brother Angel's radio he listened to the strange mantra of tides and winds, gale forces and storms out there beyond this island. Finesterre. He remembered hurricanes. He would rub his hands and say, 'It's chilly today', and hear how he sounded.

The young brother looked out of the window, but there he saw only the darkness; himself and Benedict reflected in the orange light. There was an amber hum where the town glowed on the horizon. Ashton; it was on fire.

'It looks like a fire,' Aelred said.

The wine must have gone to his head, because he realised that he was talking a lot and telling Benedict all about growing up in Les Deux Isles. 'My mother is wonderful. She's very beautiful. Kind. Loves me. When she comes down in the evening she smells of *l'herbe à* Madame Lalie.'

'What's that? Who's that? And where does your mother come from, that she comes down?' Benedict chuckled at the young novice's enthusiastic gush.

'Oh, it's no one. Questions! There is no Madame Lalie. It's a tree. It has a sweet-sweet smelling flower, white, yellow and white. It opens like a lily. We've got one in our

garden. Right in the middle of the lawn. They make perfume from the flower. She dabs it on her neck and on her
wrists. She strokes her long neck with her finger. My mother
comes down from her bedroom for drinks with my father
in the evening. When it is just getting dark. It gets dark so
quickly. A green flash, and dark. Very dark. You can't see
anything.'

'You must miss her. But you have wonderful sunsets?'

'Sunsets? Yes, yes, boy, red-red-red, and yellow. Like
fire. Cane fire. The whole sky burning up. Yes, I miss her.'

Benedict smiled.

Aelred saw him smile. 'You laughing at me?'

'No, sounds kind of French, kind of Welsh too, the way
you speak, especially when you're excited.'

'And you, you sound funny too, not like limey people
in Les Deux Isles.' He wanted to hit back at something.
'Tell me about yourself. I know nothing. You come from
London?'

Benedict laughed. 'No, not at all - well, I've been all
over. Up north. I was born in the valleys outside a large
city. A valley of mines. My father was a miner. Lots of us.
Nine. Poor, really. I escaped south. Seems a long time ago
now. Studied. Became a teacher. Ended up here. My
parents are dead now. My father, in an accident. In the
mine. My mother, pneumonia. That's my life.'

'God. All of it?'

'Well, not quite; perhaps I'll tell you more. There's a
beauty in the valleys. Suddenly they open up whole hillsides, not all besmirched. Some other time. When we get
a chance. And you must tell me more about your sunsets.
What your sunsets say. Another feast day perhaps. We
must mix now.'

Before he turned away to speak to a group of young monks who were fellow philosophy students, Benedict took the novice's hand in his. He held it in both his palms. He looked straight at him, into him, Aelred thought. 'We'll talk again.' Then he ruffled his fast-growing, cropped hair playfully. 'Your hair grows quickly. You'll soon have to be shorn again.' The novice felt embarrassed. He felt that Benedict shouldn't do that. But he was also happy. He was nervous and happy at the same time.

'What sunsets say? They don't say anything,' he said.

Besmirched, Aelred listened to how things were described. Benedict was already speaking to one of the other monks.

Aelred sat with the other novices, listening. Then he talked with Brother Stephen about the farm. He was excited about being put to work on the farm. The farm was like the estate, his father's work with animals.

He saw Benedict on his own, which was unusual, because in observing him, he noticed that he was the life and soul of the party; he was popular with the older monks, and the young monks were eager to talk and share opinions on their study.

Aelred found himself feeling jealous. He didn't feel he had anything interesting to say to him. He wanted Benedict's attention. The way he spoke, the way he looked at him: it made him feel special.

Later, when it was almost time for Compline, Benedict and Aelred found themselves together again. Benedict beckoned him over to where he was sitting. Right away, he was direct, picking up where they had left off, as if not to lose any time. 'It can't all be sunsets. What do you miss the most?'

Without deliberately thinking it out, Aelred answered, 'Ted.' Ted was so often in his mind, on the tip of his tongue, like a secret. He had to bite his tongue.

'Ted? Who is Ted?'

He had not told anyone at Ashton Park about Ted. He looked down at his boots. I'm standing in him, he thought. Always, I have him.

'Ted. He was the best at everything. The way he swung a bat, bowled a ball. Football season, he was the fastest on the left wing. Captain. We played tennis for hours. Sun and sweat like salt. Then we swam. Best, we climbed into the hills and swam in the river pool where the water fell twenty feet sheer. Like falling glass. Frothy like crystal, shattering. He dived, jackknife.' He said the words, painting the picture of another world, lost, dreamt. 'We were the best. Two of us.'

The young novice found himself staring into the murky glass of orange light and darkness and the faces of himself and Benedict superimposed, each upon the other, mixed and distorted. Then he looked at Benedict, staring at him, talking about Ted.

'He meant a lot to you?' Benedict said, concerned. But his eyes had an astonishment about them, as he heard the young novice in front of him tell of his young friend.

'He meant a lot to all of us. All who knew him. He had a way of making you feel special. He was the best and brought out the best in others.'

'But he was your friend? Your special friend, was he?'

'Yes, he was my friend.'

'And you gave that up too? You left him with your sunsets?'

'Yes. I gave him up.' As he spoke, he thought he felt

Ted's boots pinching his toes. 'These are his boots.' They both looked down at the black boots. 'It's a secret. Can you keep it? Is that OK, you think, to have them?' 'Let no one presume to give or receive anything without the Abbot's leave, or to have anything as his own, anything whatever, whether book or tablets or pen or whatever it may be; for monks should not have even their own bodies and wills at their own disposal.' That was the Rule.

'Oh, yes, I'll keep your secret. If you'll tell me more. But we must go.'

The Abbot and prior were preparing to go into Compline. The community was forming a procession out of the chapter house.

That was it, Aelred thought: he made him feel special. Then he thought of Ted. In the darkness of the choir he felt the tears rolling down his cheeks. He pulled out his handkerchief and blew his nose.

The acolyte of the choir asked for the blessing, bowing in front of the Abbot and then standing in the middle of the choir. He read the lesson: '*Fratres...* ' 'Brothers, be sober and watch, because your adversary the devil, like a roaring lion, goes about seeking whom he may devour... Resist him...'

The next day, as Aelred looked out on to the fields while the mist of dawn was lifting, he waited for the bell to announce the Conventual Mass. He saw that the snow was indeed melting and the grass was lucent beneath a light film of ice. Where there was a sun catch, there was a patch of fresh green grass. It would be spring again. All this was a kind of miracle, this change of seasons, an entirely new experience which seemed to grow instantly in him. But at the same time, his head was filled with Benedict, not because of anything that Benedict had particularly said, but because of a vast multitude of things which being with Benedict, and talking with him, had made him feel, especially telling about Ted. So there was comfort in his homesickness, and he found that it disappeared with the coming of the spring and with his feelings for Benedict.

There was a growing desire to see and be with Benedict, but this was not going to be possible. Benedict had already taught him all there was to know. The other customs he would pick up from the other novices, or be told by the novice master. He would have to lose his guardian angel.

the same time, his head was filled with he really not
because of anything that he did; he had positively said,
but because of a vast multitude of things which he [...]
with benedick, and talking with him, had made him feel,
especially telling about Ted, that there was comfort in his
homesickness, and he found that it disappeared with the
coming of the spring and with his feelings for Benedict.

There was a growing desire to see and be with
Benedict, but this was not going to be possible. Benedict
had already taught him all there was to know. The other
curators he would pick up from the other novices, or be
told by the novice master. He would have to love his guardian angel.

The Guest House:

24 September 1984

> Already now the shades of mist are thinning
> And dawn is rising from the skies...

Lauds, praise! I pick my way in the darkness around the cloister, up early like a good cocoa planter. The temperature can drop even in the valleys around Malgretoute.

In the silence, the bare stone, the arch of the sanctuary reaches and curves. The round solid pillars support space. The church is central to this complex, this monastery. An enclosure wall holds all in: workshops, farm, chapter house, scriptorium (library), refectory, cloister, cemetery, gardens. Silence. These men move quietly, businesslike, happy, smiling: like the men I had as teachers at school. What were they up to that I didn't know about? Once or twice we joked about a couple of them.

Take care Dom Michael in Maths, boy. He like to touch you up.

A rough cowl scrapes the worn and polished stone. A hooded man, bowed, walks near the wall. I think I see my religious brother, then I don't.

I am learning about this life, about this ritual. From so young, J. M. knew it all. There was the fervour since that first dawn going down to the abbey church and hearing the Gregorian chant. It took away his homesickness during his first week at boarding school. There was that fervour and then there was Ted. When I was very small I saw something. I'm not sure, now. I put it out of my mind.

There they are, in the choir to which he once belonged. There is Benedict, still there in the same stall where

Aelred always knew he would be at Matins, Lauds, Prime, Terce, Sext, None, Vespers, Compline. When J. M. entered the monastery, Benedict was ten years older than him. Ten years! He found that out when they were washing up one day during one of those rare moments, stolen moments, out of the monastic silence. I never imagined that this was the life he was leading. I didn't dream it could be this way.

Boy, I don't know. I don't know nuh. I was twelve, going on thirteen when he left.

Yesterday afternoon, after my walk, after I had threaded my way back through the silver birches and the wood the other side of the stream, I joined Benedict in the orchard. I like the way this park is like an estate. He's so thin. J. M., Aelred - what do I call him? Here, I call him J. M.; in my reconstructions, Aelred. I've got to get my bearings, keep my mind, sort out what I really think. J. M. described Benedict as strong and well built, at least in the early days.

J. M. writes in his journal:

'This is Dom Benedict,' Father Justin said, introducing me. 'Our new Brother de la Borde, from Les Deux Isles,' he said to Dom Benedict. I opened my outstretched arm to shake his hand which was still hidden beneath his black scapular. But instead his arms extended to my shoulders, clasped them tightly and drew me towards him, first to the right side and then to his left in the kiss of peace, the monastic kiss, and I could feel my full crop of hair brush against the shorn side of his head and cheeks. He was strong. Strong arms, full chest.

My heart beat fast.

'We prayed for your safe flight,' Dom Benedict said. Father Justin smiled.

'Dom Benedict will be your guardian angel. Show you the ropes.' We all three smiled.

The geography of the abbey and the grounds was my first guided lesson, the afternoon after Brother Chrysostom's funeral.

We kept calling him J. M. at home, even after his clothing. Mum read his letters at dinner. He was special to Mum; something different from what the girls and I had, even I who was her baby. I know my father didn't like it. Now I remember feeling ashamed. When he left I didn't want to go to the airport to say goodbye, not after what had happened. I never felt that I could make it right again.

There is a feeling of autumn in the air, early autumn. Light in autumn has a great intensity which is then distilled. It is the angle at which it falls. But there is also a breath of cold in the air, and a haze like a veil through which it filters. I notice this change in the light, new to me. I see it in his words, feel it, like his skin feeling it, feel him feeling it.

I learn these new seasons through his words, under his gaze, seeing with his eyes, his fingers on my pen. This English park comes off the pages of his journal. Then in my memory the bush opens. The mountains of Les Deux Isles grow and climb to peaks. The cocoa hills of Malgretoute creep like iguanas.

I was telling this to Joe and his sister Miriam, who've given me such a warm welcome as friends of J. M. It was Miriam who said that J. M. continued with his notes on landscape and flowers and birds. I went walking with them along the Avon between Bristol and Bath. It was spring then.

There, a kingfisher, a flash of blue under a bridge, Miriam said.

I just caught it. It was when I had first started reading
the journals. Reading of J. M.'s first spring, when the snow
didn't begin to melt till March. The winter wouldn't go
away.

We had fun, Joe, Miriam and I, discovering the first
cowslip, the wild violets and the primroses. Miriam
loves those. I think Joe brought her along so I wouldn't
just have to be with him. I think he thought I was self-
conscious just being with him alone, though we've
spent a lot of time together alone sorting through J.M.'s
papers and things.

I must get back home. I've well overstayed my intended
time. The phone calls back to Malgretoute get more and
more expensive. Krishna called from the agricultural
college. He can still oversee the estate for me. He's very
good; spent some time before as a kind of trainee. Now
that he is fully qualified they want him to teach at the university. He's almost a friend now. I feel confident in him.
But I need to get back. I can tell that he wants me back: I
really like him.

Yesterday afternoon, with Benedict, there was also the
fact that we were throwing bundles of blackberry cuttings
and raspberry canes on to a stack for a bonfire. The flame
and the smoke, a plume of blue rifling up in the afternoon,
made the time undeniably autumn.

This is the real smell of autumn, Benedict said.

I speak of it now with such confidence because of J. M.

An owl hooted. Benedict turned and looked in the
direction of the copse. The hoot came again, but we did
not see its flight. Benedict looked so handsome as he turned towards the light. At fifty, he's still handsome, but thin.
Why so thin? He hasn't mentioned any ill health. Yes, he's

handsome. I can see that. You can see that a guy is hand-some; nothing wrong with that. But more difficult for me to see how it all went on as a daily occurrence. I know what the journals say. But he seems just a nice fella. And he might be like one of the priests to whom I would've gone to confession. I don't any more. That's my own affair.

They would seem closer in age now, both older. But then, when J. M. first came, so young, a boy still, Benedict was a man. This couldn't've been right. I remember again that laughing about Dom Michael at school touching up boys. I don't want to think that it was like that with them.

Benedict is glad that I've come and wants me to come down to stay for a another week, a kind of retreat. I'm apprehensive. He wouldn't try something with me, would he? Now, as I reflect, I feel OK about it, but then I suddenly want to be back in the flat in Bristol. When I talk with Joe and Miriam I think I begin to see Benedict and J. M. like anyone else - well, nearly.

Look at Joe. He's my brother and he is who he is, Miriam says.

I like her. She's not as hard-hitting as Joe. I suppose I could come back and make a kind of secular retreat, an excavation! I'm here for J. M. I'll ask Joe what he thinks.

I can hear him say, Keep an open mind. They were dif-ferent, he would say.

Though it's seventeen years since J. M. left, I feel self-conscious, and wonder what some of the other monks think. Do they know who I am?

Benedict says I must not worry. He wasn't a criminal, he said.

Why did he use that word? He knows everything. But there is a kind of guilt I feel. Guilt can still be so pervasive, without particular reasons. Inherited? No, I 've got my own measure of guilt. I've got my own reasons.

Who were the criminals?

We hardly talked about J. M., Aelred, as he continues to call him. Benedict wanted to know about me, and asked a lot of questions. Eventually, all the stuff about my divorce came out. He was surprisingly sympathetic, though not really approving. I felt that it gave us a certain equality in terms of virtue and sin. I don't really feel good about it. Annette and I were young, too young, and did the expected thing. It didn't work out, and it's easier now. It was easier to do once my parents had died. Thank God there are no children. Makes it lonely, sometimes, up at Malgretoute. I will try again to draw Benedict out. I must find the right moment. It's why I'm here, after all. I didn't think Benedict wanted the whole thing dragged up again. I'm worried about his health. He'll probably be very sympathetic.

Benedict brought me the letters which he found in the archives. So strange, so neat, so formal. I let myself cry for the first time. I didn't even when Joe first showed me his room. I remember peeping over his shoulder at first drafts of that first letter to Ashton Park, not understanding anything then, and Ted looking over his shoulder too in the study hall. They got rid of me.

Skeidaddle, J. M. said.

Never rough, he ruffled my hair. I remember I always tingled for his attention. Then felt odd about getting it. Ted didn't want J. M. to go. So many changes in what they thought they wanted and what they thought they should do. I don't think I knew about anything that was going on. I must've known, or felt something. When it all broke, I was there. Of course I was. What am I saying? What am I hiding?

The letters don't tell of that time.

PAX

St Maur's College
Saint Pierre
Les Deux Isles
Antilles
British West Indies
6th May 1962

Dear Father Abbot,

My name is Jean Marc de la Borde. I am seventeen years old and I am a pupil at St Maur's College, which is a boarding school run by the Order of our Holy Father St Benedict. I am at the moment completing my O Levels in English Language, English Literature, History (West Indian, but I have done British History), French, Latin and Mathematics. My teachers expect me to do well. I will be sitting my examinations in June of this year.

I am writing to you because I want to apply for admittance to the novitiate at your abbey, St Aelred's, when I have completed my schooling. I have always wanted to be a monk, ever since I was a little boy when I made my first communion. Since then, I think I have had a vocation to the monastic life. First of all, I was encouraged by my parish priest, Dom Maurus who is a monk at the Abbey here, and then, since I have been at the school, I have been encouraged in my vocation by my English teacher and confessor, Dom Placid. I feel that I am at a stage now when I can make a decision to give my life to God. I want to join a monastery which devotes itself to manual work and prayer. I do not want to join the monastery here because I do not want to be a teacher. What I have read of St Aelred's attracts me to the primitive interpretation of the Rule of our Holy Father St Benedict. This is the life I want to lead. I am attracted to the way manual work, study and the celebration of the Divine Office is described in your brochure. I want to lead the enclosed life.

I know that I am still quite young, but I am sure that I am doing the will of God. I hope you will allow me to enter the novitiate when I have finished my schooling.

Dom Maurus and Dom Placid would be very happy to give references on my account.

I look forward to hearing from you as soon as possible.

I remain,
Yours sincerely,
Jean Marc de la Borde

PAX

St Aelred's Abbey
Ashton Park
Ashton
Somerset
Great Britain
12th June 1962

Dear Jean Marc, Son in Christ,
Father Abbot received your letter of 6th May with great pleasure and has passed it on to me as the novice master. He asks me to thank you and hopes that in God's time he will be able to meet you, and hopes particularly that that will be as a postulant who knocks at the door of the Abbey of St Aelred asking for admittance.

I have noted both your desire to enter the monastic life and the age at which you feel that you have been called by our Blessed Lord. I must point out to you the rigorous nature of our life, which, though it gives great joy to the soul and adds to the power house of prayer in the world for the salvation of souls here and in purgatory, is nevertheless, or rather because of that, a life of abstinence in which you are asked to surrender your will to the will of God through obedience to the abbot as Christ on earth. It is a life lived in common with your brothers. This 'conversion of manners' is the way our Holy Father St Benedict describes the life of a monk. The life of poverty and chastity is assumed into that vow which I hope you will eventually make among us.

Our physical life is very hard. Father Abbot and I did think immediately of the warm climate from which you are coming. We notice your urgency to enter after finishing your schooling, but would ourselves urge you not to come in the winter, but more preferably in the spring or summer months. But we do not wish to dampen your enthusiasm and so would leave it to your judgement and that of your parents and directors.

I have written to your parish priest and spiritual director to get the references which are needed. I trust that all will be well, and as I have mentioned before, Father Abbot will have great pleasure to admit you among us.

Please accept my kind regards to your parents.

I leave you in the name of Christ and our Holy Father St Benedict.

God bless,
Father Justin Simmonds, OSB,
Novice Master

PAX

The Presbytery
Notre Dame de Grace
San Andres
Les Deux Isles
Antilles
British West Indies
20 June 1962

My dear Father Justin,
I'm an old man now, but, yes, of course I
remember Jean Marc. He was a wonderful child
with a marvellous mother from one of the good
old families out here, who inculcated in her son
from a very early age a special love for our
Blessed Lord and his Immaculate Mother, the
Blessed Virgin.

I christened the child in their village church.
But it was when he first came to our little school
next door to the big church, as we always call it,
that I was able to notice him. He was always very
devout, making daily, sometimes I think twice-daily
visits to the Blessed Sacrament, if I recall my ever
watchful housekeeper who kept a good eye on all
the children. He was always at communion
during the school Mass on Thursdays. Regular at
confession.

Jean Marc, poor little fellow, was always
remembered because he used to faint frequently,
a slight physical weakness at the time, maybe not
eating sufficiently at breakfast, having to come
from the country into the town to school. Also, at

times he was a little nervous, a little highly strung. This is not meant to detract in any way from a fine boy. As you see, the ramblings of an old man, father. But we do remember his faints because it was Mrs Goveia, my housekeeper that is, whom I've mentioned, who took especial care of the children, and who cared for him when he had one of these bouts and one of the school masters brought him to the veranda of the presbytery to get some cool breeze and the master in his anxiety for the poor boy filled his own hat with water and doused poor Jean Marc. He soon recovered. It is very hot here. Mrs Goveia always made him a special lemonade with lots of good brown demerara sugar. But less of these tales, good father.

I've known of Jean Marc's desire to give his life to Our Lord in the monastic life. I'm a little sad that he does not want to join our community here, but he is resolute on an enclosed life devoted to manual work and prayer. We are a teaching and parish community out here in the missions. It is inspiring to see such zeal in one so young. I think you will find him a devout young man who is open with his thoughts and feelings and thoughtful of his neighbours. He comes from a good Catholic family with a brother and sisters and a mother who is exemplary in her church work and duties as a mother, and a father who is a pillar of the church, as we say. He is from one of the very best families. Not that I wouldn't recommend a boy from one of the poorest of our good Negro people.

I have no hesitation in recommending this young man to you.

I leave you in Christ,
Dom Maurus de Boissiere, OSB
Parish Priest

Malgretoute Estate
Nr Felicity
Les Deux Isles
Antilles
British West Indies
21 June 1962

Dear Father Justin,
Thank you very much for your letter, introducing yourself and conveying Father Abbot's wishes. Please extend to him our best wishes, those of my husband and myself. It was very kind of you at all to write in this way. It makes us feel very much more in touch with the realisation of our son's ideals. The whole tone of your letter makes us feel very secure that Jean Marc will get the very best advice in this enterprise of his. I say his enterprise, but maybe I should really say, God's enterprise for him. I know that that is what he wants to do, the will of God for him. This we pray for each day. He is our eldest boy. We feel honoured and chosen for this great gift our Blessed Lord

has bestowed on our son, to give him a vocation to leave all, father and mother, brother and sisters, home and country even (though of course we are only a colony, sadly to be given so called independence soon), and follow him. To tell you the truth, father, I am quite overcome at the thought of my boy, not quite my Benjamin, my Joseph, let us say, doing this, but of course I am absolutely prepared to support him in his ideals and to give him up as it were to our Blessed Lord, as Abraham was called upon to sacrifice Isaac. But as I said before, my husband and I are secure, after getting your letter that Jean Marc will be well advised. And I am sure if the day comes that he leaves us and finds a home in your community, he will be well looked after by wonderful older men like yourself.

His father, not a man to show his feelings much, is proud of his son and said to me this morning, and I quote, 'My dear, if that English monk says that Jean Marc will make a good monk you can rest assured that he will, and with good discipline.' My husband sees things so clearly.

Jean Marc is a good boy, father. Yes, he is devout, but you know, father - and I feel I must be open with you, because I know that you will understand and will know how to help Jean Marc - he's still very young. He is quite emotional, and quite headstrong too. I think these qualities can be good if well directed, but can cause problems. I would never detract from my son's character, but I feel I am talking to you, father, who will be his novice master and spiritual director, and who will have the care of his soul. I feel as if in giving him into your capable hands I am giving him into the hands of God. I know that you will understand me, father, when I write like this. I speak as his mother.

My husband asks to be remembered to you and Father Abbot.

So, father, in God's time, if it his will, Jean Marc will be a son in your home as he has been here in our home.

I remain,
Yours sincerely and most gratefully,
Chantal de la Borde

PAX

St Maur's Abbey
St Pierre
Les Deux Isles
Antilles
British West Indies
30 June 1962

Dear Father Justin,
Thank you for your letter concerning Jean Marc de la Borde.

I have known Jean Marc since he was a young boy of twelve and first came to our college. I have been his English teacher since then and his spiritual director.

I am fully convinced of the sincerity of Jean Marc's vocation. My only regret is that he has not chosen to enter our abbey here, but I respect his desire for a more primitive interpretation of the Rule of our Holy Father St Benedict.

Jean Marc is young. While I think he can make this decision, and it is a big one, to leave his country and a very close family, he will need a lot of kindness and support. He is an emotional boy, pious, sometimes vaulting too high the hurdles on the course of the spiritual race. While his enthusiasm must not be dampened, he will need guidance to avoid consuming himself. He is fired by the lives of the saints, but can sometimes misinterpret the symbolic significance of these examples of spiritual attainment.

Jean Marc will adapt well to community life and values, and to the support a brotherhood like ours can give. He values friendship and has a generous heart, but should be advised very closely in this. There is a tendency to let his emotions get the better of him.

I fully support his application into your community. If I can be of any other assistance please do not hesitate to write to me.

In the fellowship of Our Holy Father St Benedict, I remain,
Yours sincerely,
Dom Placid Marcus, OSB

This was the official life. Of course, I'd never seen any of the letters; only that time, looking over his shoulder. I didn't understand Ted's anger, Ted's sadness. One needs to read between the lines. I bottled up what I knew, twelve going on thirteen. Then I couldn't any longer. They were such an exercise in euphemism, dear old Father Maurus mentioning his fainting. One must read between the lines. Was there a hint here, and a wink there? And Dom Placid's letter, mentioning enthusiasm and friendship and need for counselling: there was nothing explicit. They all wanted so much for him; all so intimate and knowing at one level, and knowing nothing at the same time. He was himself so bland. And that letter written with Ted looking over his shoulder. No one knows. Well, some do know. Not even I know the truth, still. I know my own truth. I hadn't always admitted it; tried to hide it away. I should've talked about it. He was too odd both times he returned, for the funerals of our mother and father. I think I knew what he was, but I didn't want to admit it. Certainly, I didn't want to talk about it. It made everything awkward. My truth, that's what I have. That's what I can go on.

There is the silence of directors, confessors, parents, lest they be scandalised.

I can only reconstruct, tell his story, use his words.

It was Joe's letter which changed everything. It hurt me that it was Chantal that he wanted to write to.

19 St John's Way
Bristol 8
Avon
England

15 March 1984

Dear Robert de la Borde
I have been a friend of your brother Jean Marc's
for years. I found your address among his things.
I am sorry to be the bearer of sad news. Jean
Marc died on 5th March in the early evening
here at his flat in Bristol. He had been ill but said
that it was not necessary to write to anyone in Les
Deux Isles. He said he would if he felt up to it. I
didn't agree with him, but I respected his wishes.
But now I think I must tell you of his death. He
said that if he wrote he would write to your sister
Chantal. I don't have her address so I am writing
to you. I have some things which belong to you. I
was very fond of your brother. And please extend
my sympathy to your sisters. I know that both
your parents are dead. I enclose a phone
number, 0179 412567, in case you want to call.
Do get in touch one way or another. I will keep
his things here for you. Please accept my
sympathy and that of my sister Miriam, who also
knew Jean Marc.

Best wishes,
Sincerely,
Joseph Gore

The Portrait

I am black but lovely...
Song of Songs

Once again, Brother Aelred was at his daily chores of housework between the hours of Prime and Terce. After he finished dusting the banisters on the first floor this morning, he paused to dust the frame of a painting which hung two or three steps down from the first floor to the mezzanine. The library was through the tall heavy doors off this landing. The painting was the portrait of a man dressed as an eighteenth-century gentleman of wealth, and presumably, as it occurred to Aelred, one of the early owners of Ashton Park before the monastery was built, and maybe, even the owner of the original house. There was gold lettering at the bottom. It was a name, but many of the letters had faded. He could decipher the word 'Duke'.

But it was the small boy who knelt in a decorative manner at the duke's feet who held Aelred's attention as he wiped the glass and dusted the goldleaf of the frame. He was a black boy. As Aelred dusted and wiped the frame his mind wandered and his imagination mused as he stared into the wide open face of the black boy. He lost himself. He was Jean Marc again.

'Jeansie, Jeansie, come boy, come nuh man, come and play cricket in the savannah, nuh man!' It was Redhead from down in the village near Malgretoute. Ramnarine from the barracks was running behind him, pitching the cork ball into the air. He was bowling it up the gap to the big estate house. 'Throw it, Jeansie,' Redhead called.

After play, he waved goodbye. They hung back to talk at the bottom of the gap. He didn't invite them up to the house.

'Ei, Jeansie, let us come and play nuh man?'

He kept on walking up to the house. He waved from the high verandah.

'I've got to go in. My mummy's calling me.'

'You mummy calling you?' Redhead and Ramnarine sneered.

Aelred stared. The portrait drew him into its world. It was a triumphant landscape of fields, lakes and mountains, dark and sombre, unfolding behind the figures, through arches and the rich folds of drapes. There was a town in the distance with towers and spires. This was England. There was a port from which a tall ship was setting sail. As he stared, he saw this little black prince, for so he seemed to Aelred, smiling up to the duke. The little black boy was dressed in red satins and gold silks. His coat and pants were made of blue taffeta. He mirrored and mimicked his master. He was a diminutive, his master's doll. The boy was offering the duke a purse of jewels, or a purse encrusted with diamonds or pearls. The duke was accepting it nonchalantly. He was not even looking at the boy; he looked out over the world beyond the frame of the painting.

The admiration in the boy's eyes was the same as that in the face of the master's dog which knelt at his feet on the other side of the painting. It was looking up plaintively.

Aelred stared and wondered. Then he saw his own face reflected in the glass of the portrait. His face was superimposed upon that of the boy whose face shone from beneath, so that the black face seemed to be his own. 'Who all you white boys think you is?' It was Espinet at Mount Saint Maur. He was sitting in the pavilion alone. They weren't letting him into the game of cricket. 'All you think all you superior. You think this make a difference.' He was jabbing at his face pointing to the colour of his skin. 'And you, de la Borde, all you French creole!' It was then that Aelred saw that the boy in the portrait wore a collar. Or was it a trick of the light? It looked like a dog's collar. Then he thought it was a reflection of the light in the glass. It was tightly fastened like a choker. Now it seemed like a thick iron sphere. It seemed it encircled his neck and glinted above where his satin cloak shimmered and fell in folds like those of the duke above him. 'Why all you so, eh de la Borde? One minute you nice nice, the next you with the others on your high horse.'

Aelred continued to stare. And as the boy's face grew in his mind, so did the voice of Toinette, his nurse and his mother's old servant grow in him, so he spoke to himself in her voice. '*Dou-dou*, come let me tell you a story.' And she told a story she had heard from her great-grandmother. 'This is what my great-granny tell me right up here in these cocoa hills overlooking them same sugar-cane fields.' The breeze whispered through the serrated leaves beneath the cool hills. Aelred looked down from the steps of the Malgretoute house to the village of Felicity. Aelred had heard this story from Toinette many times. 'Tell it, tell it, Toinette, the one about the little boy.'

'His name is Mungo and he come from Africa,' Toinette began.

'From Africa.' Aelred heard his own boy's voice repeat.

'And they bring him here to Malgretoute.'

'To Malgretoute.'

And so the story always started.

Aelred was behind in his housework. He saw Brother Patrick climbing the stairs with the hand bell in order to give the signal for the end of manual work. 'Now, don't you go and fall, brother,' Brother Patrick warned as he passed by. Aelred stretched to dust the top of the picture frame and was intent on returning to his duty. He missed those friends: Redhead, Espinet, Ramnarine and Mackensie.

While he was in an awkward position to reach the top of the large portrait he became stuck for a split second. He noticed the intense silence of the abbey and himself there in this early hour of the day with Toinette's story going in his mind. 'Mungo was a runaway.' He turned from stretching up and prepared to place his foot securely on the step to return to the first floor. As he turned, he saw the door off the mezzanine into the library closing. He heard it click shut. It closed softly, clicking in its brass mortise.

In the light which had poured from the partially open door, he noticed the back of Benedict and the door closing behind him. It startled him. It was like an apparition. He immediately thought of a childhood fancy. It was a sudden déjà vu. He thought he had had a vision when he was fourteen. It was Our Lady of Grace, dressed as if she was in the parish church next to his school in the old rusty racatang town of San Andres. She wore her blue veil and a white and gold mantle over her shoulders. Grace, like light, poured from her hands. She appeared to him just as he was waking from sleep and disappeared down the corridor to his mother's and father's bedroom in a flight of light. He remembered crying out, 'Mummy.' She came and comforted him and together they said the Hail Mary. 'There, now, dear, Hail Mary, full of grace.'

He had to finish his chores on the first floor and still had to continue up to the second floor. His mind began to play back what he had seen.

It was as if, now, he wasn't sure what he had seen, so powerfully did the image of the small black boy stay in his mind with the accusations of Redhead, Ramanrine, Mackenzie and Espinet, with the story of Toinette being told to him again. Mungo carried a scar on his neck. He now wondered what it was that had startled him the most: the image of the black boy or the image of Benedict disappearing behind the library door. It seemed as if he remembered that on turning, in that fraction of a second, taking his eyes off the black boy, he saw Benedict standing in the open door of the library staring at him. It was not as Benedict would do normally, smile and say something. He was lost in his staring. Then he turned and closed the library door behind him.

Aelred went over the scene several times. He was convinced that when he first turned around he saw Benedict staring at him, and what he was staring at were his legs, which were exposed because his light denim smock had ridden up his leg, exposing his naked legs in his effort to dust the top of the picture frame. He had been unaware because of his concentration on the face of the black boy in the portrait.

Aelred became agitated. The black boy's face, Benedict's disappearance, and then the distinct sense that Benedict had been staring at his naked legs distracted him.

'Brother Aelred. The bell has gone for the end of

manual work. You need to get ready for Terce.' It was Father Justin. He felt that he had been caught doing something wrong.

As he stripped off his denim smock in the washroom he saw de Leger. He was a boy whom he had once caught staring at his legs in the chapel at Mount Saint Maur. When he looked back at him he saw the blue of his eyes, which were like the blue of the veins which ran in his legs, the blue in marble, the blue in the veins of Dom Maurus's arms, blood like Quink ink. Then the bell for the consecration tinkled. '*Hoc est corpus meum.*' They all looked up at the host and then bowed their heads. When he screwed up his eyes he kept seeing the boy with the blue eyes who had stared at his naked legs.

Aelred felt worried but excited by the realisation that Benedict had been staring at his naked legs. But he was also a little embarrassed about how he would be next time he spoke to Benedict. Perhaps Benedict would tell him to check that his smock did not ride up when he was working, because it could be a distraction or embarrassment to others. Maybe he would tell him that he should have worn his overalls. Perhaps he was himself embarrassed.

Aelred washed his hands and face in the washroom of the novitiate. He stared at his wet face. He could not get the face of the black boy out of his mind. He could not get the face of Benedict out of his mind. Benedict had been so absorbed. Later de Leger had waited for him by the woodwork shop behind the college. 'I want to kiss you as if you were a girl.' But he never did and he kept himself in a state of anticipation whenever he saw him. Then once, very quickly with only the dim night light in the dormitory, he came to his bed and kissed him on his mouth, as in the pictures, while the other boys slept in their beds in rows.

Ted and he had never kissed when they were small. They had been small when it started. It seemed as if it was as far back as he could remember that he and Ted used to play games which were to do with touching and other things. They used to undress together.

'Rub my totee.' He heard their boyhood word.

'Suck me now.'

'Yes.'

'Put it in.'

'Where?'

'In my bottom.'

'My finger?'

'No.'

'Come. Come. Push it in. Push it in.'

He remembered when their first orgasms started. 'Let's jock together.'

'You break yet?'

'Yes, yes.' They held each other, hardly breathing. It smelt like the smell of swimming pools.

Then they had to go to confession. It was impure, a mortal sin. They would go to hell. 'Lick, suck,' Aelred heard those words from far away. He could not settle down to his Lectio Divina. 'Break', another word of childhood, threaded itself through his thoughts. *Le petit mort*, someone had once told him it was called when he was grown up. He wanted to tell all this to Benedict.

He was alone in his cell. He would not see Benedict till he looked across at him in choir. He drifted and nodded.

'His name was Mungo and he come from Africa.' He heard Toinette's voice. He was roused by the bell for Terce.

After Terce and the Conventual Mass Aelred decided to go to the library to look up any books he could find on the history of Ashton Park. He could not get the face of the black boy out of his mind. Toinette's story which had lain buried for so long, now came back to him with a peculiar force. He took comfort in her voice.

Dom Gregory, the librarian, directed him to a section of the library on local history. 'There are one or two books which discuss the history of the house,' Dom Gregory explained. Aelred promised himself that he would come back to the library after dinner and spend the siesta time there. There were other books on great houses of the West Country.

Maybe Benedict would come through the library and he would stop and talk to him. He could tell him of his interest since seeing the black boy in the portrait on the staircase. How would he explain his own disappearance through the library door?

Aelred went to the library straight from the refectory. He would have until the bell went for None. 'Take your time, brother,' It was Father Abbot, whom he met on the staircase as he bounded up three at a time. Aelred smiled, lowered his hood as was customary when you greeted the Abbot, and slowed down his ascent to the library.

The house was once called Ash Wood. Aelred remembered Brother Stephen telling him one afternoon when they were working in the wood behind the cemetery that ash was very common on the estate and that it was a nuisance. There was a house at Ash Wood. There had been the original medieval house, which had had the medieval chapel that still existed in the cemetery. It was built by a printer to the King, a Mr Walter. He had the King's head carved above the door to the great hall. But that house no longer existed. Another house was built, but that was burnt down at the end of the seventeenth century. The Ash Wood which interested Aelred was the house which first existed in the early part of the eighteenth century. This house was owned by a merchant, a Mr Dewey who had a son named Master Walter Dewey who went out to the West Indies. Mr Dewey had made his original fortune in the 'South Sea Bubble'. Mr Walter had an estate on the island of Antigua, near to Ashtown, a small coastal town on that island.

'You're very absorbed, brother?'

Aelred looked up from his reading. It was Benedict. 'Oh, yes. I've found something really fascinating about Ashton Park. You know that portrait on the staircase? Just outside the library. Where you saw me this morning?'

'Did I?' Benedict looked embarrassed. But at that moment the bell for None startled them.

'Anyway, I'll tell you about my discovery some time.'

Benedict pulled on his hood and left the library first. Aelred put back the book he had been reading on the shelf. It was a reference-only book. He would have to come back. As he passed the portrait on the staircase, he heard Toinette's voice: 'Mungo is his name and he come from Africa.' He watched the bright young face of the boy and his heart first rose, but then fell.

The Guest House:

*The flame of love grew brighter yet
That spreads its love to all we meet...*

Since J. M. left they have done away with Prime. Terce is tacked on to the Conventual Mass. Odd the little bits I've remembered. I myself find it difficult to follow the Mass now. I can still follow the chants, appreciate the beauty of the chant, even now, in English. But the Mass doesn't mean what it used to. Something J. M. and I obviously shared without me knowing it. Not even that we shared when he came for our mother's funeral.

It's hurt me to find out that he would've written to Chantal and not to me. She's the eldest. Was that it? We boys came at the end. The girls almost looked after us. I'll always be the baby brother, I suppose. The girls wanted me to come to England. Neither of them thought they could face it. Had they suspected something, and were afraid of what they would find?

I sit at the back of the church and feel very out of it. Am I being judged? I've not talked to Benedict about my faith, or the absence of it. It's not that formal. I'm lapsed. It's the divorce. I let it all drop because they've rejected me. I had a simple faith, no real instruction or development beyond confirmation. Mine was a penny catechism faith: the little blue book, questions and answers parrot fashion.

During Mass, I'm distracted by my own reconstructions, by what I find in the journals; the unutterable words, as my mother would call them. I'm not that strait-laced, but I don't really want to think of my brother doing those things. Touching, yes, lots of boys somewhere along the line touched each other's totees. Rub totee, as we called it. We all joked about jocking in the bath queue.

Watch you slip and break your neck, boy, someone sniggered as one boy followed another into the shower.

There was lots of laughter and pushing, but lick, suck! Yes, they sucked each other, some of them. But the other? I always think of dogs stuck together in the heat. But J. M. writes of it as something so hidden and secret, something so precious, savoured from childhood; something that came back like a perfume. He knew that it was a sin.

Can you find any of that in yourself? Joe asks.

I don't know. .

Miriam says, You must look into yourself.

Joe says, You must keep an open mind.

Something in the life I'm discovering moves me. They ask if I would accept all those things between men and women. I shrug a yes.

So it's not the acts in themselves? they ask.

Acts! Well, I'm not sure about that.

I can see Benedict looking at me. Looking for J. M. in my face, in my gestures. He smiles when I talk because of my accent. I suppose it's like J. M.'s when he first arrived at Ashton Park. I do look a little like him too. Not his unusual beauty. I can see my mother's eyes on him, her gaze. J. M. was something quite different.

Too beautiful! That's what my mother used to say.

Well, there is that family resemblance. I can see it when I get out the old photographs. I have my favourite one of him and Ted in my wallet. Looking at it, you would not know what had happened. I've always kept it since he went away. I hardly took it out; my guilt, I suppose. But it would be there as I flicked through my cash cards; fresh-faced, open-eyed boys, haircuts like James Dean, white T-shirts, sleeves rolled up over their muscles. You can almost hear Bobby Darrin in the background: 'Every night I sit here by my window, staring at the lonely ave-nue.' The past comes back as Pop! Early rock-and-roll.

I found the photo among his things in his room at Malgretoute after he left. Yes, the old forty-fives were there as well. Mum decided to pack everything away. There was this box in the press which had J. M.'s things. I often wondered whether he had taken a photograph of himself and Ted away with him. There is no photograph of Ted among his things now. There is the one of me. I expect Mum sent him that, a school leaving photo.

Mum has written on the back: Robert, eighteen years old.

Very English, Benedict. He calls me Robert, pronoun-cing it in the English way. I feel it's not me. I expect J. M. must've talked about me to him. I know he prayed for us; got the community to pray for us all: our parents, our sis-ters. He would say in his letters that special prayers had been offered for us. We had this sense that he was looking after us. My mother would often say that J. M.'s going to have a word for us with God, when there was a family problem. We didn't know what J. M. was up to, did we?

I get angry. I'm angry because I don't know what he thought of me, what he felt about me during that time and after. Why the hell should I bother about this whole quest? What good is it going to do? Who is the quest for anyway, and why?

I spent the morning reading and making notes on

Aelred of Rievaulx's life and theology of friendship. It's a difficult kind of language for me, but there is no doubt to me that he thought masturbation was disgusting. But he says surprising things about monks holding hands and kissing in a spiritual way. I expect that a lot of things went on then, too, and he's dressing it up, trying to make it spiritual.

I hope I'll work with Benedict in the orchard again this afternoon. Then we're supposed to have a quiet session in my room. See how it goes. Where will we begin? Aelred? Ted?

Walking around the park, I returned to his words. My anger left me. I have the words for everything. Everything? He moved between here and Malgretoute, Les Deux Isles. I have brought the journals with me, the letters and the book of dreams. I let his words stand on their own. I change nothing. This is not my paraphrase. I have been going over things.

Coming down the drive after a visit to Ashton this afternoon, I thought of him back then. He would've got the train to there from London via Bristol. I thought of his arrival that winter more than twenty years ago. I change nothing. I listen to his young voice. This person I'm reading about was so young, my brother. We missed him. I remember our mother missing him. At times, it was as if he had died.

He has died to the world, Mum would say.

He was sort of frozen in time; would always be the guy who left. Then there would be a letter. He wrote all his letters to her. They were addressed to my father and us as well, but they were to my mother. She shared them with us all, me mostly, the last one at home, her Benjamin. I remember now I used to feel sick and have to leave the table.

I am now back on my first morning, a winter's day, at Ashton Park, 1963. The afternoon before, Father Dominic, the guest master, had met me in a Land Rover at the top lodge where the taxi from the station had dropped me, prevented from entering because of the high drifts of snow. 'Brother Chrysostom was very old. Ninety. He died last night and we are keeping his vigil,' Father Dominic said as we drove down the narrow winding drive from the top lodge down to the monastery in the small valley of Ashton Park. I couldn't see anything because the banks of snow were so high. And though it was only two in the afternoon, it was as dark as night.

It was like night. I think I said, 'It's like night,' and then I thought that Father Dominic thought that I was stupid. I've never seen snow before. I had never felt cold. It was like putting your hand in the ice compartment of the Frigidaire. Before, cold was the drop in temperature in the mountains at school. My mother had given me a bottle-green cardigan.

When we got to the front door with my trunk, Father Prior said, 'Ninety-five in the shade is it, where you come from?' He laughed. I smiled, shyly.

The house smelt of boiled cabbage. The panelling on the parlour wall was dark oak. Dark oak: I read that in books about England, about the time of Henry VIII and Anne Boleyn. 'Is there a priest's hole in this house? I learnt that when I was doing English History. Then we changed to West Indian history, no longer kings and queens, Cardinal Wolsey, but slavery and emancipation. Wilberforce. Slave ships, black people packed in rows like bananas, and the islands changed hands many times between the European powers, like pawns in a game between the

French, English, Spanish, Portuguese and the Dutch,' I babbled.

'Well, you'll have to have a look,' Father Dominic said, tapping the panelling, smiling. 'And maybe there is even a secret tunnel, a runaway's escape.' Then we went into see Father Abbot and I had to kneel to kiss his ring.

'Father Justin, this is your new charge,' the Abbot said. The heavy door closed behind a broad monk, who smiled without opening his mouth, his lips a thin line. His hand felt like sandpaper. He smelt of pomme aracs. Later I saw the bulbs on the windowsill of his cell. Hyacinths, I learnt. I breathed in the smell of my childhood, the red fruit which looked like pears whose pulp was like cotton wool, smelt strangely like these flowers, blue like Quink ink, which grew from bulbs into fleshy leaves and petals like skin. The scent hung heavy in the room on the windowsill above the black, hot-water pipes. Father Justin took me up to the dormitory of the novitiate wing.

'We've put an electric blanket in your bed. It's not usual, but Father Abbot thought it best for the first night. You may dispense with it when you think you can cope.' That night I woke thinking I had a raging temperature. I had forgotten to turn the blanket off. I was hot and then cold.

He tells his life like a story. He wanted it told, even then. I will tell it.

I see now that there were other things which bothered him, for instance, the special significance he gives to those boys: Redhead, Espinet, Ramnarine and Mackensie. Obviously looking back he felt guilty about the colour business. He didn't have to go through all that we had to go through with Black Power. It doesn't seem natural, his preoccupation with race. I mean, they are like anyone else to me. Like Krishna who works for me: he's like any other guy. He's a friend really. But it wouldn't have been like that in his day. Yes, things had to change. I don't get too wound up about it. Some black people still do. Miriam asked me the other day about it. She asked whether there were any memorials to what happened. I didn't know what she meant at first.

I mean, it's nearly two hundred years ago, I said.

But the repercussions are still there, she said. Think what it would be like if we had erased the holocaust. Slavery is like that to black people.

It hadn't occurred to me that she was Jewish. Things like what Miriam says make me think that these are J. M.'s adult friends; make me wonder about who he became.

Spiritual Friendship

*Feed me with raisin cakes
restore me with apples...*
Song of Songs

Because of the strict rule of silence throughout the day,
other than at recreation in the common room and out of
necessity at work, Aelred did not have many opportuni-
ties to talk with Benedict. They might meet on the farm,
in the apiary, in the orchard or walled garden, or at any
of the other work places where the monks laboured to
bring in their simple fare, speaking only when it was absolutely necessary, or with the signs of the hands. 'Let leave
to speak be seldom granted to observant disciples. In
much speaking thou shalt not escape sin,' said the holy
Rule

It was not possible, Aelred felt, really to feel you were
ever getting to know these men who were around you. Yet
he did feel close and at one with the community at work,
in the chapter house, in the refectory, chanting and listening to reading. When the lights went out and there was
only the wind in the copper beeches outside the window
of his cell, he felt that they slept as a brotherhood.

Copper beech, he whispered. It was a word in a dream.
England. Aelred slept, caught between worlds.

The jacaranda swayed beneath the verandah.

'I don't feel that I'm really getting to know anyone,'
Aelred said to Father Justin at his weekly meeting with
the novice master.

'It takes time, brother. It'll come without noticing,

without having to be told, or without much talking. Be observant of your fellow brothers' needs. Their characters will reveal themselves. You will know them in Christ.'

'Yes, I try that, but I mean like having a pardner.'

'Pardner?' Father Justin looked at Aelred quizzically.

'Oh, sorry, that's our word back home. Like a friend, someone you really get on with. Someone you feel something special with. You find it easier to talk to them about problems, feelings. And isn't the love of God in the love that we show each other?' He tried to sound knowing and mature in his conclusion.

'Yes, but appropriately, in line with our vows, in line with our rule of silence. You can talk to God, brother. You can come and talk to me. What you are suggesting is the communication of the world. And I must warn you against particular friendships. There's much danger in them.'

'Yes, I remember that from school. In my boarding school my confessor warned me of those. But that was when I was just growing up. Will I not be able to have a friend ever for the rest of my life?'

'Did you heed your confessor?' Father Justin avoided answering Aelred's question directly.

'I tried, in a way, but it didn't work.' Aelred could feel himself censoring his thoughts.

'Your heart should be for God, brother, and for all your brothers equally.'

Aelred listened and thought Father Justin's words a hard doctrine. He remembered Dom Placid at school saying that love was painful. But he did not seem to be suggesting he should avoid it. He wanted to ask Father Justin about what he had talked about with Dom Placid, but he didn't feel encouraged to do that. He certainly didn't feel he could mention Benedict. He wanted to love all his fellow brothers, but that wasn't the love that seemed to be the most difficult. He would try and follow Father Justin's way and concentrate on his private prayer with God. But it seemed that there was one self which was trying that way and then another self that wanted something quite different.

He had not clicked with Father Justin. He found talking with him difficult. What was he going to do about that? The Novice Master was very important.

Since the moment in the library with Benedict, and noticing the portrait of the black boy on the staircase, which he could not get out of his mind and which distracted his meditations, as did thoughts of his relationship with Ted, he had not spoken to Benedict. Their formal meetings as his guardian angel were now over. 'You know the ropes now,' he had said at the end of that final formal session. He hardly saw him, except for choir and refectory. He talked to others at recreation. He had fleeting glimpses of him in the cloister. Benedict walked with his head bowed and hooded. He tried to meet his eyes, but they were downcast or averted. He had been embarrassed the last time he spoke with him in the library in passing. Then he thought he shouldn't try to get his attention. That was precisely not Father Justin's way.

Was Benedict weaning him? He felt that he could at least smile at him. Had all his attention been solely because he was his guardian angel and Aelred had been his charge? Was that all there was to it? Had it only been a duty? That would be in line with Father Justin's way. But he had felt other things with Benedict. There had been a kind of charm. He had not imagined it, had he?

Aelred began to feel homesick again. So, the spring had not changed his feelings, nor Benedict. The spring had continued with surprises. The flowers Aelred had learnt the names of - snowdrop, crocus, forsythia, daffodil, tulip - burst and burgeoned into the full shade of trees, as well as a host of flowering plants and shrubs he could not name and pin down. There was magnolia. This world was too different and he did not know enough of it fast enough. Ashton Park was growing too quickly. He leant against the rough stone wall of the cloister which caught the sun. All around was cold despite the sun. But this one spot was hot. He thought of how lizards lay in the sun at home. He warmed himself. The lizards moved among the dry almond leaves.

The new blossom suggested other colours, other shades, other names: poui, bougainvillea, flamboyante. In his mind the colours were too lurid for this light; smells were too rank for this soft powdery air.

Words are a world, he thought. Muslin is for dresses, linen for sheets, cotton for shirts and aprons, broderie anglaise for bodices. He heard his mother and Toinette. His father wore a pith hat for the sun, a rim of sweat on his brow. His arms were the colour of pawpaw. His horse was sprinkled with the colour of cinnamon and flour. And she, his mother, before she came down from her room, dipped her comb in a glass of water. It was light like a hummingbird's flicker, hovering like a halo over her hair. She smelt of *l'herbe-à* Madame Lalie; yellow-white lily flowers on a green lawn, collected by a black woman in her white cotton apron. She knelt and smelt of ginger and bayrum. It was Toinette. Toinette was black like bark, glossy like coral. Blue butterflies pinned themselves to a hedge of sweet lime. *Marbleu*. Between jalousies he could see the birdbath on the lawn at Malgretoute. Water is a mirror for a sky of enamel-basin blue. Breeze moves green palms. Palmistes! Breeze moves green hills. And again he heard Toinette's voice: 'Mungo have a scar right there on his neck. Like when you sweetheart give you a kiss on the neck and you could see the bite. But is no kiss. Mungo have to run. Mungo have to break his chains and run away.'

Snatches of the story were coming back to Aelred. They reminded him that he must go back to the library and carry on his reading about Master Walter, who had an estate in Antigua. He had made a fortune in sugar and added on a wing to the house at Ash Wood. But he never stayed there long. Old Sir Dewey, his father, could no longer make the journey, and Master Dewey always had to make yet another voyage to the West Indies. He could not trust those half-breed overseers with the running of the place. There had been a fire last time he was away and the darn niggers had almost ruined the place. There had been expensive repairs to be done to the sugar mill.

'Grandmammy say they always tie Mungo because he always running away and the Master can't afford to lose a young able-bodied boy.' Toinette's story threaded itself in with Aelred's readings in the library of Master Walter Dewey and his voyages to the West Indies.

'But where he get the scar on his neck, Toinette?' Maybe if he spoke in secret, in confession, he would get some help with his other preoccupation. Aelred wrestled with his dilemma. He began in the usual way, kneeling at the prie-dieu at the side of Father Basil's desk. 'Bless me, Father, for I have sinned. It has been a week since my last confession.' Then he was silent. He didn't know how to start. It was not like before, with a list of sins: pride, jealousy, losing his temper, impure thoughts. He wanted to talk about a condition.

In the end it was Father Basil who spoke. 'Is something worrying you, brother? Is there something you would like to talk out? Take your time. We can wait like this till you're ready.'

'I'm homesick, father.'

'Well, that 's only natural. And that's not a sin.' Father Basil smiled.

'But it's something else.'

'Yes.' Aelred kept staring at a statue of a donkey on Father Basil's desk. He remembered the sermon Father Basil had preached one Sunday of how the donkey that had carried the Virgin Mary and the child Jesus to Bethlehem and then on their flight to Egypt had experienced its sweetest burden. He then developed this long meditation on the donkey, a beast of burden, and of the burdens that we must be thankful that we have to carry. Father Basil had a simple childlike faith and devotion. The statue of the donkey was homely and comforting. 'And what do you miss the most, brother? '

'My friends.'

'Any particular friend?'

'Yes, in a way. 'Aelred did not want to talk about Ted. 'Having friends.'

'Yes, that's a big thing to give up and you're still very young. You've a lot of growing to do. You mustn't be impatient with yourself.'

'But I'm not allowed to have a friend, am I?'

'Do you think you know how to treat a friend? What care you must take? Why do you think you mustn't have a friend?'

'That's what Father Justin says. That there's a danger in particular friendships.'

'There are dangers. That's very true. That's why I ask you whether you know how to take care and how to treat a friend in a true friendship.'

'I want to be able to.'

'Well, go ahead and try within our rules and with care. Think of the other. Maybe, and this is natural in one as young as yourself, you're thinking too much of yourself and what you want. What does your friend want.? Think about that.'

Aelred left Father Basil's room feeling freer. He felt that Father Basil had mixed Father Justin's way with another possibility. Once he was careful, he could try. Yes, there were the rules of silence. But there were moments when it might be appropriate to talk to Benedict. He seized his chance in the laundry one Monday morning.

Working in the laundry room meant being confined all day in the hot steamy room with the tubs and washing machines, the electric driers, mangles and roller irons. Then the rules of silence were relaxed slightly. Brother Fergus, who was in charge, would give the signal and then they could have their break. When they had their coffee break it would be appropriate to exchange a few words.

But Aelred could have bit his tongue to stop himself once he started speaking. Hardly were they out in the courtyard, outside the laundry room, and he found himself, coincidentally alone with Benedict, when he blurted out, 'You've hardly smiled at me. You look away now.' This was not following Father Basil's advice. He was thinking of himself. But it did not stop him. 'I know the rules, but you don't have to be so cold.'

Benedict said nothing at first in reply to this unexpected outburst. 'There are others here. Please take care. I think of you. I pray for you at the beginning of your novitiate. It wouldn't be right to distract you. I don't mean to be cold.'

'Well, you are. You've already distracted me.'

'What I did, brother, was as a caring guardian angel, within the custom and practice of our community. That relationship is over now. We must meet appropriately in community. Certainly not like this. Not speaking to me like this. You must examine yourself.'

'And what about the other day on the staircase outside the library? You looked embarrassed last time I mentioned it.'

'What, brother? What do you mean?'

'You know what I mean. When I was standing looking at the portrait.'

Benedict would not continue. 'We must get back to work. Don't think badly of me. I've got your interests at heart. Be patient with our life, with the new life you've chosen.'

Aelred knew he had gone about it all wrongly.

At recreation that evening, Benedict made a point of sitting next to Aelred on the bench in the sunken garden where the novitiate met for recreation now that the weather was warmer. 'I've hardly told you about myself, have

I? You've told me so much already about your home and your young friend, Ted.' Aelred was immediately transformed from his depression, which had come upon him in the laundry earlier in the day.

'You said that you were from the valleys up north.'

'Yes, you remember.'

'Then what?'

'I studied at Oxford. That's not too far from here. Read English. Then I became a teacher for a short while. After visiting here I loved it so much I decided to join. That's the simple version.'

'Is there a more complicated version?'

They both began to feel at ease. This was appropriate, Aelred thought. This was what Benedict was teaching him. He had to keep biting his tongue. There was so much he wanted to tell Benedict.

The bells went for Vespers. And as they strolled up through the gardens, Benedict said, walking close to Aelred, '"Glory be to God for dappled things .../ All things counter .../ Whatever is fickle, freckled (who knows how?)." Gerard Manley Hopkins, a Jesuit and a great poet. Look for him in the library.'

This little moment enlarged the spirit of Aelred. It felt as if something special was being said to him.

The next morning after study and just before the bells went for the Conventual Mass, there was a knock on the door of Aelred's cell. '*Ave,*' he hailed.

Benedict put his head around the curtain of the novice's cubicle, which served as a cell. Aelred was so surprised that he leapt to his feet. Before he could speak, Benedict raised his hand and put a finger on his lips. 'Not now. Don't speak. Pray.' His finger traced Aelred's lips. 'I've brought you this. Read it. I think you'll find it help- ful. Some of the language will be strange at the begin- ning, but you'll get used to it. Read it more than once. Read and hear. Let the voices speak to you. It will be good for Lectio Divina. You can have it passed by Father Justin. I'm sure he'll approve.'

The bells for the Conventual Mass resounded through the abbey. A huge, joyous sound from the throat of the bells filled the valley of Ashton Park.

Benedict raised his hood and smiled. He turned and left the novitiate.

Aelred put his present on his desk. *Spiritual Friendship*, by Aelred of Rievaulx. He remembered. He was the same saint about whom Dom Placid had told him at school when he had gone to him about Ted. His namesake. He flicked the treatise open and read: 'When I was still just a lad at school, and the charm of my companions pleased me very much I gave my whole soul to affection and devoted myself to love amid the ways and vices with which that age is wont to be threatened, so that nothing seemed to be more sweet, nothing more agreeable, nothing more practical, than to love.'

He flicked again and read: 'And so, torn between con- flicting loves and friendship, I was drawn now here, now there, and not knowing the law of true friendship, I was often deceived by its mere semblance.'

As Aelred raised his hood and left his cell, he brought his fingers to his lips and traced them where Benedict had touched him. He kissed his fingers for the fingers of his friend. *He* understood.

The Guest House:
26 September 1984

The glory of the morning light
The burning heat of noonday sun...
The fever heat within the blood.

The monks have gone to Sext. I make the rhythm of their day, his day, my day. I notice the young monks - not many of them now. The community is much smaller than when J. M. was here. The youth of today don't come in their numbers any more. But I hear a passion in those voices. They breathe in, breathe out, young voices, old voices. And in the 'Salve Regina' at Compline last night, pitched in the darkness, their voices reached to the heights of the nave. What is this all about? He called it passion. When I think of J. M., just nineteen, think of all that has happened, I can't accept that this is the way for young men to grow. But I will keep an open mind, as Joe asks. I will. Has Joe got an open mind? I ask myself.

What Benedict and J. M. had they tried to keep well within the limits of Aelred of Rievaulx's theology of friendship. Even I can see that, though I find it strange to think of a medieval saint advocating it would seem, homosexual love, in thought at least, if not in deed. I never realised this existed in the writings of the church. This was Benedict's way of coping. I read that in the journals. Maybe I can talk to him about that, something objective. But can I ask him about himself and J. M.? How can I? It's too private, and too many years have gone by. Why should he talk to me about this part of his life? Can one talk about these things easily? I wouldn't want to talk with just anyone about Annette and myself, about the divorce. No way!

This morning I returned again along the trail to the quarry, testing the boundaries, the depth of the excavation. I got lost again among the silver birches. There are ghosts. They walked here. Earlier ones; ran. There are these layers of history. I keep coming back to these two things, sorting out in my mind my brother's love for a man and his guilt about race. These are the two things I have to sort out in myself. The first because it's to do with him, not me, the second because I grew up in the same world as him with the same history. His views broadened on both these issues. It happened differently for me, living up on a cocoa estate on a small island. I stayed and went to university on the island. Unusual, but there is a very good Department of Tropical Agriculture. I was following my father.

Benedict and I didn't work together yesterday, but we did manage our first quiet talk here in my guest room. We had about three-quarters of an hour before Vespers. He is mainly concerned about me, to talk about my loss of faith. He can't understand how I've let the whole thing go. I said that I felt rejected by the clergy and the community. It was a matter of how the church dealt with what it called sin, in particular, sexual sin. I suggested that this was similar to what had happened for J. M. He skirted round that. I have to be careful with how I talk about J. M. He was sympathetic, like he was through the whole thing in the end. He said that he would not condemn, but that he could not condone and he did not approve of how J. M.'s life had developed.

But I can see it disturbs him that I have J. M.'s journals. He must know that I know more than I talk about. As a way of life, it disturbs him. I think it disturbs me. It does disturb me. Probably because of the way I learnt about it. There hasn't been anything in my life till now that would encourage me even to think about homosexuality as acceptable in any way at all. Homosexuality was messing about at school or older men touching up young boys. But I've never had to take it on as a seriously considered way of life which people have noble thoughts about; certainly never considered it as something that could be part of my family. You read Aelred of Rievaulx and you see it was an intrinsic part of his religious life and love of God. I might see it as a phase. Benedict says it's something you have to accept in yourself. It's something not even to get rid of, but to accept, almost God-given, to be borne, a cross. It is an occasion of sin, but also an occasion of grace. Something to be denied. The more powerful, the more it is to be denied; the richer the grace for the greater denial. I felt he was protesting too much. Was he telling me about himself? Is this how he dealt with his homosexuality and his celibacy, his chastity? Would he call it that? Would he admit to that?

Even on J. M.'s last visit to Les Deux Isles, even then, I didn't put two and two together. He was a loner. He went off on his expeditions. This was when he was visiting Amerindian sites in Oropuche and Arenas. Now I understand: even then he was interested in the presence of Africa in the Caribbean, as he called it. The Amerindian stuff interested me, and I would've liked to have gone with him on a dig, and in that way try and make some sort of relationship. I had an interest in the early history of the island. But he never made it possible. He said he preferred to be on his own. There was something, but I put it out of my mind. I couldn't quite put my finger on it. I put it down to someone who had lived in a monastery. So it didn't seem odd that he wasn't running behind women. Now that I think about it, he mentioned a woman who was also an archaeologist in England. That was why Miriam's name rang a bell when I first met her, so I thought maybe she was his girlfriend. Anyway, I was busy with the estate.

About African history on the island, I said, there was nothing.

J. M. replied, Wasn't that significant?

He asked me didn't I think it was interesting, disturbing, that there were no African names of any real significance, no place names? Had I not thought about why that was?

At the time, I said that I hadn't.

We wiped out their history, he said.

Long ago I might've said, And a good thing too. I don't think that now. But 1970 and Black Power was still a memory for all of us at Malgretoute, a hard lesson.

Late one night we stayed up talking on the verandah high above the cocoa hills. The night was full of fireflies. On the plains, St Pierre twinkled in the distance near the gulf. I remember it well. He used to enjoy me playing the cuatro, all the old-time calypsos. Like he hadn't changed. He got a bottle and spoon, I an old grater, and we made music together. That night he had quite a few rums, which surprised me. But I could see that he had found our father's death and funeral difficult. He had arrived just in time. A day later, and he would've missed it.

At the actual moment of death it was just J. M., me and our mother; the girls had just left. I could see his mouth moving over the Hail Mary and Our Father of the rosary.

He wouldn't be silent and hurt her. He prayed as if he
believed. Maybe, somewhere he still did. Maybe somewhere there was still that special link with her, that thing
which had to do with religion and just the way he was.

Too beautiful, she would always say. I mumbled my res-
ponses in my usual way.

She was accustomed to that. Robert, darling, open your
mouth. It is God you are talking to.

It was our father's heart that gave out in the end. But
he had been going steadily downhill over the last couple
of years. J. M. said he didn't really want to hear about it,
that Mum had written about it in a letter. But I had had a
few rums myself. Emotions were raw because of Dad's
death and the funeral the week before. So I launched
into my story. Electricity and phone lines had been down,
so there was no communication. Imagine it! We were all
out here on the verandah, like now, I told him. It was
after dinner and Toinette had already cleared the table
and gone downstairs. There was no TV to watch. She used
to like to sit by the pantry door and watch the TV from
there. She had got very old. I could see J. M. register that.
He had missed Toinette's death. He asked where she was
buried. He wanted to visit her grave. Mum had written to
him about that. I had to get out the cemetery plan for
him. They buried her outside the family plot.

You missed something, I told him. They came right
into the yard, about a hundred people, Indian and
Negro. Their leader shouted for Dad to come out and
talk to them. All the time the crowd shouted, Power! They
called for la Borde. Mum took to her bedroom with the
rosary. I stood just inside and Dad went out on to the
verandah. The chanting of Power continued. Then the

most extraordinary thing happened. Toinette came out from under the house and started shouting in her weak voice.

What all you people want? All you young boys don't have work to do? All you don't have mother and father to go home to? You not shame coming up in Mr La Borde yard at this time of night.

The crowd went silent. Dad went down into the yard and stood next to Toinette, and put his arm around her shoulder. For a moment they stood there, the old cocoa planter and his servant, the old black woman, with a crowd of Negroes and Indians ready to start chanting again, but gone strangely quiet.

I was looking down from the verandah. Dad and Toinette just stood there. Someone tried to make a speech about wages on the estate, about the state of the barrack rooms that still existed. But it was Toinette standing there that dampened the crowd. I swear they might have burnt down the house. Then people began shuffling and filing out of the yard. Dad and Toinette kept standing there till the last man and woman left. Dad indicated to Toinette to go back to her room and then he came back upstairs.

I heard Toinette muttering, Well, what you expect if you treat people so. What you expect? She knew. But at the same time she came and stood next to Dad. He was shaking. He didn't speak. He went to his room.

Later in the night, I heard a noise, glass shattering, so I came out on to the verandah. Dad was sitting alone. He was sobbing. Someone had flung a flambeaux on to the verandah, where it had smashed. The flame ran for a bit then petered out. The banisters got scorched.

They want to burn me out, I heard Dad say.

Only one odd drunk fellow coming back late, I told him.

But it cut him up.

After all these years, they want to burn me out, he said.

It was the final end of the old ways. I remember J. M. saying that. I could see that he thought we deserved what was coming to us. But then he said, Poor Dad.

Strange all this coming back as I sit here in England unravelling these stories. We don't know what will turn out when we are kids and growing up.

Before J. M. left to go back to England we sorted through Dad's things. I had flashes then of how it had been at school. He had been a kind of hero for me to begin with and then it changed. I didn't guess his life.

You were the one he really loved, J. M., said, meaning Dad. Funny, the one thing he took as a memento was an old Yardley shaving bowl in which Dad kept his school rowing medals. He took the bowl and the medals. They were part of the clutter on the desk in the flat in Bristol. For some reason I put my face in it and it still held that Yardley fragrance, the one perfume he allowed himself.

I unearth. I unlearn. I'm an earth digger. I'm a word eater.

Typical Benedict, as I'm learning: as he stood to leave the room for Vespers, he pulled me towards him and hugged me. He really held on to me.

I will pray for you, he said. Have an open heart.

His body was so thin. I could feel the ribs beneath his habit. Benedict used to be well built, J. M. said. He sees J. M. in me, he says. I felt a bit awkward there being hugged and him saying that. There is a way you hug a man. You embrace and keep firm. If one of you relaxes into it as you might with a woman, he gives himself away; you know something is different and you withdraw. We held it firm. I expect they used to relax into it.

My Lectio Divina is the *Song of Songs*, a favourite monastic text, interpreted metaphorically. I didn't know the Bible could be so hot. I continue to read Aelred of Rievaulx. I have the journals and now my own stories. I reconstruct. I tell his life. It begins to change something in me. It begins to change me writing this. Write it to understand it: that was his method. I hear Miriam's voice.

I eat his words.

He moves between there and here.

I stood on the tarmac of the airfield below the green mountains which changed to blue when I began to walk towards the steps up to the plane. When would I turn around and wave to my mother and father, brother and sisters, to Aunt Marie who had just given me a bound volume of the Old and New Testaments, and a bouquet of pink anthuriums wrapped in cellophane for Aunt Julie in England? They were so pink and looked unreal in the cellophane. Like plastic. I felt awkward carrying them, but I couldn't refuse. When would I turn and wave? That was what important people like Princess Margaret or the Governor did when they got to the top of the steps before they entered the aircraft. I turn. There is Robert. Did I ever make things clear to him? Did I leave a burden on young shoulders? The sun came out from behind the clouds and the mountains were green again.

'My dear man, you can't possibly expect me to unpack this boy's case. But I will, because I will certainly not pay the over-weight.' My mother was in charge. She spoke to the black BOAC

*attendant. My father had his back to us at the check-in desk, at
the window, looking out into the car park. He was smoking a
cigarette. 'Jean Marc, it's those boots and you have insisted on
those books, darling. You can get books in England. There will
be lots in the library of the abbey. Let's take the books out. Leave
the boots, otherwise your poor feet will freeze in that winter.
Remember what Father Justin said in his letter. They are worried
about you. I can't send you without shoes, darling. And Mrs
Salter was so kind to let you have Ted's boots. Your friend. Open
up this case, my dear man.' My mother threw up her arms with
impatience.*

*Ted's mother had said I could have his boots for the trip to
England. Ted. Poor Ted. And would I die too? We swam under-
water till we got to the rock. 'Come on out now,' someone shouted.
Our bodies shining in the afternoon sun. Ted died when he was
seventeen. I was a bearer at his funeral. We went from school in a
procession all along the promenade to the big church.*

'Bless me, father, for I have sinned. Father, will he go to hell?'
'Why, my son?'
*'The week before he died - died - we were playing in the pool
and we...' When I looked into the coffin he looked as if he had
been covered with white powder. He didn't look like Ted. I had
been dreaming of Ted. Poor Ted. I could see in the dim night light
which shone from the dormitory ceiling, his boots, next to my
desk. I woke to the other novices being knocked up,* Benedicamus Domino, *and their sleepy answers:* Deo gratias. *I
was being allowed to lie in this first morning. Then falling asleep
and waking again to bells. Matins...* Domine labia mea aperies ... *and then I fell back to sleep. Thoughts and dreams.*

*I lay under four blankets and an electric blanket on rough
cotton sheets, my head on a bolster with what seemed like a rock
stone inside it. The cotton curtain of my cubicle cell moved in*

the cold draught I felt when I stuck out my hand, and then it moved again with the draught of passing novices in the corridor. I woke when the novices came back from Matins. Then I got up. It was dark like night. The water was as cold as ice. Thank God for Uncle André's coat, thick and grey. It smelt of mothballs and cuscus grass, the little sachets which Aunt Marie had tucked into the sleeves and pockets preserving it from the penetration of moths after Uncle André's death. 'He loved you like a father would love a son; he would have wanted you to have had it.' I had lain the coat right on top of all my blankets. Its coarse herringbone scratched my face, as did the rough feel of the jute blankets.

I hugged it around me now, far from home, that first morning after my first night in my monastic cell. I pushed my woollen-gloved hands deep into the pockets. The notes of the Sequence for the dead trembled in the lattice of naked branches. The measured tread of the monks following Brother Chrysostom's coffin crushed the gravel under the ice, which crunched at the entrance to the small oblong of green lawn that had once been a medieval cemetery. Funny, I thought, it looks like dry season, but so cold, so cold. The dead leaves in the hedge which the snow had not covered, like dry season, but cold, so cold. Father Justin had been right about coming in the winter. I didn't feel homesick though, not yet. But it was only my first day. My throat tightened. I wasn't homesick, yet.

To find my name years later, his thoughts of me, amazes me, moves me. It was like he had died then. They had both died. I kept a low profile at school, except I learned tennis, and got really good, for his sake. He wanted that.

He tells a story moving over the sea, migrating in his mind. I follow.

The pelican's young pick at its breast. They drink blood. Images I'm reminded of.

Drink this... words, words change everything. Blue veins the colour of Quink ink. A poetry of pain.

The Grave

Take no notice of my swarthiness,
It is the sun that has burnt me.
Song of Songs

Aelred came to the cemetery at siesta time. It was a quiet, secluded spot above the abbey. It was a sun catch. That was what he liked about the spot. He brought the work he was doing on the translation of the psalms and sat on the grass in the open among the graves. The graves were in rows; a simple wooden cross over each plot. The only inscription was 'PAX' and the name of the dead monk with the date of his birth and death. He would be able to listen for the bell for None from here. His concentration flagged in the warmth and after-lunch drowsiness. He struggled with his translations.

In a corner of the cemetery was the small medieval chapel. Aelred wandered around it, reading the inscriptions on gravestones which had been leant up against the walls. One stone in particular caught his attention. There was a stone carving of a head. It was a young head, a boy, with curly hair. Under the head was the letter J. The other parts of the inscription had faded. He could just read part of a date, 17– As Aelred continued to stare at the face, he realised that it was an African head. He could tell by the lips, the nose, and the woolly hair the stone carver had given to the head. The portrait on the staircase came immediately to his mind. Could he be the same boy? Something in him wanted it to be the same boy. His fancy ran away with him. He invented a name for this head. Jordan, like the river. 'The River Jordan is mighty and

cold, halleluia, chills the body but not the soul, halleluia.'
As Aelred hummed, he heard the singing and clapping,
the chanting and wailing coming from the Baptist chapel
down in the village of Felicity below Malgretoute. Toinette
bound her head in a white cloth and went to pray there
on her evenings off.

Jordan. He said his name. The wind whispered in the
cedars of Lebanon. Jordan. He heard waves breaking on a
beach without care. He heard the chuckle of salt waves
meeting the fresh water current of a river. Then, there
was an ocean.

Aelred thought of Father Dominic's remark about the
secret tunnel and about the runaway. His fancy enlarged
upon a story building in his mind. He was filling in from
his study of West Indian History at school in his last year.
He was filling in his recent reading in the library of
Master Walter Dewey's exploits on the island of Antigua.

According to Amy, an old woman who worked in the
Dewey house at Ash Wood, Master Walter had arrived late
one night from one of his voyages. The ship had berthed
in Bristol. They had had to put in at those islands called
the Azores because of storms. Amy heard Master Walter
grumbling to the groom of his many trials as he left the
horse to be watered and stabled for the rest of the night.
They might've lost a valuable cargo. And that would have
been a cheer for the abolitionists, she heard Master
Walter sneer. They'd rather them in God's hands than in
chains doing work in my household or in my sugar fields.
He had galloped all the way from the port to Ash Wood.
But there was a great commotion in the courtyard that
night of his arrival and Amy, that Somerset woman, was
left to assuage the wounds of a young black fella who had

had to run alongside Master Walter's horse, often dragged behind along the lanes and fields, stumbling and
falling near the hedgerows.

Then all at once, Ted entered this story. Certain
moments just came back, kinds of coincidences they must
be, Aelred thought. He and Ted had been playing one of
their secret games. Then they had gone to the grapefruit
trees below the estate house. They were climbing and picking fruit, peeling it with their fingers, pegging it, they
called it, and sucking on the fruit so that the juice was
sticky on their hands and faces, dribbling on their merino
jerseys.

Sometimes little quarrels would break out between
them. He couldn't remember now what the quarrel was
about. But suddenly Ted blurted out, 'So, my grandmother's black.'

'She can't be black, because you're not black. That's
stupid.'

'She is black. I should know.'

'Which grandmother is it - your father's or your mother's
mother.'

'She's my father's mother.'

'But your father's not black. '

'His father is white.'

They were shouting these statements at each other as if
they were swear words. The words 'black' and 'white' in
particular, 'father' and 'mother', were ringing out, with
venom and insult mixed with incredulity in J. M.'s voice,
and a stoic assertion in Ted's.

'Anyway, you aren't black, so,' J. M. hit back.

Then Ted said, 'But I'm blacker than you. Look.' He
stuck out his arm and lifted his merino and showed his

chest and belly. 'Look, I'm much blacker than you.' He was saying this boastfully. Till quite suddenly, they were almost fighting with each other, grappling and almost falling out of the fruit tree from whose branches they were hanging.

'I know what you're like. I've seen you. You don't have to show me. Don't show me,' J. M. shouted.

'Don't you like it ?' Ted teased.

J. M.'s anger brought tears. He walked away and went out from where the fruit trees were into another part of the estate. He hid among the young canes. He remembered the smell of ripe guavas.

Now as he wrestled with his nature, his sin, his love for Benedict, he sort of made a pact with Jordan. Like having an imaginary friend, a friend from home. It was his black skin, reminding him of Ted and the black school pardners whom he had left behind. He repeated their names like a litany. Surnames: de la Borde, Espinet, Mackensie, Redhead, Ramnarine, Salter. Like a roll-call at school. Present, present, present... their voices faded in the yellow sunlight, motes of dust caught in the bands of light coming through the open windows of the school room smelling of coconut oil in San Andres.

They were all in the same school in the racatang building next to the church of Notre-Dame de Grace. He could smell the coconut oil which the Indian children used to use. They were all together: black, brown, white and Indian, all mixed together till three o'clock and then they went their separate ways. They didn't come to his home to play; only Ted did. 'He's a nice boy,' his mother said. 'His people are good people.' Now Aelred could begin to admit to himself the coded words of his mother's statements and questions. 'Have you met all the family, dear?'

He held the memory like a photograph: the day he saw all of him standing with his back to him, his dark curly hair, his strong neck and shoulders, his curved back and slim hips, his buttocks rising, the muscles climbing his back and then his long legs, muscled calves. He just had to recall it and the vision was there. His brown skin. 'I'm blacker than you.' He turned and smiled. He could now see his developed chest and the darker, browner marks around his nipples, his flat hard belly, the black curly hair around his thick prick and tight balls, little tight curls on his legs. 'I'm blacker than you.' He smiled a smile of white teeth and full red lips. They locked together, hard against each other and then relaxed into that embrace they began to know so well; then held fast till they could hardly breathe.

The images of Ted and himself swarmed and hummed like the bees and wasps already beginning to feed on the new flowers in the warm after-lunch heat of his secluded sun catch. He could hear the noisy playground when they were younger. He could hear Dom Maurus's voice: 'de la Borde, Salter.' They would run to meet him and be caught up in the swirling folds of his white habit, his scapular like a Hindu prayer flag in the breeze. They were Dom Maurus's favourites. Dom Maurus smelt of incense, communion wafers, the scent of wine, the blood of Christ on the breath. He gathered them into the white clouds of his monastic habit as they swirled in play in the school yard of the parish church of Notre-Dame de Grace.

Jordan. Aelred began his story. He was Jordan of Ashtown in Antigua. His portrait was on the staircase. He was the duke's slave. What kind of life had he had before he was buried here? Jordan was blacker than boys he had known at school. He had the blackness of Africans. There was something pure about the colour of his skin, the mould of his face, the dome of his brow, the spread of his nose, the white of his eyes which shone against the black of his skin. The full curl of his lips was red like rouge.

Who had painted him? Had he really looked like this?

Aelred began to remember facts and figures from the history he had learnt in the last year of school, when the syllabus changed from British History to West Indian History. Father Julius had chosen to teach the slave trade. There were etchings, artists' impressions of Africans being captured on the shores of the dark continent. That was what John Buchan had called it in Prester John. It was a green and black book and published by Blackie. He remembered that.

Then he saw Jordan beneath the deck of the ships. He was put into a hold for small boys. In the holds of those charnel galleons, they were packed in, head to head on their sides with other boys, chained at the feet and the hands, with collars round their necks. Many peas in one pod.

'Lord and Master, in the River Jordan wash me clean, as white as snow.' He heard Toinette praying in the kitchen after Baptist prayers, peeling onions so it made her cry.

'What you crying for, Toinette?'

'Child, don't be stupid.'

Sin was black. There appeared to be nothing more

beautiful than Jordan's blackness. There appeared to be nothing more beautiful than what Aelred felt for Benedict, his love for him. That too was a sin, Aelred's sin. His first love was Ted. It became a prayer. Don't go from me, dear friend. They had hardly known what life meant. He did not want to betray Ted's memory. He felt again how unjust that he should have been snatched out of his sight. He jackknifed into the bronze pool; the River Jordan, bled like flamboyante. Then there was his bruised white face; powder over his face. The lid came down on the coffin in Paradise Cemetery. '*Dies irae, dies illa*'... it was a hot afternoon with a procession of schoolboys. Wreaths smelt sweet like frangipani. Still a boy, one of the old ladies of the parish whispered. He prayed. I will not betray you. I'm adult now. Here, unasked for, unimagined, quite unpredictable, I came across the ocean thousands of miles following a dream, then another dream, not knowing, and here, this man, this kind man. Nothing has happened. Nothing I can put my finger on has touched me so. I know nothing like it. Not what we had, Ted. Do I betray you? Not just that touching and those pardner feelings, those little-boy pleasures. And even when it came out all sticky and white and smelling of swimming-pools. Was it love like this where there has been nothing? There is nothing to speak of, but glances and smiles, the restraint of the monastic kiss, the brushing of cheeks at the 'Agnus Dei'. 'Lamb of God, who taketh away the sins of the world, have mercy on us.' There is the acknowledgement of the bowed head, the tilted hood, hands put back into the safety of cowls, or folded beneath scapulars; averted eyes.

This was how he chose to remember him. Jordan

reminded him. Ted, Benedict, he called upon all three.

Jordan would help. It was his name which first came to him. Because of the river? Because of the river and the crossing over, Toinette called it. Because of the black boys he played with, because of the comfort of blackness: it was these things.

Toinette say, '*Dou-dou... Dou-dou.*' He heard her voice in the wood pigeon. He saw her black breasts. Her polished, purple arms like melangen enfolded him.

He smelt Jordan. He smelt of bayrum and talcum powder. He smelt of Ted.

Because of the river in the valley which flows beneath the school he called him Jordan.

Aelred was jolted out of his reverie with the bell for None. He scrambled up his books. He had not got far today with the translation of the psalms.

The Guest House:
27 September 1984

May evening time be calm and clear...

Since eleven this morning the house has been smelling of boiled cabbage. That was something J. M. always remembered; still the old cabbage. The diet has not changed in twenty-one years. Siesta; I doze and read. I was reading, but also re-reading what J. M. had read twenty-one years ago, trying to make sense of the passion of his youth. I read of how Aelred of Rievaulx lost his heart to one boy and then to another in his schooldays. I reflected now, like the young abbot of Rievaulx, that J. M.'s youth had brought with it many problems concerning the question of love. That really seems an understatement. But I can see why J. M. identified so closely with this twelfth-century Cistercian.

I'm changing inside myself. Joe's advice is proving to be good advice. As I read and reconstruct I'm beginning to see it J. M.'s way. Well, not completely. I'm not sure about all the physical stuff. I can see you can really be close to a fella, kind of love him. But the other, I don't know.

I wait for the bell for None. This afternoon I will work again in the orchard with Benedict. I hope. He whispered at breakfast that he had not had a good night, whatever that means. I must confront him about his health. He was so pale. I didn't see him eating anything: he was only drinking coffee, his head bowed over his brown bowl.

The events surrounding Ted's death came back to me again last night, so I didn't fall back to sleep till almost when the bells for Matins went. I must've been wakened by the bells for Matins and then again for Lauds. I was half dreaming, half going back over the events.

What is still so extraordinary is that even now the monks at college don't know the truth, or won't divulge it. If I had not gone down to the river that afternoon, no one would've have had a chance to hear the truth. Not that they listened, or wished to believe. It was a scandal. Above all else, scandal must be prevented. What is truth? I've put all this aside for so long that I find it difficult to recall it precisely the way it happened. Then Joe's letter came, announcing J. M.'s death.

When he went away I gradually forgot everything. His letters to Mum and Dad used to bring it back but, even then it faded eventually. He was like a frozen image, my brother who went away. J. M.'s journals astound me in how much they remember, as if it had all happened yesterday. This is disturbing for me. I'm beginning to see how he saw it.

Now, I should've seen it coming, the afternoon of 'the Raid', as J. M. called it. That should have been a sign enough, but I should have seen it even before that. I can't imagine, though, how anyone dared to start it. It spread like wildfire. To say it of Ted! He didn't deny it. But he chose silence which meant guilt to everyone. Then his standing in the college, as head boy, and captain of both the football and the cricket team, was at its height. He was everyone's hero. But who was the sad boy who thought he had to destroy him? I read that question all these years later. Did even I know, who saw him dive? Saw them both dive? Standing away from the bigger boys, I see his fear, hear jeers, taunts, the dares of all the others jostling around him. Dive, dive! Those others stood around me.

No one owned up to the writing on the wall. A jealous boy? I could always swear I knew who it was. Was it someone who wanted to hurt J. M., jealous of him, someone who wished to destroy the one whom he desired? But he knew that if it was said about J. M. alone it would peter out, last for a day or two. Linked with the name of Ted, that was dynamite! Headmaster, dean of discipline, house captains, parents, everyone was involved. But they let it run. No one said a word. No one dampened the stamping feet in the study hall. No one put a stop to the hissing in the refectory.

Psst!

And then those words hurled!

Ted's authority was threatened and challenged everywhere. Ted remained in his positions. No one seemed to take on the refusal of the teams to practice. No one seemed to take on the self-fouling that took place on the football field.

Is this why I'm here? I saw and heard all that and I said nothing. You forget how it was. J. M. must've gone over these events many times. They are dated early on in the journal.

Ted Salter is a *buller*.

The word we boys used for sodomites, the double-backed beast. Everyone went scuttling to their Bibles for the words: Sodom and Gomorrah.

The word got taken up, '*Buller, buller,*' the chant leaders looking around to see who was not joining in.

Then there were the writings and drawings. An arrow pierces a heart, like those chalked by teenage sweethearts. It was a lopsided heart scratched with a penknife into the door of one of the cubicles in the seniors' lavatories. You sit there and scratch away at the wood with the smell of farts and urine, running water gurgling like a fountain in the urinal. There can be silence and escape there. It can be as silent as the silence of a confessional. You read the other words; words that are written then scrubbed off, written again, 'Timothy de Gannes has the biggest prick. Eight inches. Fuck. Suck. Cock. Balls. Ted Salter loves Jean Marc de la Borde. XX for kisses in a heart. Love me tender, love me true... ELVIS.'

I had crept in and looked at the graffiti now that everyone was talking about it. My face burned with shame; a smaller boy, a younger brother. My allegiance was challenged, my ideals attacked. Athletes, heroes. His beauty, their beauty, was destroyed.

It took a while for either of them to understand why it had started. They were sure no one knew. No one saw anything. Then a friend told them. They each, separately, found the right cubicle and saw the heart and kisses. They read the words. There was a feeble attempt to find the culprit with a threat of detention for the whole school, the suspension of the Saturday night film. This was allowed to happen to a head boy!

They thought no one knew anything.

No one knew. No one saw. Their love was a secret, confessional. It hid in the silence of the night, in an owl's hoot, in the head boy's room after lights-out. He was the trusted one. The window of his room opened over the wide valley, the sky encrusted with constellations. Jagged stars, Look, a comet.

One boy tilts his head back over the window in the darkness. The other boy has his lips on his mouth, his hands on his neck.

Look, Orion, the Plough, the Rosary. They navigate with the stars.

The world swirled. They risked everything. The plains beneath were smouldering with cane fires. The smell of cane juice was on the night air.

They had permission to swim late at the river pool. They picked ripe cashews, stained their shirts with the juice. The shade of the cocoa trees hid the yellow and red sunset, hid their naked bodies. It was siesta when their cries were drowned by the cigale in the gru-gru tree, when their sighs, their kisses, mixed with the sawing cicadas in the whispering casuarinas.

J. M., Aelred. It is Aelred the young monk, not my brother J. M., who found this poetry in himself even here in the cold of winter. He found these high words, as he calls them, in the high hills, from the tall palms, from the palmistes. He called them that, 'high words'. He had begun to mix it all up. 'In the valley below, the River Jordan over blue-veined rocks like the blue of Quink ink.' High words. He writes them, the kind of words he writes as poetry, the kind of words I saw in the lavatory: lick, suck.

I hear his voice: Push it in.

They walked back in the darkness holding hands.

I eat his words. I am drunk with his blood. Words of blood soak into desk tops, on to lavatory walls. Messages. They were marooned in their desire. I become a poet.

Cocoa planter sing your calypso boy. Leave these matters to the poet. Then a world litany of abuse: queers, faggots.

What's strange, what lights a fire?

Pouf, fairy. Pretty, funny, light as a feather.

I talked with Joe and Miriam and they explained to me
these things. I'm beginning to understand a bit. Like Joe
says, you can still see written up in public lavatories, 'Who
will kill a pouf for me?'

Then, when I return to J.M's journal, he's recorded it with
another gaze.

*There was the boy who touched my knee while he was sitting close
on a bench, umpiring tennis. Then he left me. He looked back
down the road at me after the game. He went the way the seniors
went and would not talk with me. He would not say what that
touch meant. There was the boy who dragged me below the water
of the swimming-pool, so fiercely, that he could have drowned me
and I thought he must want to. There was the boy who preened
himself like a rock-and-roll star and hit me all the time to prove
his toughness. I thought, it is because he knows that I know, that
what he really wants to do is to kiss me, what he really wants to
do are things he can't even imagine, so he preens and preens and
loves his own image. There was the boy who lay awake at the foot
of his bed while I lay at the foot of my bed. We stared into each
other's eyes in the night-light of the dormitory. This was the boy
who had stared at my legs and noticed there the blue in my veins.*

*One afternoon, while the wood smoke rose above the valley,
smelling of the resin of cedar trees, this same boy leant close to my
neck and told me that he wanted to kiss me as if I was a girl. He
then went away and never did kiss me.*

*There was the boy with whom I lay in the heat of siesta reading
comics. We leant against each other until our weight was as
heavy as the heat which bore down on the croton hedges and
made the frangipani and the poinsettia droop. In the midst of
that moment, the cigale cried for rain. We leant so close that our*

lips, at first dry and then wet, kissed and kissed and kissed. We spoke not a word of what it meant.

After the holidays, I carried a letter for this boy, a letter of the utmost sincerity, declaring a love which never got told. The letter was eventually torn into shreds one afternoon in the forest on one of my secret pilgrimages to the shrine in the forest. I lit a small fire of dry leaves and burnt his letter, burnt my words.

These are testaments he found in himself, years after. Now I find them.

I was there, twelve, thirteen, and did not understand.

The Walk

For see winter is past, the rains are over and gone.
The flowers appear on the earth.
Song of Songs

It was a time of glances, smiles, tilted hoods and '*Agnus Dei*' kisses. Aelred liked it when he got to stand next to Benedict in choir and would receive the kiss of peace from him; when he would get to be held on the shoulders and he could hold him under the arms and they could rest their cheeks one upon the other, first to the left and then to the right: 'Lamb of God, who takest away the sins of the world...'

'Peace be with you,' Benedict greeted Aelred.

'And with you,' Aelred whispered.

The seasons had changed from winter to spring and the first signs of summer were beginning. The copper beeches in Ashton Park were putting out a new sheen. The liturgical year had unfolded with its own colours: green, white, purple, gold and red. It unfolded with its own times of the year: Advent, Christmas, Lent, Easter and Pentecost. Then there was green, the greening of the year. Aelred looked forward to Sunday walks.

What increasingly became important for Aelred was his attachment to Benedict; everything else fell to this, or found meaning in this as yet unspoken bond, this attraction. He felt that this was Aelred of Rievaulx's *affectus*. This attraction was in a glance, a smile, a gesture, meaningful coincidences if put to work together in the garden, weeding or folding linen in the laundry. Their eyes met in choir. They exchanged smiles during meals.

They spoke in signs. The limitations put upon them by the rule intensified these wordless communications. They worked under Brother Stephen's supervision. 'Come on now, brothers, we need that weeding finished by the end of the afternoon.'

Aelred felt that his desire was straitened.

Benedict had become Aelred's model: the way he walked, hooded and bowed; he way he stood in choir; his singing; the way he served and read in the refectory; the way he kept his silence and studied in the library; his meditations in the cloister. He watched him. He followed him. 'I'll make myself like you,' he said impulsively one day while Benedict taught him the rituals for cantor in choir.

Benedict smiled. 'You'll be yourself, I'm sure.' The older man kept with his lesson.

Aelred's imagination was fired by the reading of Aelred of Rievaulx's book *Spiritual Friendship* which Benedict had given him. Lectio Divina was now a special time. Aelred began to imagine the dialogues that he could have with Benedict, fired by the dialogues between the Abbot Aelred and Ivo his monk. He read and ruminated: 'to live without friendship was to live like a beast'. Those were Aelred of Rievaulx's words. Dom Placid had told him the story as a boy and now he needed to know more. He had come this far, leaving mother, father, brother, sisters and land.

As recreation ended one afternoon, Aelred said to Benedict, 'Thanks for Aelred of Rievaulx's book. I'm deep into it. Though I've still got to speak to Father Justin about reading it.'

'You see the parallels with Aelred of Rievaulx's life?' Benedict asked.

'Yes, of course. I see a lot of things. Do you think we can talk more?'

'In time. Don't rush it. And we've got our rules.'

He needed all the help to grow to understand his nature, to understand his sin.

'But you've not committed any sin,' Father Basil said to Aelred during his weekly confession and spiritual guidance time.

'Aren't my feelings sin? Feelings like, wanting to kiss, to hold hands and more. More feelings, I can hardly describe to you. I just tell you that they're impure.'

'Brother, you're young. You've got the passion of youth. Not because you've joined the monastery and desire to live the chaste life are you going to be immediately changed. It's a *life* that you've entered. It will take a life.' Aelred looked at the old man with the statue of the donkey on his desk. He thought of him as a young man. Did he know what he was going through because it had also happened to him? Had it taken him a life? Was it still taking him a life?

'Sometimes I feel I should punish myself. Do you think I should ask permission to use the discipline?' Aelred was referring to the whip which monks customarily used on themselves on Friday nights.

'No, brother,' Father Basil smiled. 'We don't think that's appropriate any more. Some of the older monks who were trained in the use of the discipline from when they were young can sometimes get permission to continue. But not someone as young as yourself. It would not help you brother. You should not dwell on these things too much. Keep the rules of our life going. These will help you.'

'But maybe pain? Something painful could stop me feeling what I feel. So, if I whipped myself? If I fasted, maybe? That's what the saints did.'

'You must come and talk. You must thank God for your passion. He wants those who give their life to him to be wholehearted about it. In time, this passion will be fully changed and directed only to God.'

Aelred always felt better after meeting Father Basil. Not like when he had to see Father Justin. Then everything had to be clamped down. He felt muzzled by Father Justin.

'Why don't you read Francis de Sales, St John Boscoe?' Father Justin asked Aelred at his weekly novice master's meetings. 'Do you think you are able as yet to understand the monastic authors of the twelfth century? It may be better to keep to tested spiritual teaching from texts which have been tried repeatedly.'

'I thought you would be pleased with me reading monastic writers, rather than the religious life of other traditions,' Aelred answered, trying to take the bull by the horns. He wished he could be more honest with Father Justin.

Instead Father Justin reiterated his old warning, 'Never in twos, always in threes.'

'What? What do you mean? Who are you talking about?'

'Brother it's my duty to notice these things. I've noticed you and Brother Benedict. Is this wise?'

'But you know he was my guardian angel. You know that it must be because of that .'

'Never in twos, always in threes. If followed, there can

be little danger.'

Aelred did not reply immediately, but became alert and, without admitting it to himself at the time, angry. 'He was my guardian angel. Who else should I talk to?'

'But he's a man, not an angel, brother.'

'I know he's a man. What do you mean? Of course he's not a angel.'

And, as he left the novice master's cell, Father Justin smiled. 'Beware of particular friendships, brother. Follow the reading which I've advised.'

Aelred closed the door behind him. Then he opened the door immediately again, knocking simultaneously and standing in the open doorway. He said, 'Is that all you can offer me: don'ts, bewares? Are there no positive things to do?' He felt a rebellion which went right back to college.

'Next week, brother, we will take up this subject again. Meditate upon what I've told you. I don't think this kind of outburst helps, brother.'

'Yes, father.' Aelred closed the door as quietly as he could. He felt like banging it shut.

The change in the weather brought the longer days and a day off a week from the normal monastic day. A non-day, or a *dies non,* the monks called it. It was a hot, windy day and the monks tramped along the narrow country roads of Somerset, across fields and over stiles, all new to Aelred. Time had galloped on from the winter and the early spring with its surprises. And now the signs of summer, with the heat almost as of his home, were already here in May. Aelred longed for it to stay this way before the days of rain set in.

Benedict was careful to spend time with his other fellow monks and not too quickly spend his time with Aelred. They found themselves getting closer and closer on the walk, so that they could quite naturally be next to each other and it not seem in any way different to being with any of the other monks.

At last they were with each other. The rest of the group had walked on, so that there was a gap between the other monks and Aelred and Benedict. They walked, Aelred listening to Benedict, who was telling him of books he had been reading and books that he should read, and telling him about the countryside which was new to him. 'Have you read that poet I once mentioned to you?'

'Gerard Manley Hopkins?'

'That's the one.'

'Yes, I enjoyed "Felix Randal".'

'"The Farrier". '

' "Big boned, and hardy-handsome." '

'And "Pied Beauty" from which I quoted to you last time.'

' "All things counter, original, spare, strange;/ Whatever is fickle, freckled (who knows how?)" '

'Who does know how?'

'What?' Aelred felt nervous.

'What is not quite right.'

'Is that what it means?'

'I think he is glorying in the imperfections of nature and seeing beauty in them. Maybe even in the flaw in nature from original sin.'

'Yes, I see,' Aelred said, but uncertain what he was understanding.

'You've been reading carefully.'

'Yes, right away. And Aelred of Rievaulx.'

'Things don't always grow the way they should. Have you seen Brother John in the walled garden tying up the canes and training the fruit trees along the wall? They would rather twist and go their own way. They've got to be trained. Otherwise, they take their natural path.'

'Things are different, not uniform.'

'That's it, absolutely. Even if they seem like they should be. And they've got their beauty in being so.'

'Why then do they have to be trained?'

'Perfection? The world can't take all that variety of beauty, maybe. Nature and art. Nature and grace. One has to form the other. One is given, the other is prayed and worked for with good works. But mostly it's given to us: grace, a gift. We have to be redeemed.'

'I can't wait to study. Isn't it precisely the difference that Hopkins is praising?' Aelred said enthusiastically, learning quickly, enjoying the debate.

'But that's Hopkins,' Benedict was skating round Hopkins. 'And then there's Aelred of Rievaulx.'

'Yes. He's – '

'A different story, but maybe the same struggle.'

They were walking close and their shoulders were brushing against each other. Their closeness was as stifling as the heat, and they were both glancing at each other and then looking away as if something should be said beyond this debate, something to shatter the peace and the innocence of what was happening on the walk and their controlled exchanges up to this time.

'This boy, Ted? Tell me more about him,' Benedict said.

'You remember me talking about him at the party? He was my friend. My best friend who died.'

'He's dead? I'm sorry. How did he die? How old was he?'

'Seventeen. Too horrible to talk about.'

'You can talk, if you want, when you want. Just come to me.'

'Thanks. But you know I can't do that now.' Aelred wanted there and then to tell Benedict everything, but he didn't want to recall Ted's death, not now. Not at this moment, this happy moment with Benedict. Was he betraying Ted?

'Is having a best friend important to you?'

'Yes, at school I lived for that, for time with my best friend.'

'Were you not told that it was dangerous?'

'Dangerous, yes. I was told by Father Justin the other day that you were dangerous, because he saw us walking down to the orchard together. Always in threes, never in twos. That's Father's Justin's favourite tune.'

'Brother, rebellious already? You must be patient with Father Justin. But what did you say?'

'I said that you had been my guardian angel.'

'And what did he say to that?'

'He said that you were a man and not an angel. I know that,' and Aelred looked at Benedict and smiled. 'As if I didn't know.'

The hot wind pulled at their cassocks and scapulars, flying in the breeze like Hindu prayer flags.

'I think of you as a friend,' Benedict said, turning to look at Aelred. 'I do, and I keep thinking of you and wanting to speak to you of it. I'll be your friend.'

'That's like my namesake, Aelred of Rievaulx. Is that why you gave him to me to read?'

'Yes. And what do you feel?'

Aelred felt shy. He was inwardly exalted, but at this moment, shy to respond to Benedict's confession. It was also as if he felt he could not cope with the knowledge. He could cope with his own desire, in his own mind, his fantasy. But as he had already admitted to himself, this was not as he felt for Ted. This was different, and it was so powerful and good that he immediately wanted to reject it, to deny it, not to have it said. He might lose it. He could not be loved, not by someone so good. He had not said he loved him. He had said friend. Was that the same thing? He felt flattered that the older man loved him, almost a boy still.

He wanted to say that he didn't feel like this. He wanted to hurt Benedict for the first time. He couldn't understand this sudden confusion. Was this not what he had wanted all the time, the friendship with this man who had been so kind? Why was he doing this?

Suddenly he felt powerful. It felt cruel. He wanted to hurt Benedict.

'What do you feel? What does it make you feel?' The older man had to take all his courage in his heart to say to the young novice that what he felt was a powerful feeling which was dangerous. 'I'll say it then. I love you. I've fallen in love with you, I think.'

Then, without thinking, Aelred blurted it out: 'I don't feel like that for you.' Aelred turned and smiled in a cruel way. He looked about him and noticed that they were still alone. The other brothers had walked on ahead.

He didn't understand why he was doing this, but only that, now that it had come to this, after all these months of his own imaginings, he couldn't deal with the actual knowledge of it. What could they do with this knowledge? 'I'll keep it in my heart,' Benedict said. 'I'll keep it for both of us.'

Aelred did not reply.

They parted and rejoined the other monks, each choosing to talk to one of their other brothers. Eventually, they stopped near some lakes for their picnic lunch. Before they ate, Aelred and Benedict again found themselves alone while the other monks went for a dip in the lake. They sat under the copper beeches and Aelred noticed the veins under Benedict's skin like the blue in marble, blood like Quink ink. They did not speak. They had all the time now on their *dies non* but they did not speak. Aelred could not. He did not know what to do with this now new and certain knowledge.

Aelred got up and left and went to sit on a rock a bit further off. He turned and looked back at Benedict. Why couldn't he tell him that he loved him? Is that what it was? Did he love him?

Benedict dropped his habit on some rocks near by and prepared to walk into the shallows of the lake. Just like that, after all the restrictions of monastic life, Aelred was now looking at Benedict's body, almost naked, except for his black trunks. He looked at his white skin, the blue veins beneath his skin. He liked his body, the way it was formed: his arms and legs, his stomach and his chest, the dark hair against the white skin. He was trying not to look. But he saw his black hair curling around his navel. His skin was so white. Along his arms, where the muscles were on his legs the veins were a dark blue. He was so different from him, so different.

'Why don't you strip off and have a go?' Benedict encouraged.

'It's too cold. It'll be too cold.' Aelred felt that he could not show *his* body.

'Nonsense, see how hot it is in the sun. You'll feel wonderful and tingling when you get out of the water. Come on.'

'No, I don't want to.' Aelred put his arms into the sleeves of his habit.

'OK.' Benedict smiled, but looked disappointed. He walked towards the water. Then he was part of the light as he dived suddenly and swam out into the middle of the cold lake. How could his body stand such cold? Aelred thought.

Aelred sat and looked at him getting smaller and smaller.

'Come for a dip,' Benedict shouted from the middle of the lake.

'It's too cold. Too cold,' Aelred called back. He sat and hugged himself.

Aelred felt wretched that he had rebuffed Benedict. Benedict had been brave enough to be open with him. He had not been open about the secret feelings which he had been having about Benedict over the last few months. Why? Why, when what he had desired was offered him, had he appeared to reject it, to feel now that he wanted to destroy it?

The Guest House:

So now as darkness closes in...

This afternoon warmed up. The day had begun with wind and rain. The Bath stone darkened because of the wetness. The fields were filled with low-lying mist, though by Lauds, the herd of cows could be seen processing into the fields after early milking. Maybe I should offer my services. I'm getting out of practice. I need to be out and about on the estate.

Spoke to Krishna yesterday. The rainy season has caused flooding in the ravine, below Malgretoute, he said. Boy, when you coming back? he asked.

Soon man, I said.

He would hang on a bit longer, he said.

The farm and the park here are like an estate. They remind me in a way of Malgretoute. I know that J. M. saw the parallels. God, I find myself, at times, quite spontaneously, crying. It's having to go over all of this. I could never take his leaving. There were things I couldn't, wouldn't admit.

I can see how one place is kind of fashioned on the other. The idea of the estate house is based on the great house. The original great house of Ashton Park is now the guest house up past the cemetery and the medieval chapel, near the lodge.

Later this afternoon, the light was golden as Benedict and I entered the orchard. It was russet-coloured. A word I didn't know; early autumn, clearly there. The rows of apple trees in the orchard, red brick walls of the garden, the grass of the fields, all picking up this last brilliance of the day. The distant copse seemed charged from within, electric. Yet with the growing chill, a softness floated and breathed over the surface of things. A bonfire in the market garden curled its smoke into the air, the smell of burning wood and grass reaching us where we stood. I'm writing with J. M.'s words. Aren't I? He's getting under my skin. He's getting under my skin in many ways. All of this so new to me, only here for a few months. Of course, I know about England. We learnt its history, saw pictures, envied snow. England is a carol. 'Earth stood as hard as iron, water like a stone.' We sang carols from house to house on the estate, imagining it was cold.

Cold no arse, boy. We joked as kids. It was a colonial pretence.

I was called from my room to the phone. It was Miriam. She wanted to check how I was doing. She said either Joe or she would come and pick me up when I had decided when I wanted to come back to Bristol. She asked whether I was enjoying the changes in the season. It's very special, the light, she said, at this time of the year. Then she said, By living the seasons, you'll live his life.

It moved me, her interruption, just when I was writing this. Maybe I'm really getting in touch with J. M. She also asked whether I had found the slave boy's grave. She had never seen it; hoped she would if she came down to collect me. Did I have enough jumpers? I could borrow something from Joe. They're really being nice, really kind; don't know how I'll repay them. Maybe they'll come out to see me in Les Deux Isles. I look forward to seeing them again at the flat in Bristol.

The fields beyond the orchard were a lucent green. The sheep as still as stones, only one or two moving, grazed imperceptibly. Benedict and I did a lot of standing and staring into the distance without speaking. This is calm, prosaic, but another vein is running here, filled with blood, an excitement of the spirit, something which had started the first night I arrived. The blue air of this afternoon, light like burning bushes, hips like electric bulbs: I feel it and see it and read it. Through him I feel it all. This is for J. M. I want to feel it. Feel him again.

I regret so much. So much I still don't want to face.

Benedict and I talked, bundling raspberry canes for the bonfire. I'm beginning to see something of the attraction that Benedict had for J. M. Well, not quite, not the erotic attraction. Was it erotic? He has this way of listening and being there for you. So I begin to see my impulsive brother always wanting to be listened to and this kind man obliging but then always reminding him of the rules.

Joe asked me the other day when he called, Is he still attractive? I was embarrassed. I didn't know what to say. If Miriam had asked me I might've been able to answer more easily.

Can you imagine your brother getting the hots for him? he asked.

I began to laugh. I'm on the phone near the Abbot's room, I said.

Come on, Robert, loosen up. You have to try and see him how J. M. saw him.

I said I would try my best. It sounded weak. He's an older man now, I laughed.

He sounds special, though, Joe said.

Joe pushes me. I've not seen men in that way.

Have you ever allowed yourself? Joe asked.

I have close friends, pardners. Like Krishna is a pardner. Some other fellas I play tennis with. You laugh and mess about when you have a few drinks in you. But there is an energy, a closeness. You wouldn't dream of touching or holding hands. But you might put your arm on his shoulder, or even on occasion give a bear hug. But the other sounds like what I want to do with a woman. That's a kind of softness which I don't associate with men, a kind of tenderness. It's not been physical. Once, I think, messing about. Well, we all did a bit, as boys, rub totee, as they say. But you grow out of that.

Funny how things come back. I saw them once. They must've been twelve, thirteen. I was seven or eight. I knelt and peeped. They were in the bathroom, the one out in the yard at Malgretoute behind Toinette's room, a shower and an open latrine. There was that smell around there of the latrine and those wild white lilies which Mum got us to pick for the altar of Our Lady, and which always grew in the seepage behind the latrine. It was a sweet smell, a perfume, and then that faint smell of shit. I know that smell even today on the estate when I smell those lilies. But this moment has been lost to me for years. I knelt and peeped and listened. J. M. was kneeling in front of Ted. They had their merino jerseys on, but their shorts were curled around their ankles. J. M. was sucking Ted's prick. I remember Ted's face. He had perspiration above his lips and he was licking it with his tongue. He was look-ing straight at me. For a moment I thought he really saw me through the crack in the door. He was lost, his eyes soft and half closed, and he had J. M.'s head in his hands rubbing his hair. It was so quiet I hardly breathed. My heart was thumping. I watched till Ted then knelt and sucked J. M. Then I was looking at J. M.'s bottom and Ted's hands were holding his bottom and pulling J. M. towards him. His fingers were finding the crack of his arse. I was so scared. I got up easy, easy, backing away on my tiptoes. I must've made a noise, because I heard J.M. say in a loud urgent whisper, Someone's there. I ran like hell across the yard and into the house. I remember I found it hard to look at J. M. for days after that. Then one day I said to him I would tell Mummy what I had seen if he didn't let me ride his bike. Something silly like that.

Quite some time after, it just came out at table with all my sisters there. Celine put her hands over my mouth. J. M. blushed.

Mum put her hand on Dad's arm, saying, It's OK dear.

Chantal giggled. I was told to leave the table and not talk like that, otherwise I would have my mouth washed out. Later I saw J. M. on his own, pelting stones at nothing. He just kept bending down, picking up a stone and pelting it as hard as he could into the air where the garden fell away to a bank of orange trees. A train clanged along the line in the gully. In the heat, the perfume of the lilies rose in the hot air; perfume and the stench of the latrine. J. M. turned and saw me standing behind him, watching him. Then he continued throwing stones. I went and stood next to him and began pelting stones as well. We slowly began competing with each other. Of course, I couldn't pelt as far as he did. Then he got me in a lock, clenching his arm around my neck.

No, no, I screamed, but he was playing. I realised he was playing.

There was something I didn't understand. Of course, it got worse.

Benedict takes such an interest. I told him about J.M.'s return to Les Deux Isles, his research. He had become a serious academic, I said. I told Benedict how I had lost touch. We had not bridged the years.

I didn't know him, didn't know his life.

He and I had to go through the whole thing. I let him talk. I could see he was anxious and that he would be late for Vespers. Then he said that he would see me after Compline. He would get permission and then we could talk without interruption. He had some of J. M.'s letters he would show me. Too many painful moments to listen to, too much that's awkward to find the words for, particularly as we hardly know each other. But he makes you feel as if you know him quite quickly. At least he didn't ask about the worst of those moments. I've just begun to talk in detail with Joe about those. Even he is reticent. What's a worst moment like?

I see his room now in the flat in Bristol the day Joe met me at the station. I had taken the tube into London from Heathrow and then the train from Paddington to Bristol.

I'll meet you under the arrivals board, Joe had said when I phoned from the station.

The windows were open in the room. It was chilly.

You can stay in here if you like, but there's another room. We've made the bed. We thought we wanted to leave J. M.'s room like it was.

The first thing I saw were the red notebooks with black spines on the shelf above his desk. They would become my daily reading.

Benedict suddenly asked about Ted, what I knew of that time. I nodded, that I knew. We both probably assume we have the same information. This time I think he understood. He understood that adolescent pain. His old and original sympathy which J. M. talks about came through remembering those young times, romantic times. But he couldn't approve of the later life.

But, yes, he knew, of course he knew, what it was to love a man. He knew what it was to feel sexually attracted to a man, he said that. We were just nearing the basement where we changed our boots. I was amazed. It was strange for me to hear it coming from this old monk. Well, he isn't young. It was also invigorating. I felt good about J. M. I felt that by saying it he was making it good. I'd felt that a bit when Joe talked, or, when Miriam talked about Joe. I moved between incomprehension, disgust, received ideas of sin and then this feeling that it was good. Then I felt sad. I regret so much. I wanted my brother back, the brother who left.

Benedict felt that God wanted it expressed differently, Aelred of Rievaulx 's way. Did I know his writing? I said I had the books in my room and I was looking at them. He felt the church was right, though at times harsh in how it advised. He tempered that official rejection, with an understanding for passion and growth. He felt that, yes, even physical passion could be a start on the way to spiritual passion. One must not hate what God has made. Ours is an incarnational religion.

' "Glory be to God for dappled things.../ All things counter," ' I said.

He smiled recognising that I had read J. M.'s journals and remembered them. You're an attentive reader, he said. He was so intuitive, your brother.

He asked again about J.M's return to Les Deux Isles, his need to understand that atrocious and horrifying history. I said that things had changed. It was a different society.

Yes, what J. M. was affected by was true. There had been injustice. There was injustice. But he had not grown with it the way I had. He hadn't been there for 1970.

And that secret history? I think Benedict meant Ted. Which makes me think he doesn't know everything, or else he means a secret from others.

He was following Jordan, he said, laughing and smiling at J. M.'s imaginary friend.

So he knew about that too. What a tangle! What it must've been like living this through! You remember Jordan? I asked him. I think he did exist, I said. He looked sceptical. I could see that he had been impatient with J. M.'s fancies. After all, he was only nineteen going on twenty. There seemed to be a resignation in Benedict's eyes. I'm not sure about what. I thought that somewhere he felt that J. M. had deserted him, but knew that he had had to leave him then. It had been years ago.

You'll come back, won't you? he asked. It's good talking to you. As you look like him, the eyes.

Yes, I would come and stay for my secular retreat. I would come back. You're not well, are you? Tell me. I want to know, I said.

You know how strong I am, he said.

I felt at that moment that he thought he was talking to Aelred. I knew how strong he always was. When he was younger. Are you ill? Or are you fasting again? I asked. I was being bold, divulging what I knew. Is the Abbot allowing you to fast? I can't believe it. I think it's so wrong. It's wicked. I felt myself getting angry, suddenly. Angry for those years, angry for what he denied my brother. I was surprised that I should feel this.

Who are you to be angry? You don't believe. You don't know. What do you know now? Look at what it has all come to. Benedict got angry.

Don't say that. You mustn't. Don't ever. You know that that isn't true. There's no logic in that. That's the most awful kind of avenging and revengeful God that you have, if you say so. Those aren't your feelings, your true feelings. I went on. Then I was suddenly aware of a double-think in myself. These might be my feelings, couldn't they? You were hurt. He hurt you. You're still hurt. I'm sorry, I said.

You're right. He hurt me. My friend in Christ. My young bonny lad. My brown-skinned boy. He was, you know. When he first appeared. He transformed my life. You have his eyes.

But you don't have to kill yourself, I said. He stared through me.

When we parted, Benedict drew me to him, into the monastic embrace with a kiss, brushing his cheeks on mine, both cheeks. Our father used to do that. I liked it. J. M. didn't. Now the right side, now the left side. '*Agnus Dei*'... 'Lamb of God, who taketh away the sins of the world.'

Then and only then did I want to kiss him. Fleetingly, for J. M. For J. M.? For myself? He withdrew, with decorum. Would I kiss him on the mouth? What a thought! My childhood wasn't J. M.'s. Do I tell of that? My story? I tell some of it. I'll have to come to more of it. I'm here for him, his world, how he saw things.

I was never able to reconcile myself to his leaving.

Someone had said that the spring was here at last and I saw the green grass out on the fields shining in the sun under the melting ice. I remember that the homesickness stopped soon after. I had never let anyone know. I never said anything in my letters to my parents. But when I got a letter from home, I went to my cell, and before I could even finish it, I was crying and feeling desolate. I felt as if I really was sick with a terrible illness that would never, never go away, eating at my stomach and choking me. This was the biggest mistake I had ever made in my life, to leave my mother and all my friends and my country.

It was crop time, hot, dry and windy. The dust was blowing up from the savannah under the tamarind trees. My father was on his horse riding up the gap. He always had lime juice, iced, in a glass jug wet with condensation. My mother was fresh after a cool shower and her hair set and tied up in a scarf. I missed them all.

I missed Toinette too, my black nurse and my black friends, Espinet, Redhead, Ramnarine and Mackensie.

When would there be some sun?

I wear Ted's boots, black leather, and they come right over my ankles and keep me very warm. The leather soles clatter on the wooden floors, and click on the black and white tiles in the sacristy. Sometimes I cry myself to sleep thinking of Ted. I saw his powdered face, the face that wasn't his. And then the dream would change to sunlight and Ted and I were in a boat, alone, stranded in the middle of the ocean. We were naked and diving off the side of the boat. Then Dom Maurus, our parish priest, was blessing us because we... 'Will I go to hell? I will go to hell. I will go to hell to be with Ted, put in chains, lowered into the fire.'

Along the side of the silver fuselage, what I could see beneath the wide expanse of wing, were the cane fields like I had never seen them, a patchwork quilt, an English image. Now I knew what they meant, the fields laid out with the hedges in between. These were hedgerows. It was a new language, new feelings. The cuckoo, which had only ever lived in a clock on the cream dining-room wall, I heard one morning after Prime when I walked out on to the terrace and the fields were appearing out of the mist. 'The cuckoo is a usurper,' said Father Prior.

My worlds were inside each other.

Below the wing, the forests and the mountains were as impenetrable as I had never seen them before. And then we were leaving the land, the edge of the land, the swamp, the islands of mangrove, the sea, the little archipelago of islands between Les Deux Isles and the mainland.

I touched Ted's sunburnt shoulder where the sea water fractured like crystals and trickled like mercury down his arms. His sweat tasted like salt on my tongue. When I looked down again the light had changed; through clouds the sea was black. Then all that I loved went out.

The face that wasn't Ted's was covered with powder.

I, his brother, now taste salt on my tongue.

The New Novice

...like a young stag,
See where he stands behind our wall,
He looks in at the window, he peers through the lattice.
Song of Songs

'This is Brother Edward Boswell.' Father Justin introduced the new novice at recreation in the sunken garden under the arbour covered over with wisteria just beginning to bloom. They had come down the stone steps from the terrace with Brother Benedict. 'This is Brother Angus, John, Dominic, Charles.' He went around introducing the group of novices and simple professed monks with the new novice shaking hands. 'And this is Brother Aelred.' Aelred had come from late kitchen duty, so stood outside the circle of the novitiate. They also shook hands. 'Brother Benedict will be Brother Edward's guardian angel,' Father Justin said, looking around the group of his novices, smiling. 'But I hope you'll all lend a helping hand to show Brother Edward the ropes if you find him lost.'

Brother Edward smiled and everyone said, 'hello,' and 'welcome' to the new novice.

Brother Charles, a young Irish brother with a ruddy face, said earnestly, but nervously, 'It's a grand time to join up because of the grand weather. He pointed to the full summer of the park splendidly lit by the bright afternoon. 'It's grand,' he said, beaming.

Brother Edward smiled and agreed. 'I'm lucky to have had good weather for travelling.' He looked spanking new in a smart black cassock, buttoned right up to his neck. The long leather monastic belt was pulled in tightly at his waist, knotted and allowed to hang down his left side. He was tall with blond hair. He had bright blue eyes and very white skin. He stood out. All the other novices wore varying degrees of tonsure, as their shaven heads were called. The actual circular tonsure, the bald pate, had been dispensed with some years ago, but the full-haired new novice was strikingly unshorn.

Brother Angus asked politely about Brother Edward's journey. They exchanged reminiscences, discovering that they both came from Shropshire. Immediately, they were outcoing each other in praise of the Shropshire hills and boasting to the other novices. 'I expect you've done all the big walks up to the Stiper stones and the Devil's Chair and over the Burway.' Father Justin looked on approvingly as Angus obviously made Edward feel at home.

'Oh, yes, and Caer Caradoc and "All around The Wrekin", as the saying goes.' Edward turned to the other novices, clearly enjoying an immediate familiarity with Brother Angus. 'I was walking on the Long Mynd only yesterday.'

Then the other novices got on with their usual recreation conversations concerning their studies, the farm, gardening or some tid bit of gossip someone had picked up from one of the lay workers in the pottery, being careful that Father Justin did not hear. News from outside the monastery was not encouraged, particularly in the novitiate. Brother Charles was always keen on folk music and had been allowed by the Abbot to play his guitar. So he liked to pick up news of popular music. The lads in the pottery were talking a lot now about Bob Dylan from America. Brother Charles was allowed to bring his guitar to recreation at times and this afternoon he picked away

at a new tune. 'The answer, my friend, is blowing in the
wind...' A couple of the other novices joined in, learning
the lines of the lyric.

Brother Dominic suddenly asked, 'And what about
the Beatles?' Edward was about to answer but picked up
his cue from the other novices, who had at that moment
turned to Father Justin to see his reaction.

'I think Brother Edward has left all that behind?' His
statement turned on the inflection of a question and was
said with a frown and a smile at the same time.

The novices returned to their usual conversations.

Aelred tried to get close to Benedict. Their conversation on the walk some days before was still worrying him
and he felt that he wanted to put it right, and say something encouraging till they could steal a moment to talk
properly. But Benedict was already engaged in his guardian angel duties and was in a huddle with Edward on a
stone bench outside the arbour. Aelred felt left out. He
had not got into conversation as yet with any of the other
novices, because he had been late from the kitchen.
Usually what happened on these occasions was that one
sat next to Father Justin and made formal conversation.
'Come and sit here, brother.' Father Justin indicated a
space on the bench next to him. Aelred was not keen to
do that today. He had felt a tension growing with Father
Justin since their last weekly session, and felt that he was
keeping a careful watch on who he mixed with and whether
he mixed properly with all the novices equally. This too was
something Aelred felt frustrated about, having to make
conversation. He never felt that the talk was real.

So, he declined the offer. 'I'll just pass the tea and cake
around, and continue my kitchen duties, which I've been

enjoying.' He busied himself with pouring out the tea from a large brown enamel teapot and offering around the fruit cake which he had helped make this afternoon, tutored by Brother Felix.

'This is Brother Aelred.' Benedict introduced Edward. 'Aelred is from Les Deux Isles in the Antilles.'

'The British West Indies. Oh, how exotic! I remember collecting those wonderful colourful stamps of all kinds with pictures of exciting flora and fauna. And the unusual names like Antigua, Trinidad and Tobago. Those two always went together,' Edward joked.

Benedict smiled to encourage the new novice but glanced at Aelred, gauging his response. 'Exotic? Oh, yes. Would you like some fruit cake which I made. It's a very beautiful island, Les Deux Isles, but I've never thought of it as exotic.'

'A long way away,' Edward continued, frowning at Aelred. 'A desert island.'

'Yes, it is,' Benedict interjected. 'Aelred's been very brave. And it's a little exotic to us, you know. Remember those sunsets you once told me about.'

'Yes, I could see at once you weren't English,' Edward continued.

'Oh!' Aelred looked at Benedict for explanation and support. Aelred was feeling awkward. It was the new novice, Edward, but it was also that he had not spoken to Benedict since the *dies non* walk. Aelred passed on, offering cake and tea. The sleeves of his habit were rolled up to his elbows, showing his brown arms recently heightened by the sun from working on the farm and in the garden.

Father Justin tugged at his sleeves when he got to him

with tea, and indicated that he should roll them down. 'Brother, brother,' he said playfully but in an admonishing tone.

'Sorry, it was so hot in the kitchen.' Aelred acted out his complaint. The other novices nearby smiled.

Then Aelred overheard Edward say to Benedict, 'He's very dark,' looking at Aelred.

The bustle of out-of-door recreation was soon over when the chimes for Vespers filled the park with its hypnotic music. Then everyone began clearing up and helping to pack up the tea things to take them back to the kitchen.

'I wanted to talk,' Aelred said softly next to Benedict on the path to the terrace when he had stopped talking to Edward for a moment. Edward had moved off to have a word wirh Father Justin. 'I wanted to say, I've been thinking about what you said.'

'Not now,' Benedict interrupted. 'Not now.' Then he resumed talking to Edward and walked on ahead into the cloister.

Aelred felt desolate. He watched Edward and Benedict conferring with each other and remembered how sweet the feeling was when Benedict had been his guardian angel.

Under his cloak with his hood on he felt dejected as, in the queue along one side of the cloister, he turned his mind to Vespers. He prayed, 'Dear God, help me with this. Help me when I feel so alone.' He snatched at a stalk of lavender from the bush along the cloister and crushed it in his fingers under his scapular. Then he felt Edward behind him. Edward coughed and Aelred could smell the new smell of his cassock. He was now no longer the last in the queue into the choir. He was now no longer the new novice.

There never seemed to be a moment now for Aelred to speak to Benedict. So much time seemed to be passing since he had confessed his love on the walk. It seemed as if it had not happened. Aelred kept going over the scene along the road when they had dropped behind the other monks and when they sat together near the ponds. He could still see his wet black hair against his white body as he came out of the water. He was full of regret because of what he had said and wanted to put it right. Their eyes met each other in choir and in the refectory, but they did not talk. Each day Aelred looked hopefully at the notice-board too see whether the cellarer had put him to work with Benedict in the garden or on the farm. He was always being detailed now to work with the new novice Edward, in order to show him the ropes about manual work or the various rituals of the day. Aelred was always bumping into the two of them in the common room, poring over a book of psalms, or going through a ritual like serving in the refectory.

'Oh, brother, *benedicite*,' Benedict called, giving the formal opening to conversation as a good example to the new novice. Aelred was coming through the common room on the way to the novitiate cells after housework that morning. He was about to change the flowers before Our Lady's statue in the novitiate's corridor shrine. He had adopted this as an additional chore, which he did as the junior member of the novitiate.

'*Benedicite*,' Aelred responded formally. 'Morning, brother.'

'*Benedicite*, good morning,' Edward followed the example of Benedict.

The three brothers smiled and acknowledged the

humour which at times monastic rituals, like the custom of 'bendicite' before speaking, held for the new monks in particular. They were stumbling over each other with the formal greetings.

'A lot of the time the *"Benedicite"* greeting was dispensed with "Brother",' Benedict continued. They all smiled at the continuing pun on Benedict's name.

'Yes.' Aelred was happy to have been invited into conversation.

'I was thinking it might be good for you to give up this duty of changing the flowers for the novitiate's shrine and let Edward take that over. As you remember, it's always been the duty of the junior member of the novitiate. Remember you took over from Charles?'

'Oh, yes, fine. I've just picked some wild buddleia which grows in the rocks by the quarry. There are already some early blooms. Do you like buddleia?' Aelred addressed this to Edward, but smiling at Benedict.

'You've been all the way to the quarry this morning already?'

'Oh, yes, I love to walk out there for some quick exercise. It's glorious along the path with the gorse all out and the silver birches which I love. I had to climb the rocks for the buddleia.'

'Don't go and fall.'

'Do I have to take this duty on? Brother Aelred clearly enjoys this chore. I'm not great at flower arranging.' Edward smiled at both Benedict and Aelred.

Did Aelred pick up the very slightest inflection of sarcasm in his tone of voice on flower arranging?

It was possible that Benedict did. But he carried on showing his concern for Aelred's safety on the rocks of

the quarry, alone out there in the early morning. 'I
don't think you should go climbing out there at the
quarry alone. Anyway, I think it's best if Edward takes
over the flower arranging.' Benedict emphasised the
word 'arranging'. A new novice needed to begin to
learn humility. He was also feeling protective to Aelred.

'Oh, that's fine. Maybe Aelred could just show me the
rudiments, and the best places to pick flowers and where
the secateurs are kept.' Edward spoke precisely.

Aelred could see Benedict's face taking on a stern look.
He himself felt hurt by Edward's tone of voice. He was
very polished and sounded slightly snobbish, Aelred
thought. But he wanted to be good. He wanted to be
good for Benedict.

'Certainly, I'll meet you here after house duties tomorrow
morning and then we can visit the garden together. I'll
enjoy that. I'm really enjoying getting to know England.
And the coming summer.'

'Maybe you can show me your rock face one day, if
that's OK. I'm quite a good rock climber, actually. I was
trained on the sheer side of Caer Caradoc. England is
more than its flowers, you know. It's more than a garden.'

'Anyway,' Benedict said, 'I'd just keep to the flower
beds on the terrace for the moment. But don't hack away
at all Father Kevin's horticulture. Well, there 's the bell for
Prime.'

Edward left to change for Prime.

'Benedict.' Aelred carried on speaking, wanting to
address their need to talk.

'The bell, brother. Let's give a good example.' Benedict could be cold sometimes. Then he turned and said
quietly as he raised his hood, 'I still feel the same. I do

what I said. I keep it in my heart for both of us.'

'And I, I ...'

Benedict put his finger against Aelred's lips as he had done once before. 'Soon.'

Aelred went off to his cell feeling hurt and confused. Some of it was to do with Benedict refusing to let him speak, but there was this nagging feeling that he was different. He didn't like the tone of Edward's voice. He hadn't liked the way, now that he put it altogether, that this morning's conversation and the first meeting at recreation went, when Edward joked about Les Deux Isles being exotic and talking about the stamps of the islands. He had a way of talking down to him, he felt. Then he remembered his remark about how dark he was. Aelred could feel himself being homesick, like he used to get when he had first arrived.

The following morning before Prime, Aelred got the secateurs from the cupboard in the common room. While he waited for Edward to meet him after housework he picked out the dead flowers from the vase in front of the Lady statue. He did this as he knelt at the prie-dieu in front of the shrine. Hearing footsteps behind him in the corridor he turned, still in his kneeling position, and saw that it was Edward. He got up, making the sign of the cross.

'I'll just get rid of these,' Aelred said, depositing the dead flowers in the large hearth of the common room fireplace.

'*Benedicite,*' Edward said formally. He had a new work smock, which was crisp and creased where it had been folded in the linen room. Like when he was in his cassock, Edward exuded a smell of newness. Now it was the brand-new denim work smock.

'*Benedicite*, brother.' Aelred smiled. 'I'll just get the secateurs,' and he returned to the prie-dieu where he had left
them.

'You've been doing your devotions?'

'Yes. Do you have a special devotion?'

'I prefer to keep my prayer life within the official
liturgy, rather than keeping up all these side devotions.
I've always thought of them as sentimental and belonging
to old women and the Spaniards.' Edward spoke in a tone
that Aelred now recognised right away.

'I see. Oh, actually, my mother is half Spanish. Well,
let's go to the garden, on the terrace.' They pulled up
their hoods and processed out of the novitiate through
the cloister and out to the terrace in silence.

There was a mist still lying in the folds of the park,
though the bright sun they had had over the last few days
was beginning to break through. There was a chill in the
air. The new light breaking through played on the walls of
the abbey. There was shadow and light in the cloister and
on the lawns beneath the terrace.

'I don't care what you say. It's a garden to me,' Aelred
said pointedly, remembering Edward's remark the day
before, as he inspected the beds to see what they could
pick and, at the same time, not denude Father Kevin's
hard work. 'I suppose the thing is not to pick from one
place. And any greenery you need, try and get it from different bushes. The greenery usually lasts a week or even
more.'

'I'd think you were Welsh if I hadn't been told that you
came from Les Deux - what's its name?'

'Les Deux Isles. The two islands. Yes, that's what everyone

thought when I first arrived.'

'It's the lilt in the voice.'

'Yes, kind of sing-song. Maybe the French in the dialect.'

By now Aelred had a bouquet of white daisies in his arms. 'What's this look like?' He held the flowers up to the sun, which increased through the mist.

'You're the tutor, brother. I'm the apprentice.'

'You're always joking, aren't you?'

'Brother?' Edward was taken unawares, confronted unexpectedly.

'My father had a dry sense of humour. It can be misunderstood, can't it? At times?' Aelred said.

'You're - excuse me asking: I was wondering, and remarked to Benedict that first afternoon I met you - you're not coloured, are you? Because you don't seem so, and yet - ?'

'Now I really love red roses but I daren't pick any of these first buds. Do you think we should?' Aelred turned around and held a small red rose up to Edward. 'Smell this.' As Edward took the stem of the single rose his finger caught on a thorn.

'Ow!' He handed the rose back to Edward. 'Take this.' He sucked on his finger where the thorn had punctured and where it bled.

'Are you OK? I used to faint as a child for things like that.'

'I'm fine. I'm fine. Don't you think we have enough now?' Edward blushed and Aelred noticed his mounting irritation with his dryness, which was now mixed with sympathy. He remembered what it was like to be new. Everything was strange. One wasn't oneself.

'Yes, well, why don't you take them? Arrange them in the novitiate. The bell for Prime will go soon.' Aelred handed Edward the bouquet. 'Mind the rose.'

'Wish you were doing this.'

'It'll be fine. You'll get the hang of it. Benedict will be pleased.'

'That's important, isn't it? Pleasing Benedict?'

'Very.'

'Oh, yes, where's the quarry?'

'Over there.' Aelred pointed into the distance, the other side of the orchard. 'Over there, beyond those fields. It's just out of view. No rock climbing, though. And by the way, you could say that I'm a creole.'

'Creole,' Edward repeated, getting his lips around the word.

'Yes, like Joséphine.'

'Joséphine?'

'Joséphine Beauharnais.'

'Who's she when she's in choir?' Edward looked down his nose at the red rose.

'Napoleon's first wife.' Aelred smiled and swept up some cuttings from the verge near the flower beds. 'You know, from the exotic island of Martinique.'

Edward looked confused and Aelred chuckled.

As they reached the cloister, and before raising their hoods to process back to the novitiate, Aelred noticed Edward look him over. He folded down the sleeves of his work smock over his brown arms. He was very handsome, Aelred thought.

They parted. Aelred could smell Edward's newness as he followed him.

On fine days the monks were allowed to spend siesta on the lawns below the terrace. It was there that Aelred found Benedict some days later. He was lying on the lawn near the monkey-puzzle tree. He came up to Benedict and stood over him. Benedict looked up from his philosophy books, which were spread open on the grass around him. There were three big tomes: Being and Nothingness and Being And Time.

'Existentialism: Jean Paul Sartre and Martin Heidegger.' Benedict pointed at the tomes.

'Yes.' Aelred smiled, not being able to respond. He did not know any of these authors.

'You'll read these one day.'

'I hope so. I want to study and know more about myself and the world.'

'In time. You must do your novitiate reading first.'

'I'm sorry about what I said the other day. They're true, the feelings which I expressed. They were true at the time. I felt confused.' He was talking quickly, blurting it all out before he felt tongue-tied again as he had on the walk. 'I love you.' Aelred continued to stand over Benedict, who was now sitting up. He looked into the distance towards the quarry. Aelred felt awkward standing as he was. He didn't want to sit on the grass next to Benedict, because he shouldn't be there: he was out of bounds. He made as if to leave.

He was surprised when Benedict said, 'Sit a while. Don't run off.' Benedict could see that the younger monk was agitated and had taken all the courage he possessed to come here and confess his love. It seemed like that to both of them. It was something to confess, secretly, something which had been made close to sin since childhood.

Now he was telling his love: all that love which had been pent up for his friend Ted who had died, and about whom Benedict had questioned him on St Aelred's Day soon after he had arrived, and again on the walk.

That first love had come with the first spring of sex. Benedict imagined this for the young novice, barely a man, and seeming to Benedict to be in between man and boy, his face as smooth as a girl's. As he looked up at him, he seemed to be a person who was questing and struggling for virtue.

'Sit, sit by me.' He knew this struggle in himself. 'I understand.'

Was this not like their patron saint of friendship, Aelred of Rievaulx, whose loves in his youth were characterised by conflict and distraction? Hadn't that Aelred seen himself as needing to be cleansed; and wasn't it the honey of his love for the boy Jesus which had saved him?

'I love you,' Benedict said, raising his hand to hold Aelred's and tugging at his sleeve for him to sit by his side. 'Thanks for your love.'

Aelred lowered his eyes in shyness and confusion. 'Good, I just wanted you to know, because I felt terrible after the walk. For so long now since we've had a chance to speak. I don't know why I felt like hurting you. There's no reason I can think of.' He couldn't get it right - couldn't get it to sound right, what he wanted to say.

'These things are difficult. And in time we must talk more, but we must keep to the rules.'

'I'm so glad you spoke. I love you. I've never talked of this kind of love before, not even to Ted really, because we were so young. Not like this. I was younger.' Then he felt he was betraying Ted.

'And remember Aelred of Rievaulx. There are those who have gone before us and are our guides,' Benedict said.

They smiled, and then the two men left each other. The older man knew that for the first time in his monastic life there were feelings for one of his brothers which had not manifested themselves before, feelings which he had to contain, the extent and true nature of which he had not even told Aelred. He felt that he had responsibilities, now that he had confessed to one so young. This was a love which he knew to be more than the love he had for all his other brothers in the community.

The younger man felt happy, and already yearning for the next time they would meet. When they did, they would look at each other in choir, in the refectory, on the way to the garden, when they shared the washing up: the daily chores of their simple life. Glances would carry so much more; looking and the language of the eyes would mean so much more.

Aelred began to feel for the first time that the burden of his feelings had been lightened. He heard what Benedict said. They had their rules. He felt like the young Ivo, in Aelred of Rievaulx's treatise on friendship, who wanted to open his heart, pour out his thoughts. He felt that Benedict had noticed him in the same way that the medieval abbot had noticed his young friend Ivo. He returned to the treatise on friendship with added enthusiasm to find solace and advice for this new thing in his life.

'Come now, beloved, open your heart. Just a little while ago I was sitting with the brethren, you alone were silent. At times you would raise your head and make ready to say something, but just as quickly, as though your voice had been trapped in your throat you would drop your head again and continue your silence. Then you would leave us for a while, and later return looking rather disheartened. I concluded from this that you wanted to talk to me, but that you dreaded the crowd, and hoped to be alone with me.'

These were exactly Aelred's feelings, to be alone at Benedict's feet, his model monk. Now his friend who actually said, I love you. He took the words away with him, treasuring them, excited and frightened.

Later, as they were queuing for None, Benedict came up to Aelred. '*Benedicite*, brother,' he smiled. 'On another matter. You must be supportive to Edward. Remember what it is to be new.'

Aelred nodded, as Edward joined the queue behind him and the community began processing into choir for None.

The Guest House:

As shadows lengthen into night ...

Compline: 'Brothers, be sober and watch, because your adversary the devil, like a roaring lion, goes about seeking whom he may devour... Resist him, strong in faith...' The young monk who is the acolyte of the choir read the lesson and afterwards lit the Lady candles. He is so young, so handsome. He reminds me of J.M. I try to imagine him then. I left Compline sad, so sad for losing my brother, for his way of dying, not knowing how to retrieve him. I get some of him back.

Back then, there was Benedict. They were all younger then, both of them. I feel that the older men had gave him, gave them, so little direction, not the right kind at the right time. He shouldn't have had to lose this life. I feel that so much of him wanted to go on with it. But, in the end, he had to go and seek the meaning of that love, that friendship, that passion, in the city, as Joe calls it.

They were without support, surrounded by treachery, bigotry, like criminals. That's what it was like then, Joe says. You were arrested. You were imprisoned and fined. You were shamed, insulted, beaten up. Not that it does not take place now. There were some pubs which you knew you could meet at. There were actually one or two clubs, particularly in London, and just opening up in the bigger cities. There were growing liberal attitudes, but essentially you were still a criminal. Odd to think of the ideal they were forging in this cloister.

The '*Salve Regina*' at the end of Compline was pitched into the darkness, and the candles threw long shadows.

I keep going over what Joe and Miriam have described to me, trying to imagine him going out into that world of public lavatories, back alleys, waste ground, odd pubs and underground clubs, away from this safe cloister; imagine them losing each other. But then, here, they were branded sinners.

Of course, back on Les Deux Isles we knew nothing of this. My parents would turn in their graves.

There is a history, Joe says. It happened for a reason.

And, Miriam adds, now we know that the concentration camps were also for those with pink triangles. There was a systematic elimination of them too. They need memorials too.

I will leave tomorrow for Bristol. But I will come back. I've told Benedict that I will. Already, I hear the hum of the traffic on the main road beyond the fields. The city's sodium amber hum. Joe or Miriam or both will pick me up after lunch.

Making sure not to make any noise, I went out into the night and again circled the enclosure walls. I knew the trail by heart now. Using my former knowledge, I didn't have to depend upon the yellow arrow trail. My trousers got caught on the gorse bushes. I passed through the little wood of oaks. Again I was on the brink of the escarpment, and opening up in front of me were the sheer, steeply descending layers of the Bath stone quarry, with the pool of water on its deepest floor. I could see the crevices where the wild buddleia grew. The arc lights hummed and floodlit the vast underground, busy with its own industry. There was blinding clarity and shadows and then encircling darkness. I descended the bank into the silver birches.

That night, I read of his heroes.

I admired the sprinting athlete, the diver as the champion swimmer, the jumper through the invisible air, a figure of perfection - perfection in that turn and twist. I saw perfection in the swift cycler, and in the serve of the tennis player, long and stretching and delivering deftness and power. I had come close to some of these arts myself, failing and succeeding in order to touch the essential beauty in myself and in Ted; his perfect beauty.

I admired the dash of the footballer on the wing, the drive of the turning batsman with the ball driven to the covers. I examined the sprinting fast bowler, with that trick of manhood; the feminine dance of the spin bowler, that trick that man could be so like a girl and be a man. This was a richness which I sensed, tasted and knew to be there, but could never fully have.

Ted and I placed questions in the hearts of each other. We placed them in our wrestling young bodies, like athletes in an arena we did not understand the rules of. We placed them in our clinging to each other, swimming off the boat when we were alone in the sea and could not see the land. The salve of life was to lick the sweat from his shoulder, those salty crystals, which then I took with my lips to place eventually, in that audacious way, upon the mouth of my best friend with a kiss like those I was shown in the pictures, like Warren Beatty and Natalie Wood in Splendour in the Grass.

His images entered my dreams.

The Quarry

like a gazelle,
like a young stag.
Song of Songs

This had become Aelred's favourite walk. It led through a
gate at the bottom of the apple orchard, frothy still with
the last of the white blossom. The late winter had slowed
the spring and then there had been a quickening, a feeling of juice and joy in growing things. Then he learnt that
the cold could suddenly come and interrupt the season.
Once he left the grassy orchard, the path was a mixture
of gravel and soft verges with beaten-down leaves and
bark chippings. At this time of the morning, between
housework and Prime, the grass and flowering cow-
parsley were ladened, fresh with dew and early morning
drizzle. Banks of white lace tumbled from the hawthorn
and the air reeked with the wild perfume of the hawthorn
and cows' parsley and the wetness. Everything was shooting
long, seeming lovely and lush. Aelred walked quickly. His
heart raced with an enthusiasm which was born of
excitement in feeling loved by Benedict, his ardour for
his monastic duties and the newness of the season. It
was a short interval, stolen in the tight schedule of the
monastic day.

Where the path narrowed it was prickly with gorse
bushes crowding the edges, catching on the sleeves and
legs of his denim work smock. He leapt over the puddles.
He liked the fact that when he saw things now, he knew
their names. He knew and could feel the difference between
the open blue air, the shade in the wood of oaks and the

glade of silver birches, dappled with shadow. It was chilly, he thought.

He was alerted. He looked up. Just there, beyond the hedgerow at the edge of the field, level with a row of poplars, was a hovering hawk. Where and what was its prey? It might be a field mouse, or a rabbit, or, a small bird. Phrases from a new poem he was reading came with his stare. 'My heart in hiding stirred for a bird - the achieve of, the mastery of the thing.'

Time was running out. His stolen time would be abruptly cut off with the bell for Prime. He could not be late. There was just enough time to reach the quarry. He liked to descend to the bottom, circle the glinting pool, climb out the other side and return along the escarpment down through the silver birches.

In dips, where things had begun to grow again, a purple lilac was in bloom. Buddleia, not yet in flower down here, sprouted from stone crevices as if living on nothing but the air.

He had entered this new world and was learning to name it, but through the poetry he was reading he read the landscape with exhilaration and gleaned the glory of his Lord.

Then Aelred saw him. His first reaction was to call out, he was so startled. But then he checked himself, in case his outburst should surprise the rock climber and he should fall. Aelred walked fast and drew closer to the face which was being climbed. It was Edward. Aelred found his denim work smock, weighed down by a rock, with a bunch of freshly cut lilacs near it. He had come out to cut flowers. But really he had come to climb. What was most startling was that he had on a pair of tight black shorts and a white jersey. His arms were outstretched and his hands worked at grips in the small crevices on the face. His legs stretched and his feet found a sure footing, slipping and finding it again, stepping up and up. All the time he was moving, and testing the firmness of his grip and the sureness of his hold. Aelred stood below and looked up. He was afraid that the quarried face might not hold the climber. He was not sure whether Edward had seen him. As he looked, he could see the straining of the muscles in his calves and along his arms. Aelred was scared and he was worried that if he stayed any longer he would not hear the bell for Prime. Had Edward thought of that? Had he lost a sense of time? He was so absorbed in his climbing, in the acute concentration in that moment. Aelred stared at the movement of his body: his legs, his calves, his buttocks, his arms. He was an extraordinary cohesion of strength and co-ordination of purpose. Edward's blond hair was waving in the breeze at that height. Bits of rock fell away from the footholds and clattered, bouncing on jutting rock further down, being pitched to the bottom and shattering into small pieces where Aelred stood, staring, as Edward continued to prise with his fingers and feet and raise himself up. He was almost at the top. That was the hardest. Where would he get a grip at the top, where the tufts of grass clung in loose earth, ready to give way? He might just lose hold and fall back.

Freefall like a hawk.

Aelred began his climb out the other side. He would go and meet Edward where he would reach the summit. Then he thought to go back and gather up Edward's work smock and the bunch of lilacs. By the time he got to the top Edward's hands were clutching for a firm hold. The bell was ringing for Prime.

'Here, grab hold of my arm.' Aelred lay down on his stomach and reached over the edge. Their heads were close together.

Edward looked up. He was breathless. Aelred could have touched his face.

'What're you doing here?' Edward spoke between gasps. He had not noticed Aelred at the bottom. 'I'll pull you over if you lie like that and we'll both be gonners.'

'What should I do? Don't you need a hand?'

'If there is a root or a stump just here, I might be able to grab for a hold. What can you see?' He scrabbled with one hand, holding with another. 'Or, if you can secure yourself with one hand, you can offer me the other.'

Aelred dug with his fingers where he felt that there was a root, possibly from a young oak a little further off. He dug around it so that he could get his hand through it like a handle. He held fast to the root with his left hand, also digging his feet into the ground to secure himself. Then he stretched out the other arm to Edward, who raised himself a little further to the summit so that his head was over the top. The bell for Prime had stopped.

'Here, now you can grab hold of my hand. I'm secure.'

Edward let go of his hold on a tuft of grass which was already giving away, gravel spilling from under it and shooting out over the quarry beneath. He grabbed, holding firmly to Aelred's hand. 'Pull,' he gasped as he himself pulled and pressed with his legs from his last foothold.

Aelred pulled. 'I've got you.'

Edward was heaving and sliding himself over the edge on his stomach. Aelred was lying stretched between the root and Edward, his face close to the ground. Then Edward's legs and feet showed over the edge. He was up.

'We've done it.' They both panted and shouted together. Then they lay back. First the bird song and then the wind and the echo of the stillness below reached them.

'We're late for Prime.' Aelred said. 'Hurry. Put on your smock.'

'What'll happen?'

'We'll have to explain to Father Justin. We'll change quickly without washing, and then when we get into choir you have to kneel by the Abbot's stall till he knocks his hammer indicating that you can rise. He can keep you kneeling longer than you think.' The two novices hurried back to the abbey along the path, and then, as a short cut, they cut across a field, running, so avoiding having to go through the orchard. Edward had forgotten the bunch of lilacs. Aelred carried them.

'I can't admit that I was rock climbing. Can you keep a secret?' Edward asked, as they reached the door of the choir.

'I'll leave it to you to explain yourself. I'll say I misjudged the time back from the quarry.'

'It needn't come up that we were together?'

'We must go in. I'll go first. You can see what I do,' Aelred whispered.

'Thanks.' Edward straightened his cassock.

Aelred was distracted during the chanting of Prime. He kept seeing Edward climbing the rock face above him. He saw his strong body in his tight black shorts climbing and stretching up the rock face surrounded by the blue air. He could so easily have fallen. He closed his eyes, repeating the verses of the psalms by heart He looked across the choir at Benedict. Their eyes met. Benedict had a question for him. Why had he and Edward been late? He thought that that was what he was asking him. It had all happened so quickly. It was odd, what Edward had done. It was not appropriate to strip off out at the quarry alone and climb. He would not say anything about this. Father Justin would find it highly irregular. It was. Would he do it again? It went with the way he spoke. It was a kind of arrogance. He had been exhilarated by helping him. He had been frightened and he had been aware of the Prime bell tolling. What would Edward say to Father Justin and Benedict as his guardian angel?

'Your lateness at Prime, brother?' Father Justin was standing in the doorway of his cell as Aelred passed along the corridor to the novitiate, eager to get washed after his tugging and pulling and the sweaty run back from the quarry.

'I misjudged the time back from the quarry, where I went for a quick walk after housework,' Aelred said matter-of-factly.

'And Brother Edward? You came into choir together?' Father Justin looked under the rim of his glasses, frowning. It reminded Aelred of his headmaster at school, censorious. He did not like it.

'I'll leave it to him to explain. I think he was probably absorbed in cutting lilac bushes for the Lady in the novitiate.' Aelred pointed to the bunch of lilacs lying on the common-room table. He could see through the doorway from where he was standing.

'I expect Benedict will sort him out.' Father Justin

smiled. 'Very well, brother. You better get along to Lectio Divina.'

'*Benedicite*.' Aelred pulled on his hood and walked away with his arms under his scapular.

As he passed through the common room, he noticed Benedict with Edward. He wondered what Edward had said. How would Benedict take the news of the rock climbing. He had never presented him with such a difficulty. Then he felt a tinge of jealousy that he couldn't be talking to Benedict.

Edward joined Aelred in the washroom. Aelred looked up for a moment from his washing, but then kept his silence. He was bending over the sink, his smock off, standing in his overalls, washing behind his neck with a flannel, up and down his arms, under his arms and his chest. Though he was not directly looking at him, he could see Edward: glimpses reflected in the mirror, out of the side of his eyes. They were alone in the washroom. The other novices were at their Lectio Divina, as they should have been, but because of their running back from the quarry they were in the washroom outside the usual routine.

Edward had dropped his smock on the ground and was standing in his overalls, their straps hanging at his sides. He stood bare-chested and bare-backed. He was wiping the nape of his neck with the wet flannel under his long hair. He was soaping and then wiping his arms, his chest and under his arms. Through the slits on the side of his overalls he was wiping the uncovered part of his body, his groin and buttocks.

Aelred felt irritated. There was something indulgent in the way he washed, the way he splashed water and had thrown his smock on the ground. He did not smell new now as he did in his cassock. There was a smell of sweat and soap. Aelred got his soap, toothbrush and towel together and made to leave the washroom.

'Thanks for arranging the flowers.' Edward turned and faced him, wiping his chest and towelling under his arms. His hair was falling over his face. 'You'd better keep that duty. I'm obviously no good at it. Were the lilacs OK?'

'I think you should see Benedict. Should I pick this up for you?' Aelred picked up Edward's smock and hung it against the wall, where there were pegs for that purpose.

'You didn't say anything about the rock climbing to Father Justin?'

'I accounted for myself.' Aelred had picked up a rag from the corner of the washroom where the cleaning things were kept and started wiping down the sinks. 'I think we'd better clean up in here and get back to Lectio Divina.'

'You disapprove of me?'

'You must take advice from Benedict. He's your guardian angel.'

'I do. I do, brother. My guardian angel! You like all these little ceremonies and titles, don't you ? Arranging flowers, guardian angels. Don't you? And you are dark, aren't you. All over, it seems.' Edward looked Aelred over as he stood there clutching his smock to his chest. Edward tossed back his long wet blond hair. 'Yes, I think you disapprove of me.'

'I think we should keep the silence now, brother. *Benedicite.*'

'*Benedicite.*' Edward pulled strands of wet blond hair off his face.

Aelred was relieved when he settled down at his desk for his Lectio Divina. He sat with his hood up. He was alone but he was not at peace. Novices used the washroom together. But they did not strip off quite in the way Edward had done. They did not enter bare-backed. Aelred forced his concentration on his Lectio Divina.

It was in Lectio Divina that they cultivated their imaginations. It was at this prescribed time, a time set aside from the very beginning of monasticism and developed through the ages, that the monks read the scriptures and the fathers of the church. The reading now included those books recommended by the novice master for the training and uplifting of his charges.

Lectio Divina - holy reading, divine reading - was to be a meditation, a listening of the heart and the mind to voices from the pages. Ancient monks were encouraged to read aloud, to move their lips in reading. The public reading in the refectory, the chapter house and in choir were integral to this Lectio Divina. This was to be listened to in silence. The monks were instructed by their rule to see to each others' needs and to communicate quietly by signs at these times.

But the heart and core of this reading was here when the monk was alone in his cell, moving his lips silently. He was encouraged to read and to hear: *legere et audire*. His entire attitude was a turning of himself towards God, a conversion. He was to hasten in this turning and take flight from here. It was with this desire that the reverberations of what he had read had its lasting effect on the quality of his mind. For Aelred, it was this that worked on the quality of his imagination.

The purity of his mind and actions, the flight of his

desire, was to create something as close as possible to the angelic life, the life of angels, the vita angelica. He sought wings to fly. He was like a bride in anticipation of the heavenly bridegroom. This was his bridal chamber. The monastery was a cloistered paradise.

Here, in Lectio Divina, was a place to rest: busy rest, a waking sleep, upon a bed of flowers. Like bees which sucked the nectar, the most nutritious food. The idealism of all this fired the young Aelred along the path of his beloved Benedict. When would he be able to talk to him?

The habit of reading was formed in the custom of the ancient monks, and the habit of writing too: both together were the tools in the science of salvation. Aelred felt that he was stepping out from the tradition of the ancient scriptorium, where monks deciphered and copied, corrected and illuminated, painted and bound their manuscripts with extraordinary beauty, enhanced by the extravagant flights of their calligraphy and illuminating pens. The monks who did not take up the plough took up the pen. It was the work of the fingers and the mind, an ascetic art. In the almost silence of scratching pens and quietly moving lips, Aelred ruminated, meditated and remembered. He kept his journal. He wrote a letter to Benedict. He had one back in return. He sipped on this nectar, the words he sent to his friend. Aelred wrote in his journal then copied it out for Benedict.

> Dear Benedict,
> Because we can't talk I want to drop you a line. I think of you.
> And when I do it feels good. I think of your love

for me and mine for you as the love which Christ
had for his disciples and the love we must have
for him. He is in our love. When I feel frustrated
that I can' t talk to you I offer it up and know that
that makes our love deeper. It will help me love
all my brothers. We can talk with our eyes. I write
about you in my journal.

Yours in Christ,
Aelred

Dear Little brother,
Yes, we can talk with our eyes. Yes, our love is that
great love we all strive to exist within. I know it's
difficult for you as it is for me.
But this is the boundary we have to set ourselves, a
boundary made by the holy rule and the customs
of our community. This is our dangerous chastity.
There will be moments that we can have.
And they will be more precious because of the
waiting. Keep reading Aelred of Rievaulx.

Always in Christ, my bonny lad,
Benedict

Aelred pasted the letter into the pages of his journal.

The Flat, Bristol:

It was Joe who came to pick me up. I was glad. There were things that I felt I wanted to share with him right away. I know I used to feel more comfortable with Miriam, or when Miriam was there. Not that we didn't spend time together alone, Joe and me. But I was really glad to see Joe. I'm still amazed at his kindness. He's part of what I am excavating. He was very excited to visit Ashton Park. I was surprised that he'd not visited before with J. M., or even on his own. It's not that far away. Quite apart from how it is linked with our lives, it's such a beautiful spot.

Joe said that he would be arriving at two thirty, but it wasn't till after three that he arrived. There'd been traffic and he had taken the winding country roads.

I was waiting in the guests' parlour so that there would be no difficulty in finding me when Joe arrived. The porter came and collected me. Joe was out in the car park.

Where is he? Joe whispered. Immediately, he wanted to see Benedict. I've not come all this way just to pick you up, you know. He laughed. I've heard about this guy. You know? You've read the journals. I've heard J. M. talk so much about him. So this is the place where it all happened. God! I can't imagine it, despite all the evidence. It must've been quite a few days for you. Can't wait to hear about it. Joe was beside himself. Miriam had wanted to come too, he said, but she'd got an important dig this week down in Devon.

I had said to Benedict that I would come and say goodbye. He said that he thought he would be digging spuds in the walled garden, not in the field where most of the others were at this time of the year. We found him with Brother Stephen.

Oh, there you are. Benedict hailed us, lifting himself up from his work with the potatoes. I thought you'd gone.

This is Joe, I said. He's a friend of J. M.'s. Benedict rubbed his hands on the side of his work smock to clean off the mud from his hands. He shook hands with Joe.

From Bristol, are you? he asked. Joe nodded, suddenly shy. We talked about the garden. So much going on inside all of us. We had so much in common and we didn't speak of it. But J. M. was there, standing between us. He was the reason we were all there together. I could see Benedict looking at Joe, sizing him up.

Well, we must go, I said. Leave you to your work and some peace without me bothering you.

You know you've never bothered me, he said, smiling. He drew me into his embrace, giving me the monastic kiss on both cheeks. He shook Joe's hand. You must come some time and stay. We've got good Benedictine hospitality. He smiled. And you'll come back soon. Benedict took my hand again.

I was really sad to leave. But relieved, too. I need some time away. I keep thinking of our parents. So many regrets.

Joe and I didn't stop talking all the way back to Bristol, even though Joe took a scenic route to show me some of the countryside. Wonderful autumn colours!

I can see something of the young Benedict J. M. talked

about. But he's a broken man, Joe said. Can't you see that?

I said, Yes, I could see that in a way, although talking to him had given me another view. But he had been ill once when I was staying.

He's a broken man. He's denied himself something fundamental about himself. It's eaten him away from within.

I was irritated with Joe's going on.

He's betrayed himself all his life.

In the end I didn't argue. But isn't that the life he's chosen, a celibate life, chastity? For whatever reason.

Yes, for whatever reason, Joe said.

We don't understand, I said. But there's a lot to him. I've grown fond of him.

We've come a long way, Joe said. He was thinking of the gay movement. I thought about what he said, and wasn't sure if I agreed. It wouldn't bring my brother back. I didn't say that.

I know that Joe still has a story to tell me.

Things are as I left them, what's left in his room. The red notebooks with the black spines are still there. I hadn't taken all of them to Ashton Park. It's good to be here with him, my brother. Joe has gone out to a club. He wanted me to come along. I said I was tired.

Maybe some other time. Not sure I'm up to that. I think he was disappointed. He said that Miriam might phone from Ilfracombe in Devon.

I get post.

St Aelred's Abbey
Ashton Park
Ashton
Avon

7 October 1984

Dear Robert,
Your visit has brought about a most extraordinary
recall of events which I had hitherto put to rest, if
that was possible. You may have found me evasive.
Yes, I was grateful for your discretion. It has not
been easy to hold in balance the conflicting
claims on my emotions and on my beliefs,
brought about by the relationship I had with
your brother. Just before Aelred, J. M., eventually
lost touch, his letters came less often, I remember
him writing to tell me that he had returned to Les
Deux Isles to research some history, the history
of the island and the house. I was glad to hear
that he had become a history lecturer, or did
some lecturing. That seemed purposeful.
Altogether, I don't know what you will find in
those journals. There are the writings of a very
young man.
Funnily enough, your stay has revived my interest
in the earlier events of J. M.'s life. I suspect those
must matter to you as well. He was J. M. then, not
Aelred. I never got the Ted story in full, as it
were. He never told it in one sitting. I always had
it in fragments, sometimes the same fragments
retold - an indication of his distress. I am now
convinced, with your corroborations, that those

events are what put a particular pattern upon J. M.'s questing. His directors had been remiss. The church has to take responsibility for an enormous amount of bad judgement and wrong advice, being far too concerned with possible scandal and not enough with the particular help needed for the individual soul. Nevertheless, we have to judge the events in their time. I wonder if J. M. came to that conclusion. I doubt it somehow. I think his sense of history was more to unearth buried histories, legitimise illegitimate behaviour. Far too ideological, I think.

Your brother was very needy for human affection. The loss of Ted and the particular circumstances of that loss marked him for life. He was bent upon avenging that secret.

As you see, I have not changed, no matter what the journals say. Yes, I was charmed by your brother. I loved him and I tried to keep that within ideals set by St Aelred of Rievaulx. It was something I had to control because of my vows. That in itself was a radical thing to attempt. I invited him to do the same.

My dear Robert, you yourself are charming and remind me greatly of your brother, though you have a lighter personality. He was driven. I respect your endeavour in putting together his story. I hope I can be of more assistance. I hope you will not be disappointed. I hope you'll look after your faith.

I hope to see you again, God willing. Look forward to your arrival on the Friday. You will stay away

from the retreatants, being at the lodge, not the
guest house this time.

Yours affectionately,
Benedict

Yes, I thought he had been evasive. I do not
reprimand him for that. I'm grateful that he has
agreed to talk to me at all. Now that I've had a
chance to go to Ashton Park, to think and read, I
think I know what my brother was doing in his
journals. I think he was trying to redeem acts that
were in Aelred of Rievaulx's writings, described
quite luridly as evil. He wanted to redeem them
with the quality of his love, the genuineness of
his passion. That could be called ideological. I
think I can weigh up what was youthful about my
brother's journals, that's not to say untrue, and
what can stand the test of time. I can genuinely
feel that I think this way now which I didn't six
months ago. No, I don't expect Benedict to talk
to me in detail. My God, how many years has it
been? It says something that he wants to continue
talking. He must feel very compromised that I
have the journals. He's not helping with accounts
of Ted. That's something I have got to face up to
on my own. Benedict's been perceptive recognising
those events as important to me. I think I know
more than he does. I will have to trust my boyhood
perceptions and the journals. I agree: the church
and his directors at the time were at fault. I'm not

sure whether time excuses, but then what difference does it make to say it doesn't excuse? It should not happen again.

I reply. Receive my own words back again.

19 St John's Way
Bristol 8
Avon

12 October 1984

Dear Benedict,

Thanks again so much for having me down for the week. Thanks for your letter. The visit meant more than I can describe, too. I should've written first. It has brought up so much, so much more than I at first thought was the point of my visit with you when I planned it. I say planned, but you know it was much more haphazard than that, and it was really an idea which had been taking root for some time and growing more interesting each time it came up. As I said to you, yes, I had kept putting it off. It seemed presumptuous. But having embarked on the reading of the journals, skipping and dipping, making my own chronologies, my own story as it were, it began to seem right, appropriate that I should meet you, for J. M.'s sake. To think that I have been so near, here at St John's Way.

I'm sure you did stay here, the evening you went to the Mozart concert in the Pump Room in Bath –his very favourite Horn Concerto too, the music you taught him to love. I play it in the flat now, where I am alone with his things. New to me. I'm a calypso man. I must play my cuatro for you some time.

Do you remember that you climbed up the hill with the folly outside the city when it was still quite light, that brilliant summer of '67? I paid a visit yesterday. How reckless it sounded then! As I read, I snoop. This is why I had to meet you and say I know. Give you a chance to change the account. Or to say yes.

And now, here at night, writing you in the room at 19 St John's Way, everything comes back.

I must stop rambling. But you see how grateful I am to you for bringing it all back. This is to thank you again for that, and to say yes to the 'retreat'. Well, yes, I do qualify it, because as you said I needn't think of it as a retreat proper, but as a quiet time to think out things.

At one time I thought you might not still be there. No, I didn't just think you had left. Well, yes, I thought you might've died. When I thought that, I really panicked. I felt then it would be impossible to put it all together without meeting you. You meet someone, talk lots, and then afterwards you wonder what the hell you've said and what they've made of you.

I agree that the old lodge would be a better place to stay rather than in the main house. Then I'll be away from the real retreatants.

Expect me about four o'clock. I'll probably come by car. I might want to take some drives. Joe will lend me his car. I'll certainly want to take some long walks. What was that place with the lakes? You took a dip. He found it cold.

Have you been to the quarry yet? I was surprised you hadn't taken that walk, right there on your doorstep, recently. Do you know I crept out on my last night and went back to it? The excavation!

I remember, you'll leave the key for the lodge under the grate where the milk bottles are left.

Look forward to seeing you again.

Long ago, he was worried about your letters being read.

All my love, dear friend - that's what I think you have become to me,

Love,

Robert.

P.S. Come on a Friday, isn't it? Drop me a line if I've got it wrong.

I write more than I might speak, if he were there in front of me.

More post.

St Aelred's Abbey
Ashton Park
Avon

20 October 1984

Dear Mr de la Borde,

I am the bearer of sad news. Father Benedict died yesterday afternoon during None. I thought you should know. Your address was among his things near his bed. And I knew that he had arranged for you to return.

I must say that I feel that we must express our sympathy to you who have obviously lost a dear, though recent friend, and someone to whom your brother Jean Marc was close. God's ways are mysterious, and we must wait for that mystery to be revealed in His time.

I hope that you will still keep to your plan to visit and stay for the little retreat you were planning with Father Benedict. We would welcome you.

I enclose the letters from your brother you had asked Father Benedict to make copies of. They were in a collection all ready to send off. I also enclose your last letter to Father Benedict, which he did receive and read before his sudden death. This is not something we normally do, but in the circumstances, and Father Benedict having promised, I will agree to send them.

I look forward to meeting you.

The arrangements you made with Father Benedict to stay in the lodge can still stand. Everything will be made ready if you confirm your visit. Just phone and Father Dominic can make the arrangements.

Father Benedict's funeral is on the day before you planned to come. We've decided to keep it a bit later than usual to coincide with All Souls' Day on 1 November. If you would like to come down earlier for the funeral that would be quite convenient for us. Please confirm with the guestmaster, Father Dominic.

I hope to see you soon.

Yours in Christ,
John Plowden
Abbot.

I am shocked. I can't believe this. It's as if he wished to join him. I will return. What can I learn now? I have only the journals, the letters and the book of dreams. Those early letters are different to this last letter. I thought he was ill, so thin. The Abbot sounds approachable. How did he die?

I hear Joe's words. He's a broken man. It's eaten him away from within.

How did it all come to this? This is my story to tell.

your visit. Just phone and Father Dominic can
make the arrangements.

Want to hear? Is there if I can discuss before you
planned to collect. We appreciate to keep the list
later than usual to correlate with all points this on
November. If you would like to come down earlier
for the appointment would be quite convenient for
us. Please confirm with the guestmaster. Father
Dominic.

Hope to see you soon.

*Yours in Christ,
John J. Plunkett,
Abbot.*

I am sure he'll can't bear to meet. He'll be placed but
into him, I will return. What can I learn now? I have out
the journals, the letters and the book of dreams. These
early ones are different in this by term. I thought he
would sort him. The abbot seemed approachable. However did
he die?

I hear low swords. He is at motion pause. It is quiet film
near from within.

How did it all come to this? That's my answer felt.

The Sanctuary

Your lips, my promised one ...
I sleep, but my heart is awake.
I hear my beloved knocking.
Song of Songs

The monks processed into the choir from the chapter-house for the last office of the day, Compline. '*Fratres ...*' Brother Charles, the acolyte of the choir, intoned the lesson. 'Brethren, be sober and watch, because your adversary the devil, like a roaring lion, goes about seeking whom he may devour... Resist him, strong in faith... You, however, Lord, have mercy on us.'

The choir replied, '*Deo gratias ...*'. 'Thanks be to God.'

Compline was sung in the darkness as usual, with only the two standing candles on either side of the high altar flickering against the bare stone of the sanctuary. Before the 'Salve Regina', which completed Compline, with the community processing to stand in front of the Lady shrine, Aelred, who was the second acolyte of the choir, lit the candles on either side of the statue of Our Lady of Ashton Park.

At the end of Compline, the monks, in their customary way, paid their visits to the side altars which venerated St Benedict, St Aelred, Our Lady and the Blessed Sacrament. Aelred returned the lectern from the middle of the choir to a side chapel, where it was stored when not in use. As he turned from leaning up the lectern against the wall, Aelred was suddenly confronted by Benedict, whom he had not seen kneeling in prayer when he first entered the Chapel. Benedict rose and stood in front of him. They faced each other in the darkness without speaking. The only light was the red flicker of the sanctuary lamp which signified the nearby presence of the Blessed Sacrament reserved in the tabernacle. The real presence was signified by the flickering flame, its wick feeding on the oil from he lamp.

The two monks did not speak. The Great Silence had started.

Benedict put out his arms to draw Aelred to him. Aelred felt himself held in a way that felt good. His heart began to beat fast. He liked the tender feeling of being drawn close to the warm cowled body of Benedict, and to feel his cheeks against the rougher cheeks of the older man. He thought of his father's cheeks. He used to feel frightened, but now it felt good and exciting. He felt suddenly nervous of others near by, whom he could hear leaving choir. But Benedict continued to hold him close to his body. They were hidden by the darkness and the alcove of the side chapel. Everything stopped as he felt suspended there, embraced. He did not want anything to hinder where he was going. It seemed as if this was the beginning of an enormous journey, which encompassed everything he was looking for in himself: monastic life, God, this love for a man - all of it folded together in this embrace. Lost, but extraordinarily alive to all that he was feeling, he let Benedict hold his face in his hands. He let Benedict put his mouth on his. 'Let him kiss me with the kisses of his mouth.' He let Benedict open his lips with his tongue. He let him put his tongue into his mouth. With his head tilted back, Benedict's hands on his neck, he saw the face of Ted in the constellations above him created by the flickering sanctuary lamp on the bare stone walls.

One of the old monks coughed in choir. Aelred was

going to speak. Benedict put his finger on his lips to silence him. 'Shh.' His lips hardly moved.

His whisper was the wind under the door.

Benedict freed his arms from the folds of his cowl and bent to lift Aelred's habit. His hands stroked his naked legs under the loose cassock. Aelred stood, without moving. He did not respond, letting the older man guide him. He let the older man kiss his mouth and touch him where he had not been touched since Ted had touched him the night before he died. He remembered a boy touching him in the showers and having to hide his erection behind his towel. This seemed a funny thought now.

He felt now that all this was good. He began to feel extraordinarily happy. Happy and nervous. Benedict had pulled down his underpants and his hands caressed his penis, which grew there. He held his tight balls in his hands, and then his palms ran over his buttocks. He pulled him into himself, and still Aelred stood and let himself be guided. He could feel Benedict's erect penis against his leg, then pushing into his groin.

Another of the other monks coughed in choir and Benedict broke away abruptly, whispering, 'We mustn't go on.'

Aelred held on to him. He began kissing him. He was now active in this new love. But Benedict now seemed agitated. He pushed Aelred away. He rearranged Aelred's habit and his own. But before he turned to leave the alcove of darkness and enter into the spill of light from the sanctuary lamp, he pressed his mouth once more on Aelred's. 'Meet me outside.' Then he turned abruptly and genuflected before the Blessed Sacrament. Aelred heard his tread and the sweep of his cowl along the floor of the silent choir.

Aelred waited a moment and then followed him out of the choir. As he descended through the choir stalls, he noticed the Abbot bent in prayer. All this under his very nose, Aelred thought, as he bowed to him and shut the choir door silently behind him.

All of a sudden, knowledge seemed to be running fast upon experience, and with that knowledge innocence seemed to be disappearing. He wanted both to be integrated: innocence and knowledge, reason and feeling.

Aelred met Benedict outside the choir. The older man drew him aside into the darkness of the cloister and spoke urgently to him. 'You must confess immediately. This mustn't happen again.'

'What, what's there to confess? I love you. What's wrong? What've we done? I feel good. I won't confess. You touched me but we didn't go further. We love each other. We haven't sinned.'

'Don't be naïve. It is a sin. Confess, then we'll make a new start tomorrow,' Benedict insisted, and Aelred saw the trouble in his eyes as he raised his hood and turned away to go to his cell.

'Benedict,' Aelred whispered loudly.

Benedict did not turn back.

Aelred could not sleep. He crept back out of the novitiate when the lights were out. He didn't think anyone noticed his leaving, though he could hear Edward still moving around in his cell. He was always the last to turn off his lights. He raised his hood. He took off Ted's boots before he passed Father Justin's cell. He moved nimbly on his woollen stockings. His hands fumbled along the walls,

down the dark corridor. There was a short cut through
the library. The floor creaked. One reading lamp was on.
It was Father Cuthbert who was a biblical scholar, poring
over a manuscript. Nothing would disturb him. Even if he
looked up, it would not bother him. He was a kind man
who was utterly obsessed with his research. He might even
engage him in some esoteric connection he had made
between the Hebrew and the Greek script. Ordinarily,
Aelred would want to be detained.

Cuthbert did look up. 'Good night, brother.'

Aelred smiled, bowed and swept on. '*Benedicite*,' he
whispered as he opened the library door softly, leaving
Cuthbert to wonder and muse for a moment, but then
return to his texts.

Outside the library, he made his way swiftly pass the
infirmary. There was a light on. Aelred could see the glow
through the glass above the door. It created more visibi-
lity in the corridor. Brother Sebastian was dying. The
community had been asked to pray for him before
Compline. Brother Hugh, the infirmarian, would be keeping watch. But there would be a rota of watchers to pray
with the dying monk, so anyone might be coming along
the corridor at any moment. The novices were not asked
to keep night vigils. It was meant not to be good for their
health. They needed their sleep.

During this swift and furtive journey from the novitiate,
Aelred still felt all the feelings that had begun in the side
chapel with Benedict, churning inside him. Suddenly, it
was all different. It was not just words spoken on the walk,
words exchanged on the lawn under the monkey-puzzle
tree, letters exchanged, the language of the eyes. Now, it
was Bendict's lips on his, Benedict's tongue in his mouth,

his hands under his habit, his smell enveloping him. He wanted it to continue. Then Benedict had run off, calling it a sin.

Always a sin! He heard his own outrage buried in himself.

Aelred arrived at Father Basil's cell. Being his confessor, he would not turn him away. He could see light seeping from under the door. He knocked quietly, so as neither to disturb others along the corridor nor draw anyone's attention to him if one of the monks should come out of his cell to go to the toilet or bathroom. He was sure that Basil would not mind, and that he would make an exception for him despite the Great Silence.

'*Ave.*' The old man's voice hailed the customary greeting from inside the dimly lit cell.

Aelred opened and peered around the half-open door.

'Yes?' Father Basil was not yet certain who it was.

'It's me, father. Aelred.'

'Not in bed yet? Young men need their sleep.' He looked down where Aelred was still holding his boots in his hand. 'Are you about to abscond, brother?'

'No, father.' Then he realised about his boots and sat on a chair by the door after closing it and put his shoes on. 'I didn't want to disturb anyone.'

'Or be noticed by anyone. What's all the secrecy about?'

'I should be in my cell.'

'Yes, there are a lot of things which should be, brother, but they're not, are they?'

'No, father.'

'Have you prayed for Sebastian? I've just given him Extreme Unction. He'll soon be on his way. "Like a thief in the night", the Gospel says.' Aelred heard a tremor in the old monk's voice.

'Father?'

'Not you, little brother. Come and sit here. Our Lord in his mysterious ways comes like a thief in the night.'

'Oh, yes. I wanted to confess.'

'Confess. Weren't you here the other day?'

'That was my weekly confession. This is special.'

'What terrible crime have you committed now?

'Father, you're teasing me.'

'Brother, I'm tired. Let's sit and talk. You tell me all.'

'Shouldn't I kneel?'

'Kneel if you wish, brother.' Basil sighed. 'But I think sitting here closely we can talk better.' Basil drew two chairs close to his desk. Basil was also the Dean of Studies so his cell was bigger and the walls were covered with books.

'So? You look quite agitated. What has happened? Tell me.'

Eventually, at first stumbling, but then in full flow, Aelred told Basil quite graphically what had happened, though he did not mention Benedict's name. Aelred felt that he suspected. Sometimes Benedict confessed to Basil. Wouldn't he put two and two together? 'Are you shocked?' Aelred ended his story. 'I love him.'

'No brother, I'm not shocked. I think the first thing to help you is to realise that this has happened before and will happen again, through the long history of monastic life.' Aelred watched the old man smile wryly. 'The walls won't come tumbling down. But let's start with your last statement, your assertion of love for your brother. I don't doubt it, or his for you. But the question is what do we do with that love here in our community, which is vowed to a celibate life and above all to a chaste life. I don't doubt for a moment that your intentions are chaste.'

'It felt good,' Aelred protested.

'It *is* good, brother. Everything that God has made is good. It is what we do with what he has made that can be imperfect. Your attraction for each other is good. You can admire each other. If that makes you act well to each other and helps you to act well to others, that is good. By their fruits you shall know them. That's what St Paul tells us. But you see, while it makes you feel happy and good, it has disturbed your brother. And, I dare say, it's disturbed you. Now let's look at his reactions.'

'He broke off. He called it a sin. He turned his back on me. He just said, go and confess. You'd think I'd done the most terrible thing. And it was him.'

'Him, brother? What about him? A strong passion has taken hold of him and now he's in distress. Possibly on his knees now at his bedside. He was thinking of your soul. But, too, it may represent a terrible thing for your brother. It may be part of a terrible struggle in his spiritual life. You can't judge him.'

'So, it's fine for me but not for him.'

'Well, not quite. In a way. You're young. Look at how young you are. How handsome. We must not omit that.' Basil smiled. 'He's taken vows. He has vows to honour. Have you thought of that? These are not easy matters, brother.' Basil looked at the clock on his desk. 'We've Matins to think of. And I wonder how Sebastian is doing?'

'But do I have some terrible sin on my soul?'

'I can give you absolution, brother. If it makes you feel better. But absolution is not magic. It's your intention, your firm purpose of amendment, as you know, that cleanses you, gives you the grace to change. You're not a child. But you must realise that you're young, you're attractive. These things exist. You must examine your wish for chastity. But believe me, what has happened is also beautiful. Use your passion for your prayer, for good acts. Use your passion. I absolve you in the name of the Father, the Son and the Holy Ghost.' Father Basil made the sign of the cross over the head of Aelred. 'Sleep tight, brother. Sleep tight, don't let mosquitoes bite. I'm sure your mother said that in your hot country.'

'Good night father. Thank you.'

Aelred went to bed thinking of Benedict and looking forward to seeing him opposite him in the choir at Matins. He was not sure that he understood everything Basil was arguing. He seemed to be arguing for Aelred of Rievaulx's way. But he felt better. He felt that he must talk to Benedict. He must comfort him. He looked so troubled. This was to be a debate within himself, his own soul, and with Benedict, about the quality and the boundaries of their friendship - their dangerous chastity. What could this love mean? Where could it go? How could it express their highest ideals?

I am black but lovely, daughters of Jerusalem,
like the tents of Kedar,
like the pavilions of Salmah.
Take no notice of my swarthiness,
it is the sun that has burnt me.
My mother's sons turned their anger on me,
they made me look after the vineyards ...
Tell me then, you whom my heart loves ...

Aelred read from the *Song of Songs* and fell asleep in the dim nightlamp of the novitiate dormitory.

Jordan appeared out of the painting on the staircase. He was running along the terrace, chased by the hound at the duke's feet from the same portrait. There was terror on the face of Jordan. The terrace became the gravel yard at Malgretoute. The duke became his father, then became the Abbot, became Father Justin, his novice master, riding on his father's horse, Prince, urging on his hound from the portrait. Aelred was dusting the portrait. His father was looking down at him from his horse. Jordan was joined by other black boys. Pardners. They were all being hunted. Young boys running, hunted. Aelred joined his friends, pursued by the duke cracking a whip and urging on the baying of the hounds. The place was both Ashton Park and the house high upon the morne at Malgretoute Estate on Les Deux Isles.

There was the smell of molasses, cane trash. There was a high wind. He tasted syrup, cane syrup. A train clanged along the line in the gully.

Then there was a fire, a sunset fire. Flamboyante and flambeaux, and cries of freedom. The town was burning. Saint Pierre was burning.

Then Aelred was with Ted. They were in a boat in the middle of the sea. The sun was baking. They were fishing off the side of the boat. Then he was close at Ted's side, so close that he licked the beads of sweat off his naked shoulder. The sweat tasted like salt. Ted turned to look at him. They were both naked. They stood together on the seat in the stern and then dived into the sea. They swam away from the boat. They swam down under the black water. When they came up they were far from the boat and Aelred could not swim to the boat. He saw Ted ahead of him, but, thrash as he might, he could not move. They were clinging to each other.

Again, with Ted. It was their last holiday before he died. He kept moving between Ashton Park and the island home where they were on holiday. They climbed rocks, then they were in bed, like the last time. Ted didn't want to, then he did. 'No, yes, lick me there, suck me.' Then they did what they used to do as small boys, touching their totees, sucking each other's. Ted was in his bed in his monastic cell and then again in his bedroom at Malgretoute.

Then Aelred was kissing Benedict. Then he was at the quarry. Benedict was falling, falling, falling. Benedict was Edward, falling, falling, falling.

Aelred awoke, afraid, falling off his narrow bed.

'*Benedicamus Domino.*' The acolyte of the choir was knocking at the entrance to his cell, waking Aelred for Matins.

'*Deo gratias,*' he answered.

He had had a wet dream.

…way from the boat. The steam down under the black
water. When they came up they were far from the boat
and had to fight not to go to the boat. He was terrified
of line fish, things he no might imagined he … had. These
were all ghost to each other.

Again, with faded … wash … he holds a before … bed.
He kept turning between Ad and Pa and the … the island
home where the … the humble. The … humble, he …
there … was in bed, than the last time, but didn't want
to … then he didn't do just like to there and know. Then
they said that they used to do as small boys mumbling …
there … roaming these such … or … they did … they … he
… his … mid and hear … arm in his … he'd never …
slight … …

Then Aobad was kissing Kendall? Then he was at the
quarry. He didn't … was filling, filling, filling … filling …
Edward filling, filling, filling.

John Lawde … … … influence … new methods of one
… … reports, concise? The … no … of the … clean was
knocking at the … … … … … … water. Where he
Mum?

… … … … … … … … …
He had had a wet dream.

The Lodge:

I persuaded Miriam and Joe to bring me to Ashton Park and stay for the funeral. It meant that I wouldn't have the car here, but I didn't want to be on my own for this. After all, Benedict was J. M.'s friend. We were doing it for J. M. Miriam loved the chant. She said J. M. used to often sing and hum snatches of Gregorian chant, right up to the end of his life.

He had monastic choirs on cassette. The music, if nothing else, still took hold of him, she said.

It seems so strange, me here all the way from Malgretoute with these two people who were best friends with my brother, attending the funeral of the lover of his youth. Lover - what a word for me to use. Listening too much to Joe. He remembers how awkward I used to be when I first arrived.

Today, as we walked up to the cemetery behind the procession of monks who walked in pairs, black-cowled and hooded, behind the six monks who shouldered Benedict's coffin, I thought, how appropriate that he should leave this world in glory. I hear his words. He called it that, glory, the fulsome ripening of autumn in Ashton Park, redolent with copper beech, horse chestnut, the turning oaks, the spruce and the flashes of light shooting through the woods in the silver birches. I feel that that is what J. M. would've noticed. Now I notice what he would notice.

'Glory be to God for dappled things.' That Jesuit,
Benedict had once said, was a passionate man.

His conversation was threaded with reference,
information and the most startling insights for me in the
week I knew him. I want to remember him for J.M. He shocked
J. M., just nineteen and very young, mostly because he hardly
understood anything at first. Not that he meant to shock him as
he smiled and gruffly wiped his ruddy face, as if to clear away any
obstacle that would prevent him from pinning down the insight.
He licked his full red lips, running his hands back through his
thick black hair, forgetting to have his tonsure shorn, revealing a
dome of brow, furrowed, and impressive to J. M.

This is a picture from the journals. One I want to recall
now. That was the man in his prime. Not the man I knew,
the diminished ascetic I met. Ascetic?

I hear Joe's voice: a broken man, eaten up from inside.
Fasting, starving himself to death.

Killing himself. Is this what he did?

I have J. M.'s words alone. I would no longer have
Benedict's verifications, perspectives or whatever else he
was suggesting to me. It seemed like an evasion at times.
Why should he have spoken to me? I had been terribly
presumptuous. I had him only in J. M.'s words now.

It was Aelred who wrote the journal. Not the J. M. I
had known, my older brother; not the J. M. of the end,
either. I keep having to remind myself that I'm recovering
a brother who was still just a boy.

When Joe talks it's quite a different picture. Joe has a
story to tell me. Little bits creep out - the brother I never
knew. I don't know whether I want to know. I've not read
any of the post-Ashton Park journals, on purpose. I will
have to soon. And Joe wants to tell his story.

J. M. had been excited with everything Benedict thought and said. He presumed that he understood and in that way he came to understand everything with the confidence of his youth and the wisdom of Benedict being older ... 'All things counter ... /Whatever is fickle ... (Who knows how?).'

He came to appreciate much of it later, when he needed it, Benedict used to say.

He had been like a sower sowing in a most fertile field. J. M. was receptive, intuitively empathic, susceptible and passionately struck by this man whose body his brothers now carried to his grave, as we mounted the short hill to the small patch of green, marked with its rows of simple wooden crosses bearing the names of dead brothers gone before, buried under the whisper of cypresses and yew trees where J. M. first learnt not to fear death when he dug his first grave.

I could see that this was bringing back J.M.'s death for Miriam and Joe.

Death had held him as a child, coming as a punishment for sin. Was that not St Paul's thought? He knew the sting of death. Ted, his boyhood friend had died, as a punishment, he had thought. Had he changed his mind about that?

So much had happened here in such a short space of time, which now seemed like quite a life apart - another life, the enclosed life. But for me, what had happened here in those four years, and in particular that first year, was a chapter in a story begun much earlier, the conclusion to which I was writing down for myself. Presumptuous with his words? Brotherly love? I was scared of what I knew I would have to face up to.

'*Dies irae, dies illa ...*' the sequence for the Requiem, the attenuated tones of celibate men, inflected antiphonally according to the inspired chant of St Gregory mixed with the wind. For J. M. they were mixed with the waves on the beach at San Souci. I knew the chants so well too, as a boy educated within a monastic school. But J. M. had learnt them as a boy with a passion. He tells of the first strains in the darkness of dawn, with Dom Placid chaperoning him to early morning Mass in the abbey church, down the hill-side path, through the garden with the goldfish pond, under the arch of bare earth near the sacristy, as the monks concluded Lauds and the Angelus broke the dawn over the hills and plains of our island.

I find my world in his. I find it described in journals, red notebooks with black spines, stacked on a shelf in an empty room in Bristol.

I stood behind the circle of monks at the side of the grave, Benedict's grave. I could hear the coffin scrape the sides as two monks lowered it, with bands of canvas loo-ped about the polished wood with a simple silver cross. 'Requiem eternam done ei Domine ...' Ted, poor Ted. So long. J. M. Then, Benedict. Names remembered.

There still wasn't any sun as we left the cemetery to pro-cess back down to the monastery. I still didn't understand the seasons: four, not just the dry and wet. After the asperges and the incense, the Abbot picked up a handful of dirt and threw it into Benedict's grave.

When the monks dispersed, Miriam asked to see the grave of Jordan. We went over to the chapel wall and found the stone with the African head and the letter J.

So it did exist, she said. And the story that helped

him - was that true?

It was true enough, I said. I suppose. We stood together and looked. There is a truth, Miriam said, which in its entirety eludes one. I'm working on a dig at the moment, in Devon. An admiralty-chartered barque, 'The London' foundered on the rocks in Rapparee Cove near Ilfracombe. Its captain, Robertson, was a not very reputable character. It's a lovely spot. Lush fields fall away to the jagged rocks down to a small beach. In 1796 the 300-ton vessel tried to put in at the cove during a storm. It was returning from Saint Lucia to Bristol. It had captured booty and slaves from the French. Some reports suggest that there may have been as many as 150 slaves in her hold. Their full fate has not come to light. Storms and erosion have begun to unearth something.

Miriam told her story while we looked at names on stones. Joe was inspecting the monks' graves and found Basil and Sebastian next to each other.

It was his passion that drew me, his beauty, which I always saw, Joe said, as we had coffee in the parlour. J. M. was always trying to make meaning of his nature against all established traditions. Joe spoke precisely. Excavating pieces of buried traditions, outlawed traditions - this is what kept him going. He called it migrating for meaning, migrating for food, living in another country. Words were his food. Eating words - you've read about it, Joe said. Joe kept looking at Miriam while he spoke. She kept smiling. He looked at me. She stroked his arm.

She's a sensitive, attractive woman, very intelligent. I hadn't heard Joe speak quite so emotionally. Miriam was allowing him to open up.

It was what I had begun to think: Benedict had not

been eating. It had been going on for years, starting, it seems, after J. M. left. There had been a series of long fasts which steadily affected his health. The Abbot let it slip out. What a strange synchronicity.

In the afternoon, after Miriam and Joe had left, I returned to the quiet cemetery, which had once been here from the original country house, to work with Brother Leonard, whose afternoon task it was to fill in Benedict's grave. We worked in silence till we had filled the six feet, each spadeful crashing on to the polished wood with the simple silver cross. Then the sound became the thud of dirt on dirt. I felt suddenly that I too had grown to love Benedict: the Benedict of the journals and then the man I met. This visit, this retreat, was to be with him. But then he died. Here he was, gone to earth.

Before we had packed down the last of the earth that covered Benedict's grave, and replaced clods of turf, Brother Leonard and I sat on a small bench in silence: a silence that quite soon took you to its very centre, a deep drone of a wind in the high surrounding trees. We sat, wonderfully exhausted by our gravefilling.

They had been lucky to have Father Basil, I thought. I see his grave.

My whole plan has now changed. I am on my own, except for meals, when I go to the refectory and sit at the high table with the Abbot and the other guests. My planned talks with Benedict are now no longer possible. I regret that.

Of course, I have more time to read and write. As Benedict said in his letter, I'm going over again the fragments of the Ted story. Yes, I too think that it had

set a pattern to his questing. That lad at school, as Aelred
of Rievaulx would have called him. What do I remember?
I know I don't like this part of the story.

After the graffiti incident, which broke the scandal, it was
an embarrassment to be even seen in the toilets, to be
there with others. After that burning shame, which the
monks and lay teachers ignored, and Ted and J. M. tried
to pretend hadn't happened, I lived with my brother's
reputation, not fully understanding, and not wanting to
betray him, but tempted, when the teasing got too much.

I was solitary in my shame, solitary in my love for him. I
could not tell tales at home. I spoke to no one. There
began a growing rebellion on the part of the other pupils.
One night, late, I went down in the darkness and scraped
off the burning words in the silence, broken only by the
gurgling water in the lavatory cistern. My fingernails
peeled the paint away. They were sore. Tears rolled down
my cheeks.

I looked up the rank of tables in the refectory at J. M.
who was on the senior tables. I looked from under my
lowered eyes, my head bowed, during grace before meals.
The stamping got worse and worse as Ted entered to sit at
the high table and lead the grace before meals: 'Bless us,
O Lord, for these thy gifts which we are about to receive.'
He could not start. They would not let him. The stamping
became banging. I could see boys looking at me to see if I
was joining in. Knives and forks were lifted and banged
down on the table. More eyes looked me. I could feel my
feet lifting and falling. My hands were on the knives and
forks. I was banging them down on the table too. I was joining in. My eyes moved between Ted's and J. M.'s. They

did not look at each other.

Eventually, Father Julius took over. You could hear a pin drop. Then suddenly in the silence, a loud voice shouted: buller man! I could feel the shout coming up from my belly. It tasted like food I could not digest. It was like bile coming up and then out into the open as a shout. Everyone laughed and jeered. Father Julius shouted for silence. The silence continued. Then there was the scrape of chairs, the clatter of sitting down. There was the smell of school food. I retched. Food was being passed down from the prefect. The clatter of knives and forks was because everyone had started eating, but some boys were carrying on the banging under the usual din. My shin hurt. The boy opposite had kicked me. I looked up the tables at my brother, then at Ted. I saw others look.

A boy opposite said, He's your brother- aaggh, making a vomiting sound. I smiled and banged my knife and fork. I stamped my feet on the ground. The boy who kicked me and the other boys near by laughed.

These facts seem so trivial, now, so small, as I understand so much more. Then it was a burden of shame. How could the taunts of small boys cause so much pain, so much havoc? No one understood the enormity of what we were doing. No one did anything about it. I did not understand what I had done. Everyone hissed as they left the refectory. Someone kicked me behind the knees. I hissed. Is this what they wanted to do to J. M., to Ted?

J. M. must've told Benedict this story, as he had written it out in his journal. Rehearsing? I read to see if he had noticed me joining in.

He says, I see Robert down among the juniors.

He sees Robert. Did he hear his shout of buller man?

This is one of the few times my name appears in these early journals. Did he see him stamping and banging and hissing? I'll never know.

I must get out and do some manual work. It's stuffy in here.

I feel sad and lonely. I wanted to take care of them now. I wanted the details of their love to be named. Aelred of Rievaulx had tried to name his sin, writing to his sister. This is a hagiographic tale, not a pornographic story. It is of the passion of those whose young love was inspired by saints and who were wrestling with their nature. His words lead me. I eat them, before I can digest their meaning.

I look out on his world. It falls under his gaze, now my gaze.

Vita Angelica

I charge you,
not to stir my love, nor arouse it,
until it please to awake.
Song of Songs

Wild violets glinted purple, close to the ground, under dry leaves and new fresh moss where Aelred crouched. Each day there were new flowers, new names to ask Brother Theodore about. 'You bring me a flower, brother, and we can match it with the picture in our book,' he had said at recreation. He had directed Aelred to a miscellany of English wild flowers. Brother Theodore had a simple faith, combined with his individually acquired knowledge of wild flowers. He had been known to place *The Little Flower - A Life of Saint Thérèse Of Lisieux* in the botany section of the library.

Aelred felt slightly ridiculous here, out at the quarry, hiding behind a boulder and a small tree that had persisted in growing even though all its roots were exposed from a piece of ground that had been quarried some time ago. It flourished; flowers were bursting from a cluster of buds. Elderberry, he thought Brother Theodore had called it. He would check. He would take back a specimen. One cluster was fully open and looked like a lace doily; it had a creamy colour. Last time Theodore had been very pleased with his observation. 'You're making splendid progress. I've asked the librarian to get us a book on tropical plants, so that you can tell me which ones you have at your home.' Aelred was touched.

On the ground, a yard away, near some rocks and anchored by a jagged stone at the bottom of a very steep ascent, were Edward's clothes. His overalls and top smock were bundled together. Aelred could not see Edward as he had done before, but he knew that he must be near by. He had just come upon the clothes on the ground, suddenly. Then he had retreated to his present hiding place. There was a clatter and thump of falling rock. Aelred looked in the direction of the sound. The rock had fallen from high above him. There, clinging to an even more sheer rock face than last time, was Edward. What was he holding on to? Aelred was about to call out, but stopped himself. Edward seemed suspended there, except that he moved. His strong legs and arms moved, and his buttocks strained in his tight black shorts, lifting his body up into the air and pressed against the rock face. He was almost spreadeagled, or an angel in flight pressed against a hard place. This time he chose each move more carefully, it seemed. Now and then he would glance over his shoulder to judge his height. The wind caught his blond hair. Then he looked up to assess the ascent. He found another grip for his hand, and another one for each foot in turn. He moved according to touch and grip, guided by contour and surface, like the bumps of braille for a blind reader. Aelred was captivated. He might fall. He wanted to say, Don't climb further. Had Edward told Benedict that this was why he had been late for Prime last time? Was he going to be late again? Would he always be coming here to climb in the early morning before Prime? Had he got special permission? There were no cut flowers immediately visible. But there, as Aelred looked more closely, in the folds of the denim overalls on the ground was a little bunch of wild violets, purple against the denim blue of the overalls.

Aelred was now crouching near Edward's clothes in order to get a better view. He could still smell a trace of newness. Edward was climbing very fast. Without knowing why, he put his hand on Edward's smock. He lifted it and took it in his hands. Then he smelt it. He buried his face in it and smelt it. It still had that new smell, but there was also the smell of sweat in the armpits. There was the smell of olive oil where some had spilt from working in the sacristy, filling the lamp for the Blessed Sacrament. Aelred then lifted the overalls, and stroked the legs and played with the buckles on the straps. Then he smelt the crotch and the seat. There was a musty smell of sweat and a distinct odour - Edward's odour, his secret odour. There was the song of a singing thrush. There was the wind in the nearby oak above the quarry. The intermittent clatter of stones from Edward's climb continued to startle him. He looked up and still Edward was climbing. He looked around him. He suddenly realised that he could have been seen.

There was an acute sense of this especial scene for Aelred: the rock climber, his clothes, the smell of his clothes, the silence, himself in the silence, and the sound of the wind and of the birds. This was shattered by the tolling of bells.

Aelred realised that it was not the bell for Prime. These bells were being tolled. There was a single loud gong, an interval, then another gong, and so it continued. Brother Sebastian must have died. He could see that Edward had stopped and was listening. He was beginning to descend. It was almost as if his climb was engraved on his memory, prompting the rapidity of his descent. His hands and feet felt for their grips and holds. Aelred left quickly. He did not want to be noticed. He took the path through the silver birches to hide his walk back to the abbey. The bells eventually stopped tolling. They were soon followed by the usual bell for Prime. Aelred hurried.

Sebastian had died. There was a visible sadness on the face of many monks. Sebastian had been an old and revered member of the community. Aelred noticed Basil with his face in his hands, kneeling in choir before the start of Prime. The news of the death for Aelred was mixed with his meeting with Basil the night before. He still had to meet Benedict. No occasion presented itself. Benedict had kept his eyes downcast during Matins and Prime. At breakfast there was the slightest glance from his worried eyes. There was no reassuring smile. They did not speak. Meeting at the coffee urn Benedict drew back. 'After you, brother.' His hand prompted Aelred beneath the elbow. His touch made Aelred burn. The coffee overflowed and he was flustered with wiping up. Benedict knelt to help with the slop pail. Their eyes met, their fingers touched.

After Prime Aelred noticed the bunch of violets in a small vase in front of the statue of Our Lady in the novitiate. Edward had done his duty. He knelt at the prie-dieu and said a decade of the rosary. The sight of the small flowers, where they had lain in the folds of Edward's smock, brought back what he had done. He remembered Edward's odour and it surprised him. It made him nervous, what he had done: pressing his face into the new novice's clothes.

That morning, instead of his usual study, Aelred was detailed to work in the cemetery with Leonard, to dig

Sebastian's grave. This was the second grave he had helped to dig. Breaking the surface was the hardest. Then it got easier. They were almost halfway, taking it in turns to use the pickaxe, when Basil arrived to help. While one dug, the other shovelled away, and the third rested.

At one point Leonard had to slip away to help at the pottery and the grave digging was left to Basil and Aelred. 'So, Sebastian has gone.' Aelred said, wanting to open conversation with Basil, remembering the reference to the brother dying and receiving Extreme Unction the night before.

'It was a long night.'

'Did you watch after I left your room?'

'I was called at twelve, and then every hour on the hour I seemed to be called.'

'Were there no other monks to watch?'

'Oh, yes, the vigil was well looked after. But at each hour the new watch came to say that Sebastian wanted me there.'

'Were you his confessor?'

'I was his friend, brother.' Basil looked directly at Aelred when he said this, resting from his shovelling.

'A best friend?' Aelred looked up from his digging, his face alert with questions.

'Yes. You see, I wanted to help with the grave, though I'm not up to the hard part.'

'I'll do that,' Aelred answered eagerly.

'I wanted to help.'

'Here, you shovel. I'll dig. When you're tired, take a rest.'

'We joined together, you know. Straight from school. We were your age, just nineteen at the time.'

Aelred looked at Basil and thought he must be in his seventies.

'He'd always been frail.' Basil shovelled and spoke. His breathing was laboured. 'At one point he nearly gave up. But we managed to find a way.'

'You mean recently? He's been dying for a long while, yes?'

'Yes, that, but no, I mean when he was young. He was frail even then. Our life was harsher in those days. There were long fasts. The heating was poor.'

'I'd never thought of that. I expect things have been changing through the years.'

'Yes. At times I think we forgot that we were men and thought we were angels.'

'The *vita angelica*?' Aelred was showing off his reading in monastic theology.

'He was as beautiful as an angel.' There was a whimsicality about Basil, the same monk who had the donkey on his desk and gave sermons on donkeys carrying their sacred burden on the flight into Egypt. 'Delicate, soft spoken, sensitive. A talented painter, but very modest. The Stations of the Cross in the abbey church are his.' Basil had stopped shovelling and was looking up into the soughing trees. He put his shovel down, took a handkerchief from his pocket and blew his nose. Aelred continued digging, embarrassed to watch. When he looked up from his digging, from where his head was down, hidden at the bottom of the grave, nearly finished, he realised that Basil was crying. He had put the shovel down and had walked away towards the medieval chapel in the corner of the cemetery. Aelred could see his shoulders shaking and he could hear his sobs between the blowing of his nose.

Aelred carried on digging and shovelled out the last of the dirt. It seemed to him that the grave was the required depth, but Leonard would have to give the final judgement. He pulled himself out of the hole.

'Are you OK?' Aelred joined Basil on a bench under the shady cedar of Lebanon.

'Yes, brother. He was a brother to all of us. It's a common loss, but I'll miss him, and no one will ever know how much. For who can I tell?'

'You can tell me,' Aelred said boldly.

'Yes, I can tell you. It's worth it, brother. It's worth carrying on, trying hard. That's what we did. We came through all the stages.' Aelred saw the old monk's eyes fill to brimming. He watched the lines in his face, the wrinkles on his hands. But in his eyes and from his lips he heard the story of youth, of the passion in youth of the sins of youth, of the body of youth. 'I know your struggles, brother, and these are your struggles. I can guess. This is the grief of an old man. But believe me, if you've been given the gift, this kind of love, you must take great care of it. It's a fire which can consume you. It's a battle that can destroy you. It's continually fraught with temptation, but the rewards are sweet, so sweet.' Basil had cleared his eyes and throat and was speaking with strength in his voice. 'It's so sweet, so delicious. It's the food of heaven. Look at me, with all these feelings and memories as if they were yesterday and I was your age.'

'Yes,' Aelred sat and looked at the old man. He was astonished at his openness. He listened.

'There will be those who take a strict line and will seem as if they don't understand, but there'll be those who will understand, the way that I understand. Be attentive to that kind of sympathy. Look at last night. They let me sit each hour with him, his hands in mine. In the end he lay in my arms and gave his soul to God.' Then he looked Aelred directly in the eye and said, 'There was one time, a wonderful hot summer like the summers of the past always seem to have been, that we spent a *dies non* together, alone, near that village, I forget its name, and lay together in a field talking and reading. We lay in each other's arms then. We took our chances. We came through.'

'I'll remember that, father.'

'Come and talk any time that you're worried. There'll be the temptations and there'll be the struggles with your superiors. There always are.'

Leonard came back and was inspecting the depth and width of the grave. There was a little more digging to be done and shaving of the sides. 'You've dug him a good grave, brother,' Basil said to Leonard. 'I'll be leaving now.'

'You can return to your studies,' Leonard said to Aelred. 'I'll finish up.'

Basil and Aelred walked back down to the abbey. 'Just when you think you've got it sorted, there will come a surprise which pulls you up short, and changes everything.' Basil looked at Aelred.

The poplars at the bottom of the drive rattled their leaves in the wind; turning white and then green, a fresh young green. Aelred remembered the words from 'Binsey Poplars' :

> *My aspens dear, whose airy cages quelled,*
> *Quelled or quenched in leaves the leaping sun,*
> *All felled, felled, are all felled ...*

They lay in each others' arms, Aelred thought.

Aelred found Benedict in the library after his theology
seminar. He was sitting in the alcove below the window
that looked out over the fields towards the quarry. Aelred
stood at the entrance closing the door quietly behind
him. He stood and stared at Benedict's back, bent over
his books. He moved to one of the shelves and pretended
to look for a book. In the silence, Aelred heard Benedict's
pen scratching as he wrote his notes. He admired
Benedict's hard study and looked forward to the day
when he would be taking philosophy and theology. The
library smelt of old books. Musty. A fat tome slipped from
his hand and thumped to the floor. Benedict turned.
'You startled me,' seeing Aelred standing there with his
hood pulled up.
  'Sorry.'
Benedict sat, turned towards him. Aelred bent down
where he stood to pick up the old tome, the *Conferences of
John Cassian*. Benedict saw the title. 'We won't find him
helpful, unless we forget all we've said and done, and pursue our vocation quite differently. He was against cliques,
as he called them, but not altogether against feelings, passion, as Evagrius was.'
Aelred looked at the title. 'Sorry, I don't know what
John Cassian says, or Evagrius. Is that how you pronounce
his name. Who was he, anyway?'
  'He would have us resist this friendship.'
  'So, he's different from Aelred of Rievaulx?'
  'Much earlier. Cassian, like Augustine, his contemporary,
thought human bonds too fragile. Come over here - we
can't talk across the library.' Aelred went and stood near

Benedict's desk. Benedict took his hand from his side and held it. 'These fathers of the church would advise us to resist human bonds.'

'And Aelred would have us hold hands.'

'Yes.'

'Who do we follow?'

'This is our struggle in our time. We've got to sort it out for ourselves. That's what Aelred of Rievaulx did, I think. He was true to his experience, but he listened to the fathers also, and then created his own way, the *De spirituali amicitia, Spiritual Friendship* which I gave you. So Aelred of Rievaulx's work is part of what we've got to look at and be helped by.'

'Do you feel better after last night?' They kept on holding hands, but Aelred had his ears pricked up for the sound of possible footsteps approaching the library. They should not be talking during study time.

'Yes, I saw Basil before Matins. He was in the corridor outside the infirmary when I got up to ring the bells. He's so good. He never refuses me. I confessed. I feel good about us.'

'I saw him too, last night, as you asked me. I didn't want to at first. But I did.'

'I'm glad. See how I hold your hand.'

'Yes,' Aelred's hand held more firmly and then caressed Benedict's arm under the sleeve of his cassock, and then again held his hand. 'Yes, Basil has made me think of you and what you want. I know you want it Aelred of Rievaulx's way.'

'I think that must be the way. We don't deny how we feel. We don't want to deny this passion. But it must find - what do the fathers say? Augustine, I think. It must find its *forma et meta*: its formula, its method and its boundaries. I broke the boundaries last night. I made you break the boundaries. I mustn't do that again. It's dangerous, but it is the way we must proceed. Otherwise what is our chastity? But our love is real, too. In all that it is. It's a dangerous chastity. Aelred of Rievaulx tells us that he wants us to be always afraid, never secure.' While Benedict spoke he had risen, and he and Aelred had moved while holding hands into the alcove to the side of the window, beneath which was the desk at which Benedict worked. They stood in the alcove, hidden from the open library. 'We can never be secure.' He lowered Aelred's hood and ran his hand up and down his soft smooth brown cheek, cupping his face in his hand. Smooth, he thought, like a a boy still, almost like a girl. 'We must always be afraid.'

'Yes, yes, I know.'

'See what happens even as we talk, even as we're afraid,' and he put his face close to Aelred's and placed his lips upon his. 'See how one thing can lead to another.' But then he withdrew as the younger monk opened his mouth. 'No, that's our boundary.'

Aelred could hardly breathe. 'Yes, yes.' He wanted to kiss more. He resisted. But there was no control over all his other feelings, no control over his erection. No control over his heart beat, over his hands running up inside the sleeves of Benedict's cassock.

'Brother,' Benedict whispered, backing away, disentangling his fingers. 'See what being alone can do.' And as they parted and came out of the alcove, Benedict returned to his desk. Aelred stood at his side. The door of the library opened and Father Justin came in. He was obviously surprised to find Benedict and Aelred together.

Aelred should have been in his cell at study.

'Oh,' Father Justin glanced at Aelred as if to say, what on earth are you doing here at this time, but directed what he said to Benedict. 'I was just wanting to talk to you, Benedict, about Edward. I see he's having trouble getting to Prime on time.' Aelred slipped away and left the library for his cell. He could feel Father Justin's disapproval by his look. Aelred felt that he should have continued looking at the library books. He felt that his slipping away was an admittance of guilt. He felt naughty. What had Father Justin realised? He expected that Father Justin would follow this up with a request for a talk. He might have seen them kissing and holding hands.

It was a blue May. It was warm. Aelred spent the siesta back at the cemetery, on the same bench where he had spoken to Basil during the gravedigging. He had brought with him his *De Spirituali Amicitia*, and a book of Aelred of Rievaulx's letters. He felt torn between the goodness that Basil had made him feel the night before coupled with the sense that he was now embarked on some deep adventure with Benedict, and conflicting feelings, sexual and spiritual, to go further with Benedict. These feelings thronged his mind with images that distracted his reading. As in a dream, the most unusual connections were made. It was like a strong force independent of his feelings for Benedict.

Aelred read again where Aelred of Rievaulx wrote to his sister:

'Remember if you like, that filthiness of mine for which you so often pitied and corrected me, the

girl the boy, the woman the man. Recall now, as I
said, my rottenness when a cloud of lust was emitted
from my slimy concupiscence of flesh and from
the gushing up of puberty, and there was no one
to snatch me away and save me.'

It was that hot Good Friday afternoon when he accompanied his mother to the Good Friday Mass of the pre-
sanctified. They had to wait in the hot three-o'clock-in-the-
afternoon sun on the gravel road for a taxi into the
town, as there was no Mass in the village church.

Holy Week had pulled a black curtain over his mind.
There were purple shrouds over the statues and cruci-
fixes. Since Palm Sunday, thoughts of the impending
crucifixion of Jesus accompanied his play, his mealtimes
and his inability to fall asleep. The family rosary was
always the Five Sorrowful Mysteries, when he would have
to meditate upon the agony in the garden, the scourging,
St Peter's betrayal, and Jesus being spat upon, crowned
with thorns, having his face wiped by Veronica and his
arms and legs nailed to the cross, pierced with a lance,
being raised on high, crying out of severe thirst, being
taken down by Nicodemus. This was a passion. He had to
meditate on the fate of the two thieves who had been
crucified with Jesus: the one who had asked for forgiveness
and who had been promised heaven - 'This day thou shall
be with me in paradise.' The other thief had jeered, and
challenged Jesus that if he were the Son of God he could
free himself and them. He would go to hell. All during
Holy Week, he had had to meditate on the last seven
words of Christ from the cross, and the profound loneliness
of Jesus, who had felt abandoned by his father.

'I thirst.'

Now, on the gravel road in the hot afternoon sun, with the taxi not turning up, he panicked that they would not get to church on time for him to be able to go to confession. He and Ted had jocked together. The new sensation had entered their play, their boyhood love. They had slipped from play, climbing trees behind the house, eating pomme aracs, stripping off and bathing in the ravine. School had broken up for the Easter holidays. They dived. Then, scrambling up the muddy bank, they slipped into the pool. Their naked bodies fought in the water, in the mud, where their bodies first held, then slipped from each other, and became a pleasure they did not resist, till they fell back into the water released, pleasure satiated.

'It is accomplished.'

Ted had gone back home. J.M. had jocked on his own the next day after lunch, knowing that it was Good Friday, knowing that that act put nails into the hands of Jesus and crowned him with thorns. He knew that his sin was what made Jesus suffer. He was responsible for the crucifixion. He had been taught that the Jews had only been agents of history a long time ago, but Jesus, with sins like his, was continually being crucified. 'Father forgive them for they know not what they do.'

Weighed down by the complications of this theology of guilt and remorse, it had not occurred to him how retrospectively he could be held personally responsible.

'Mother, behold thy son. Son, behold thy mother.'

He and his mother had arrived late for the liturgy and there was no confession. He kept pondering whether a firm act of contrition would do, to cleanse him of his sin and so allow him to go to communion; or whether to take that chance with fate, and be damned even more for a double mortal sin that would condemn him to hell fire in a most dangerous and dire way. All this on Good Friday, the day of the Lord's death!

Father Gerard mounted the pulpit for the sermon. In the midst of lurid descriptions of sins and the suffering they caused Jesus, he came to speak of the dreadful betrayal of Judas, who had sold his Lord for thirty pieces of silver; then he had gone out and hung himself. The church was stifling hot, smelling of cheap scent and the talcum powder of the women parishioners, and the mothballs of the men in their Sunday-best black suits. He was sweating through the back of his shirt and the sweat was running down the sides of his cheeks, and his hands were all clammy as he kept weighing up the state of his soul. 'My God, my God, why have you forsaken me?'

Then Father Gerard compared the betrayal of Judas to anyone who would come up to the communion table and who knew that they were in a state of mortal sin, and so, like Judas, would be damned for all eternity to the fires of hell.

He was ashamed. He did not know where to put his eyes. He could not pray. He felt like a criminal in the dock, being condemned by the judge. He was sure that Father Gerard knew the state of his soul, because he had confessed the sin of impurity to him on many occasions before and received the penance of one decade of the rosary. But this time, on Good Friday, it was worse, much worse, and he was sure he was looking at him and speaking to him personally, to warn him not to contemplate any idea of approaching the communion rails. But even in the midst of his fear, the moment in the ravine came back to excite him, so that he moved between that excitement and guilt. Pleasure and sin: they lived side by side. He could not bear it any longer, and before he fainted, he got up in the mêlée of those approaching the communion rails and left the church. 'Sweet Sacrament Divine ...' The congregation wailed. He ran out on to the promenade and sat down on a bench, letting the cool breeze blow over him. He was drenched with fear and sweat.

He would have to confess before Easter Sunday. But at least he had been rescued from committing a second mortal sin. He just had his jocking and sin with Ted to be sorry about, not the betrayal which was like that of Judas.

'Father into they hands I commend my spirit.'

Aelred dipped back into his reading.

> 'The chain of my worst habit bound me: the love
> of my blood overcame me, the bonds of social
> grace restricted me and especially the knot of a
> certain friendship, delightful to me above all the
> delights of my life. The gracious bond of friendship
> pleased me, but always I was afraid of my offence,
> and I was sure that it would be broken off at
> some time in the future. I thought about the joy
> with which it had begun, and I awaited what
> would follow, and I would foresee the end.'

Benedict's hands were in his hands, his lips on his lips, as he read on:

'I realised that its beginning was reprehensible,
the middle state offensive and the end would
inevitably be damnation. The death I awaited
terrified me because it was certain that punishment
would await such a soul after death. And men
said, looking at my circumstances, but not
knowing what was going on within me, 'Isn't he
doing well! Isn't he, though!'

Aelred stared at Sebastian's grave.

St Aelred's sin, those vices? Could they be just what
Aelred now was feeling? Were they the sins he had to confess and which he had committed with Ted? How could
he have done so much, known so much, yet be still so
innocent and unknowing, be so guilty? But guilt did not
enter how he felt for Benedict. Guilt entered about how
he felt for Edward. He kept smelling the smell of his
clothes and seeing him in his tight black shorts climbing
the rock face. There were things which he wanted to do
with Edward which he did not want to do with Benedict.
They were now crowding his mind. He kept thinking of
things in this way, this way of not actually naming what he
wanted to do. It seemed now as if he had tasted something
sweet with Ted and then Ted had been taken way from him
in death as a punishment for that sweet thing, which was a
sin. Father Basil said it was sweet, but not this kind of sweet.
He wanted to know of that. He wanted to break
through the form of medieval hagiography that hid what
he really wanted to know, to move from the implicit and
the metaphorical into the explicit and literal. He needed
the details, to know that his desires had some precedent.

He had not found it elsewhere. Aelred's sanctity was clearly described, but he wanted Aelred's sin to be described. He wanted to know what kisses were like for him, what touch felt like, where he touched. He did. He wanted to hear his voice saying, touch me where it is forbidden, where the ancients have put up a gate. He wanted to know what he did. He wanted it described: what fantasies were unleashed in his mind when he looked at a boy, at a young man, at Simon, Ivo, Bernard. Aelred of Rievaulx felt these things, did these things. They were recorded for all time. Buried in metaphors. Aelred read between the lines with his own desire as guide. In time, he came to know that the nature of a twelfth-century boy and the nature of a twentieth-century boy were essentially the same.

From across the cemetery in the eaves of the chapel Aelred heard and saw the swallows darting in and out. They must have a nest below the eave, inside the roof, he thought, as he had first seen them in the barn on the farm. 'They've flown all the way back from Africa. They summer here, leaving us in the winter,' Brother Theodore had told him one evening after milking. All the way back from Africa. They swooped and arced and then Aelred heard a voice, another young boy's voice: Jordan's voice.

I is eleven years old when they tear me from my village and from my twin brother. I lose half of myself. They flog me for not eating their nasty food. I see a white seaman flogged and then they throw him into the waves. I see black bodies like meat fling into the swelling waters. Red water. Blue water.

I is the property of a Mr Newton then. I belong with his other chattels. He has me on a list in a ledger.

On the coast they sell me for two yards of tartan. Then I hear rattling chains and the crack of whips. They take me by the hand, like a pet. Some of them nice. Then like a mangey dog, some nasty. They strike me. They call me little nigger. Other words sting me like cayenne. I get licks. A good flogging is what I deserve, say Mr Newton. He pinch me. Night was like day, all waking. And the sea, groaning beneath.

There is a preacher man on the ship. He does fling words about. I baptise you, he say, throwing water over my head, Jordan.

How I come to this house? It was in Antigua that Mr Newton sell me to Master Walter Dewey. I nearly get take by another who run into the arena and grab me, and want me for hardly any price at all because I is small. He haggle with Mr Newton and Master Walter Dewey. I remember well the morning he inspecting me like some cattle he want to buy. Some other man bring me from the port. My lips swell, my arms and legs ache.

I homesick for my village.

Then the time come that they have to lay the bit on my tongue. They muzzle my mouth. I starve. I want to tell the others I meet there about the voyage. But is the boot on the back, whip, rope, cow-skin. Salt on the lips, sun like fire, blisters.

Then there is the time when I dive beneath the sea for rocks for my master's wall in Antigua, for the house at Ashtown. That is the time when the dogs pursue me. One hound get me by the ankle and the master cry off, off. Though I sure he set it on me. Is the same hound lick my wounds, the same hound which look up obediently to the tall master.

Is here in Ashton Park I tell them the story of where I come from and the voyage I make. She say, suck your thumb and sleep. That woman is called Miss Amy from Somerset, and she nice nice. My thumb crack.

I take up my pen. I put down my pen. I make my book for him. In memoriam? Yesterday was All Souls', the day before, All Saints'. Is that it? Is this what it's come to?

I see now that my story is of that first year. Lovers in May. That's what it is, really. I feel happy that he had this falling in love. Yes, there was the Ted relationship, but that was so fraught. This is fraught too, but there's something like falling in love here, like me falling in love with Annette - what we all know about falling in love. We often used to talk among ourselves at home about what happened to sexual feelings among nuns and priests. It didn't seem possible that everything could be as neatly dealt with as the official descriptions indicated. The vow of chastity couldn't keep it all under wraps. Not that we wanted to think about all that, I know.

Benedict talked in his letter about the unreliability of the journal. I must say that the first time I read it I was really taken aback. In the light of everything that subsequently took place I saw it as the slippery slope; not surprising really, given what then happened. That is what I first thought. But now I'm seeing it differently. Yes, there are Joe and Miriam and how they talk about things, but it's also me: I find myself getting angry on his behalf, wanting him to have the right to his life.

I feel that when Benedict writes he is expressing a shyness, or embarrassment, understandably, at seeing himself

represented. He would've been afraid of his superiors reading the entries. He must've felt acutely embarrassed
about me revealing that I had access to them. He must've
wanted to defend himself. I understand that. How much
of the journals does he know? When would he have read
them? He may have done at the time of the breakdown.
He may even have thought of getting them out of the
reach of the novice master or the Abbot. There are large
absences at the time of the breakdown, torn out pages
even. I don't expect Aelred wrote much then. There is
what he called 'the Night of the Rain'.

So extraordinary that Benedict should die at this time.
I haven't quite got to the bottom of that. Too much of a
coincidence.

In my reconstruction I attempt chronology, but in here,
at the end of the day, it is all fragments, dust, residue, bits
I'd rather not be reminded about.

Another Ted fragment surfaced in my readings today,
retold on its own, out of context. Not sure what prompted
it. Strange to have it told when I can judge it against my
own experience.

The study hall: it was some nights after the refectory
incident. Ted was the prefect in charge. He began the
prayers before study: 'Come, Holy Spirit, fill the hearts of
the faithful ...' We were made to pray for wisdom. Then as
we sat down, the banging of desks. A note was being passed from desk to desk, and boys scribbled additions. It
said: 'MEET THE BULLERS BEHIND THE LAVATO-
RIES TONIGHT. WHAT WOULD YOU LIKE TO DO TO
THEM?' It was to the question that boys were scribbling
their answers. I was in such a hurry to write my addition,
so as not to seem to not be doing what the others did. I

scribbled, 'KISS THEM!' Even then I had felt the irony of my words, I think. Not sure what I was saying. It was a tender word next to 'KICK, HIT, SMASH, CUT OFF THEIR PRICKS, FUCK THEIR ARSE HOLES WITH A KNIFE, KILL THE BULLERS.'

Then it started at the back with the seniors. Their heads inside their desks and chanting, BULLER MAN, BULLER MAN, BULLER MAN. J.M. was struggling with the prayer. I stuck my head under my desk and shouted and banged. Ted walked out. Then I saw J.M. follow him out. There was an uproar, till Father Julius came in and restored order.

I have so many mixed feelings: shame and anger and sadness. I couldn't go out. I wanted to run out.

On my way to the dormitory, a boy kicked me. Two boys held my head between their legs while others kicked me repeatedly. Let's put his head in the lavatory bowl. Your brother stinks.

My words and actions hadn't redeemed me. My betrayal had not paid off. Then I heard them planning. Something else was afoot.

Phrases plait themselves through time; Aelred of Rievaulx's: 'cleanse the leper, carnal darkness'.

The Abbot mentioned at coffee in the parlour after lunch that he would like to talk to me. I'm going to try to stay a little longer than I originally planned, despite a call from Krishna that he really needed me back and that he had to return full time to university. I begged him to stay on. They were in the middle of Petit Careme and the weather in the cocoa hills was lovely. I can hear the river. Sometimes I can't combine the me of there and what I'm doing here. I write to Chantal, but I don't tell her what I've found. It'll take a long time to go through all this with the rest of the family.

I've asked to do some manual work. I need to get away from my desk. Sometimes, I feel I can't go on: ravelling, unravelling, ravelling up again. I scratch and find his story written beneath mine. At last, our lives blend. Was he writing his story for himself, or for me? And me, am I writing for him or for myself? I'll never get his forgiveness, but hopefully, because words were important to him, this will make a difference.

The swallows have left the barn for Africa. That I should read and write that stuff! It shows what's happening to me. I'll be like one of those professors at UWI.

Where history will lead you, eh, man? What a voyage!

Krishna say, I go have a nice dalpouri for you when you reach back. He looking after the mango trees in the back. Good.

Pink anthuriums, blue skies, yellow keskidees perched with their questions on the electric wire. *Qu'est-ce qu'il dit?* I miss home.

Stolen Time

My beloved thrust his hand
through the hole in the door;
I trembled to the core of my being.
Song of Songs

Aelred stared at the bulbs drying in a green plastic tray below the black heating pipes of Father Justin's cell. It was his weekly conference with the novice master. 'There's just one more thing, brother.' Father Justin detained Aelred as he was about to get up from where he was sitting next to Father Justin's desk. The geraniums which had been pricked out earlier in the year were now flourishing: red, white and pink in small terracotta pots on saucers, crowded on the small windowsill. While in March and April the scent of hyacinths thickened the air in the cell, now it was this hot geranium fragrance that took away the mustiness of the novice master's cell. Father Justin was standing at the window, his hands among the leaves, nipping off a few here and there which had turned yellow. The perfume broke from the plants.

'Yes, father.' Aelred stayed sitting with his hands beneath his scapular, his head bowed, continuing to stare at the dry bulbs.

'I think it would be better, brother, if you returned the writings of Aelred of Rievaulx to the library.' Father Justin delivered this like the first line of a sermon he had prepared beforehand.

'Are they overdue? I thought I had a couple of weeks left.'

'That may be, but, no, what I mean is... I mean, I've discussed this with Father Abbot.'

'With Father Abbot?'

'Yes.

'What's happened? Is there a shortage of these books? There were more than one copy, both of *The Mirror of Charity* and *Spiritual Friendship*. When I borrowed them I think that there was only one of *The Letters*, though. I'll make sure that gets back soon.'

'*Spiritual Friendship*. That's the one. I must say I'd quite forgotten about that text.' Father Justin did not sound convincing to Aelred. 'Then, now I think of it, we did talk once before of you reading the monastic fathers so early in the novitiate. By the way, how is your reading of Francis de Sales and John Boscoe? What about Jean Pierre de Caussade?

'I've been trying de Caussade this morning.'

'I see. And there are, for lighter reading, one or two excellent lives of St Dominic Savio and Aloyious Gonzaga and, of course, very recommended for young people is the *Life of Maria Goretti*. All examples for young people, though I think that last one is a little flagrant by implication. You know what happened to her?' Father Justin crushed the dead geranium leaves through his fingers. The perfume still lingered in them. It brought the hot day into the room and made Aelred feel he wanted to be outside. He felt trapped by Father Justin.

Edward climbed the rock face. His strong legs moved as he climbed in his tight black shorts.

'She was killed because she resisted sexual advances.'

'Yes, a martyr for the youth of our time.'

'I read these at school, father.'

'Yes, well, I hope they did you some good. Anyway, the Abbot has decided to ban Aelred of Rievaulx from novitiate reading. Maybe ban is too harsh a term. He wants the books returned to the library. I think I agree. I think it could be misleading unless you have it carefully interpreted. Who was it recommended this text? Not me. I don't remember, *Spiritual Friendship*, is it? I should've acted on this earlier. I blame myself.' Father Justin knew very well he had not recommended the text.

'For what, father? It was Benedict.'

'Yes, that reminds me of another matter.'

'What reminds you of another matter, father?'

'Yes, well, you must get those books back at once. Other copies are out as well. Who else is reading these texts? I must say they weren't of great interest in the novitiate in my time. I'll bring this up during my next meeting of the whole novitiate.'

'I don't know father. You were saying.'

'What?'

'Another matter.'

'Another matter? Yes. I don't think you should be alone with Benedict in the library during study time.'

'I was talking to him about John Cassian,' Aelred said abruptly.

'John Cassian? Yes, now he's very relevant. In fact he's to the point. Cliques are very dangerous in our life, brother. I think I've spoken to you about this before. Always in threes, never in twos. That's our little mnemonic.' Father Justin bent down to the wastepaper basket and brushed off his hands the crushed geranium leaves which he had shredded into a fine dust all the time he was talking.

Aelred felt his hands in Benedict's, his mouth on his. Benedict's neck smelt of the yellow soap which was customarily used. It was a rough ration. His neck was white and soft.

'We're not a clique, father.'

'I know. And Benedict is exemplary. But of course he's not your guardian angel any more. You must let him devote his time to Edward.'

'He does. I hardly get to talk to him.'

'You must think of talking to others at the appropriate time. And I think it would be good for you to see Father Abbot. You haven't had a good meeting with him since the first visit just after your arrival. Father Abbot likes to keep in touch with the novices.'

'Yes, I'd like to see him.'

'I'll arrange that. Very well then. And get those texts back to the library. I'll have to see who's got the other copies. Aelred of Rievaulx! I've never understood the interest. What do you think of my geraniums?'

'They're fine and smell so strong.' Aelred closed the door of the Novice Master's cell.

The geranium pots at Mount Saint Maur were by the goldfish pond near the arbour with Barbados Pride. The pods, like mangetout, were called deadman's flesh.

As Aelred made his way through the common room to the dormitory, he noticed Edward sitting on the window-seat near the novitiate shrine. There was a fresh bouquet of flowers in the vase. 'Oh, prickly.' Aelred quickly pulled back his hand from trying to rearrange Edward's arrangement.

'*Benedicite*, brother. Hawthorn. Is the arrangement not to your liking?'

'Yes, no. No, yes, I mean the white is like lace, but I

love the pink, which seems rarer around here for some reason. From near the quarry?' Aelred adjusted one of the sprigs of the pink hawthorn.

'Yes?' Edward questioned Aelred's question and what lay within it.

Aelred noticed that Edward was reading *Spiritual Friendship*. 'A dangerous text, brother!' There was a note of irony in the tone of his voice.

'What do you mean?'

'Who recommended it?'

'Benedict.'

'Benedict?' Aelred raised his eyes.

'Yes.'

'I see.' Aelred felt a pang of jealousy, because what he thought was a matter of intimacy between him and Benedict alone was shared with Edward. Obviously Benedict's guardian angel duties, he thought. But it still made Aelred wonder. Did Benedict recommend Aelred of Rievaulx to all the novices in his charge?

'When did he recommend it?'

'What's the point of this inquisition, brother? And, "dangerous text"? What do you mean?'

'Oh, it's nothing. Don't pay attention to what I say.'

'How can I not, when you burst in with your questions and statements, your raised eyes and smirks.'

'Smirks? Return to your Lectio Divina, brother.'

As Aelred made off, Edward said, 'You've got really dark. You're almost black.' He said this when Aelred was already halfway down the corridor. Aelred heard it. He turned and came back to where Edward sat on the windowseat.

'Black? Have you ever seen a black person? Black? Does

it bother you?' Then Aelred returned to his cell, leaving Edward flummoxed, and mumbling.

'I've seen coloureds in our town,' Edward raised his voice. Aelred did not turn back.

Aelred gathered up the texts from his cell and went directly to the library. 'Coloureds?' He asked, as he passed Edward still on the windowseat. He did not wait for an answer, but he puzzled with snatches of newspaper pictures he remembered of black people from the islands coming to England for work. There was one of a group of steel band men playing on a wharfside next to a big ship. There was another of a man and a woman knocking on a door under a sign which said 'No coloureds'. There was a way in which the world had been shut out, and then suddenly he became aware of it. Just beyond the walls Ashton Park was another world and he hardly knew anything about it.

'Some say Mungo get ship away.' Aelred heard Toinette's voice. As he opened the door to the library, he looked back at the portrait of the black boy on the staircase. He looked back at Jordan. 'Black boy for sale.' He heard the cry in the streets of Bristol.

He deposited the books he had brought from his cell on to the shelf for returned books. He felt angry. He felt jealous. He felt homesick. He stood at a standing desk built into the bay of the window looking out on to the front lawn. The fresh grass was embroidered with daisies. He heard his mother's voice in her last letter: 'Sweet heart, we miss you. And Toinette said, "Tell Master Jeansie I say hello." We all miss you, darling.' Aelred wished he was still Jeansie playing at Malgretoute as a boy, playing behind the house near the servants' rooms under

Toinette's all-seeing eyes.

He heard her voice. '*Dou-dou* child.'

'Where Mungo get that scar?' He heard his question.

'Mungo get hang in Hangman Alley.'

Every Sunday after Mass in Felicity, they passed the avenue of mango trees coming up the hill above the sugarcane factory. They passed under the trees where they said men had been hanged and men had gone to hang themselves. And the only thing that took away the fear as they passed was the nice warm hops bread from Mr Gomes's shop by the railway line. And there were also the warm plaited loaves his mother got specially for Sunday breakfast after fasting for so long before Holy Communion.

Stories and memories plaited themselves. Mungo is a spirit flying in at the window. 'See that scar on his neck,' Toinette say.

Then there was this other story in the book he did not want to put down, did not want to return to the library.

During those first days at Rievaulx, the young Aelred was caught up in the new routines of the men who had first enchanted him. He had come upon them in the small wood near the river, dressed in their rough brown working habits, sawing wood, clearing a space near the River Rye for an extension to their humble dwellings. And though he had not expressed it that clearly to himself, he saw in them the possibility of men living together for love. Rising in the night for Matins and then private prayer, before returning to the church for Lauds, tired him. All his energy was exhausted in keeping up with the rigour of the day, the hours of waking, prayer, manual work and

Lectio Divina. He felt that his body was being fashioned in a fire which was also tempering the spirit within him, so that he hardly turned his mind to the life which he had so suddenly and abruptly turned away from with his companion at the court in Scotland. He remembered the morning of his conversion. He remembered the morning of their departure after their brief visit. He looked back from on top of his horse, climbing the ridge above the valley and the river. He saw the monks processing out to work, and decided, or rather, he let his companion decide, that they return, taking the other young man's zeal as confirmation that he should follow his own passion.

But the other passion had not left his mind, nor had it given up its power to tempt his body.

One week later, he woke to his heart weighed down with sadness, missing the friend whom he loved above any other, in the far distant northern kingdom.

Aelred comforted himself with the story of his patron saint, which he remembered his childhood mentor, Dom Placid, telling him in his mountain school. He retold it to himself now, a young man growing up and experiencing love. He remembered then, at his teacher's feet, how he had asked Dom Placid whether love was painful, and the older man had nodded agreement. He wondered now what Dom Placid knew. Had he been a man who loved another? Was he like Basil and Sebastian? Had he been telling him this story because he knew, through the boy's confessions, of his passion for his friend Ted and had wanted to prepare him for a life in which it is not easy to love another man? Had he loved him, himself, and was sublimating his desire for the boy into his celibate love?

Was this what he should now do? Aelred strove for sublimation, his chaste and celibate ideal. Benedict called it a
dangerous chastity.

They could not take the story from him. They could
not. It was a love story. He took the books again from the
shelf and read, absorbed, standing at the window till he
was interrupted by the bells for Conventual Mass.

'Flaming June. That's what we call it.' Brother Stephen
outlined to Aelred his part of the walled garden to work
for the collection of the soft fruit. The remainder of the
morning timetable had been collapsed to bring in the
rest of the harvest ... 'and in the morning we will go to the
vineyards'.

The whole novitiate were particularly involved.
Everyone went out after the Conventual Mass. They
stayed out all morning. They broke to recite Sext,
standing in two rows opposite each other. Benedict
began the office, '*Deus in adutorium meum intende.*' They
all made the sign of the cross.

'*Domine aduvandum me festina,*' the rest of the group responded. Then all bowed at, '*Gloria Patri et Filio and
Spiritui Sancto,*' rising at, '*Secut erat in principio et nunc et
semper et in saecula saeculorum, Amen.*' The monotone
chant droned like the wasps and bees around the strawberries and raspberries.

Festina, quickly. Aelred savoured that word, *festina.*

Aelred remembered photographs of monks chanting
the office like this when he used to pore over books on
monastic life at Mount Saint Maur. He was fired by the
romanticism of it. Now he was actually doing it. Then
they had a picnic lunch under the mulberry tree. After

lunch they had a brief recreation. They went and lay in the field outside the walled garden just beyond the stream with the watercress beds for siesta. There would be a second shift to take them into the afternoon, after reciting None. Then if necessary, a third shift, finishing with the fall of darkness, before which they would recite a shortened form of Vespers. Aelred loved this time. It was a respite from the routine of monastic life - though he was still as enthusiastic about it as ever. It gave him an opportunity to be with Benedict with less tension. Not having to worry about Father Justin finding them, as in the library. He knew that they could not hold hands and kiss, but they could just talk. Stolen time. They could talk while sitting in the garden, as the nature of the work allowed for pairs to work closely at one patch for a while. The relaxation this afforded was exhilarating to Aelred.

He was always keener than Benedict to steal moments together when some of the other monks were busy elsewhere in the garden. Benedict wanted to include the other monks and not appear to be exclusive. He spent time with Edward, which made Aelred jealous. But it was also the temptation, the occasion of sin, that these moments could present, that sometimes deterred him from Aelred's games. To have other monks near by was safe.

In their work smocks, their bodies seemed to be more exposed. The smell of the grass, the heat and the open air conspired to make these moments most difficult for Benedict. He admired more than ever the beauty of Aelred as his skin tanned to dark brown in the summer, reminding him of when he had first arrived. His arms and cheeks were glowing with the blood of his exhilaration in moving quickly around the garden, collecting up the

punnets which lay near the strawberry beds and raspberry canes, and carrying them in a wheelbarrow to
Brother Stephen's shed, where they had to be packed to
be taken into the nearby market town.

Aelred knew that he was being admired. He turned
and smiled.

They had found a sun catch at the top of the field
behind a full-flowering hawthorn which was losing its
bloom. Aelred wanted to talk. In his spontaneity, he
touched Benedict on his arm. He held his hand, impetuous
to make his point. Benedict restrained the boy, as he
thought of him at these times, still enjoying his at least
seeming innocence. He seemed to have no will to change,
even though Benedict made it clear that they should be
careful.

The summer's exhilaration, the hot sunshine - these
offered their own explanation.

They lay together where they could not easily be seen.
'This is good. What are you afraid of? We're just talking.
No one else can see what we're doing.' Aelred was sliding
his hand under the folds of Benedict's smock and tickling
his ribs.

'But you're still a novice. Anyway we must always be
careful.'

'Aelred of Rievaulx says it's fine, to touch, to hold
hands, to look at another monk, to admire his beauty,
the shape of his body, the look in his eyes. These things
are good. I've read about this. You gave me this to read.'
Aelred saw a question in Benedict's eyes. 'Why did you
give it to me to read then? To excite me and then to
punish me? This desire is essentially good.' Aelred
broke out into a kind of tirade, but not really angry, just

forceful. Gradually his tone became more cynical, when he remembered Father Justin's voice.

Then Benedict could not help but flirt. 'You look beautiful when you get angry.'

'Don't talk nonsense.'

Benedict smiled, not recognising Aelred's mounting seriousness, and then lost himself, putting his arms around the boy, pulling him in with an embrace and holding up his head by lifting his chin from where it was buried against Aelred's chest. He looked into his eyes, and, very slowly, brought his face close to his and kissed him on his mouth. His lips were cracked by the heat, dry with their hard work. They held each other, and then broke off, feeling suddenly exposed in the field the other side of the copse where Aelred had contrived that they could snatch the last half hour, before they would have to meet again in the walled garden to recite None under the mulberry tree.

'You see, you go further than I would,' Aelred said.

'That's why I must be careful, as I said in the library. You're not aware of what you do? I notice it even with the other monks. You disturb some of the other monks. Even Edward. You must be careful. Careful with what you do with your hands, with your eyes.'

'You sound like Brother Marcus. Do you know what he said to me the other day? He said I wore my habit like a girl. Can you imagine? What can you do with a sack? Can you imagine it?'

'You're being silly. You've got to take responsibility for what you do, your effect on people. For instance, Edward ...'

'They must take responsibility too. What's going on in Marcus's mind? And what do you mean, even Edward?'

Benedict did not reply directly. Then he said, 'We're meant to avoid the occasion of sin.'

'If you call it a sin, it becomes a sin. It's rules and laws that make sins. That's what St Paul says.'

'You might find Aelred of Rievaulx sympathetic, but don't quote Paul on the matter. There are other texts. And you must think of yourself and the preparation for your vows. We're supposed to be chaste.'

'We are chaste. I love you. That's chaste.' Aelred meant what he said. He knew that there was a difference in him, in the feelings which he had for Benedict, into which no guilt, or sense of sin had entered as it used to with Ted. He would gladly have gone further with Benedict because of his love, if Benedict had not all the time confronted him with his doubts. He could convince himself that this was not unchaste, that the vow of chastity was more to do with freeing oneself from a family to lead the contemplative life. What harm would there be if they went further? What would it feel like to go all the way with one you loved? Not like with Ted - only boys and clumsy.

'But you must be aware of what you tempt me to do?'

'I wish you would do it sometimes, like now, when we're alone here. I wish you would do it. It sounds mad. I know it sounds as if I don't know what I'm saying, but it doesn't feel wrong. It doesn't feel like a sin. It's not like when I was made to feel it was a sin when I was a boy and a teenager with my friend Ted. It doesn't feel like that. I don't feel anything like sin when I'm with you. I feel good about what I want to do with your body. It just seems to me to be an extension of our love - that it is our love - and I can't see why I can't do it. I don't really agree with St Aelred. He talks so violently about hating his body. I feel good about my body. Though even he allows for holding hands.' Aelred developed his theories as he reached for Benedict's hand and pulled him closer.

'But what about chastity? We take a vow of chastity.'

'But that's not the reason why you don't want to. You wouldn't think this was good if we were not in the monastery and were not taking the vow of chastity. That's not why you think it's wrong. You think it's wrong because we're men.'

'I'm not sure. I'm not sure what I think. Part of me thinks it's wrong, but I know I love you. I love you as a boy, as a man. I must admit that. I gave you Aelred of Rievaulx to read. It's what I believe too. How can you say that I think it's wrong because we're men? Aelred of Rievaulx believed that we could transform the carnal into the spiritual. Yes, we can kiss, not on the lips; we can hold hands, but not the other. What does our chastity mean if we do the other?'

'Then don't be afraid. Love; love me. I won't push you any further than you want to go. I want only to rest my head on your shoulder, to hold your hand, to be embraced when I feel sad, or hug you when I'm happy. It's bad enough that I can't do this when I want to. It's enough to keep that within the rules. But when we can, why not? It's good. Please, Benedict, kiss me once more before we join the others.'

The older man took the younger man into his embrace and kissed him on the mouth. 'How do I resist you?'

'Don't.'

Benedict withheld his tongue. 'No more.' They turned towards the walled garden when they heard the bell announce None.

'Listen, Father Justin says Father Abbot is banning Aelred of Rievaulx's writings from the novitiate.'

'What? Where did you hear that?

'Father Justin, this morning at my weekly meeting.'

'Why? What's happened?'

'I don't know. He just says I shouldn't read it now because it needs careful interpretation. We've just been interpreting it.' Aelred laughed.

'Don't joke. What else did he say?'

'He asked who had recommended Aelred of Rievaulx in the first place.'

'And?'

'Well, I said that you had.'

'And?'

'Then he said that I shouldn't've been talking to you in the library the other day.'

'Did he? Oh! I know. He had a kind of word with me about that. I didn't want to worry you. He was quite cross really. It makes me wonder how long he was in the library before we noticed him. Or whether he entered the library, realised that we were in the alcove and then went back out again, embarrassed to catch us, as it were, and then re-entering when he heard us talking louder by the desk. He didn't talk directly or fully. It's Father Justin's way to be irritable about something, not tell you, and it sounds as if it's something else. He was complaining how much time I spent studying and reading existentialists and not getting on with the syllabus. I'm now sure it was this matter. You see, he wouldn't want to talk about it. It's hard, isn't it. He's never questioned me at our weekly meetings about what I recommend to the novices. Have you returned the texts? He did say he wanted to see me specially. But he hasn't called me.'

'Yes, immediately, reluctantly. All the books I had are back.'

Aelred and Benedict had arrived at the watercress beds and were crossing the small rustic bridge in order to get back to the walled garden in time for the recitation of None. The rest of the novitiate had already formed themselves into two rows opposite each other beneath the mulberry tree. The hymn had already been intoned. They slipped into their places, taking their small breviaries from their pockets.

After None Brother Stephen detailed Aelred to work with Edward on the early soft fruit in the lower half of the garden. As they worked at their separate bushes, plucking and collecting them at once into the punnets, Aelred wondered what Benedict had meant earlier by saying that he disurbed other monks. Even Edward, he had said. He and Edward worked silently. Their discussion this morning had not been concluded. Aelred was still wondering what he had meant by noticing his darkness, calling him black, and mentioning coloureds in his town. Was he against black people? Did he think that he was and was that the reason he was hostile? He remembered that some of the hostility to Ted at school was because he was coloured, to use Edward's word. Ted was mixed. This was the second time Edward had commented on the colour of his skin. He was aware of himself now, with his sleeves rolled up and his brown hands among the bushes. There was Edward close to him. Their hands were almost meeting among the bushes. His strong arms moved, with the blue veins running beneath the skin. Where he bent his neck, Aelred could see the smooth white nape beneath his blond hair. When he looked up he saw his blue eyes. They were so different.

He knew Edward's secret was rock climbing. He had observed him again just yesterday morning. He had arrived earlier. He noticed Edward arrive and undress himself. There was something audacious the way he stood in the open, pulling his smock over his head, getting out of his overalls and standing almost naked in the open, in his tight black shorts and white vest, running his hands through his blond hair and pulling the strands behind his ears. What did rock climbing mean to him? It frightened Aelred. Not only the possibility of falling, but the feeling of naked flesh against the hard rock, the body's utter vulnerability. It was something daring, like attempting to fly - a kind of hubris. Scaling height. Conquering vertigo. Falling, always that possibility. Free-falling! He picked the gooseberries assiduously and lost himself in this reverie among the hum and drone of bees and wasps in the heat. There were some hives just a way off whose bees worked the garden, among the flowers that Brother Stephen had planted with the spring onions, lettuce and celery. There was a wonderful sense of order about the beds and paths, but the random flowers gave a sense of wildness. Full-blown red poppies fell on to the small gravel paths between the beds. Honeysuckle climbed the trellises between the walled plums and apples. The top of the wall was a tangle of Russian vine. It reminded him of coralita back home, falling over the rusty galvanised fences. Aelred felt proud that he was doing so well with the names of flowers.

As he continued to pick the early strawberries, Aelred

tried to keep his mind on what he had been reading in Lectio Divina that morning. The writing was encouraging him to abandon himself to God, to mould his body into a place for God to dwell. His body was the temple of God. There seemed to be writings which emphasised a relationship with God which was lonely and another which included others, and included love of others, like Aelred of Rievaulx, who said, 'To live without friendship was to live like a beast'. Aelred of Rievaulx had faced head on the risks of this, but nevertheless advocated it. The writings which Father Justin advised sought for the most part to leave out others, or at least to have them not as real friends, more as acquaintances, to love them with detachment, not with passion. Aelred of Rievaulx seemed to want to work through passion.

'I see what you mean,' Edward broke into Aelred's meditation, 'about the dangerous text.'

'Oh,' Aelred stood up and stretched and then arranged the full punnets in the wheelbarrow near by. 'Sorry, I was somewhere else.'

'I shouldn't've interrupted your meditation.'

'No, it's not frowned on to exchange a few words. You were saying?'

'About this morning, what you said about a dangerous text.'

'Don't bother with what I say.'

'Well, Father Justin instructed me to take my book back to the library. Why do you think that is?'

'Did he not tell you?'

'He said that it was not appropriate for me at this time of my novitiate and that I should be reading the more traditional books that were in the novitiate library.

Aelred of Rievaulx needed interpreting.'

'Yes, that's what he said to me.'

'What do you think it is about Aelred of Rievaulx?'

'Well you must realise, surely?'

'You mean what he says about sex?' Edward was blunt.

'He recognises that attractions exist between monks. That they're good.'

'He doesn't mince his words about the dangers and what shouldn't take place. '

'True. But he allows for much more than we are encouraged to explore. Never in twos always in threes. Hasn't Father Justin said that to you?'

'No.'

'Well, maybe you're different.'

'Maybe you're different,' Edward countered.

'You think so, don't you? You think I'm coloured. You think I'm -'

'Hang on.'

'I think we'd better get back to the fruit picking. We'll soon have to be taking these down to the shed.' Aelred was thinking of what Benedict had mentioned about Edward finding him disturbing.

Edward volunteered to take the wheelbarrow down to the shed after they had loaded all the punnets. Aelred watched Edward and noticed every movement of his arms and legs and hips as he strode off. Then he saw him again in his tight black shorts and white vest pinned to the rock face; then falling away, falling, falling. How did he disturb him? he wondered. What had he actually said to Benedict?

The sun had gone behind the hill at the top of the park.

Aelred was now on the higher ground of the garden, where you could see over the wall into the fields beyond. There was still a rich light, which was descending into a soft powdery haze at the bottom of the valley. Against it, every trunk and branch, every shadow was distinct. Beyond the spinney was a pond, which held the reflections of the trees that grew at its edge. There the light was khaki. A duck webbed its way across the pond. The ripples in its wake crinkled the reflections of the trees. The novices moved quietly among the bushes. This great settling down of the day was momentarily jangled by the bells for Vespers. The novices made for the mulberry tree. Once the bells had quietened down, they recited the evening office.

Above them swallows and swifts darted and swooped like bats. In the distance two wood pigeons called to each other. '*Dou-dou, dou-dou.*' Aelred heard Toinette's voice. He told himself the story of Jordan.

Miss Amy of Somerset tell me to come that night by her room and she go make a comfy bed by her fire. I must not be sleeping in the damp of a cellar she tell me. Miss Amy come like a mother to me. She put aside food from the kitchens and she mend some old clothes she get from the son of the master of the house. A boy like you needs a good breeches, she says to me. And at night by the fire, Miss Amy and her old father, who she must look after all day, say to me, tell that story again, boy, of your voyage. They want to hear about my journey from St Kitts, my voyage from the island of Barbuda. They like to hear the names of islands. While those places have a horror for me and a sadness and a loss, they are like wonders to Miss

Amy and her father. They like to hear of storms at sea, of
shipwrecks and escape. They like to hear of the fish that
fly. But when I speak of my bondage, of the flogging with
rope and whip and cow-skin, they say it's better to sleep.
And Miss Amy start to clear up the fire. Any big logs she
put to one side to save for the morning. I see a world in
that fire as I curl up and watch it die down. I see a sunset
over my village which is by a big river. I see pink flamingos
in the shallows. And there in the centre of the fire I see
the eyes of the tiger. When a log falls I hear the ostrich
run, like the sound of the wind in the chimney. The
sparks light the fire that burn my village down. I, Jordan,
is in England now. I, Jordan, is with Miss Amy from
Somerset.

The novices made their supper together in the warm kitchen. There was hot tea and bread and cheese and then
some of the fruit they had been picking that afternoon.
They stood at the counters and ate quietly. One or two
took their plates into the refectory. When they had cleared up they went and said Compline privately before reti-
ring to bed.

In the novitiate, Aelred heard someone at he door of
his cell and opened it. It was Benedict. He put out his
hand. Aelred took his hand and brought it to rest on his
cheek. Their eyes held all their longing. Benedict withdrew; turned and left. Aelred sank to his knees by his bed
and prayed for a peaceful night. He heard Edward
moving about in his cell. He had a distinct cough.

Tomorrow they would bury Brother Sebastian. Aelred
thought of Basil and what his thoughts might be that
night. They had joined together, he had said. They had
been his age, nineteen. They had had a lifetime together.

The rain dripped on the outside windowsill. A soft rain which did not last long. He heard the drip drip in the cocoa at Malgretoute.

Mungo could fly. 'He fly back to Africa,' Toinette say. 'He climb the hoe in the field and fly.'

The Lodge:

Most of the leaves have gone now. The drives and walks
around Ashton Park are deep in dead leaves. The poplars
have shaken themselves out and stand bare. I got detailed
to work with Brother Malachi in the hothouses in the
kitchen garden. We work in silence; words only for
instructions. He smiles a lot, though. He points and uses
sign language. He brought me a mug of tea he makes on
the stove. I'm grateful for this time: the autumn air, the
smells, the earth on my hands.

I'm part of this place, doing jobs J. M. did. Yes, my
rhythm is his. I rise early. I follow the offices. I read his
texts. I immerse myself in his journals, his life, their life,
the whole story.

The whole passionate story, as Miriam says. This is the
way to resurrect him, remember him.

I understand more. I feel more. I change as I write it
out, as I make up the story that I hear. I scratch and read
and write over his words. It's beyond me to record the
details of the theological debates, the subtleties of the
moral questions. The young Aelred tried. But it is the
sheer persistence in trying to unravel emotions that
impresses. I admire them. They got so little help from
directors or confessors in that first year. No, they got help
from some confessors. There were one or two who had
been through it, gone before, leaving a path. The
church's teaching is so black and white, so without

understanding, with so little compassion - always sin. I remember that impurity, the obsession with masturbation. A different light falls on all this now. Today, there is still the exclusion.

And the spurious distinctions between the state of homosexuality and homosexual acts, as Joe puts it.

Of course my change has to do with Joe and Miriam. They point me to history: histories that challenge centuries of moral assumptions. Joe is a social historian. He talks about an ironic freedom, which was given to gay people in the war, and then he talks of the clampdown, in the fifties and early sixties, the linking of homosexuality with crime and the underworld.

Prejudice drove it underground.

He talks of the Wolfenden Report and the reforms that did not take place.

Hypocrisy, prejudice, blackmail, he says.

I think of how lucky J. M. and Benedict were in their cloister by comparison.

There would be raids on public toilets, Joe says. Prominent people caught, not to mention all the ordinary blokes.

Joe is so intent on me loving my brother as he was that he shoves anything my way that will clean the air, as he insists. Brush out the cobwebs, he says, with a flourish. Centuries of accumulated lies and half lies, misconceptions and misinterpretations.

I'm amazed by what I read. I get to read interpretations of Aelred of Rievaulx which were not available to J. M. This is a sort of revolution for me: a leap in time to reach my brother. I have the advantage of hindsight.

History. You mustn't internalise the filth society has

made us feel about ourselves. You must reach through that to your brother, Joe insists.

Brother Malachi broke his silence. You are the brother of the ex-Brother Aelred? he asked.

I nodded.

He smiled. A good one, he said.

I smiled.

You look like him, he said. And smiled again. It's them eyes, he said.

I understood how much can be said in a smile, with the eyes. He put his hand under my arm at the elbow to usher me out of the hothouse at the end of the afternoon. Touch and looking; speaking with the eyes: I was getting to understand.

I walked up through the apple orchard and looked back at the barn, metallic and blue, and the flames burning down. The sky burnt, all flame over Ashton, England. I walk the paths and fields of their story, my story.

And there are the other stories which insert themselves. Extraordinary coincidence, that it is here in this English park that I've had to come to reflect on the colossal history of cruelty in our islands; to confront even more deeply than in 1970 for my family, what our politics, government, judicial system and trade have been founded on - what made the West Indian Estate.

Yet human compassion can confound us. It is here that Jordan met Miss Amy of Somerset. It is here that I read my brother's journals and in them the black woman, Toinette, echoes her '*Dou-dou, dou-dou* child' down the years. As boys, we got a lot of loving from black women. It is here that I learn my brother's story of Jordan, a story he told himself, a story of this place, a story that told itself. Yesterday afternoon I went and looked at the portrait on the staircase. I saw the African boy. I unlearn, learn anew.

The new Abbot seems different from the one recorded in the journals. I spent a little time with him before Vespers. It's shocking. Benedict had hardly been eating. Over the years, it seems, some times worse than others. A little to drink, enough not to draw attention to himself. It was a condition that had become worse over the years. John Plowden, the present abbot, was a novice soon after Aelred had left. He didn't know my brother. But he spoke of him. Extraordinary: it now appears that the stories are passed down through a generation of abbots. The events in the barn; the 'Night of the Rain.' Aelred's phrases are now my phrases. It was all tidied up though, in neat phrases: a mental breakdown, lost his vocation, lost his faith. Though I think this new Abbot does not wholly go along with those simplifications. They still trot them out: neat words, empty, emptied.

You must strive to empty yourself. The things we were taught.

But Benedict, fasting? Sounds more like anorexia; odd, at his age. A history of self-abuse, diminishment. Sounds almost like suicide.

The Abbot was being discreet. I could tell. There was more, much more. I did not want to ask. It shocks me, the destruction of his body, the negation, the denial, the punishment. Now it shocks. I get angry for him. What kept him going? Words. 'Man does not live by bread alone, but by every word which comes from the mouth of God.'

'*Domine labia mea aperies ...*' 'Lord, open my lips, and

my mouth shall announce your praise.' I hear it each morning, echoing along the naves. All words now. I feed on words. I eat words.

He lived on words, his own journals. I wonder what's in Benedict's journals? I saw a brother clearing out what must have been Benedict's cell. I had been detailed to polish the corridors this afternoon. He was taking out boxes of papers to an incinerator outside the kitchens. I was so tempted to rifle through the ashes for a corner of unburnt script, for a word that had not curled in flame. Oh, for a scrap of word, something left after the incineration! What's in ashes? Sometimes the quest is too big for me. His death comes over me!

Miriam says, Everything got used: gold teeth, rings, hair, fingernails, skin. They were all used for industry.

She showed me a picture: a room of shoes. She has her story, which she returns to.

We have these stories we have to tell. Joe has his, Miriam hers. And I've found my story, my brother with his stories. They are stories larger than him, than us.

Deaths transfigure each other. Meanings are laid one on top the other. My grief does this.

Thank you, Amy of Somerset. There's always one to comfort us in the most wretched of circumstances.

Rock Climbing

I opened to my beloved,
but he had turned his back and gone.
My soul failed at his flight.
I sought him but I did not find him,
I called to him but he did not answer.
Song of Songs

As the bells began their tolling, filling the whole valley with their sorrow and respect, their great solemnity, in memory of Brother Sebastian, they echoed and rechoed against the stone of the quarry. With each toll, Edward continued his climb up the steepest of the rock faces. Aelred watched him. Because of the heat, even though it was still early, Edward climbed in only his shorts. His skin glistened. The sweat forming on his back and arms trickled down his legs. His shoulders and arms, which had been burnt red, were now turning brown. He was climbing faster than usual. He moved nimbly, surefooted. Bits of shale flaked from under his boots as they pushed away. The shale clattered and fell the awful drop to where Aelred crouched, smashing into small pieces on the gravel clearing in front of him. The falling shale tore at the wild lilac and the newly budding buddleia. The purple flowers were broken and scattered. Edward's denim smock was buried with broken rock and tatters of strewn lilac: green leaves and purple flower. Edward's white vest hung on a branch. Aelred walked towards it, took it in his hands and buried his face in it, inhaling the smell of sweat, the odour of Edward. He opened the soft jersey and hung it again on the branch by its straps. This had become his ceremony.

The bells were now on their last toll; single tolls with ringing silences in between. Aelred looked up and was alarmed. Edward was not on the rock face. For an instant, Aelred thought he had fallen. A hawk hovered overhead. Then he realised that he must have reached the summit and must be making his descent the long way round back to his clothes. At the crunch on the gravel, Aelred spun round where he was standing, his fingers still caught in the strings of the vest. He gasped, 'God, you gave me a fright.'

Edward was standing in front of him. He stood in the full light, bare backed, in only his tight black shorts and his climbing boots, with thick grey socks crumpled round his ankles. His soft blond hair glistened, blonder in the light on his legs and chest, thicker where it curled around his navel. Blue veins ran along his arms. His hair was wet from the sweat on his face and brow and was drawn back behind his ears. He was wiping sweat from his upper lip with the back of his hand. Aelred could smell him. He stood in front of him, confused, caught.

Edward broke the ice. 'I can teach you to climb.' He was still breathing heavily from his run back down. 'Any time. We'll have to get you some boots. Maybe Benedict could get us those from the Cellarer.' Edward was pulling on his vest, which he shook out when he had taken it from the branch. He put his nose to it and smiled over its soft whiteness at Aelred, who was tongue-tied, standing there awkwardly, with an ear cocked for the bells for the Conventual Mass which would come soon after the tolling. He was an acolyte for the Requiem Mass. He had to be back in time. 'I was an instructor at my school. I've got certificates. It would be perfectly safe. It's a great sport. I think of it as religious. Coming out here in the early morning is uplifting. It's like the spiritual ladder to heaven. You've got to take it gradually. You've got to learn on gentle climbs at first. Then they get steeper and rougher. More sheer. You are the rock as you climb. You almost enter the rock. What do you think?' Edward smiled from where he was bending down and pulling up his denim overalls and pushing his head into his smock as he stood up. He pulled his leather girdle tight around his waist. 'It would be something! Wouldn't it? I could teach you. I'm no good at this flower arranging.' He bunched the tattered lilacs into a bouquet and held it out in front of him. 'What do you think?' Then he flung them into the bushes.

'You've got burnt.'

'Oh, yes, almost as dark as you.' Edward smiled.

'I think we should get back. I'll be late and I'm acolyte at the Requiem.'

'Brother Aelred, the perfect novice. At the sound of the bell, drops everything. You'll beat Thérèse of Lisieux to perfection. '

'You mock me. You get me wrong.'

'No, brother. I think we're different. I find it harder than you. This is what I live for.' He glanced up at the steep rock face he had climbed. 'I'd always had a sense of a vocation. I don't know why. It was always strong. Particularly since my entering the church. I used to be C. of E. Then I became interested in the old rites, the old traditions. You know, the Sarum Rite. Maybe I won't last.'

'We should walk back. The old traditions? Things are changing fast now. Since the Second Vatican Council.' Edward picked his way among the gorse bushes and the broom was already beginning to turn a glorious yellow.

'The Second Vatican Council! Modernisation! It'll

destroy the mystery of religion. I've noticed you, you know. You come out in the mornings and watch me climb.'

'I always come out here. Remember, it was me, I told you about the quarry.'

'That's right, you did. But I've noticed you.'

'So?'

'Speak to Benedict. I tell him my difficulties. We're lucky to have Benedict, yes?'

'Yes, he's a good guardian angel. The best. I'm frightened of heights.'

'I could tell, that first time you helped me. That was brave of you. And you didn't let on. That was sporting of you.'

'Discipline is up to Benedict.'

'Yes, I suppose so. The giver of dangerous texts.' Edward smiled. 'But I can't give this up.' He looked up again at the steep rock face. It was a cloudless blue sky, high and lucid. It must have been the same hawk, now hovering over the field. Aelred ran the lines of the Hopkins poem through his mind:

> *I caught this morning morning's minion, king-*
> *dom of daylight's dauphin, dapple-dawn-drawn*
> > *Falcon, in his riding*
> *Of the rolling level underneath him steady air, and*
> > > *striding ...*

'Striding.' The word got enunciated.

'What did you say?'

'Nothing.'

The two novices parted as they came out of the silver

birches into the wide open field and the track which cut across to the apple orchard.

The bells for the Conventual Mass hastened Aelred in his preparation in the washroom. *Festina,* he said to himself. Quickly! Images thronged Aelred's mind. He noticed Edward's arms. They were strong arms. Sinewy where Edward rolled up his sleeves to wash himself. They glinted with blond hair. When wet, the hair was sleek against his white skin. Aelred had noticed the novice's arms when they were digging together in the walled garden and just now at the rock climbing. He noticed the muscles, the way his fingers went red at the knuckles. He glimpsed and stored parts of Edward's body: his waist with his tight girdle; his slim hips; his strong legs in his denim smock; the movement of his body in his work smock; his hair above his stockings on his calves in the basement. He smelt his fresh sweat. When Edward took off his cassock to wash his neck and opened up the front of his cassock in the washroom, Aelred noticed the white of his neck and the blond hair which grew on his chest, curling up to his neck. Each revelation was a source of wonder in a world where the body was hidden under cassocks and cowls and hoods. Hair. To stroke hair, to feel it over skin. His hair would soon be shorn. Now he had thick falling hair on the nape of his neck. Under the blond curls at the edges was a pure white skin. He had never seen skin so white - white like marble with veins running blue.

Each of these glimpses was buried beneath Aelred's dislike for Edward. He was jealous of the time he spent with Benedict. Now he talked about Benedict as if he was as intimate with him as he was. He could hardly admit all this to himself. He did not like to think of himself having these uncharitable thoughts, having impure thoughts; having thoughts of pleasure about someone he didn't think he liked. A terrible spiral of hate and attraction began to take hold of Aelred, so that he wanted to behave in a cold way to Edward. Yet he went out to the quarry each morning to look at him. He was becoming obsessed by him. He told no one. He hardly admitted it to himself. What had Edward noticed? What had he told Benedict?

He knew that he blew hot and cold. Sometimes, he talked to Edward at recreation; other times he ignored him. He contradicted him in novitiate studies without any real reason. The new novice must think of him as immature. Edward still teased him about his funny accent - funny Welsh-sounding French. He still made remarks about his colour. Benedict sometimes joined in the humour at recreation. Edward used his Englishness over him - something Benedict had never done, nor any of the other monks. He laughed at his mispronunciation of words in the refectory when it was his turn to read.

Edward came from a posh background. That's what Benedict said, one day in passing. He spoke differently from Benedict. He had a different accent. They laughed at each other's accents. They laughed at the Irish brothers' accents. Aelred was picking up these differences, picking up about English class.

Maybe Benedict felt the same for Edward as he did for him, giving him Aelred of Rievaulx. So he wanted to rival him for Edward. He felt that Benedict must notice Edward's physical beauty: his blond hair, his blue eyes, his white skin, how tall he was, his arms and legs. Like an athlete. He made him think of Ted. Athletes yes, but one was blond and white and the other was dark and nut brown.

Aelred remained distracted throughout the Requiem Mass, which was celebrated by Father Basil. He heard the break in the old monk's voice as he came to recall those who had died. 'Let us pray for Brother Sebastian, our dear brother.' The community bowed their heads. Aelred remembered Basil telling him how he and Sebastian had lain in each other's arms in a field. Later, at the cemetery, Basil was the first to throw a small handful of dirt on to the coffin. Aelred knew that the old man would be back in the afternoon to help fill in the grave, as he had been there to dig it. Theirs had been a whole long life together from nineteen till this death.

Father Justin had arranged for Aelred to meet the Abbot after the Conventual Mass and the funeral. Aelred let the heavy door knocker drop. It was the head and shoulders of a Franciscan friar. It was made of brass. It glinted as it looked at him. It was a joke. Why would Benedictines want to be knocking a Franciscan on the head? It knocked against an open book with 'Pax Vobiscum' scrolled across the open pages. 'Peace with you,' the knocked head said. There was a pause and then the Abbot's voice came from deep within. '*Ave.*' Aelred opened the door, shut it quietly behind him, and stood there dropping his hood and straightening it, then putting his hands under his scapular, staring into the Abbot's study. The room smelt of furniture polish. The Abbot was not in his study. Aelred had forgotten the Abbot's room. Then his first brief visit soon after his arrival came back to him. He was confronted by a large lifesize crucifix with a naked Christ in a scant loin cloth. The Abbot's chair was under this crucifix behind a wide open highly polished desk, which had hardly anything on it. There was a large blotter and an old brass inkwell with a pen standing inside it. There were some sheets of paper and obliquely, with its back to him, a bust of the Virgin Mary made out of marble. On the other side of the desk was a black telephone.

'Is that Brother Aelred?' Without waiting for an answer, 'Have a seat, brother.' The Abbot's familiar voice echoed from within, behind a door to Aelred's left. Aelred knew his voice mainly from sermons in the chapter house, from blessings given in the choir, prayers intoned in the refectory. It was a voice that spoke from a dais, from a throne, from the high table. It seemed odd to hear it uttered from behind a door, which was the Abbot's bedroom, hardly a cell. He could hear water running into a basin. Then he heard a lavatory flush.

'Yes,' Aelred answered to the first question. Then, 'Yes, thanks,' to the invitation to be seated. But then he felt awkward sitting without the Abbot being there. He would have to get up when the Abbot entered. He sat on the edge of a leather upholstered chair. A tall clock tick-tocked, standing against the wall between two windows to his right. Red, green and yellow stained glass captured the light in scenes from the lives of different English saints whom he did not recognise. On the wall opposite, built around the closed door behind which the Abbot's voice had called, were bookshelves stacked tightly with leatherbound tomes with Latin titles. One long shelf held the *Summa Theologica* of Thomas Aquinas, each volume numbered. He could hear the Abbot moving about behind the closed door. He expected him to burst out at any moment. Once or twice he heard his cough. It seemed an interminably long time. He looked up at the lifesize crucifix that was looking down at him. Looming over him, it reminded him of the Christ on the cross in the famous Salvador Dali painting, with Christ on the cross hanging above the world, over the sea or a lake with a small boat putting out from the shore in the foreground. There was a fisherman pushing out the boat. He looked like St Peter, the boat was the barque of the church.

Then the door suddenly opened. Aelred jumped up. The Abbot came towards him. He was a small man, jumpy. He tugged at his abbatial cross, which hung on a long gold chain about his neck. It had a stone which looked like a ruby in the middle. It glinted. He was noisy. His black heavy shoes clattered on the slippery polished brown parquet floor. He dropped a book on to the desk. 'There,' he said. 'All that we need to know in life.' At the same time he held out his hand to Aelred, with his abbatial ring.

Aelred dropped to his knees to kiss the ring. Out of the side of his eye, as he knelt at the height of the desk, he caught the title of the book the Abbot had dropped there thunderously. *The Imitation of Christ*, by Thomas à Kempis. Aelred remembered the small black volume given to him at his confirmation. It had not helped him then; would it now? He got up from his genuflection.

'Yes,' he said, almost inaudibly.

'Well, I like to hear from my novices.' The Abbot spoke in a businesslike way, pulling out his chair, almost tipping it over and indicating with a thrust-out hand to Aelred to sit again, opposite him. Aelred folded his scapular carefully from behind him and sat. He found it difficult to fill the chair. He felt his feet would leave the ground if he sat right into it and leant back into it. So he sat up, without leaning against the back. He sat with his hands under his scapular. The Abbot fidgeted with his pen and straightened his blotter and inkwell. He lifted the sheaf of papers, knocked them together and packed them into shape, holding them up and knocking them against the desk top, dropping them repeatedly. 'You've settled in now. I think you've done splendidly. Father Justin tells me all is quite perfect.' The Abbot smiled.

'Yes, well ...'

'Of course. It's bound to be a little difficult at the beginning. And you've had huge adjustments to make. Quite beyond what most novices have to contend with. Not least, the weather.'

Aelred kept trying to form a thought in his head into a speech. He thought the Abbot's habit seemed far too large for him. It almost swallowed him up and he looked minute, sitting in his large abbatial chair. Aelred wondered what the Abbot's body looked like under his habit. He glanced up at the crucifix. The face of Christ was handsome, though gaunt and sorrowful. Edward's barebacked body flashed through his mind, blond hair curling around his navel.

The Abbot took off his glasses and cleaned them with the tip of his scapular. 'You were saying ...' The telephone rang. The Abbot picked up the receiver gruffly, throwing up his eyes at Aelred, indicating his irritation at being interrupted. 'Yes, Father Mark. That's what I decided. That's what I told you yesterday.' The Abbot glanced at Aelred. Aelred felt embarrassed overhearing a conversion with the Cellarer in which the Abbot was being patronising, obviously irritated by something Father Mark had got wrong. 'Anyway, see me in half an hour, I have a young novice here at the moment.' The receiver clattered in its hold and fell on the desk, and then the Abbot had to put it back properly. 'Where were we? He rubbed his ring against the palm of the opposite hand. This was ostensibly to shine it. Why? Aelred thought. But it was also like someone sporting for a fight.

'I don't mind the weather. I quite like it. It's a novelty.' Aelred said tentatively.

'Yes, well, that's splendid. But there's one little matter.' The Abbot tidied his sheafs of papers again. 'The Imitation of Christ.' The Abbot picked up the book as if it had come to hand miraculously at that moment. 'This is the book that will help you. It has been tested. It is uncontroversial. A tested spiritual guide.'

'Father?'

'No need to say anything, brother. Father Justin has told me the whole story. Yes, I think Benedict had the best intentions in giving you Aelred of Rievaulx but I'm sure you understand now ...'

'No,' Aelred blurted out.

'I'm sure you see the sense of this.' The Abbot spoke over Aelred's attempt to speak. 'And I must insist, brother, from what Father Justin has described, that you and Brother Benedict should not meet alone. I don't think that would be wise.'

'Father Justin said that you were banning Aelred of Rievaulx from novitiate reading. He didn't say anything else was wrong.'

'Brother, we don't need to spell this out. As you well know, even Aelred of Rievaulx would agree that dwelling on the description of sin is in itself a way to encourage it.'

'Sin? What sin, father?'

'Well, you know what I mean, the occasion of sin. "In much talking thou shalt not avoid sin". 'The Abbot quoted the holy Rule.'You know that. You did very well at you examination on the holy Rule before your clothing. The whole council was very pleased with you.'

Aelred felt humiliated. He felt like crying. He felt angry. The Abbot was not listening. The Abbot was not allowing him to talk. Then what could he tell the Abbot? He was right. But at the same time Aelred felt something was wrong. This man should be helping him. Father Justin should be helping him. There was only Basil. Not to see Benedict alone! What did the Abbot and Father Justin talk about? What did they really know? What were they not saying? Or were they just guessing, trying to avoid anything happening. Father Justin would have his eyes peeled for every transgression. This rule was going to be impossible. How on earth was he going to obey this rule?

'Father, I ...'

'I think you must just obey, brother. That's the hardest part of our life, the vow of obedience. You will take this vow in a few months. You must practise this now. Father Justin says that you have the making of a good monk, but there are these few things to get right at the beginning. In time it will be more appropriate to see Brother Benedict as you would any of your other brothers. But for the moment a little restraint in this matter is needed, it will be good for you and for him. You must think of him. You are very young brother. Very enthusiastic. Impulsive. Maybe it's the hot climate you come from.' The Abbot smiled. This was a joke, Aelred thought, but then he felt that the

Abbot meant it. 'Anyway our rule was written in Italy, so it's well tested for those in the sunshine.' The Abbot smiled again, getting up from his desk, indicating that the meeting was over. They walked together to the door. Aelred knelt and kissed his ring. The Abbot gave him a blessing, making the sign of the cross over his head. 'Thomas à Kempis, brother, *The Imitation of Christ.*'

Aelred tried to smile. He closed the door behind him inadvertently lifting the 'Pax Vobiscum' knocker, then grabbing it tightly before it knocked again at the Abbot's door. He put his hood on and made for the cloister. He walked near the wall of the corridor, as was the custom. He walked with head bowed, his eyes downcast. He needed some air. He needed to walk. He needed to run. He couldn't go to Benedict. He did not want to bother Basil today. He thought he might visit him later in the week. He had to get some help. Now he felt that Father Abbot and Father Justin knew everything that had been happening.

He remembered again bowing to the Abbot that night when he and Benedict had kissed and embraced in the side chapel. The Abbot could not know the details of that. It must have been what Father Justin had heard and even seen in the library. He tried to settle his mind by saying the rosary as he walked around the cloister. As he came back into the corridors on the way to the novitiate, he noticed Benedict going into the Abbot's room and Father Justin coming out. What was going on? All these meetings? Something serious, much more serious, was happening.

Maybe he could still get a mug of coffee, Aelred thought,

or had he missed the mid-morning coffee break? He was
just passing the pantry and, as he passed, he heard music
coming from inside. Then he remembered that Brother
Angel, who was blind, worked in the pantry and was
allowed a radio. Aelred retraced his steps and put his
head round the door. The monks were encouraged to do
that sometimes, to say hello to Brother Angel, to cheer
him up. Edward was sitting on the edge of a table in the
middle of the pantry, sorting out a cluster of tins of fruit
and vegetables. Obviously he was on dinner duty. Brother
Angel was at a smaller table, shelling beans into a basin.
On the radio was the tune, 'Love, love me do. You know I
love you'.

Edward looked up. His lips were formed into a whistle.
He smiled, humming the tune. He paused. 'Benedicite,'
he said pointedly. 'The Beatles, brother.' He whistled
along, pointing at the radio. Brother Angel chuckled.

'Are you being distracted, brother?' Aelred put his arm
on Brother Angel's shoulder. 'How are you today?'

'Not at all, not at all. Fine, brother. It's a catchy tune.'

'Is this the station you want, brother? Not your usual?'

Edward laughed. 'He's taking a break from the Home
Service, aren't you, Brother Angel?'

'That's right. Who's that?' Brother Angel indicated to
Aelred that he did not recognise Edward's voice.

'A relatively new postulant, brother. One who's not far
off his clothing. Who hasn't quite given up the world.'
Aelred looked at Edward smirking. Brother Angel
chuckled.

'It's just a bit of innocent fun,' Brother Angel said
solemnly, scratching his beard.

'Is there any coffee left?' Aelred said to Edward who

would have cleared the refectory earlier to lay the places for dinner - an expression Aelred could not get used to. He still thought of it as lunch. Dinner was what he had with his parents, a fine meal which Toinette cooked and served. White linen and silver!

'Yes, I think the urn is still warm. You might be lucky.' Edward continued humming. The Beatles sang, 'Love, love me do. You know I love you.'

Silence settled on the siesta of the monks. The heat shimmered over Ashton Park. Aelred could not rest, could not stay in the dormitory to rest, could not lie three cubicles away from Edward, whom he could hear shuffling at his desk, not resting either. All the windows of the dormitory were open. The cool breeze, coming off the hillside beneath the cemetery, blew the white cotton curtains of the cubicles. They soared to the vaulted ceiling of the dormitory. If only he could speak to Benedict and find out what had been going on this morning.

Aelred went to the common room to browse among the bookshelves there. He was soon distracted from that. He was preoccupied with his meeting with Father Abbot, his last meeting with Father Justin and all that seemed to be implied in what they had said. He stood with his face against the glass of the tall windows in the common room, looking out on to the thick laurel and holly hedges. Suddenly, there was a thud. A swallow had flown straight at the closed window, stunning itself against the glass, and had fallen to the ground. It had all happened in an instant. It took Aelred completely out of himself. He opened the window and looked down at the ground below the window. He watched the small bird. It lay there panting, moving its legs. Its head shuddered. Its wings folded. Then its legs stopped moving.

Aelred went and got his work on the translation of the psalms. Then he took himself to the grave of Jordan, to kneel in the shade and translate his psalms. On the way he picked up the dead swallow. As he entered the cemetery he stooped down and buried it under some dead leaves and twigs.

Brother Sebastian's grave had still to be filled in. That would be done after None. Maybe he would be detailed again for grave duty.

On the soft green turf below the whispering yew trees, a balm for his hurt, he was soon distracted from his translations. Overhead, he heard the sharp clicks and whistles of the swallows, which were darting at a furious speed, weaving in and out of each other above the cemetery and darting to their nests below the eaves of the chapel. He noticed one swallow in particular. It swooped and arced. It darted into a weeping ash tree, and was out again and then under the far eave of the chapel. It continued this journey back and forth, building a home.

You're like those swallows, the travelling you've done, Miss Amy say.

Yes, Miss Amy. Master Newton point them out at sea. He say we'll see you in England, talking to the birds. We up on deck when I hear him say that. They call it Bristol. You must know Bristol. That is what we hear when we still on the sea. Bound for Bristol. Everyday I so sick, I happy to be going anywhere and stopping anywhere. What a clamour there is when we out on to the deck. We still in chains down under. Lots of fellas sick and womenfolk crying. One morning, not far from Maderia, I wake up. It calm for the last hour or two. This fella, his name is Joseph, or that is what the white sailor who loose our chains call him. They just call us by a name. But he dead, Miss Amy. I think he asleep, leaning on me. But he is slump against me because he is dead, Miss Amy.

It is early morning.when we dock in Bristol. But people know we come. Such a clamour when we come out into the cold and have to stand up. Six of us chain together get push to one corner where a number of gentlemen come to look at us. But Master Walter pick me out and say, I is one of his breed. The man who speak with Master Walter sound like a man I hear speak in Virginia. He come and look us over and poke us with his walking stick, which has a silver top, I notice. It shine like a candle in his hand in that dark, cold, early morning. And he have a watch in his pocket. I know his voice well, for once I go there. And once to South Carolina, on a boat on a river called Waccamaw. Me and a boy called Jack, we try to escape there into the swamps, which is wooded with oak and pine and cyprus. We hide there among the reeds and rushes. Me and Jack. He come like my twin brother I lose when they take me from my village. And is a solace, I remember, the beauty of a flowering magnolia. But we get catch and take to Charleston. Then I get take back to the island and find myself with Master Walter once more.

Because I is a runaway he beat me, Miss Amy. He hang me up and beat me.

Then when we arrive in Bristol we is in these narrow dark streets and I hear the cry, Black boy for sale. Master Walter, and the man who speak like that man I hear in

Virginia, follow the cry down the narrow streets. There is this clanging of signs, each proclaiming another black boy for sale. Well limbed and fit to serve a gentleman, is the cry. The clanging of the signs mix with the sound of iron, the iron of the contraptions. The man I hear like a man in Virginia, he telling Master Walter about more contraptions he can show him from Virginia, like the ones he has back in a home in Kentucky. Never can do without them, when leaving them niggers with the · womenfolk. That is later when we come to this house that have stables out in the back and we get to lie down in some straw, next to where there are some horses. I hear the gentleman like I hear a gentleman in Virginia sound, call a little girl, Bessy. He tell Bessy give some hot drink, some bread and dripping. We eat and drink anything they give us, and me and the five fellas sleep. One of them I hear Master Walter call Jonah. I never know his name is Jonah.

Then I wake from a dream of a ship sinking in the sea, from a storm and a ship crashing on the rocks. I hear the gentleman like that gentleman in Virginia talking to Master Walter. I peep through a hole in the stable and I see into a room hang with saddles and stirrups and reins, and this same gentleman is showing Master Walter his contraptions, which he is taking out of a trunk mark Bristol. These are his contraptions from Kentucky, which he is saying Master Walter needs to use on the young breed that he buy. He show him the muzzle, then he show him the mask and last of all he bring out that thing they call the bit, and he explain to Master Walter how to use it. And how confounding good it is to keep that breed in control if he wants to get his money worth, for they are natural lazy, natural indolent, and wish all the time to run away.

Miss Amy say, tucking her sick father into his chair by the fire, some of you darkie lads must be scoundrels, I suppose. You better watch for the young Master Walter. There is no knowing what young Master Walter might do when he flies into a fury, Miss Amy say, going out to fill the kettle at the pump in the yard. I can tell you some tales myself, my lad. That is what Miss Amy of Somerset say that evening when she go out into the yard where the swallows still darting and swooping, clicking and whistling. They've come back home, Miss Amy say, looking up into warm May evening. I swear them is the very same birds that was here last year, Miss Amy say with authority in her voice.

Swallows persisted with their darting and making a swooping arc above the cemetery, in and out from under the far eave of the chapel into the ash trees and back again, building a home in England while Aelred struggled with his translations.

The bell for None brought Aelred back to the same Ashton Park. He made his way quickly from the cemetery to the novitiate to put down his books. The novices were shuffling from siesta along the corridor to choir. Aelred went via the library and the oak staircase. He had this fancy to check the portrait of the boy he called Jordan. Then he went to his position as acolyte of the choir near the holy water font. Aelred dipped his fingers into the holy water font and offered them to Benedict as he entered the choir. Benedict's face was blank. He could not read any explanations for the questions he had crowding

his mind. Last of all in the procession was Edward.
Edward's eyes met his for a second, then were lowered
again as he entered the choir. The celebrant for the week
intoned: '*Deus in adutorium meum intende.*' The community responded: '*Domine aduvandum me festina ...*' 'Lord,
make haste to help me.' *Festina*! Quickly.

The two novices, Aelred and Edward, were put to work at
haymaking that afternoon. Aelred had wished to have
Benedict near him, because, whatever the new rules
Father Abbot and Father Justin were making for their
relationship, he had to speak at least one more time.
Aelred delayed his departure to the fields and lingered in
the basement where the monks changed from their
house shoes into their work boots. At first, the basement
was busy with monks coming and going. Aelred pretended that his laces were in a knot and sat fiddling with
them.

The last to leave was Edward. 'I'll see you in the fields,'
he said.

'Yes. I won't be long.'

'We must get those climbing boots.' Edward lingered
by the door out into the courtyard.

'Yes, maybe.' Aelred did not look up.

As Edward closed the door behind him, Aelred caught
a snatch of the tune he had heard that morning in the
pantry. Edward was whistling it as he closed the door. The
words came to him: 'Love, love me do. You know I love
you.' When Aelred looked up Edward had left.

The basement was dark and cool and smelt of dirty
socks and sweaty boots. A tap dripped into the basin in
the corner. Where was Benedict?

Brother Theodore came down to the basement and changed into his boots. He smiled at Aelred. 'Any new wild flowers, brother?'

Aelred looked up, pretending hard to be working on his knot. 'There's campion and speedwell in the hedgerows. I've got those.'

'Yes, pink and blue. The speedwell runs under the white daisies and cow parsley. A river of blue. I checked with Father Christopher about the tropical plants book. He says it's ordered. What's it like in your country now?'

'Rainy.' Aelred thought for a moment, as if he doubted himself, and then said again, 'Yes, it's rainy season.'

'Rainy. Well, we've got a lot of that stuff here. But we're having quite a dry spell. We need it after that winter. Well, I'll be off. And you keep your chin up, brother. You look a little glum this afternoon. Make hay while the sun shines.' Brother Theodore chuckled as he fumbled with the door knob.

'I'm fine,' Aelred said, looking up and trying to smile. Brother Theodore's remark brought a lump to his throat and tears into his eyes. When he was on his own again he found the tears pouring down his cheeks. He would call it homesickness - it was that kind of loss; but it was also all that had taken place, and most of all, it was that he was frustrated that he could not talk to Benedict. What was happening? This was not how he had imagined monastic life. He thought of Ted and what he felt at his funeral. It was his face which was not his. Then there was that smell of frangipani and asparagus fern. Ted's head was on a white satin pillow.

He forgot that he was pretending to be untying a knot in the laces of his boot. He was staring at a stream of light coming through a crack in the door, which Brother Theodore had left open. It was filled with myriad specks of dust, floating aimlessly. He remembered staring through a microscope in chemistry class, back at Mount Saint Maur, at bacteria in a glass dish. A whole life he did not understand, formed and reformed. To the naked eye it was a smudge on the glass. This was why he was here: to sort out these mysteries. He sat absorbed, right there, on the old bench in the basement. It was a prayer, not a prayer, but *prayer*, he thought.

'You're still here.' It was Benedict appearing quietly and suddenly. He was wearing his slippers.

'Oh, I didn't hear you. It's this knot.' Aelred kept his head down, almost believing that there was a knot to untie.

'Let me see.' Benedict's voice, his care, made Aelred cry again.

'No, it's nothing.' Aelred looked up.

'What? You're crying? What's the matter? Let me look at it.'

'Nothing's the matter. There's no knot. I've been waiting for you. I've got to speak to you. ' Aelred was sobbing now.

'Hush. Someone may still come down, though I think most people have gone out to the fields already. We must take care.'

'So, you've been told ?'

'Yes, this morning.'

'I know. I saw you going into the Abbot's room then Father Justin coming out. I saw the Abbot this morning. What's happening? What do they know?'

Benedict could not resist wiping the tears away with his

fingers. 'Try and stop crying and then we can talk for a little while as I get my boots on. I'm late. We mustn't walk down to the fields alone.'

'Are we going to have to live like this all the time?'

'We must show that there isn't a special attachment between us. That's what both Father Abbot and Father Justin are most concerned about, that we don't show to others that there's a special attraction between us. It's as if they've accepted that there is. They would prefer that there wasn't, but they realise that there is.'

'And they think it must stop.'

'We must be very particular. Our being together is going to be interpreted as being inappropriate, whatever our behaviour is like. So at least for a while we must stay apart.'

'This is so hard. I don't know whether I'll be able to do this.'

'You must. You must think of me. You must think of your vocation.'

'What exactly do they know about us?'

'I'm not sure. Father Justin may have heard more than we thought in the library. He may have been noticing us and wondering for some time. But coupled with this is the reading of Aelred of Rievaulx. That has alerted them to the quality of our relationship. I've not told them anything that we've done, anything that is rightly a matter for confession.'

'I'll have to talk to Basil. Only he will understand.'

'I understand.'

'Yes, but how will you help me now?'

'I'm sorry. You must realise this is a great fear for superiors. It isn't simple, what we've embarked on. Aelred of Rievaulx recognises these feelings, but he does insist that they become spiritual.'

'He allows for holding hands.'

'Yes, but we've done more than hold hands. We've kissed. He expressly speaks against the carnal kiss.'

'Carnal - it sounds terrible.'

'Come on, brother. I don't think Father Justin will be allowing holding hands at recreation. We won't see Father Abbot walking hand in hand with Brother Theodore or whoever. It's not like that. You know that. It won't happen. We mustn't be naïve.' Aelred began to see the funny side and he and Benedict began laughing and imagining possible couples among the community.

'A farewell kiss? Aelred leant over and turned Benedict's face to his and rested his lips gently on his.

Benedict smiled. '*Au revoir.* Look at me when you need encouragement. We can hold it in our eyes. But be careful. It's going to be harder than you imagine. We must go.'

Benedict left first and Aelred followed a short while later. Near the bed with with the yellow roses Aelred saw Father Justin weeding. He felt policed. He felt guilty.

Aelred was working on his own, solitary against the hillside. His confusion drew him into himself. But he had spotted Edward lower down the field. He had been concerned earlier, because he had not seen him at all. He knew that they had both been put down for haymaking duty. He wondered what had happened to him. It might take him out of himself, and his thoughts about Benedict and their problem with Father Justin and Father Abbot, if he worked with Edward and talked about learning to rock

climb. He had no intention of rock climbing, but it might
be distracting just to talk about it. Maybe this was a way to
get to know Edward. Things might run more smoothly
between them. The secret of Benedict and himself was
becoming an obsession. It seemed to grow louder and
louder in his mind, so that he thought all the community
must know something about it. Maybe all sorts of little
things had been noticed and interpreted. He felt guilty as
he went along, dragging the heavy bales and waiting for
the tractor to come and collect them.

The monks elsewhere in the fields eventually broke
from their haymaking to collect around the tractor to
have tea, which Brother Crispin had brought out in a
small urn on the back of the tractor with some of Brother
Edwin's fruit cake as a treat for their hard work. There
was fresh milk from the dairy after the first milking.

Benedict was among them. Aelred worked out that he
had been detailed to work in the barn, making room for
the new hay. That would mean that they might not be
able to talk to each other again this afternoon. But he
might, in the new natural way they must now be careful
about, while mixing with their other brothers, catch a
moment to speak.

Such a moment came when Benedict was passing the
cake around. 'I wanted to say that I think you should try
and meet up with Edward. He's been talking to me about
you and he wants to mend fences. He thinks there's tension between you about silly things. Maybe some big
things too, like changes in the church? Anyway, try and
mix with him. It's difficult being the new novice, as you'll
remember.'

Aelred had a lot of questions in his head but he

decided to just go along with Benedict's suggestion. They were interrupted by Brother Crispin who was collecting up the mugs. 'We've got a lot of hay to be bringing in, brothers.'

As Benedict turned away to go back down to the barn in the farmyard, he said, 'I must just have a quick word before we turn in this evening. I'll be down at the barn. Try and come that way.'

'Yes.' Aelred tried to smile, to look normal about their communication. Yet it all seemed so furtive, so self-conscious.

Edward had been the last to join the group having tea. He had hung back from the others, who had been chatting about the hot weather and the quality of the hay. Now the good news was that they might have to stay out longer, past the time for Vespers, because rain was expected the next day: they could not risk the new hay being soaked. This meant that they would work late into the evening, beyond Compline. Aelred was pleased by this. He felt that it would be stressful having to be back with the novitiate and the normal routines of the day. It would be a kind of holiday, a *dies non,* staying out late.

The bell for Vespers had been rung a long time ago. Now the community must be at supper. Aelred was exhausted with pushing himself. Then out of the haze which now hung over the fields, Brother Crispin arrived on the tractor to take him out of his exhaustion and daze. Riding at the back of the tractor was Edward. They had come to collect him to go down to the farm to work in the barn. Aelred kept his eyes averted. Yes, he should talk to Edward, as Benedict suggested, he thought. But now he felt more at peace within himself and he didn't want to disturb that.

At first Aelred thought that now he would be able to see Benedict, as he had suggested, before they turned in. But as they approached the farm, he saw Benedict walking up the hill to the abbey between the lime trees. He realised that he and Edward were relieving the monks who had been working all afternoon at the farm. They, he and Edward, were to take the last shift before darkness came and the last bales of hay were brought in before the rain. He suddenly realised that he would not be able to talk to Benedict. As soon as the tractor stopped, without thinking, he jumped off and literally ran up through the avenue of lime trees, calling, 'Benedict, Benedict.' He realised what it must have looked like to Brother Crispin and Edward, but he continued. Benedict stopped and looked around. Aelred was out of breath. 'You said you wanted a quick word. And I'm to stay down in the barn.'

Benedict pulled Aelred off the path into the shade of the lime trees. 'Brother, this is not a good start. In front of everyone. I wanted to say this more quietly with time, but I expect you're right. You'd realise soon enough.'

'Realise what?'

'I didn't know how to say it earlier. The reason I was late this afternoon coming down to the basement was that I was having to move my things. Father Abbot has moved me to the senior's dormitory, given that I'm not far off my profession. He thinks it would be better. He is concerned that our relationship is not the best preparation for my final vows. You would have realised going to my cell and finding it empty.'

Aelred stood quietly looking out into the fields. 'You

would've let that happen? Let me go to your cell and find it empty? I see. I see.' He turned and began walking back down to the farm.

'Aelred,' Benedict called. He met up with him. 'I was going to stay up and look out for you. I thought I would do that. I'm sorry. It's all got too much. I will find a way to meet you. Please, please take this as a sign that we need time apart. The Abbot is our superior. We must see in this God's will. Go and see Basil. Talk to Basil.'

'Yes, yes.' Aelred let his hand brush against Benedict's. 'Yes, I will. I must get to the barn. They'll be wondering what's happened.'

The rain clouds were already purple on the horizon in the late summer sunset. There was a cool breeze whipping up the valley.

The barn was still warm. Aelred and Edward worked at stacking the bales, which the conveyor had dumped in a random way. At first they did not work according to any method, but struggled on their own.

Now that they were together, Aelred could not talk. Stacking the bales took the place of talking. Aelred meditated. He noticed that Edward followed him with his eyes, hiding them when he thought he would be noticed. They worked hard till they had stacked all the bales that were brought in that night. 'Let's meet tomorrow in the common room after classes. Benedict thinks we should have a talk.'

'Yes, I'd like that.' Edward seemed uncharacteristically shy. Then he said, 'Everything OK? You seem miles away.'

'I'm tired, I suppose.'

'We must get those boots for rock climbing.' Edward

smiled, trying to lighten the mood. Aelred tried to smile. He was tired.

Afterwards, they walked separately, hooded, hands in the folds of their smocks, away from the farm. They walked in silence back to the abbey for supper. Then they went to the Abbot's room to receive his blessing before bed.

In bed, anticipating the early call for Matins, Aelred hoped that a new day would change everything.

Aelred, the young Abbot of Rievaulx, woke earlier than the call for the vigils. He could feel the cold breath of the north in the woods about Rievaulx. The cold water of the River Rye flowed over the smooth rocks. Dark brown and green. Rust bled in the bubbling foam.

He knew that he had no choice in what he should do about the raging fire that had woken him in a dream. This was a fire within him, the embers dying in his hearth. A raging fire had filled not only his mind and the wild images that played there, not only his dreams to wake him with their terror and their seduction, but also his loins. His dreams were of Simon, the young monk, who amazed him with his tenderness and delicacy, whose beauty enraptured him and who had accepted him as a friend. Though frail, the young man was zealous for the monastic life, in fasting, vigils and the discipline. He had heard the sound of the lashes coming from his cell. He imagined the welts on his back. He was a young man whose beauty had attracted him the first day he saw him, when he had first come to Rievaulx, requesting admittance as a novice.

Aelred battled to hold this within his ideals of chastity,

but the night woke him with the most sensual phantoms of this dear youth. They were phantoms he could not rid his mind of without the most extreme measures.

He saw the writing on his back, the welts, the blue veins.

He whipped himself. His monks heard and took example.

In the midst of his flagellation the images appeared.

The power of this seduction, the most beguiling of images, was Simon as the young boy Jesus at twelve when he was lost from his parents and found in the temple in Jerusalem. The boy was lost in the city. He ached with wanting to feed him fresh bread dipped in olive oil, to quench his thirst with red wine. He pined to prepare his bed with clean linens. He longed to take off his shoes, to wash and kiss his feet, to anoint them with fragrant perfumes. His longing held the boy Jesus, turning into Simon, naked in his warm bath scented with balsam. He wept with finding his lost one in the city. He hung upon his neck kisses, a necklace of red roses. He drank the blood-red wine that flowed from the roses on his ivory neck.

His dream was all feeling, a feeling to save the young Jesus from his lostness. When he held the boy in his arms, he turned into the delicate Simon whose mouth was as sweet as all the kisses in the *Song of Songs*, which tasted of pomegranates. His cheeks were dusty like plums. His breasts, where he put his hand under the coarse wool of his habit, soft, the nipples growing hard as nuts in his fingers. He heard the words of the *Song of Solomon*: 'Let him kiss me with the kisses of his mouth.' In his dream, he kissed Simon's lips with his full mouth and the kisses of the youth were from lips of scarlet, purple as the grapes from the vineyards on the hillsides of hot countries. He smelt of the fragrance and perfume of incense, a field of lilies, an acolyte of the choir, a server at the altar. His woollen habit flowed like a flock of sheep over a green hillside, the lace of his surplice frothing like the gush of water over the rocks of the River Rye.

He was a shepherd's boy, a shepherd himself; the boy Jesus, the carpenter's son from Nazareth with a cross as his staff.

He felt under the wool for his belly, a sheath in a heap of wheat.

He was one whose skin was as smooth as skin which is oiled to prevent it from the cracks of the heat. He took his hand to run into those hillsides growing crimson with the vines where the grapes are poured out. They ran where the henna flowers grew among the vines of Engedi. He pursued him with a passion as nervous as a young deer, with the agility of a gazelle. He ravished him on a bank of lilies by the pool of Heshbon, by a pool of milk. They lost themselves on the hillside where the shepherds' flocks leave their tracks for the summit of Amana, the crests of Senir and Hermon, dangerous with lions and leopards. He hears his voice asking, 'Tell me then, you whom my heart loves: where will you lead your flock to graze, where will you rest it at noon?' In the wild, like vagabonds, they wandered. In the dream, they tumbled and coupled like young chestnut horses whose cheeks were as smooth as the cheeks of the horses that drew the Pharaoh's chariot.

Then they were young men together again, best friends, with a love for each other, as Jonathan had for David.

The dangerous text which the Abbot had banned from
the novitiate to protect his young monks had already
possessed the deepest layers of their being. 'Man does
not live by bread alone but by every word that is uttered
from the mouth of God.'

There is a strange synchronicity in all this, a macabre
pattern, a common impulse: denial, punishment, death.
The pattern becomes compelling.

Something else was afoot. I heard them planning. The
sense of threat was tangible. I said nothing. I could've
gone and reported something. What would I report? How
would I talk about it? I was expecting it to be at night. But
it was in the middle of the afternoon, hot, blinding light.
The seniors didn't have games that Saturday. I remember
it so vividly now, the noise, running feet on the bottom
corridors. A roar of boys! I had detention in the study
hall. The prefect in charge left to go and see what was
happening. We were all out on the corridor hanging over
the parapets, looking down into the playground. A ring-
side view. Ted and J. M. were being pursued by what
seemed like twenty seniors. It was wild. They had taken
off from the playground and had disappeared down
the path which led to the bush, past the shrine of Our
Lady of Lourdes, and which eventually led into the
hills behind the college. We could not see anything. It
became very silent. The prefect returned and the
detention continued. I kept my head down. I could not
imagine what was going on.

'*Ave, ave, ave Maria* ...' Even now, our hymns plait
themselves in incongruously.

There was a high wind, which howled and rattled the windows. Parrots screamed. Then the silence and the scratch of pens on paper continued. Lines: I must not talk in chapel, five hundred times.

Once when I looked up, the boy in front of me turned around and signalled with his hand and fingers, flicking them so they made a clicking noise, indicating that Ted and J. M. were getting what was coming to them, what they deserved.

Licks, he said, clicking fingers like whips.

I put my head down and wrote. I must not talk in chapel. Blue Quink ink on white paper with pale blue lines, words in blood: now his poetry is mine.

When we came out of detention I saw the seniors, one or two at a time, come straggling back into the playground.

J. M. called it 'The Raid'. He had a way with titles. Like The Night of the Rain.

There is an account in the journal. Aelred going over the ground three years later?

But I heard the seniors talking. One or two were real braggers. So bragging that it was some time before they noticed me.

The brother, they pointed.

They had it coming to them. If that's what they want. If that's what they like, the bullers. If that's where they want to take it. Let them.

Did you hear them? Like they were asking for it.

PLEASE was louder than STOP. Did you hear them?

The bragger was going over the top. I saw others slink away - already ashamed now that they were back in the playground. I saw some others not even join the gang with the bragger, who were congregating into the lavatories to smoke. I slipped into a cubicle.

I heard some say, Shut up, leave it.

A fight nearly broke out. But then a core of braggers egged each other on with description. I sat in the cubicle and listened. I dared not breathe. I hardly read what was on the walls: 'K.O. SUCKS S.T. WHO WANTS A PRICK AS BIG AS A DONKEY?' Someone had written under it, 'YOU DO. FOCK YOURSELF.' An O for U. The cleaners hadn't got here with their brushes as yet.

The bragger coughed, and the smell of smoke mixed with the smell of urinals.

Did you have them both?

One and then the other.

I saw O'Connor come out and there was blood all over his prick.

Do you know what he did? He went round. And when Macdougall went in, he shoved it down one of their mouths.

I heard him say, Suck it clean, you cunt.

They all laughed. I retched. I could not help it. I started being sick.

Who's in there? They were kicking the door.

I sat bent over. They clambered up and looked over. When I looked up, four faces.

All said, It's the brother.

One jumped over and opened up the door. They dragged me out. One was about to put my head in the urinals, when another boy walked in.

Leave him alone, he's not a buller, just because he's his brother.

It was him who shouted buller. I saw him in the refectory.

You know your brother is a buller, don't you?

Maybe his brother has bulled him, another laughed and sneered.

Get out.

They all kicked me as I passed out of the door.

Get out or we'll all bull your fucking arsehole. Then they laughed again. Yes, come take this. One held his cock bunched in his pants and shoved it out at me. I was passed along the line, blows to the head.

Yes, your arse must be sore. They kicked me again.

What have I done with all that hurt, all these years? My hurt.

That is your hurt, Joe says, acknowledge it.

I did not see J. M. or Ted. The headmaster called me into his office that evening and said that my brother had been taken home and would not be coming back until the new term. There were still two weeks to go before the holidays. I could not imagine how they could come back. It was kept from me, kept between my parents and J. M.

During the next holidays I remember he did not play, as he used to, with me, even though I was younger. He wouldn't come down to the savannah to play cricket. He stayed a lot in his room, reading. Was that when he went religious? I remember he used to get up early early in the morning to go to Mass in San Andres. He would take the five o'clock bus. He had a whole set of prayer books. I remember Mum saying things like: Toinette take Master J. M. lunch in his room today.

This was when I learnt to creep around him quietly. It was like I knew what had happened and knew what it was but didn't fully bring it into my mind to see it for what it really was and cope with it. I never wanted to admit any of the things I had done and said. I suppose it was the time we were living in. Now I might've had a counsellor. J. M. would've had therapy. All that was on offer was Father Gerard's spiritual direction and confession. Inside his heart there must've have been so much shame, so much guilt. And then what happened to Ted! No wonder he left and went away. And it was hardest when they had to go back into the new term to prepare for their exams.

But before the holiday, a special assembly was called on the last evening. Two boys were expelled as ringleaders, another two suspended. They let the others stay. There was a long queue outside the dean's office late that night.

Some were strapped, some caned. All in pyjamas, dropped, naked bottoms. Ironic.

There was a new head boy. The following week there were new captains for the teams. Ted was dropped, J. M. forgotten. Forgotten?

I overheard the gym master one afternoon speaking to one of those I noticed in the lavatory, who had not been suspended at the beginning of the new term:

They had it coming to them - fairies, he said.

Now I think of angels. Wings. A fancy.

What is it Joe said that really struck me?

It's like the church has taken possession of the body. It's like a demolition site.

Then he asked: Why does spirituality have to entail the subjugation of sexual passion?

There's another thesis he developed, which I find startling. It was on one of those nights when he and

Miriam stayed up really late finishing the rum and getting me to play the cuatro. They want to come to Les Deux Isles. They took me down to a West Indian restaurant before for some good food. It was Jamaican.

Joe is so animated. The state wants to control the body, wants to say what you can and can't do with your body. Then, ironically, it now says that we can kiss and touch. Well, it's not explicit, exactly what it is we can do with our own consent, provided we are twenty-one. That has to change. We have to have the same rights for gay people as we do for heterosexuals. It will come. Sixteen! he says. Look at your story, the story of your brother and Ted. It will come because it's enlightened and just. He talks of the Stonewall riots.

I try to imagine myself having this discussion in Les Deux Isles with the family, or just with so many friends. Of course back home there's no protection under the law, no rights whatsoever.

Religion run amock, Joe says.

I agree, actually. Though Joe says that many countries give lip service to some UN charter. I didn't know that.

He says, It's barbaric. There are things afoot in this country, even now.

Miriam says, In some countries, particularly with fundamentalist regimes, it's like concentration camps all over again, and so often in the name of God. All this done in the name of God.

Maybe J. M. died for something in the end. To make his brother think straight. Straight? Words take on a new meaning. And I always have *his* words, grist for my mill. I see the forming of his complex desires and where they got hidden.

I found a substitute for my love after Ted's death among those men who reminded me of angels and would be angels in the beauty of their chanting. Their dance was so different from that of the lithe athletes.

I lingered over those pictures in those foreign books on monasticism in the library, desiring and fashioning myself on the bodies of the monks I saw there: the sharp outline of the tonsured head, the hooded head bowed in holy prayer, the folds of the cowl, the tight belt, the scapular over the cassock, the leather sandals buckled on their naked feet.

I yearned for the life I saw there. I sought to be one of those men, hard at work in rough smocks. I stared at those still lifes of hands in prayer, at a potter's wheel, bent on a hoe in the field. I put out my fingers to stroke those perfect profiles, those shoulders at a desk, those hands illuminating sacred manuscripts.

I devoured these books like a kind of pornography, my spirituality, an erotic mysticism.

I idealised them in the lace of their surplices, the linen of their albs and the damask and silk of their vestments, the chasuble and the cope. I drew near to their sacred dance, this liturgy, an acolyte.

As I genuflected, as I turned and descended the steps from the high altar, as I bowed, as I poured water from the crystal cruets on to the soft consecrated fingers of the priest, and swung the thurible of hot coals smoking with the perfume of incense; as I carried the Abbot's crosier and mitre, I fashioned my face into that of an angel.

And from where they stood, the others, who had jeered and dared Ted to dive into the pool, could not touch me on my pinnacle. From there, I could pretend I was safe.

See my poetry in the words my brother found from a distance; a long gaze.

Hay-making

... if you should find my Beloved,
what must you tell him ...?
That I am sick with love.
Song of Songs

From the moment Aelred woke for Matins, all through
Lectio Divina, his reading of the Song of Songs echoed in
his mind. It disturbed him while he was doing the house
chores, and when he found it difficult to settle down to
study that morning after Prime. He avoided Edward in
the dormitory. He was conscious of the meeting they had
arranged for after classes later that morning. He turned
his own glances away, and turned from those which might
come from Edward - in choir, in the refectory, in the
washroom. But images of him filled his thoughts and feelings and distracted him. There was a tug-of-war between
the sadness and disappointment in what had happened
with Benedict and these strong feelings for Edward now
crowding his mind and body. He did not know how he
would extricate himself from this obsession which was
taking hold of him. He had not gone to the quarry this
morning, though Edward had hinted that he should, and
that he would lend him his boots and guide him on a low
ascent from the ground. 'Your feet are much larger than
mine,' Aelred had said bluntly as he passed the buttery
where Edward was working during housework. 'Let's
drop the idea.' Edward had looked disappointed, cowed
by Aelred's apparent sharpness. 'Come on.'

But Aelred had walked away, pulling on his hood and
moving down the corridor close to the wall.

He kept his head lowered and his face hidden within

his hood as he went about the novitiate. The curtains of Benedict's cell were left drawn open. The mattress was rolled up on the bed. The desk and bookshelves were bare. The small windowsill where Benedict kept more books, the ones on existentialist philosophy, was dusty. Nothing which Benedict used was here. The cell needed to be swept out; maybe Aelred would be asked to do it. Maybe he would do it voluntarily: show his acquiescence in what he now felt was brutal, cruel. He felt angry and he wanted to cry. As always when he had those feelings, he felt homesick. The window was open and the breeze lifted the white cotton curtain. A wide band of light picked up the dust from the floor. It felt as if someone had died. The iron bed looked like a hospital bed, cleared after a body has been removed.

'Looks like our Brother Benedict has moved on. I expect he'll be taking his final vows soon. That'll be a grand day.' Brother Malachi put his head round the doorway and spoke softly to Aelred, who was standing drawing patterns in the dust on the desk.

'I'll miss him,' Aelred found himself saying quite naturally to Brother Malachi, without turning to face him and still distractedly drawing patterns in the dust - then wondering at once what he might make of that. He hated this feeling of guilt, this feeling of being policed, spied on.

'We'll all miss him, brother. He is an exemplar, a real model for us novices.'

'Yes, he is.' Aelred felt that he could now legitimately praise Benedict. Brother Malachi obviously did not have any suspicions of hanky-panky - a word Father Justin had giggled out nervously and of which Aelred had to infer the meaning. Aelred detested the word. His anger twisted

it ironically in his mind. He enjoyed exchanging reminiscences with Malachi of Benedict as a caring, careful
listener and helpful guardian angel.

The meeting in the common room between Aelred and
Edward to discuss their theological differences was con-
ducted as legitimately as possible in subdued tones. At
first, they sat at the conference table and laid out their
differences, which had been coming up at recreation and
in the novitiate studies.

'I suppose my passage from the kind of low church
Anglicanism I was brought up with makes me theo-
logically and liturgically conservative in my adoption of
Roman Catholicism. So when I see the church that I've
adopted taking on the customs of the church I've left, it
disturbs me.' Edward was speaking deliberately and carefully.

'You mean things like the Latin Mass, communion
under both kinds, bread and wine.'

'Yes. I particularly want the old rites preserved. Of
course, communion under both kinds is an old rite, so
there are some things I agree with and would welcome.'

'I suppose I'm just the opposite. Maybe it's coming
from Les Deux Isles, a missionary church, where the
whole pastoral side of things is more important, so a
vernacular Mass would really help people. I want things
to be relevant. Mixed with that are popular devotions,
which you don't like, do you?'

'That's a matter of personal taste. Education I think.
That's fine on the missions - the question of relevance,
the vernacular - even in parishes here, I suppose. I've no
quarrel with that. But we're monks, enclosed. We could

be the preserver of the old rites. We don't have a primary responsibility to the laity, as the parishes and missions do.'

'Both things can happen at once, can't they? We could mix the new rites with the old. I suppose some priests might be allowed to say Latin Masses if they preferred. We're being so reasonable now. I don't know why these points have come between us at recreation and in novitiate studies. They've disturbed Benedict.'

'Maybe they're an excuse for something else.'

'Something else? Like what?'

'Come on, brother. You're not unaware that we've found our differences difficult.'

'Differences?' Aelred was now feeling shy and nervous. Edward was being straightforward and putting aside his jokes and irony.

'Well, I mean, look at us. I don't know many people from abroad. It seems as if we speak another language.'

'Yes. I didn't think there would be problems like this. You know monastic life ...'

'We're still human ...'

'Does it bother you, really, that I'm dark and might be black. I'm not saying that I am. But ...'

'I've never seen a black person in my home town of Shrewsbury. In Birmingham, yes. Plenty of coloureds there. Wolverhampton.'

'Yes. I've read about that. What goes on is prejudice.'

'I suppose, it's difficult for people, though. A whole lot of people swamping their town.'

'Swamping? Anyway, what's that got to do with you and me?'

'But, I mean, what was it like for you in Les Deux ...?'

'Les Deux Isles. It really irritates me that you never remember the name of the place.'

'I'm sorry. They *are* little islands.'

'Yes, but - anyway, yes, there's prejudice. I had a really good friend who was coloured, as you call it.'

'And?'

'Well, he was discriminated against. I mean Les Deux Isles is not like Little Rock, Arkansas. You must remember there - you know, segregation and all that. Well, we mixed in school, and - you know, as I didn't have black friends come home, my home. Well, there were exceptions and we didn't think that was abnormal.'

'But they did. You sound a bit unsure of it all.'

'I suppose. We teased each other, you know - things like blackie cockroach. They would call us whitie cockroach.'

'But there was slavery. The slave trade, the history of all that, the politics of it all.'

'Yes, I studied that. That was a long time ago. That's true. It's very difficult - repercussions, I suppose. But me being dark - what's that got to do with the slave trade? And anyway, it started here, didn't it? In England. In Europe. Maybe even Ashton Park. Well, it didn't start here, but Ashton Park was involved. Did you know it was connected, that the original house was built on the proceeds of the slave trade?

'No, I didn't. Is there something in the library?'

'Yes ...'

'This gets to you doesn't it?'

'What? Yes - no, I mean.'

'I mean between us. You're different. The way you speak, use your hands. I don't know.'

'Well, this is what Benedict said we should do - air our

differences. We've been at this a while.'

The issues were bigger than they were. They were issues of faith and race, and Aelred heard in his head that Jordan voice, telling that Jordan story. It did get to him, as Edward put it. Edward was right. He did not know how to share with him his story of Jordan. He did not feel like going into that there and then. He just said, 'You should take a good look at the portrait on the oak staircase.'

Edward looked quizzically and said, 'Yes, I will. I'm interested.'

The time was creeping on to Sext. They might be able to grab some time at haymaking later.

Father Justin put his head round the door. 'I think you two should think of bringing this conference to an end soon.' Aelred became self-conscious but Edward started again, from another angle.

'I know that it's wrong to judge you, but I thought you rejected me for my views.' Edward, beginning to find it difficult to cope with this meeting, spoke looking out on to the hillside below the cemetery.

'Well, I did, in a way, but I feel it's about more. I feel we affect each other, and - I don't know.' They were stumbling upon their feelings.

'Yes, but you seem so strong and powerful, and with your relationship with Benedict, I felt that I wouldn't count.'

'What do you know of my relationship with Benedict? What relationship?' Aelred looked for reactions in Edward's face, the tell-tale signs. He had not spoken of it. Had Benedict to Edward? Did others notice? Were Father Justin and Father Abbot right? It was just what they were worried about. Was it that everyone knew, and there was a terrible silence? 'What do you mean, not count? What of my relationship with Benedict?'

'You know. I expect I mean that I'm the junior, that everyone seems to have the same views and I'm the odd one out. And yes, of course we know about you and Benedict. When you are in a room together it's different. I notice the difference. You make a difference when you enter a room. You both do. You do.' Edward was getting unusually agitated.

'But many of the senior monks think like you. They don't want the changes coming with the Council. What do you mean, difference?'

'There, you see I can hear it in your voice, dismissing me and my views. These things are as deep as matters of faith. I know I seem blasé. Rock climbing, joking, a little cynical maybe, but ...'

'I'm sorry. I don't mean that as it sounds. I'm sorry.' And Aelred reached out with his hand to touch Edward's arm. 'I'm sorry.'

'No, don't worry. But you see what I mean? That's like you, touching me.' His arm slipped down till their hands came together in a clasp and they stood looking at each other. 'You see, this is what you do. I notice you. You don't take responsibility for this. I see you with other monks. I don't suppose you realise what you're doing. Like your views - rash, impetuous.'

'Responsibility? And you?'

There was a noticeable clatter of someone in the corridor outside the common room and Father Justin put his head round the door again and said, 'I really think it must end here.' Edward and Aelred almost jumped apart, or so it seemed to Aelred.

Aelred and Edward looked sheepish. Aelred raised his eyebrows. Inside he was furious. He was really beginning to resent Father Justin and his ways of ordering things. He did not say anything because he didn't want to give a bad example to Edward. They both pulled on their hoods and returned to their cells.

When Aelred returned to his cell he was agitated. He had held Edward's hand. He put his hand to his face and smelt his hand, sitting at his desk unable to concentrate on his study. They had said something without saying anything. What they talked about did not seem to be what the problem was about. They needed to talk again. The bell went for Sext and then there was lunch.

After lunch, Aelred went to the library to browse the shelves. As he came into the alcove where the art books were kept, he saw Edward. He was standing at the desk in the window that looked over into a small, walled ornamental garden with a statue of Our Lady in a grotto. Edward was poring over the large open pages of a book on sculpture. Aelred had not used this section of the library before. It was what he liked about siesta sometimes: browsing and finding new books. It was exciting, like the time he found the history of Ashton Park, which talked about the old house and how it had been built on the proceeds of the slave trade. This browsing was not positively encouraged by Father Justin, but it was tolerated to some extent.

Aelred looked over Edward's shoulder. 'What're you reading?'

'Oh, *Benedicite*, brother,' Edward said solemnly but jokingly. Edward liked to be irreverent about some of the monastic customs, and the rule of preceding conversation with '*Benedicite*' always seemed to amuse him, so he used it himself pointedly. 'Rodin. I wanted to go to art school once. Chucked it in for the monastic life. I love drawing. But I like the old stuff. We had to look at books like these for A Level.'

'I don't know any of this.'

Edward turned the large pages and they both looked at photographs of Rodin's sculpture. 'He's a very important and exceptional French sculptor. He worked a lot in marble. I like his bronze, too. Once, quite exceptionally really - my first visit abroad, we were taken to Paris by our art master. He was brilliant. We saw Rodin's work: a whole museum of his work, in the Rodin House, with sculptures all over the garden.'

'Paris?' It was a kind of wonder to Aelred. His mother had told him about Paris. They had cousins in Paris. But it was like another world. He had forgotten things like that.

Edward talked about sculpture, most of it going over Aelred's head. But Aelred watched the photographs as Edward turned the pages slowly and the sensual, tactile limbs and torsos absorbed him. They leant together over the tome, their shoulders touching. 'It's very connected with rock climbing.' Aelred smiled. 'No, really. You see, you have to understand how the body works. You have to understand about tendons and muscles, about tissue and skin, about flesh and of course bone structure. You must know and feel for all the elements; above all, know how it all works. That then leads you to physiognomy and to cha-racter: to be able to judge character in the features, in the cast of the body.' Edward was speaking animatedly, as if all his young knowledge was coming up to the surface in a rush while he was looking at the pictures and turning the pages slowly, waiting till he felt that Aelred had finished looking at a particular page. 'It was all because of Toby, Mr Holme, our art master. He allowed us to call him by his first name in the studio and when we went on field trips in the countryside to draw and paint and rock climb. I wouldn't know any of this but for him. He was a rock climber, too. He was a marvellous drawer. He would draw us boys rock climbing. Instruction in rock climbing and sculpture went together. What a waste!'

'What's a waste?'

'Oh! Nothing. Oh, look, this was something he told us about. See it's a frieze around a vase.' Edward had taken down a book on Ancient Greek art. 'He talked about the drawings he had done of us boys. He talked about beauty and truth. He talked about honour. Yes, beauty and the attraction to beauty. He was teaching us about form. He brought us pictures of vases with paintings of the young heroes, athletes like this one depicted all around the vase. This tells the story of the god Apollo and his love for the boy Hyacinthus. Apollo loved this handsome boy, but Zephyrus was jealous. See, there he is. When the god Apollo hurled a quoit, Zephyrus blew it off course, so that it struck Hyacinthus. Where the boy fell to the ground, bleeding, these flowers with dark blue petals, which we call hyacinths, grew out of the earth. For some, he is the god of vegetation.'

Aelred listened enthralled. 'Hyacinths?' He thought how little he still knew.

Then Aelred and Edward, without talking, took turns to pull the large pages over. After a while, in silence, the two novices were leaning closely together over the art book.

Edward spoke again. 'It was a real waste.'

'What?'

'Mr Holme. He had an ideal. It came out one day. He said we were like young heroes.'

'Why a waste?' Aelred repeated.

'What? Oh, nothing. I'll tell you some time. He was asked to leave. It was very sudden.'

They both continued turning the pages of the book of ancient Greek art. 'You know what you were saying this morning about affecting each other?' Edward began to speak again, carefully.

'Yes.'

'Well, I think I know what you mean.'

'And you were talking about responsibility. You said that I should take responsibility,' Aelred said.

'Yes, I remember. Well, I think it goes for me as well. I've been thinking it over since I left you.'

'And?'

'Well, I think I should say this: it's because - yes, I'm in love with you. That's it.' The declaration was said plainly and hesitantly, as Edward continued turning the pages of the art book. He was not looking at Aelred. Aelred was not looking at him. He was absorbed by the photographs of the sculptures. Edward may not have meant it to come out at that point, and in a way it went unnoticed, neither of the young men wanting to deal with it: to deal with the implication of their secret, now spoken aloud, if even only between them. Love. Was that what it was, all these feelings? 'Love, love me do. You know I love you.' The tune floated in, like an ironic joke. 'So,' Edward continued, 'I've used the differences we were talking about this morning to fight against it, because I don't know what to

do with these feelings. I don't know what will happen.'
They stood still, talking quietly. Their hands had come
together at the edge of the art book. Oblivious of their
world, the two young men were caught up in something
beyond, which neither of them were prepared for, despite
Aelred's obsession with Edward's rock climbing, his
absorption in his scent and the parts of his body. This soft
word, love, uttered quietly while poring over the
exquisitely beautiful naked bodies of men and women,
had altered everything at a stroke for the two young
novices. Suddenly, everything looked different.

'We can manage this,' Aelred said matter-of-factly.
'There's experience to call on, there's advice. We must
ask for that advice and we must pray.' Then he said
abruptly, 'There's Aelred of Rievaulx.'

'Yes, Benedict has given me Aelred of Rievaulx to read,
as you already know.' They were putting their love, their
attraction, at a distance, as something to do something
about.

'Have you talked about this to Benedict?' Aelred immediately felt jealous hearing that Benedict had shared a
similar intimacy with Edward. How could he be jealous
and at the same time be here, holding Edward's hand and
implying that he was accepting Edward's love? They had
lain something down between them and now they didn't
know what to do about it. Edward closed the art book.
They began to leave the library to walk back to the novitiate. Then they walked back again to the window desk
where they had left the book on Rodin, and the tome on
Ancient Greek art. Edward returned them to the shelves.
Time was running on. It would soon be None.

'You haven't said what you feel.' Edward looked at

Aelred. 'I feel stupid now, what I said ...'

'What did you say to Benedict?' Aelred insisted on knowing that.

'Oh, hardly anything explicit. Just sort of mentioning that there can be trouble with emotional feelings between us, between men, and it's difficult to know what to do about it.'

'So he gave you Aelred of Rievaulx then?'

'Yes.'

'Did you find it helpful, the dangerous text?'

'Yes - just to see it being talked about. I mean there's a bit of deciphering to do, but he's talking about love and attraction: physical attraction between himself and his monks, between himself and a boy, or man when he was younger at the court in Scotland. Talking about, you know, even wanking. That's what we call it here. Is it the same for you?'

'Jocking,' Aelred said spontaneously. Odd this talk, he thought. Look where they had got to from Latin Masses and communion under both kinds this morning. These things seemed easier for Edward. 'Impure acts.'

'Yes, well, there we go. Impure acts. I came into the church when I was seventeen, and yes, there was that serious stuff about confession. But it didn't seem to me a problem.'

'Well, for me it was. I was afraid of hell, literally.'

'Well, it's certainly there for Aelred of Rievaulx. Pretty lurid stuff. You know, about masturbation. It's all there - quite explicit if you know how to read the text. But still there's what the hell you do about it.' Aelred was amazed at Edward talking like this. This was different from Benedict. 'He talks about that, doesn't he? We can't lead *carnal* lives, as he would put it. He would use language like that. Then he says that we have to transform these feelings into spiritual feelings, into a spiritual love, into a spiritual friendship; a carnal kiss must become a spiritual kiss. Easier said than done, I admit, isn't it? But it's there. St Augustine in his confessions talks in a similar way. But saints were real people. It's only the writing that makes them sound weird. Does this affect you?'

'Does this affect me?' This repetition of the question in a reflective way was something that Aelred noticed he had begun to adopt. It seemed a very English thing to do. 'Yes, of course it affects me. You know it does.' Aelred didn't know what to say, how to understand his feelings. He felt he was betraying Benedict - Benedict, his Benedict whom they had taken away into the seniors. Right now he was bereft. And now he was being told by Edward that he loved him. He couldn't be in love with both of them. He couldn't change. He had not stopped loving Benedict. But there was something else. Strangely, what he felt for Edward made him feel sick in the pit of his stomach. What he felt for Benedict was joy, or sadness if he was deprived of him. He felt warmth, and a need to hold his hand, to kiss him, to be hugged by him. Yes, and he would have gone where Benedict led in the chapel. But he was ready to stop as well. He could stop. With Edward it was another feeling. He could smell him. He felt if he gave into these feelings he might disappear. He might destroy himself. Carnal? Was that it? He was trying so hard to be good. Carnal made him sound evil. He was not evil.

'I've just sort of blurted out that I love you. You've not said anything,' Edward said encouragingly.

'I feel the same. I don't know what I feel. Yes, I do.

Thank you. That sounds pathetic. I thought we didn't like each other.' All this while they were still holding hands and whispering in the library. He thought of Edward seeing him out at the quarry smelling his clothes, burying his face in the crotch and armpits of his overalls and smock. He felt embarrassed that Edward had noticed him looking at his body: at the hair on his arm, on his chest, curling around his navel. He had stolen all these glimpses and stored them in a small hot tight space in his head and they ticked away like a cicada in the heat. 'I can hardly say what I feel.' Edward held himself with composure. Aelred could hardly breathe. 'I'll think of you as differently now, as my friend. We're friends.'

'Friends? It's not the first word that comes to my mind. But maybe we can hold it all together. Maybe we can make it spiritual. We've got to try and do that or I expect we won't last it out. You know I feel weak as it is. What I need to do is to go for a climb. There'll be haymaking later. That should use up a lot of energy. What was it the fathers of the desert did?'

'They whipped themselves. They fasted. St Benedict threw himself into a patch of brambles.'

'Come, brother.' Edward put his hand to Aelred's face and cupped his cheeks. 'Come brother, you don't have to do that. I don't know what we'll do, but we'll figure it out. It's good that we've talked. That's what Benedict wanted. But physical work does help. Even if it only disperses the energy.'

Aelred was on fire. He did not know how Edward spoke so calmly.

They parted just before reaching Father Justin's cell, leaving their hands to untwine just before they entered the corridor to the novitiate dormitory. At that moment, the bell went for None. They agreed to try to talk again in the afternoon during haymaking. They both processed back to their cells before leaving the dormitory to go and line up in the small cloister outside the chapel.

Aelred did not choose to listen to the voice of caution. As the bells chimed away, echoing across the valley, and all around the stone abbey, keeping out every other sound, Aelred did not hear what he should have been hearing, what he had trained himself to hear with Benedict, except it never seemed to be needed in the same way. He quickly left his cell and went straight to Edward's, pulling aside the curtain of his cubicle without knocking and getting the reply, '*Ave.*'

He went straight in and threw his arms around Edward's neck. Edward was taken aback, saying, 'No, it's not possible. Please.' Aelred was fumbling under Edward's cassock at the neck, kissing his neck, undoing the buttons of the cassock. He could feel the blood rushing to his head, and he could hear Edward saying over and over again, 'No, it's not possible. Don't do this to us,' as he was undressing himself, opening his cassock under his scapular to make himself naked. Then Edward pushed him away and left his cell. 'I said, it's not possible. Don't make me push you away. It's the last thing I want to do.' He almost shouted as he walked away down the corridor of the novitiate.

Aelred was left in total confusion, and acutely embarrassed. He could feel the semen trickling down his leg. He went quickly to his cell and then to the washroom. Making sure no one else was there, he wiped himself clean with his flannel, hitching up his habit. He returned to his cell and made himself tidy before descending to open the door to the choir, as he was acolyte to the choir that week.

As the monks processed into choir, they took holy water from the acolyte. Aelred's eyes met Edward's as their fingers touched, Edward receiving the holy water from Aelred whose sex he had sought so passionately. Edward had withheld it, not knowing what now was possible ... 'myrrh ran off my hands, pure myrrh off my fingers, on to the handle of the bolt'. Aelred closed the door into the choir, the line from the *Song of Songs* coming readily into his mind.

There seemed to be no peace for the young novice, no allaying of his passion. Now, it was not an older monk who had had years of discipline to check his fall, his temptation by a young and beautiful novice. It was a young novice, who, sensing that he was admired and loved, wished to return that love. Being loved, he wished to love. He went back to his monastic fathers, those cowled poets, *cucullates poetas*, who spoke one heart to another, to have that truth corroborated. *Amare et amari*, to love and be loved, was their ideal, according to St Augustine, who had once given himself to the love of youth. But at the same time Aelred felt that he needed an antidote. He needed the fasting and the flagellation, he needed the abstinence, the passion of his Lord.

Aelred's whole body anticipated the haymaking that afternoon. He would not be able to bear it if he could not be there, out in the open fields with Edward. The house closed in about him, the extreme claustrophobia caused as much by the humidity as by the foreboding that his desire would be denied. 'No it's not possible,' echoed in his mind. He had been overtaken by a passion which had been building.

The rains had not come, after all their effort to clear the hay the night before. The electric storm, which had been threatening in the purple clouds of the late evening sunset, had not broken. And the heat was held in the strange darkness that brooded over the whole of Ashton Park, which now seemed sunk in a deeper valley than the one in which it rested. The haze which collected after a very hot day refused to be dispelled completely, and the sun was prevented from its full brilliance. All nature seemed held in, contained before bursting. The lowering skies brooded over the climbing cottage roses, which were as big as cabbages and drenched with dew from the night before, hanging precariously as if about to fall off their stems from the extent of their own weight. The wild brambles along the verges between the cloister and the farm, and the cow-parsley like wild Queen Anne's lace, dragged their frills, drenched and weighed down, while foxgloves and hollyhocks burgeoned in wildness and profusion. Names - he learnt their names. All that grew close to the ground, the undergrowth of the park, seemed to be reaching up to the trees in their full-leaved and complete summer state. The effect of the dark and lowering skies, which became more and more suffused with the sun's heat and brilliance, was a pervasive breathlessness, which invaded the corridors and meeting rooms, and held Aelred in an extreme state of anticipation. It clawed at his throat like the heavy and tenacious green ivy which crawled against the walls of the chapel at the front of the abbey and clutched at the weathered stone.

After None the haze lifted and the park was hot with the sun transfigured in the vivid blue sky. But at the same time, cumulus rainclouds from the west were accumulating and threatening to cloud over, and eventually break with the rain which should have come the night before. There was a persistent wind.

The younger monks were called out to haymaking soon after None, and Dom Thomas waited outside the sacristy to give the instructions quietly to each of the younger monks as they processed out of the choir. Aelred, because he was junior to Benedict, noticed that Benedict in front of him had been instructed. But because Edward was his junior and processed out of the refectory after him, he did not see whether Edward had been asked. He would have ordinarily been elated to be working with Benedict, but now, since this afternoon's sudden change, he was nervous and afraid.

It was not necessary that all the novices should be asked. Some of them would be needed for the house jobs which could not be left undone, like clearing the refectory and setting it up for supper. There was washing up to be completed and vegetables to be prepared for the next day. It was also the day for the laundry to be sorted. Already, Brother Gideon had brought up the baskets from the laundry room and left them in the hall for collection by whoever had been detailed by the Cellarer.

'I need to talk to you.' Aelred hung on to Benedict's sleeve as he turned into a part of the cloister that was screened by a vast overhanging of Russian vine, which was already beginning to burgeon with its white flowers. This shady spot was hidden from the rest of the cloister. There were benches built into alcoves, which meant that it was easy to cut yourself off from much of the activity in this area of the abbey. Benedict had left his books there when he went to None. He had spent the siesta in the shade. The spot was further enhanced by a fountain under one of the arches of the cloister.

'Control yourself.' Benedict pulled away.

As Benedict knelt to pick up his philosophy books from the floor near one of the benches, Aelred sat down on the edge of the seat and bent down to be near him, so as to talk in a low voice. 'I need to talk to you. Don't pull away from me. You've got me into this.'

'Keep your voice down. And what do you mean? What are you talking about? What've I got you into?' Benedict had already gathered up his books and was making to go quickly to his cell, so as to change for the haymaking. Aelred was still sitting on the edge of the bench, with his head now between his hands. 'Hurry, because we have to be in the fields soon. This isn't what I meant by making an opportunity to see you. This is in absolute opposition to the expressed wishes of Father Justin and Father Abbot. I can't carry on in this way, particularly in the lead up to my final vows. It's as if you can't control yourself.'

'I can't. I can't. You know, don't you? You already know? That's why you're being so rough, so dismissive? You're jealous. I'm sorry. But you're jealous and so you are dismissing me. Just like that. Your cell empty. You here, me over there. What is this community?'

'I've no idea what you're talking about. Keep your voice down. You know we're not supposed to be here, talking at this time or any other time. You know I'm worried about the number of times we see each other. You must control yourself. You look terrible. What's the matter? I will listen, but you must be quick. Couldn't you've waited till we got into the fields where we could have talked in a more natural way, rather than this hiding, this furtive whispering?'

'I can't talk to you.' Aelred made to leave the cloister. 'It's no use. You're not being sympathetic.'

'Wait,' said Benedict 'Wait. You might as well tell me now. I'll listen. I'm sympathetic. I do this for you. I do this so we can hold on to what we have, for our life here. I don't want to lose you. You run the risk of destroying it. You run the risk that it will be judged irreconcilable with our vows. Truly, you must agree. Why don't you understand? You must be patient.'

'What's the point? Anyway, you aren't interested in what happened to me and Edward - how our talk went, how the talk which you set up went. You set it up. It's your fault.'

'What on earth are you talking about? I wish you would be plain and tell me, instead of ranting and not saying anything. I assume you had a good talk and sorted out your differences. I will make time to talk to both of you. I'll talk to Father Justin and get a special permission to speak to you. That's possible. I must work within the rules; otherwise I'm sure that all is dashed. But surely all this is not about your meeting with Edward. I can't believe that. So tell me what else has occurred.'

'It's OK, I'm just making a fuss. It's nothing.'

'Benedict held Aelred by the shoulders. 'You're so young. I've put all this on you. I should've left you alone. I should've coped with my feelings in another way.'

'Yes, maybe you should've left me alone.' Aelred left the cloister swiftly and Benedict did not prevent him this time.

At first, Aelred could not see Edward anywhere. It was not till an hour later that he saw him, coming down through the apple orchard on his own. He realised that he must have had to do house duty before coming on to haymaking. His heart began to beat with expectation.

He had managed to avoid Benedict, something he never thought he would want to do. He was hurt that Benedict had not immediately perceived what was wrong and done something about it, comforted him, put it all right. His own emotions did not allow him to think of how Benedict was seeing things now, or had seen them. He felt that he was sure to have hurt Benedict, with his last remark in particular, but he was not in a position to maintain this concern.

Edward worked in the lower field near the ponds, and Aelred was asked to go and work at the top field. When he was settled there, with a view of the whole park, isolated and as far as he could be put from Edward, he took it as a sign that he should not rush things. He was beginning to feel quieter in himself since the turbulence that had filled him all day. He must try to find Benedict to talk things through again, to get advice. And he must, he thought, go to confession this evening so that he could go to communion in the morning. He would have to visit Basil tonight after Vespers. He wondered whether Edward would go to communion. Clearly he had not committed a sin. No, it was he: he had had all the impure intentions. He had performed all the impure actions. He was responsible for any sin, for leading Edward on, for creating an occasion of sin. Edward was virtuous because he had resisted. He had turned away from temptation. Aelred felt quieter, but wretched.

Aelred could not see Benedict anywhere in the fields and thought he must be at the farm. He decided to be bold and went to Brother Adrian, who was in charge, and said that he had to go off to his cell. He decided then and there to take the bull by the horns. He could not stand the tension. He must get back to Benedict. He must get back to the equilibrium of his relationship with Benedict. Benedict would advise him what to do. Yes, he would be hurt and more, he would be concerned about his vocation and the state of Edward's mind, as he would think that he was responsible for bringing them together in the first place. Aelred was sure Benedict would take a pastoral attitude to this. He must risk it. There was no one else to go to. He could not trust Basil with all the facts of this. Basil, of course, could be really understanding, but he could not bring up the whole matter of Benedict and then what had happened with Edward. He felt as if his whole life in the monastery so far was up for scrutiny. He might be losing his vocation. No, he didn't believe that. But he must get to Benedict.

His plan was to go through the farm, and if Benedict was working in the barn, he would just have to run the risk of being noticed and would ask him to come and talk to him. He would not be able to cope if he didn't.

Brother Adrian was fine about him leaving. 'Come back as soon as you can, because there's still so much hay to bring in.'

Aelred agreed. 'I'm grateful, brother. I'll be a quick as I can.'

Aelred could see Edward still working in the field near the spinney. His resolution from a moment ago diminished and he felt an ache in his stomach for the young man bending down to pick up the heavy bales and carrying them to the trailer.

He was just a small blue figure in the distance. All his distinctive features were lost in the space of the park and against the trees and the water of the ponds. His insignificance was etched against the immensity of the park.

Their secret was hidden in this immensity.

Aelred felt himself soaring. The image of Edward so moved him that he ached, as he had ached in his stomach at siesta in the library for him with the longing of all his childhood for someone to love. Was love the word? He felt sick. He felt now that he loved Edward as he had indeed loved Ted. He was sick with this love. He smiled as he looked down at Ted's boots, which had now got relegated to field work. He wondered if these feelings would last until he got to the farm and was able to speak to Benedict to explain his confusion.

The feelings continued, but there was no Benedict.

All the afternoon was coiled into the whirr of the baler raking in the cut grass and delivering bundled bales on to the field in clusters. That was in the upper field, ten minutes on the back of the full tractor from the barn in the farmyard, where Aelred and Edward laboured high up on the stacked bales under the zinc roof, sweltering in the heat. They laboured in the hum of the sun, the tractor and the baler, into which the crash of the conveyor delivered the bales to the top of the barn. They worked relentlessly within this humming space, into which the conveyor dumped the bales that Brother Martin unloaded from the trailer twenty feet below. They plodded in the hay on the floor, falling over, getting up, lifting bales and stacking them to the height of the roof, shutting out

crevices of light. They worked in unison, one fetching the
bales from where the conveyor randomly dropped them,
the other working higher up on another ledge in order to
reach the empty spaces, to fill every possible nook and
cranny. Their rest came when Brother Martin had emptied
the trailer, shut off the conveyor.

Aelred and Edward feared this peace.

They did not speak: they would not have been heard.
They worked with their heads down in the space of the
hum and the heat inside their own heads and thoughts.
But their consciousness was focused on each other, riveted
so that they became one in spirit as they moved back and
forth, forming one motion in the whole business of
stacking.

They passed messages along the electricity of the heat
in their arms and muscles as they lifted and handed bales
to each other, all the time their eyes bowed. To look at
each other would have shattered the concentration that
was at once an utter absorption as well as a mad attempt
to shut out the other in these dangerous times; each was
alone in the middle of this cave inside their heads into
which they had entered. Labouring and sweating, they
both hoped that it would never stop, and that eventually
they would be delivered miraculously from each other
into a peace they craved but could not seek, as the
magnetic field they inhabited pulled their bodies relentlessly
towards each other, as all the caution they could muster
pulled them the other way.

Aelred's head was filled with his own sin and with that
sin, the desire for more - not sin, but more of what that
feeling was; and at the same time he wanted to try to stop
it, the way he had tried in the dormitory before running

into Edward's cell and pulling at his habit to undress him in order to release from him himself, his sex, to him.

He remembered now that their bodies seemed to be a barrier between them and where he wanted to reach. This was what you had to do, but this was not where you wanted to arrive. The same feelings mounted in him now in the midst of this labour, and labour seemed to be a way to satisfy it. This was a way to dominate the body. As the fathers of the desert used to fast, to flagellate themselves; they hoped to become angels. But whatever he wished to heap upon his body, his mind would not be released from the obsession the body grew with.

This very pain held the pleasure.

He had an instinct for water, to continually wash his hands with cool water, to bathe his body in the water of a cool stream, to still this mind, this body, to cleanse it all in some new baptism which would render him safe from all that he felt. And yet, at once, he desired more than anything else not to be saved from this, but to give himself up utterly to all that his desire dictated.

Edward worked now at the same time, in an attempt to silence his own words, so unconsciously slipped out the day before, that he loved this fellow novice of his. Edward did not understand his feelings in the same way. They came upon him, came out of him, as his words 'I love you,' had come out; as he said them he discovered that those really were his feelings. In the same way, Aelred's actions had made explicit his own desires. Since Aelred had fled with his words, 'No, it's not possible,' ringing in his ears, Edward regretted his actions. Not that he knew clearly what would be possible, but he was prepared to discover, or at least not to prevent it any more.

Suddenly, the clatter of the conveyor stopped, and Brother Martin shouted up, 'There's water down here for you two.'

Aelred looked down. 'I'll just have a rest,' he called down to Brother Martin. Edward remained silent higher up in the barn, where a shaft of light came through laden with dust. Aelred lay down where he sat near the top of the conveyor. He could hear Brother Martin walking off into the farm buildings.

In the distance, they heard the hum of the baler and the tractor going about the field collecting the next batch of bales. Aelred closed his eyes.

A fly buzzed.

Aelred entered a vortex of heat and humming, which seemed to create a timeless zone in which he remained a long time.

Edward sat and stared down at the other novice lying on his back, his eyes closed. He regretted his words, 'No, it's not possible,' and wanted the love he felt for this other man to be possible, and yet he didn't know how, with the hard prohibitions his conscience delivered. How, with this body and all that he had been taught, could it be possible? And here?

They would be angels.

It seemed as if they remained a long time like this, suspended in a kind of ecstasy. In this long time, Ashton Park, in the heat of this summer afternoon, held fast its secrets: secrets which had to come out.

But first, Aelred went back in his mind to home in this heat, to Malgretoute and the cane fields and playing in the sun with his friend Ted. In his anxiety and strange descending melancholia, he missed Ted and longed for the return of those days. In the heat, he descended into a reverie, a dream of Ted, when they were still boys running alongside the canals between the cane fields, bathing naked in the muddy water, entering those innocent games, playing with their totees, growing up, and those games becoming more dangerous. On the boat, that image which entered so many of his dreams, licking salt water off Ted's shoulders and their first kiss under the house, lying in the dust and watching the spiders in their webs and cracks of light between the floorboards under Aunt Lydia's house. That was the afternoon they found the chrysalis hidden in the folds of the washing awaiting ironing by Toinette. Almost a butterfly! He recalled those long clumsy kisses once they had learnt. Then there were those afternoons at the swimming-pool when no one was around, swimming naked as deep as they could go, deeper and deeper.

Ted's face as white as powder in the coffin.

Now Aelred's daydream merged with Ashton Park.

Malgretoute became Ashton Park and he was burying Ted in Jordan's grave. They lay like twins, the brown boy with the black boy in the hole in the cemetery near the medieval chapel, but the singing was from the parish church back home. 'Let perpetual light shine upon him.' His black friends, names given, names taken away, singing the '*Tantum Ergo*'. Will he go to hell, Father? He asked the question over and over of Dom Maurus, until he woke startled, falling off the bale of hay into the silence of the barn and the humming of the tractor in the upper field.

Aelred opened his eyes and Edward was standing over him, looking down into his face. He made to sit up, rising on his elbows, dazed and not quite seeing Edward's face clearly against the light and the shafts laden with dust.

'You startled me.'

'Sorry. I want to talk.'

'Yes? What? I know what you said. It's not possible. You are right.'

'That's just it. I didn't mean it. Yes, I mean, I did mean it, but that doesn't mean that I don't feel what you feel and want to do what you want to do.'

Aelred was now sitting up and Edward was kneeling in front of him. They looked at each other. They were both at the centre of the humming, the humming which was the distant tractor, the sun on the zinc roof of the Dutch barn, and the confusion of emotions that they both carried since they had last talked and seen each other in the dormitory. They were alone and their eyes said different things to the words of their first exchange. Their eyes were confused. They spoke of a tangle of emotions that needed to be expressed but were difficult to talk about, and even more difficult to control.

They wanted to control their hands as they both reached out at the same time to hold each other's hands where they were buried in the loose hay, trying to hide themselves. Aelred was sitting and Edward was kneeling in front of him. Edward lay his hands in Aelred's lap and Aelred held them in his. They stayed like this, looking at each other and waiting.

They waited for words, but no words came; no words could be found by either monk to express the intensity of his feelings, the complexity of his emotions and the con- tradictions that ran through his mind.

They had always suffered the same contradictions, but had in the first place dealt with them differently. Aelred had acted on impulse in the dormitory and Edward had resisted. But now they both suffered the same contradiction, each feeling powerfully drawn to the other but wanting to resist.

Edward, because he felt that he must make Aelred feel that he wanted this too, leant towards him, still letting his hands be held in Aelred's. At first he leant his cheek against his in the custom of the monastic kiss, to the left and to the right, their heads and cheeks touching. As he drew away and faced Aelred's full face, he took in all his fellow novice's face, brown and flushed hot by the summer's day and the excitement of their emotions. As if they each knew at the same time the intention of the other, they leant towards each other, Aelred sitting and Edward still kneeling with his hands in Aelred's on his lap.

They kissed each other on the mouth. Edward let his lips stay on Aelred's and then Aelred opened his mouth, inviting Edward to do the same, so that their tongues touched, dry and then quickly moist with saliva. Aelred beckoned Edward's tongue into his mouth, so that he could suck on it. Aelred leant back on the bale of hay so that Edward no longer knelt, but raised himself to lie on top of him. All the time, they kept kissing with open mouths deeper than ever in the vortex of the heat and the humming afternoon, electric through their skin and their denim working smocks. They lay like this, then rolled over, so Aelred lay on top of Edward, pushing his tongue into his mouth.

They inhaled each other's smells and felt the weight of each other's bodies. Words were murmurs and sighs.

They had forgotten the afternoon and their fellow monks haymaking. They had forgotten Brother Martin waiting for the new load of hay. They were lost in each other, and then suddenly jolted out of that lostness by the arrival of the tractor from the top field.

The two novices rose where they lay on the bales of hay clinging to each other, their faces wet with their kisses, their hands damp with the heat and the excitement of their transgression.

'We must stop,' Aelred said. Edward still clung and still they kissed, while the first bales were delivered. 'We must stop.' Aelred's voice got lost in the rattle of the conveyor. Edward broke away and returned to the upper level to receive the bales from Aelred. They worked furiously to catch up with the bales which were coming fast.

They worked together.

Now they looked at each other, their eyes seeking each other out. They smiled. In passing the bales to Edward, Aelred let his fingers clutch at his where they clutched at the taut string which bound the bales. They were both impelled to hold to each other. Now they were dwelling in a void in which there was no thought, no prohibition, no caution, but only a current of feeling. They worked like this till there were no more bales.

Brother Martin called up, 'That's the last load, I'll be off now.'

Aelred and Edward slumped against each other.

In the silence, they heard the monks from the field come down the gravel drive and clomp across the concrete of the farmyard. Aelred looked down to see the last monks going up to the abbey. Then he saw Benedict on his own, walking up slowly through the apple orchard. Seeing him, he felt lonely and he felt that he was betraying his friend, the one of whom he was beloved.

Aelred now understood something else about this question of love. He had basked in the glow of being loved by Benedict. The older man had wooed him and he had given in. Yes, there was the love he felt for him as a brother, and a love which was the love of a son for a father. These were mixed in with them being lovers, monastic lovers in a quest for a dangerous chastity. Benedict had forced this. He was the one who was tempted for more, a more which would make monastic life impossible. That power of feeling was then experienced by Aelred. The sexual feelings he felt for Benedict seemed integrated and pure and an expression of his love. But these feelings he had now with Edward, and which he had always felt, did not seem to be those of love - not the love which he had for Benedict. They were feelings that possessed him and left him without choice.

As Aelred watched Benedict climb the hill through the apple orchard, half of him wished to be at his side talking and feeling close in the way they had managed their dangerous chastity. Maybe, just as they passed behind the high hedges, they might steal a kiss and rest within each other's embrace. That would be enough for the flesh, as it were, as they made their love an emblem of that love of Christ for his church, in their own mystical marriage. They made it an expression of Christ's love for his disciples, his love for the beloved disciple, John, who had lain on his breast at the Last Supper. It was like Jonathan's love for David, Aelred of Rievaulx's love for Simon. It was in the end, a spiritual friendship.

It was circumscribed with prohibition. It fed on the sight of the beloved: on the touch of the hand, on the monastic kiss, and on embrace. It had to stop there.

Aelred ached for what he had achieved with Benedict, compared with what he now felt as he stood in the barn with Edward, looking at his friend disappear behind the hedges, along the path leading up to the church.

The farm was now deserted.

As Aelred turned towards Edward, the bell sounded across the valley and echoed through the estate and the farmyard calling the monks to Compline, their night prayers.

What were they still doing here? They seemed unable to leave this place, this hideaway that had witnessed their first kisses. As the bell continued signalling a way of life they were a part of, but which they were not allowing to command them, they drew close to each other. First their fingers, then their eyes, seeking, searching out, where words were not possible and thought did not exist.

They gave the monastic kiss to start with, still nervous and new to each other. They held each other in that embrace of fraternal love and decorum. They brushed their cheeks against each other and rested their heads against each other as they would at the '*Agnus Dei*' during Mass, or when they offered greetings on feast days.

They held on, waiting. In intervals of inactivity, they became in tune, learning to move with each other in a common sensation, tentative, trying out.

Aelred brought a knowledge of his body which he had learnt with Ted, and he noticed that images from the past flashed through his mind like a kind of pornography, their bright boys' bodies in the sun, perspiration and salt water on their skins.

He knew where he could be touched, and he knew

where his boyhood friend liked to be touched.

Then the image of Ted diving into the pool. He jack-knifed into the bronze pool, red like flamboyante.

Even here, even now.

But he waited. He did not want to take the lead, but then knew that he might have to.

This had not happened to Edward before, but, as in the dormitory, his own desires became embodied now in the other novice's desires. So, ever so slowly, Edward let Aelred teach him and lead the way. Their eyes took in each other's faces and they began to kiss as they had done earlier. They kissed and smelt the fresh sweat on their faces and work smocks. Together, still kissing, they lay down on the bales. Aelred, still leading, undid Edward's belt so that his smock hung loose. He ran his hands under the smock over Edward's chest and played with the hair that ran upwards from his groin. He encircled the nipples on his chest with his fingers, tracing his desire, all the time kissing his lips and looking for his open eyes.

They did not speak.

A gentle breeze came into the barn.

Edward, in his shyness, kept closing his eyes. He lay back while Aelred kept on leading. Then Edward sat up and undid the belt of Aelred's smock and raised it up over his chest. Going further than his tutor, he kissed the skin which was open between the straps of the denim overalls.

This symbolised a change: each was now as bold as the other. Their gradual undressing was mutual in its desire and in the help they gave each other, till they lay naked against each other's warm skin, wet with fresh sweat. Each together, and in turn, rubbed their hands along each other's arms and legs, over each others' chests, leaving for last their erect penises, as if scared of where all this was leading. It was as if they did not know what to do. It was as if in the midst of all this knowing, there was profound innocence.

They made a soft bed of their discarded monastic smocks in the hay.

Aelred eased himself down between Edward's legs and took his penis in his hands, stroking it and licking the tip of it and then the length of it, till he put the penis into his mouth and sucked it gently. Edward lay back sighing and then saying, 'Let me do that to you.'

These were the first words to bring them and their love-making into any kind of consciousness. Aelred raised himself and lay back on the bales of hay while Edward lay on top of him with the full weight of his tall naked body. They kissed and kissed. Then Edward, in turn, eased himself down between Aelred's legs and followed his tutor in love, in the stroking, licking and sucking of his penis.

As Aelred looked up into the roof of the barn, he noticed the cracks of light which he had noticed earlier. The bands of light which were laden with dust were gone.

The barn was another world. The evening had declined and the sun no longer shone on the open side of the barn. Aelred could see that the sky was black-blue, and just visible was the first star of the evening.

For a fleeting second, Aelred's mind went back to Benedict and to his fellow monks in choir. Instinctually, he heard the words of the lesson: 'Brothers, be sober and watch, because your adversary, the devil, like a roaring lion, goes about seeking whom he may devour.' But as the changing evening had almost eluded him, the phrases in the admonition slipped out of his mind as easily as they had entered.

He was not choosing sin. He was in the power of whatever this was, on a quest with a companion as eager as himself.

In what was a respite, but about to plunge them deeper into a current of these feelings, they both lay back on their backs, looking up at the first evening star, a piece of jagged silver.

They were now separate. This gave them time to reconstitute themselves. Their limbs were like water, or a fire that runs through young grass.

They did not choose to leave the barn. They did not debate the missing of Compline. Instinct dictated that they did not lose this moment. It felt like a moment to which each of their lives so far had been a journey, a secret quest. Their secret history. Aelred had had his companion in boyhood and lost him in death. Edward had journeyed without knowing the quest. Their phantoms had slipped away after waking from dreams.

They noticed their nakedness. They looked at each other and smiled.

Edward rolled on to his stomach and Aelred rearranged the bed of their clothes, their denim smocks, for them to lie on. Just brushing against each other made them tingle with anticipation. To look at each other's naked bodies was wonder enough: to trace a finger along a cheekbone, to run a hand over a shoulder - each gesture became a young life's journey of discovery.

Aelred stroked the nape of Edward's neck. He ran his fingers through the hair at the back of his head. He ran his hands down his back to the end of his spine where his buttocks separated and each was smooth and soft with a down of blond hair. His fingers slipped between Edward's buttocks, where the down of hair was wilder, bristly and moist. There, the skin of the anus was soft and wet with fresh sweat. Aelred lowered himself, licking the skin on Edward's back. He lowered himself to rest his cheeks on his buttocks and kissed their downy softness. Gently, he opened, with his fingers, the hole of his anus. Edward sighed with the twinge of pain. Aelred lowered himself more, in order to lick his anus and smell the fresh sweat and musty scent. Edward's anus, at first tight, yielded to the licking and the insertion of Aelred's finger. He sighed, not with pain, but with a pleasure, a pleasure mixed with pain, a pleasure that was a kind of pain. It came from somewhere he had not been before.

Edward turned over suddenly and sat up. He took Aelred's head in his hands, and he took his whole mouth into his in a joyous claim, wanting to take back what had been taken from him. Aelred yielded his possession and more, as Edward turned him over on his stomach, and like his tutor, the student in love practised his art of licking and fingering.

'I love you,' he said over his shoulder.

'I love you,' said the other: the same words, spoken at the same time, the speakers indistinguishable.

Their discoveries followed this mutuality.

But it was Aelred, knowing his body from boyhood with Ted, who was the first to spit into his hand and run his saliva over his penis. Then he eased his penis into Edward's anus, which was soft and now more yielding. Their closeness was as never before, and Aelred slipped out so that Edward might ease his penis into him. Together they alternated in this pleasure and rehearsed the ceremony they had discovered in their nakedness. Kissing, sucking and licking, they trembled within each other, till they each ejaculated into and over each other with their fresh semen, its pure strong smell mixing with their sweat and saliva, where they lay together, holding and clinging, as the black-blue of the sky with the first evening star, changed to darkness, and the whole firmament was now a constellation of stars. They lay there, beneath its immensity.

And at least now, even if later it was to be endangered or even lost altogether, the inherited fear, shame and guilt of these actions did not exist with the horror in which they had been described in ancient spiritual writings. Rather, they existed as jewels as bright as those in the firmament above them, and under which they slept the sleep of those who know and shun innocence for ever.

'It's so good,' Edward said.

'Yes, this is good.' Aelred echoed his friend.

They lay entwined together. In their dreams, they feared the sunrise and dreaded the dawn.

I sleep, but my heart is awake.
I hear my beloved knocking.
My head is covered with dew,
my locks with the drops of night.
I have taken off my tunic,
am I to put it on again?
I have washed my feet,
am I to dirty them again?
              Song of Songs

The Lodge:

My cheeks burn. I've burnt my fingers.

I used to notice Miriam leaving the room when Joe got graphic about what goes on in gay clubs or saunas, or out in the 'cruising ground' as he calls it, being ironic and a little nostalgic at the same time. Miriam explains the latter to me.

Then Joe says to me, You need to read what your brother says. You need to read those bits of the journal that are explicit about the sex he had with Edward or what he did with Benedict. That's part of your brother. That is your brother, your religious brother.

We'd gone out and bought some more rum in the St Paul's area.

There's no point reviving some sanitised, saintly, idealistic view of him. Even if that nineteen-year-old youth might've written up his wild temptations and fallings into sin as if he were a medieval or a Hopkinesque pantheist.

The rum is working. I strum on my cuatro, 'All day all night Miss Mary Ann ...'

It will not be the truth if you don't put in the dirty bits, Joe says.

Joe! Miriam exclaims.

But then, Joe goes on, wasn't he in the writing of those very bits actually placing those accounts alongside equally lurid accounts by Aelred of Revaulx in his own idiom, about masturbation, for example? What does he talk about - that gushing slime, the concupiscence? Joe relishes the word. I think, Joe says, that your brother was trying to redeem the body, take the body away from that demolition site that the church has taken it to. Church and state!

Joe and his demolition site! We laugh. Miriam comes back into the room.

She says, I find your brother's struggle moving and beautiful and tragic. He was young, fired by Benedict, by the poetry, the ideas.

By Edward's stunning good looks, Joe interjects.

By beauty, Miriam explains. He's writing about beauty and what it does to us. But she says she doesn't want to know all that goes on down by the docks or up some alley. She's not being judgemental, she says, though she thinks she has her reservations. She just doesn't want to hear the details. Some of it worries her and offends her.

J. M. doesn't offend me, she says. I think that, yes, in times of prohibition you steal your moments anywhere, but with more freedom let's leave those places, she says.

That's when Joe says, That's shit! People won't be liberated in a decade even. Anyway, PC politics doesn't change everything. There's a hell of a lot of prejudice and hate out there still, enshrined in law. There's a lot of internalised shame and guilt. I know, Joe says. He continues. Why is sodomy criminalised? Sodomy! The very word.

It's for men and women too, heterosexual sex, Miriam says.

Yes, says Joe, but why?

I listen and say, We should have this discussion in Les Deux Isles on TV. Come and see what hate is like from priests, immams, pundits and fundamentalist preachers of hell and damnation. It's like the mid-west in America.

That stuff gets beamed down to the backyard. Then I venture an opinion. Isn't sodomy, I mean anal sex, unsafe now, anyway?

It can be, Robert, of course, Joe jumps in, but it can be made safe. We make it safe for pregnancy so why not for disease. It's safe for other diseases, so why not AIDS? Yes, I agree. We must be safer.

Even for Miriam and Joe, certainly for me, the acronym can be a heavy sound in a discussion.

We must demythologise our hate of the homoerotic, Joe proclaims. Coming back to J. M. I think that's what he was trying to do. Poor bastard, at nineteen in 1963 in a monastery of screwed-up theologians and moral philosophers. Sick.

Joe! Really! Miriam says. Get a balance. You know that's not half the truth. That's not J.M.'s story. Get off your soapbox. We must respect all his story.

Miriam notices that I go silent. Miriam and I smile at each other; Joe leaves the room.

You must forgive him. You know he was the first person they met when they left. He's angry but he's hurt, very sore. He was their friend for fourteen years or so.

I know, I say. Some of it is too much for me, too much too quickly. You're both right. I'm lucky to have you.

There was an account in the journal of 'The Raid,' as J. M. called it. I call it rape. J. M. going over the ground.

I have the debates going in my head.

The ground is beaten smooth. One of the dens where we boys come to smoke. The wind in the high trees howling, crying. We are both crying and looking at each other. Made to lie side by side face down.

Stripped naked. Pinned down.

We enter each other's eyes, watery. Here in this luminous eye we see only each other. This is where we have curled, into each other's eyes. To hide. We ravel up our selves. Only the roar of the wind. All ears. The river at the bottom of the valley. Sunlight on rocks. All ears. Parrots higher than the trees. Green in the blue. Imagine for an instant. Don't imagine. We leave our bodies on the ground and ascend above them and look down. We look down. They are used by them. Utterly. We utter nothing. Someone says PLEASE. Someone says STOP. One goes in. One comes out. One goes in. One comes out. There is a crowd in there. Entrance. Exit. Pressing. How many more can fit into this room. It is a small room. It is small. It is little. Little. Very little.

The eye is the window to the soul. We climb through the eye into the soul. We leave the body.

The temple. The body is the temple of the Holy Ghost.

Now the room is so deserted. So abandoned. And the curtain of the temple was rent in two. But still it feels full as if that is its natural state. To be so filled up. Then emptied. Empty yourself. Then we can't feel. I can't feel anything, there, can you? Numb. I want to feel. I want to feel.

I don't want to feel.

Fill me, fill me up!

Cleanse me.

Empty. Be emptied.

We climb back out of the eye, out of the window to the soul, into our bodies. Only the wind in the high trees. The sound of water over rocks. How ravaged. We curl into each other. Where in the world is there a place for us? Where can we stand in the open and say what has been done here? Who will listen?

We gather each other's clothes, helping with sleeves and necks. We use spit to clean off the dirt. It smears. Makes a stain.

Stainless. Pure. Like shit. Smell of shit and blood. And numb-
ness. Will we die?

I want to feel. Don't touch me. Who says that? Where do we
go?

We stumble down to the river. Look at what's happened.

The rock pool runs red with our blood. This is my blood which
shall be poured out for you. Blood over blue stones.

We wash our bodies in the River Jordan.

That was one way in which he saw it. Who can imagine
these two young boys, sixteen, with their fellow pupils, sixteen? 'The Raid.' What state of mind was J. M. in when he
wrote that? There's an early version and then it's embellished some years later. This is the embellished version.

I was there. It staggers me. It shocks me profoundly. I
was thirteen.

Miriam says, You can't beat yourself for something you
did or didn't do when you were a boy.

I don't fully remember what I did with my thoughts
about what I heard they had done to my brother and his
friend.

The new term began as if nothing had ever happened.
There must be no scandal. There must be forgiveness. I
sometimes saw those boys queuing for confession.

Until that afternoon. They stand all around. Out of the
blue. I am there again as witness. A witness for the prosecution. But who does the prosecuting?

Words. Made to eat my words. Testaments.

Fill up. Empty.

The Abbot, whom I've spoken to again, said that there
was a tradition of fasting, but it must be done with approval, and in moderation. Benedict had gone beyond what

was recommended.

So, he did kill himself then?

Who can judge? the Abbot asks. It's a matter of judgement. Think of the common good. Lest any be scandalised.

'*Take this and eat, for this is my body.*'

I pick up all these implicit and explicit meanings in his writing. His puns. His poetry is a poetry of pain.

The Vigils

We will spend the night in the villages,
and in the morning we will go to the vineyards
Song of Songs

Aelred, Abbot of Rievaulx, kept his vigils, while his monks slept till the bells woke them for Matins. It was a warm night. He knelt at the window of the small oratorium off his cell. The black-blue sky was laden with stars. It hung as low as the trees along the Rye. It smelt of rain. The closeness of the clouds spoke of an impending storm.

Particularly, the Abbot prayed for his young novices, prey to the stealth of seductive dreams and restless nights, bewitched by evil thoughts; they might be tempted in the heat of the night to give expression to these phantoms. The novices slept close to each other, as the Rule stipulated. Their belts were undone. Their young bodies lay within their rough woollen habits, their legs and arms free.

Aelred knew of his young monks' temptations, because they had been his own, and could still be, as he watched the beautiful young men who entered the monastery seeking to sublimate their desires among men who lived to love one another. He was forced to take some of them, who were rough and prone to anger and fighting. He tamed their carnal spirits with the ideals of spiritual tenderness.

On this night, his lover from his youth, the one whom he had loved so extravagantly and more than any other, at the court of Scotland, entered his cell. He could smell him. He knew it was the work of the devil that made him enter his cell, now, at the open window with the sky lowering black and blue, beckoning him into his arms with that smile which had bewitched him as a youth.

He had stroked those arms and legs. He had kissed those lips. He had stroked that back, which he saw as the figure turned.

Aelred knelt and prayed before the naked and crucified figure of his beloved Christ hanging on the wall to take the phantom of his past away, to let him not be weakened, lest he lose the guardianship of his young monks, asleep before Matins was called.

Then the figure of Christ turned into the one whom he had loved so extravagantly. He hung naked as his beloved Saviour. He raised his lowered head. He smiled at him with a gesture of his eyes and a movement of his lips, inviting him to come and kiss his feet where the nails were driven; to come, climb up and put his hand into the wound on his side, to finger where the nails were skewered into his hands; to come and cradle his ill-used head, which was crowned with thorns. He beckoned him to do these things and not disbelieve his love like a doubting Thomas.

Aelred was torn between the image of his prayer, which was his true Christ, and this phantom lover of his past who sought to trick him.

But Aelred had fought this battle before. He had arranged his own tricks for the phantoms of evil, when he could not resist any longer the temptations which risked him losing touch with his innocent novices and their temptations.

He took down off the wall of his cell the monastic discipline, the strands of cord, each strand knotted at intervals. Five strands for the five wounds of Christ. Hard

as iron, pitted like stone. With this whip, he would drive
the tempting phantom from his cell, drive away the seducer,
just as Christ had driven the money-changers from the
temple.

He knelt in front of his crucified Lord, who was still in
the semblance of his lost loved one. His loincloth had
fallen to the ground. His sex was erect.

Aelred knelt, tearing his woollen habit from his frame.
He bent forward. With the whip, he lashed his back over
the right shoulder and then over the left shoulder. He
continued this flagellation of himself till his lover came
down from the cross and left there the image of his sweet
Lord.

Back at the window, the phantom was reluctant to
leave.

Even after he felt that he had performed his task, he
could be tricked. His scent still lingered in the cell.

Weakened and bleeding, he would begin again. But by
a strange alchemy, this very abuse and humiliation of his
flesh could be the door through which pleasure walked.
There, he was in his lover's arms again.

He went to the corner of the oratorium, where he had
had a hole excavated above the cold stream which flowed
into the River Rye. This was his ultimate trick for the evil
one. He lifted the stone cover of the hole. Still stripped
naked in the cold night, he lowered his burning body
into the icy cold water. Standing there, holding on tightly,
while the fast currents rushed about his legs and torso, he
could feel his passion leave him with the shock of the cold
water.

Naked and wet, he stood silently in the middle of his
cell and felt the night settle about him. His sweet Lord

reassembled himself on the cross.

The bells for Matins rang out over the valley, scattering sleep before dawn, and Aelred felt confident that he had saved himself and his young novices from the evil one who stalked his monastery like a roaring lion going about seeking whom he might devour.

Aelred and Edward slept in each other's arms through the first hours of the night, after their lovemaking and their belief in the goodness of their deeds. The warmth and the comfort of the barn and each other's bodies cushioned and blanketed them, swaddling them in an innocence which lasted for those few hours. Aelred was the first to wake and his mood turned to apprehension, finding himself naked, clinging to Edward in the chill of the night. He pulled his smock over his head and put his arms into the sleeves. There was the smell of the fresh hay. The inside of the barn was dark and loomed above them. The side of the barn that was open showed a faint starlight and half a moon, a slice of lime. The apple trees in the nearby orchard rustled in the night breeze. Aelred lay, looking up into the barn and letting the events of the day and night before unfold. Slowly, anxiety began to build. What had happened began to fill him with a dread.

'Edward,' Aelred whispered, 'Edward.' He shook his shoulder which felt clammy because of the heat of the barn mixed with the chill of the night.

'What is it? What is it?' Edward woke, startled and, turning, he clung to Aelred. 'Yes, yes.' He then sat up suddenly. 'Where are we?' His arms falling around Aelred's neck and shoulders.

'Don't you remember? We've spent the night in the barn after hay-making.'

'God, I didn't know where I was.' He looked at his nakedness, standing up and fetching his smock which somehow had got pushed away from where they slept. He knelt near Aelred. 'What have we done?'

'We've missed Compline. Well, we would've anyway, being late from haymaking. But then we should've got a blessing from the Abbot. Maybe no one noticed. What time do you think it is? It's still very dark. But it could be near Matins.'

'I mean, what have we done? Oh! I think it's about one or two in the morning. It will be another two hours at least before the bells for Matins.' Edward had stumbled in the hay to the edge of the open side of the barn to make his judgements by the light of the night sky. Then he turned to Aelred and said, 'You know, there's a clock above the dairy. Maybe I could go down and check the time.'

'Don't you think we should return to the novitiate while everyone's still asleep? What do you think?'

'No, I want to stay here a while, talk a while and be with each other and assess what we've done.' Edward sounded very decisive, so Aelred agreed.

'Take care as you climb down the ladder in the dark. Should I come with you? Can you bring up some water? There must be something down there. Actually, there's a metal cup left by that tap where Brother Martin said we could get water. Take care.'

Edward took off his smock quickly, and pulled on his overalls and then the smock once more. He left it loose, as he could not find his girdle. His head disappeared over the side of the barn, where the long ladder was left standing against it, leading down to the bottom of the conveyor.

It was only when Edward had returned with the metal cup of water, spilling it as he climbed back up the ladder and stumbled over the hay to where Aelred was sitting up that their mood turned into fear as the full realisation of their transgression began to dawn on them. They wiped the sleep from their eyes. They sipped the water, sharing the cup from hand to hand. The nature of their transgression grew.

'We've slept all night in the barn, been here from the previous evening, missed Compline and slept out of the dormitory.' Edward went over the events, taking stock. He had to remind himself.

'Yes, yes, yes,' Aelred said, getting agitated. 'Not only that!'

'I'm hungry.' Edward said.

'Here, have some more water.'

'I thought the storm would've broken last night.'

'No, the atmosphere is still very tight.'

'Don't be worried.' Edward took Aelred's hand.

'But it is worrying.'

'Yes, but we can't undo it, what we've done. You wouldn't want to, would you?'

'No, I wouldn't want to.' His hand stroked Edward's face. 'But another part of me wishes that we had not gone that far. It was as if we were not thinking any more. Not choosing. It chose us. I can't remember. I can't believe what we've done.'

'I can. I want to do it again. I want to make love to you again, even now.' Edward was emphatic. 'Kiss me. Your lips are cracked.'

'Edward! Let's do what you suggested. Let's talk. Then let's go to our cells so that we will be in time for Matins. I want to go to Matins. I want to see Father Basil. No, I need to talk to someone else.'

'Talk to me.'

'No, you talk to me. No, someone else who is not you.'

'Why Father Basil?'

'He's my confessor. He understands. He knows about these feelings, about these temptations; about things like this happening as well, I'm sure.'

'Why? How do you know?'

'He told me. Well, at any rate, he suggested it. He told me about himself and Sebastian.'

'Sebastian? Who? Sebastian who has just died?'

'Yes, they were friends. That's how he described it. They lay in each other's arms in a field one summer.'

'God! Did they? How old is he?'

'Must be in his seventies. But when he talked it was as if he was as young as you and I are.'

'But why did he tell you that? For what reason would he come out with things like that to a novice? What, during confession? Anyway, it's your confession.'

'It was while we were digging Sebastian's grave. He was moved, I suppose.'

'Still, I find it strange that he confided in you. He must've felt that he could. That you would understand.'

'Yes.'

'What do you mean, yes?'

'Oh, God, so many questions. We're supposed to be talking about what we've done. It's all so quick. Only yesterday.'

'Is it? So quick? Only yesterday, yes, that we began to

talk. But what's been going on before? You at the quarry each day. I wanted you there. I noticed you. I wanted you to look at me. I came to want you to smell my clothes. I wished I was my clothes, that you were smelling me. I knew. You let yourself be known. You didn't know. I'm sorry. That was cheating.'

'No. Yes, I've - there's more I've had to confess, things to Basil. Things like this, almost, what we've done.'

'With whom? With whom? No - yes - I can't believe it. Yes, of course. Benedict.'

'Don't say it like that.' Aelred recalled Benedict walking up through the apple orchard yesterday evening, when he felt that he wanted to run out to meet him and to go with him, to hold his hand, to kiss him behind the tall hedges on the path from the orchard. He had not. He had stayed with Edward. He had stayed and look what had happened. 'Don't say it like that.'

'Benedict. All the time, and me stumbling to tell him. Me confusedly talking about emotions between men. He must've known all along that it was you. Who else could it be? Who else but you and your lovely face? Who else? He would know. He had got there first.'

'Edward! Edward! It's not what you imagine. Benedict - you don't know Benedict. He's so strong. He put a stop to it. We got nowhere. He has not got there first. I love him. Please don't talk about him without respect. I love him.'

'You love him? What do you mean you love him? What have we done? What is it that you feel for me, then? You've never said, have you? I said I loved you in the library. You've not been able to say that.'

'I said it last night. I said it to you last night .'

'I don't remember.'

'No, we don't remember the words. There were hardly any words. But I did say it. What did you think I showed you? I've given you everything. I've not given him anything.'

'Yes, you have. You've given him your respect.'

'He doesn't think that. He thinks I endanger his vocation, his final vows.'

'Yes, you've given him your abstentions. You can both be monks. You've lost it with me. We've endangered ourselves.'

'Yes, we have and that's why I want to talk with Basil.'

'Who will I talk to?'

'Who's your confessor?'

'Father Dominic. I don't know why. It was suggested that he was one of the confessors for the novices. My confessions are very mechanical. I've not really talked about my real concerns, about you.'

'Well, there's no reason why you shouldn't see Basil too. Maybe Basil will talk to both of us. We must use those who have gone before. Aelred of Rievaulx, Basil and Sebastian.'

'What about Benedict?'

'I don't know. This isn't what he meant by sorting out our differences.'

'But he's no fool. He knows that I felt attracted to you.'

'Well, like Aelred of Rievaulx, he felt that we should explore it and use it for our spiritual life.'

'It must be dawn.'

'The bells for Matins will ring out soon. Maybe we should make our way to the novitiate. Have you seen my belt?'

'Yes, here it is. I long for everything to return to normal. We must try hard.'

Aelred and Edward sat at the edge of the barn and watched the first swallows emerge from the eaves above the dairy. The birds from Africa clicked and swooped. The novices watched the night turning into the beginnings of dawn.

'We call this "foreday morning" back in Les Deux Isles.'

'The dawn before the dawn?'

'Yes. See the swallows.'

They sat lost in their own thoughts.

Aelred watched the park emerge from the night into the day. 'That foreday morning they find Mungo body hanging from the mango tree down Hangman Alley.' Toinette begins to close her story.

Aelred tells his own stories to himself.

Dark clouds are moving fast in the sky above. I lie low with my heart.

I cannot let another night like last night happen to me. I cannot stay with my bundle in the stable. I cannot stay near the contraptions.

I hide last night away. But I cannot keep it a secret from myself.

Master Walter come back drunk from a drinking bout. I must watch him in that state. For then he can fly into a fury. But tonight is different. He is stumbling around in the stable with his breeches down and he is calling wildly for his little nigger boy. I want to be one of those mice that live under the straw and bite me in the night. He is standing over me, Master Walter. I pretend to sleep even when he kick me. Even when I feel the hot stream of piss over my face. Even when he kick me again. Even when he kneel and open my mouth for the hot stream of piss. Even when I choke and vomit. Even when he finish with his pissing and even when he find my mouth a soft and slippery hole for his member. And he straining and straining and it won't finish, it won't finish till what he do I cannot tell you. For my mouth is suffocated against the straw and he is humped on my back like a pig at the trough. Even then I am asleep, even then I sleep when he fall over me breathing and sighing, so that even this stinking hulk feel like some tender pig in its trough. Is the first time that I hear Master Walter sigh and mumble softly to himself. I think, is not him. Is not me. I asleep.

But I cannot sleep when Master Walter revive and he drag me to the room with the peeping hole and the contraptions and where he hang me against the wall to whip me. He remember who I is. Then I cannot sleep but remain till dawn when Miss Amy come to collect my body in a heap against the wall of the stable where he, Master Walter, drag me and drop me.

She has water and lint to sop and assuage.

I know that the darkness is my protection so I stay out in the fields all night. I crouch between the hayricks at the bottom of the field where earlier in the day I hide the small parcel of food Miss Amy give me for my journey. You must keep out of the way of Master Walter in the daytime, my lad, and at night you must not stay where he thinks you lie asleep, for then you are easy prey. You are a quarry for his hunt. You must go out into the darkness. Your blackness will help you, my lad. Out in the night he will not find you if you hide in the fields. You sprinkle this cayenne near the entrance to the hayrick and the scent will disturb the dogs, put them off your smell.

Miss Amy have everything plan for me.

When I know that my master is eating his supper and will not be calling for me, so will not be missing me, I go out into the darkness and make for the hayrick at the bottom of the field. I lie there thinking my own thoughts, which are commonly of those other times I have to save myself from a cruel master. I cannot bring myself to leave altogether. For where do I run in England? I is dependent on Miss Amy and her kindness. But for how long can I depend upon it? I must plan to run.

Dripping wet from his baptism of immersion, Aelred of Rievaulx waited in his cold nakedness for his phantoms to retreat into their darkness. In the corner of his oratorium, below the stone lid, the rushing water, normally icy cold, bubbled and steamed with his passion, in the way of the best-written hagiography.

The one whom he had loved extravagantly from the court of Scotland was still hanging from the cross where his Christ should have hung. He hung within his Saviour's figure, but was fading by the power of the Abbot's will and the grace of God. He still tried to smile and invite him to climb up into his embrace, but instead, Aelred lay down naked upon the cold flagstones of his cell in the form of a cross and waited for the last of the evil passion to leave his body and his cell.

He was woken from his prayer by a knock on his door. It continued. When he registered the knocking, it seemed as if he had been lost in prayer for hours. When he looked up at the crucifix, the image of his Saviour hung in his simple pristine state, the image of the one who had died for his sins.

Aelred rose and covered his nakedness with his woollen habit. After he had buckled his sandals and rearranged his scapular, so that all looked normal and appropriately decorous, he approached the door and the now frantic knocking. The apparition, as it seemed, that presented itself to the worn Abbot after his own personal ordeal with the evil one was of two of his young novices, Ivo and Gratian.

They were drenched and their woollen habits hung sodden and clinging to their wet bodies. Their hoods were still on, hugging their heads and shoulders. They fell to their knees. 'Father, forgive us,' they beseeched, in unison, with raised heads and forlorn eyes. They put out their arms to touch the hem of his habit. He knelt to meet them and lift them up from where they knelt abjectly, asking for forgiveness. 'Bless us, Father, for we have sinned.'

'My sons,' he interrupted them, taking their words into his mouth with kisses on their cheeks and lips, drawing them to him as a mother who suckles her young babes, as a father in heaven saves his drowning sons from the dangerous cataracts. 'My sons.' He warmed their shivering bodies, lifting them up, walking them, an arm around the shoulders of each, into his cell and sitting them near the fireplace. He soon kindled a flame in the embers of the fire of the night before and warmed a little wine he allowed himself for his arthritis.

'My brothers, sit and tell me your troubles. Unburden to me the torments of your minds and bodies, for which you beseech so earnestly for forgiveness. How can I forgive if there has been no transgression, no sin, no offence against Our Lord, your brethren, or your dear father and brother, myself? Tell me, dear friends.'

They looked at each other, their eyes holding both terror and fear. They looked at their holy Abbot. They cast their eyes into the fire. 'We were ...' They each made to speak at the same time, hoping that the other would carry on and that somehow they could be rescued now from describing what they had done.

'My sons, there is nothing to fear. You are already sorry for whatever it is you imagine you have done, and that sorrow in itself is sign of forgiveness. But draw closer to the fire and dry your damp habits. Sip some more wine and raise your spirits. Come, Ivo, my young brother,' and the Abbot Aelred drew young Ivo to him. 'Come, hold my hand, place your palms in mine and know that this is good. This feeling is good. Our bodies are good. They are the temples of the Holy Spirit. It's in these physical vessels of flesh and blood, that God sees fit to manifest himself, in the love we have for one another. Do not be afraid of this. And you, my dearest Gratian, with those angelic eyes, fear not the beauty which God has bestowed upon you; fear not that your beauty draws others to you. Believe me, brothers, your father knows your troubles before you can find words to describe them. They are already described to my eye and ear and have an ancestry in my flesh, which has warmed this very night to the phantoms that the evil one disguises himself in: masks of holiness, sometimes images most familiar and innocent. But I have prayed before them and I have, with the grace of Our Lord, staunched the flames of their rising passions, unruly, but capable of filling you with delightful feelings. Brothers, believe me, these delights leave you bereft of lasting delight, which you may have been fooled that they would give to you.'

Ivo and Gratian listened, entranced by the mellifluous wisdom and consolation which flowed from their abbot's lips.

Gratian spoke first. 'Father, how do you know these things? You don't in a direct manner say to us that you know what we have done, and yet your intimations suggest that you know almost the very details of our transgressions. The fervour of your voice convinces me ...'

'Me too,' said Ivo.

'You do indeed know, and can speak from experience, not like some of the confessors who don't seem to understand the beauty we have to resist, so that we can follow the ideals of chaste love, a love that gives and does not take.'

'You speak well, Gratian, but you must also take. We need to feed our hungry selves. All cannot be fasting and abstinence. Therefore I encourage you, dear brothers,' and Aelred drew his young monks close to him, so that the three sat huddled and warm in each other's arms. 'Hold hands, touch fingers, stroke the face of your brother so,' and he stroked their young faces and kissed them on the cheeks. 'Allow your love to gaze into your beloved's eyes. Do not resist these impulses, dear brothers, and above all put into words your love, confess your love, discuss your love, write letters of love and friendship, and allow your spiritual selves to grow in this love, which is a spiritual friendship. Cherish your friend. He who scorns friendship is an animal. God is friendship, brothers.'

'Father, I feel so good now.' Bernard took the liberty to

rest his head on his abbot's shoulder.

'And you, Ivo, you are quiet and let Gratian do all the talking.'

'I too, Father, grow to feel more reconciled to myself and to those impulses I cannot control.'

'Know, my son, that the beauty you see in Gratian, the beauty I see in Gratian is the luminosity of God's own beauty, manifested in his creation. This is good. Cherish it and cherish your feelings for it.'

'But, Father, I tempted him by my attraction to him. I flattered him so that he weakened in his chaste resolve, and because he did not want to hurt me, because he loves me, he allowed me to lead him astray. He allowed me to ...'

'And now, my sons, you must ready yourself for Matins. Don't speak of those deeds; that in itself is a way the evil one has of tempting us further: of tempting us by the power of those words that describe those deeds, to commit similar deeds, and so to be for ever entrapped by reflecting on sin rather than on the goodness of Our Lord and his immeasurable grace. So no more, and rest assured that I, your abbot, have been up all night wrestling with the evil one, so that you may be saved, and your coming straight to my door and knocking me up from my meditation is proof that God has heard my prayers and has bestowed His forgiveness upon you. Think of it no more and go get dry habits and proceed to choir for the chanting of the divine psalms.'

Ivo and Gratian left their abbot's cell in peace. Parting at the end of the corridor, they kissed each other on both cheeks and went to their cells, which they had not visited since Vespers.

The sky had lifted. The storm had broken. The River Rye was swollen and flooding the nearby surrounding fields along its bank.

As Ivo and Gratian, each in their individual cells, changed into dry habits before going to Matins and reflected on the words and wisdom of their abbot, they found themselves naked before the windows in their cells. And, looking out to the fields and the river, they each still clung to the naked body of the other in the barn amidst the warm hay and the lowing of the cattle, breathing heavily in the darkness. The storm breaking, and the rain locking them away from the monastic rhythm of the world, they could be tempted by their past misdemeanours.

In choir, in the simplicity of their church, with its bare stone and unadorned wood, kneeling, reclining, sitting, standing, chanting the Divine Office, they sought a simplicity and peace that was not as natural as the desire and passion of their night together in the barn; though their ideal was to make it so, to be angels and not men in that expression of their desire.

A thick mist shrouded the valley and all Ashton Park. The bells came to Aelred and Edward muffled, but announcing clearly enough, their call to the two novices that they should rise to sing the praises of the psalmist who rises in the night to praise his Lord. '*Domine labia mea aperies et os meum annuntiabit laudem tuam...* Lord, open my lips, and my mouth shall announce your praise ...'

Aelred and Edward rose without talking. They stood together and held on to each other. Then climbed down the ladder, one behind the other. They made their way through the apple orchard. They had to enter the house without being seen. They walked quickly and quietly. They felt like children, like naughty children, like Adam and Eve hiding in the garden in the afternoon when they heard the voice of God calling them and realised that they were naked. They had eaten of the tree of knowledge. They had yielded to the temptation of the serpent. They would have to work by the sweat of their brows. They would have to suffer. God told them so, sending his Archangel Michael with a fiery sword to drive them out of the garden.

But for Aelred and Edward, there was no burning sword, just the damp morning and a sinking feeling in their stomachs that they had lost themselves and each other, and, possibly, their vocations at St Aelred's in Ashton Park.

They had to creep up to the novitiate to change into their habits for choir.

They crept past Father Justin's room on the creaking floorboards and then they left each other, giving each other a last squeeze of the hand as they tried to make themselves invisible as they entered the corridor of the novitiate and avoid the other novices coming and going from the washroom in preparation for Matins.

Their absence would have been noticed, because on Aelred's not answering to the '*Benedicamus Domino*', the response '*Deo gratias*', as was the custom for being awakened, the acolyte of the waking would have pulled aside the cotton curtains of Aelred's cubicle and seen his empty bed. This would not have alarmed him, had it not been that he would have then had the same experience when he came to Edward's cell. Never in twos, always in threes: his novice master's voice would have echoed in his mind.

Aelred and Edward continued to hold the secret of their night together in the barn, but they felt it slipping from them and being announced as loud as the bells that echoed about the valley of Ashton Park. They saw it written on the faces of their fellow novices. They saw it in the demeanour of Father Justin, the novice master, and in that look of the Abbot when they bowed to him on entering choir before going to their stalls for the beginning of Matins.

After Matins, throughout Lectio Divina, they avoided each other. They avoided being seen together, seeking to bury their deeds by burying any opportunity for suspicion.

Of course, what would anyone have really known? Their offences were to have spent the night out of the dormitory, to have missed Compline and their special supper after haymaking. They had not had the Abbot's blessing. That was all that anyone could know. No one had seen them, but of course they would suspect much more.

Aelred wished that Lectio Divina would go on and on and that he would not have to leave his cell that day. He sat and listened to Edward coughing in his cell. Then there was silence.

Later, after Prime, Aelred stood in Benedict's empty cell. He stared out of the window. The scent of honeysuckle rose from the garden below. He stood and stared and added with his finger to the hieroglyphs in the dust on Benedict's desk from the day before. They told him nothing. He heard footsteps in the corridor. They were Edward's. He knew his tread.

'I've seen Father Justin,' Edward said, standing by the door to the cell looking distraught.

'And?'

'I don't know.'

'What did you tell him? Did you tell him the truth?'

'The truth? Yes, I suppose so. I spoke about my mother. I don't know why. About her love and how I missed it. She had to keep going away from home. It's a long story of illness. It just came out. I said that you filled up that need. I did say I loved you, or I implied it. I don't know why I said all that about my mother, or what Father Justin made of it.'

'What did he say?' Aelred insisted.

'He said that, after all, he was satisfied that no scandal had been caused. He was most particular about who knew, if anyone knew about us in the barn. I assured him that I didn't think so. He also said that it was a question of love going where it shouldn't.'

'Did he?'

'He wants to talk to you.'

'Does he?'

'You must be calm. We've broken all the boundaries. You know what you talked about - what you have with Benedict.'

They stood facing each other in the empty cell with the rolled-up mattress on the iron bed, searching each other's eyes for more and not finding it. 'You must talk to Father Basil. He will know what to do. He came through. He and Sebastian came through,' Aelred instructed Edward.

'Yes, I will. I promise.' Edward took Aelred's hand. They both stood by the window. The storm had not yet broken and all the windows of the novitiate were wide open, to enable as much air to enter into the stifling calm.

'The smell of that frangipani!'

'What did you say?'

'Oh, I mean honeysuckle. It's so sweet. Like funerals.'

No sooner had they recognised Father Justin's hurried walk along the corridor of the novitiate than he was at the door to the cell. 'What are you two doing in here?' His disapproval was in his voice and the agitated brushing off of specks of dust from his front scapular. 'Brother Edward, you should be in your cell, and you, Brother Aelred - I would like to see you at once in my cell.'

'Yes, father.' Aelred composed himself. Before he followed Father Justin, he returned quickly to Edward's cell, pulling aside the curtains and said, 'Wish me luck. Pray for me.'

Edward tried to smile encouragingly. 'I do. I will.'

'Father, you don't have to quiz me, interrogate me.' Aelred started at once.

'Brother, I think we should take this calmly.'

'I have nothing to hide and nothing to be ashamed of. I have here, myself, and my life as I know it. This is what I've brought here to Ashton Park. It could not be any different. I cannot be other than I am. This is my nature ...'

'Brother, I do really think ...'

'You don't know of this, my love for that boy since I was twelve.'

'I don't think this is at all an appropriate way to proceed.'

'I know I found that love in - no, not Edward. I know he has told you of the truth of that love. No, I first had that

love with Benedict. Yes, you once warned me, but I took
the risk with my desire and with Benedict. With his
strength we have managed to balance that love within our
monastic ideal, within what we call a dangerous chastity
according to the writings of Aelred of Rievaulx, which
Father Abbot and yourself have now banned.'

'Brother Aelred, I think we must stop this interview if
you are going to continue with this outpouring. I know
you are distraught. But ...'

'At first it was not love. It was lust. It was a sexual attraction like many boys I have known have had for me and I
for them. But it was never named. Then in the midst of
that, in the midst of giving ourselves, Edward and I, to
that, I discovered that I loved him and that he loved me
and that it could not be what Benedict and I have. It
could not be a dangerous chastity.'

'Brother!' Father Justin stood up.

'So, father, don't quiz me, interrogate or advise me,
because I have had all that. It was what was denied at
school. A confessor advised me against it, seeing in it a
sin.' Aelred was looking up at Father Justin.

'I will have to put a stop to this at once.'

'And they killed Ted. Sometimes I think I killed him,
but they did. They who jeered and they who did nothing
about it.'

When Father Justin looked at his novice - because all
the while his eyes had been riveted to his desk, unable to
bear the fire in the eyes of Aelred - he saw that they burnt
with a fury he had never seen in anyone before, and had
only read of in the lives of the saints, he thought to himself wryly. He saw that those burning eyes were filled now
with tears. They cried those tears, and the young man

stared at him openly, not even wiping his tears away, but letting them flow freely and bathe his cheeks.

He said, 'Brother, speak no more, we will speak later.' Father Justin had sat back down.

But again, Father Justin had to turn away, for Aelred stood over him and said, 'Do not silence me, father, do not silence me. I speak the truth.' He then turned and left Father Justin's cell.

Aelred returned to his cell and knelt by his bed, trying to pray, sobbing. He heard Edward moving in his cell. Then he heard the quick steps of Father Justin, and heard the novice master. 'I've arranged for you to see the Abbot this afternoon.' Father Justin pulled aside the curtains to the cubicle.

'Yes, I'll see the Abbot. Tell him I will see him, and he too shall hear the truth I have to tell.' Aelred was at his door, shouting down the corridor at Father Justin. His prayer had not helped.

The scandal which Father Justin had striven to avoid now ran the risk of inflaming the novitiate of young minds and bodies. Though the effect, to all appearances, was a shroud of silence.

Aelred remained in his cell that morning, missing lunch. The infirmarian persuaded him to take a light tranquilliser.

He woke suddenly in the middle of the siesta with a loud clap of thunder.

Edward was sitting on the side of his bed. 'Here, drink this. I've brought you some water.'

'Thanks.' He sipped. He noticed some heavy drops of rain on his windowsill. He felt terrible. 'I have to see

Benedict.' So long, it seemed, since he had seen him. He felt now as nervous and depressed as he had felt angry earlier on. His anger would try to raise itself, so that he knew that it was there, but then he felt tired and sick.

'Rest,' Edward said. 'Rest. It will work out. But you must be careful with what you say. Remember Basil. I've made an appointment to see him this afternoon.'

Aelred smiled. 'Good. Thanks.' He wiped the sweat from his brow.

Brother Stephen called to me when I was walking up through the farm this afternoon. He asked, Would I help him with a young cow, which was in the throes of calving? I said I would, though I had never witnessed this before. I was scared. The young cow was lying on its side, its stomach distended. All around the vagina area was soft, mushy and opening up. She had been in labour a long time. Brother Stephen was worried. He needed a hand to pull. We had to pull on the hooves and legs that had begun to show. But the head was stuck. Brother Stephen needed to insert his hand, his arm, to make room and coax the head out with the legs. He spoke to the cow reassuringly. He encouraged me in my efforts to pull. Then, all of a sudden, there was a rush of water, blood and transparent membrane, and the calf slipped out on to the straw, and the poor cow, exhausted, immediately turned to its calf and licked and nuzzled. It butted us off. I sat in the straw and watched, bewildered and in awe, the calf against my leg. Then we helped it to suck, Brother Stephen coaxing the milk out to make sure the calf got a good initial drink. Quite soon, it was up on its legs and knowing exactly where to go for a drink; the mother was turning and licking and cleaning it up. Brother Stephen had to get rid of the afterbirth. It was not good for the cow to eat this. The whole thing left me quite stunned. And Brother Stephen such a good midwife.

When we were washing up in the dairy he turned to me and said, I liked your brother. He liked it on the farm here. What we have just done for Marigold, he did with a young cow called Olive, and her first calf.

I smiled. Yes, he talked of you, I said. And then I wondered what he thought. Because what I really should've said was that I had read about him in the journals.

There is more to bring to light. More to come out.

Before Vespers the Abbot slipped me an envelope. It contained a letter addressed to me from Benedict. He died before it could be posted. They found it on his desk. It had escaped the lay brother's clearing up. It had escaped the incinerator.

Dear Robert,
Just a word. I loved your brother more than anyone else I've ever loved. I'm sorry we lost touch. That he died the way he died. I'm sorry for all of it. We've not been able to find a way to accept ourselves in all our splendour, understand how it all fits together. Some of it dazzles us too much. We cannot look at it. But you, I think, have the strength and youth to face it all.
Your generation can take the heat. Believe what you read. What he says is true. I hope that your research will give you back your brother, a memory which will both be astonishing and comforting. You have given him back to me. I have been denying myself his memory and all that there is to remember, of a time when we strove valiantly to love and be loved, but.. well, let

there be no buts.
I hope I see you soon; if not, you have my words.
With all my love - accept it in his place, and for
yourself,
Benedict

I could not contain myself. I was unable to go to
Vespers. On the way back to the lodge I wept. I stopped at
the cemetery. I stood by his grave and read the letter
again. I sat and wept.

Afterwards, I wondered what Joe would make of the
letter.

Poetry to the end, I'm sure he would say: all that talk of
splendour and beauty and being dazzled.

I let it work on me, though, before Joe's voice enters to
challenge me. He openly acknowledges his love. He is
sorrowful.

Joe might say, Too little, too late.

I can't say that. This is my too little, too late. It pleases
me that I was able to give him back something, that my
questing has had a point to it for him as well. J. M.'s death
has meant something. I will have to show Joe the letter.
For a while, I'd thought it was Benedict that I needed to
see and to speak to, but increasingly I know that it is Joe
who was an equally long friend, possibly the most important friend in the end. Not a lover, I startle myself, it
seems. Sometimes I wonder.

The birth of the calf and the letter said something to
me which made all my efforts seem appropriate. It was
right, this bringing forth.

They all stood around jeering, taunting. I couldn't believe

something bad was going to happen again. I saw J. M. back off and tug at Ted's arm to come with him, but Ted pulled away and went and started climbing on to the highest rock. To my eye now, Ted was, as I remember seeing him emerge at the top, thin, transparent. He could not see me hiding. I could read his ribs. I could read his blue veins. He had been getting thinner and thinner.

One day I came across him in the washroom being sick. He did not hear me. It was after supper one evening and I had wanted to find J. M. to get some pocket money. I was not really allowed up to the senior dormitory, so I was tiptoeing about. What I remember was that he seemed to be sticking his finger down his throat and then being sick, retching. I could smell all his dinner coming up into the basin and the running water gushing over the side of the basin. I don't think he saw me. He was making himself sick. I backed away. I left him. Ted, my brother's friend. I understand more of this now.

Miriam says that it is more and more common among boys.

He stood on the highest rock alone. I saw J. M. begin to climb up to him. That is when I think J. M. saw me behind Ted. He was now at the very edge. All the others were taunting, daring him to dive. To jackknife from the highest rock was to receive the greatest accolade, more than any school record at the official sports day. To jackknife into the river pool from the highest rock would prove him to be a boy like the rest of them. Last term, the raid and all that had led up to the scandalous revelations would be forgotten, for him and his friend. He could wipe the slate clean. He could be their hero again; their head boy, their captain. They would cheer for him on the left wing. The applause would ring out again for his century. The juniors would crowd around for his cap at the end of the season. He stood teetering, thin, transparent, naked but for his brief swimsuit. Blue. *Marbleu.* A blue butterfly on a black rock. His arms stretched out in front of him, then at his side. Poised. Then out in front of him again. The roar went up. High above them, J. M. shouted, Ted, don't dive! And then his thin body was in mid-air. A kind of angel. A bird. It twisted and bent for the jack-knife, then straightened and plunged into its own splash and disappeared. The roar was deafening. The roar of the boys, the high wind, the water that fell from under the highest rock in a cascade. Then there was silence, as we all waited for Ted's head to bob to the surface. Before anyone had realised, J. M. jumped from the rock, and then, there he was with Ted's body in his arms in the life-saving position, lying on his chest, Ted's head all red. Suddenly the pool was deserted as the taunting crowd retreated up the paths to the school. They deserted in fear. I was rooted to the ground. What had I seen? What had they seen? I looked down at J. M. and Ted on the rock to where J. M. had swam with him. He sat with Ted in his arms. His head was crushed, his face a red flower. The water running away was tinged with red. J. M. looked up, saw me, cried for me to get help. I ran and ran and ran. I collapsed. Father Julius arrived with first aid.

He had flown, a shaft of light, the pool like flamboyante.

Playback. It became my dream, repeated. A brown arm reaching from behind a black rock, extended, touching, gently tilted his body to the very edge, into mid-air. Its flight. Jackknifed. Plummet. Splash.

Bless me, Father, for I have seen ...sinned.

A strange synchronicity, a macabre pattern, a common impulse: denial, punishment, death. Suicide? Self-killing? Murder? I ran the alternatives and how they would have seemed. His wish to die and my wish to save face with all the others. Was that my arm, my hand ? Did I actually touch him, or had he flown? Did I get to push him or had he made the decision? It has stayed with me, because whatever he did, there will always be what I did, even if it was not the cause. Even if I only nudged what he was already about to do. Had he wanted to prove something? Was it a flight he had been preparing himself for, growing thinner and thinner, lighter and lighter? Diminished in body. Light like spirit. His flight to parallel J. M.'s flight, away from him, the island.

I remember him looking over J. M.'s shoulder when he was writing the letter of application to St Aelred's Abbey. They had had an argument. They sent me off. Skeidaddle. His fingers ruffling my hair. Tender in that moment.

Playback. A brown arm from behind a black rock. Had he tempted my nudge? Had it caught him off balance? Did he change decision mid-air? Ted. I hear J. M.'s cry. Ted, don't dive.

I had never cried. Now I find my weeping renders me inconsolable, then strangely refreshed, after all these years. Is this where I've been leading? I think so. My own betrayals, my own shame.

You cannot blame yourself for the acts of a young boy, Miriam comforts.

It's not you, Joe says, it's them: the teachers, the confessors, the spiritual advisers.

I know that in an intellectual way, I think. But emotionally, inside me, is that voice, my inner voice that tells me that I betrayed him. I am an accomplice in that self-killing.

I want my brother back. I want his forgiveness.

I know that in an intellectual way, I think. But it doesn't make sense. In my inner voice that tells me that I betrayed him. I am as incomplete as that self-killing.

I want my brother back. I want his forgiveness.

The Storm

I opened to my Beloved,
but he had turned his back and gone!
My soul failed at his flight.
I sought him but I did not find him.
I called to him but he did not answer.
Song of Songs

As Aelred walked to the library, where he hoped to find Benedict, he thought how quiet and normal everything seemed. The cloister was a little removed from him, so that he saw it as if he were watching a film. But the silence and the peace seemed untouched by the fire which had raged in the novitiate, or the one which had burnt in the barn all night. He opened the door of the library and saw that the alcove which Benedict often used was empty. He closed the door behind him, and stood outside the door staring down the corridor. Immediately, he went to Benedict's new cell. He knew this was absolutely against the rule, but he could not help himself.

Benedict got up - '*Ave*' - and came at once to him, seeing him as he had never seen him, distraught and full of pain in his face and tired eyes. 'But you shouldn't be here.'

Aelred pushed his way into the cell and slammed the door.

He had travelled a long way since last night. He was glad to rest his head on the shoulder of his beloved friend. 'My love, my love, peace, peace. Come, tell me all.' The older monk led the novice to his desk. 'Sit, but you must not stay here.' Aelred felt at once that all was going to be well again.

On Benedict's bed, Aelred saw the monastic discipline. It was a whip with five strands, each strand tied with five

knots. Five for the five wounds of Jesus. Benedict noticed
Aelred's awareness of the discipline on his bed. 'We must
not stay in here. You should never have come here. This is
seriously against the rules. Meet me in the library.' He
directed Aelred discreetly out of his cell.

Soon after, in the library, Benedict saw in the eyes of
the young novice an older person. The boy had become a
man. When Aelred told Benedict of the events of the
night before, and of his interview with Father Justin,
Benedict, too, grew into an even older man. 'You mentioned us?' But that growing was not easy, and it did not
mean that he could leave behind immediately the man
who had had to wrestle with his feelings for this novice.
He did not interrupt Aelred. The novice's tongue,
though heavy with the still reactive effects of the tranquilliser the infirmarian had given him, spoke mellifluously.
He felt that his mouth was full of honey, something gluti-
nous as the texture of honey, but not as sweet. He was still
loose with the spirit of one who spoke with tongues, setting alight the secrets of those souls: himself, Benedict
and Edward, who sought a new beginning without a past.
But it was their pasts which had returned: their personal
pasts, their collective past, the past, all here, to make this
particular present.

Benedict sat and listened in the library. He listened to
an account of the events which had happened in the barn
the night before with a composure he felt it almost impossible to keep. His heart was wrung at first with jealousy,
then disgust, then hate. 'I don't think I want to hear any
more of this.' He felt what he didn't think he had ever felt
in his life before, pure hate. He had pure hate for this
young man with tortured eyes and streaked cheeks, who

kept holding his hand, and reaching to his face and speaking with a clarity and conviction he found terrifying.

'Who else will I tell? Who else can listen as you do? Who else loves me the way you do?' Aelred clawed at Benedict's sleeves and scapular.

'Edward?'

'That's cruel.'

'Brother, you must get hold of yourself.'

Despite this hate, Benedict wanted to repossess the person he had loved, beyond any other he had allowed himself to love since he had entered the monastery at Ashton Park. The business of the love of God, or charity within the community, was hard. It gave its pain as it did its pleasure. But it did not hurt like this. It was not a pain which wrung the heart, which took the bottom out of the pit of the stomach and choked him at the throat, all because someone else had touched him whom he loved. Benedict looked at Aelred standing in front of him, a young man of nineteen.

That others loved God and were loved by him did not make one jealous. On the contrary, one rejoiced at this bounteous gift of an all giving lover.

'You let him touch you, kiss you? You kiss and touch him in ways, particularly in ways, we have made such an effort to refrain from, to abstain from for our ideals of chastity, that dangerous chastity, which did not allow us to go beyond the stolen kiss of a light touch of the lips, a holding of the hands, the seduction of the eyes?' Benedict thirsted with unquenchable jealousy. He could not get enough of jealousy to drink.

Benedict could not look at Aelred without wanting to tear out his eyes.

That Aelred had let all this happen so suddenly with another, and that he, Benedict, was in part an instrument in creating their meeting and initiating their confessions of openness wrung out of the usually composed Benedict a hate and disgust. 'I should've seen it all more plainly. I knew something was on fire here. I should've put it out.' It made him want to fling this boy, for he thought of him as a boy again, from his hands, off his chest, to tear his fingers from his face, to lift him bodily with a strength he never thought he possessed, and throw him out of the library, out of Ashton Park, so that he would never see him again. He never again wished to have his peace and his ideals disturbed and destroyed in this way. 'Don't touch me.' Then immediately he regretted that rebuff and let the boy cling again to him.

Eventually, all that he could say to Aelred were the repeated questions: 'How could you say all that you have said? How could you betray us? How could you betray me? How could you do all you've done, how? Done with another? And how could you sin so? Touch, kiss, touch.' Benedict saw all his effort crumbling. Still he held him and let the boy hold on to him.

His journey to Ashton Park, which he had never fully told to Aelred, came back with a frightening clarity. It was as if Aelred had lit a huge fire in the middle of the cloister and it was slowly burning its way through all the secrets of the souls which struggled with the meaning of love in their secluded lives.

Benedict had once loved a girl called Claire, and they had been engaged and planned to marry in a year or two when they could afford it. It was as simple as that, and as usual as that, as many young couples at the time. That was how love was. They would go for walk on the downs. In the early evening when it had grown dark, they would go for a drink in the pub. They held hands and they kissed and they petted each other, as the parish priest called it, advising against heavy petting. They talked of wanting children when they were married. He used to read her poetry. When he was away teaching, they exchanged love letters, saying more in their written words than when they spoke to each other. And then the letters stopped. Her letters stopped. She stopped replying without any reason, without a final letter. He learnt later from a friend who lived near her that she had eloped with a divorced man and had eventually married him.

All his desire, all his love, all his hope for a life with Claire had become a room with a small corner of pain which he did not let anyone into. He did not allow anyone into that small room of pain.

Then he had come on a retreat to Ashton Park. Suddenly, he felt that he had a vocation to join the monks. He felt that he could embark upon a future and a present without a past, without that past of pain. Slowly, he felt that he had almost forgotten what it was like to live in that small room, and for years he had not opened that door.

When Aelred entered the monastery, a door was opened into that room of pain, and he found himself thinking of the young novice as he had thought of Claire. His youth and his androgynous looks allowed him to imagine Claire and have fantasies he had not allowed himself. These were the fantasies which drew him to Aelred at that first feast-day celebration, had stopped him on the stair-

case to look at his legs and lifted his habit in the Lady
Chapel to feel his warm body and to confess to him his
love. Suddenly, the room of pain was opened up and here
was a second chance for human love. He thought they
had managed it, so that they could have that human love
and still manage their ideal of chastity, that dangerous
chastity, as they liked to call it.

But now the supreme trick of love had been played
upon him, because he had rationalised his desire, his
illicit desire, as the unfulfilled desire which had been
denied him with Claire. At first it had been that, but then
this boy, this young man, this androgynous creature, had
opened in him feelings he never knew existed, so that he
wanted him precisely because he was a young man. He
loved him as a young man, not as a woman, not as Claire,
but as Aelred, his bonnie lad.

This was to enter a forbidden place. It was forbidden to
think of himself in this way and forbidden for them to
be that way together. Then he had found Aelred of
Rievaulx's works, which he passed on to Aelred. These
texts would help them find a way.

But now Aelred had broken all the boundaries and
agreements and traditions, and was actually saying aloud
to his novice master, to the young Edward and to himself,
that he had a choice. He was making a choice to love
Edward spiritually and physically. He was saying this.
There was no mistake. But the madness of it was de-
troying him because it was breaking a mould which had
been offered as if there were no other. He was saying that
there was not just one, there was another mould, another
way, without as yet knowing what it was, what shape it
could have, what name.

'How could you endanger so much?' Benedict said angrily.

'If you don't understand me, I'm left all alone. Don't push me away. Hold me, hold me,' Aelred cried. These beseeching cries and kisses on Benedict's neck slowly untied the hate and disgust which wrung his heart, and he found in himself the capacity, slowly but unmistakably, to love this boy for himself, unconditionally. He would not banish him from understanding and hope, but he would not betray his vows.

This was the act for which Aelred would always remember Benedict.

'You will have to take responsibility for the truth which you speak with such conviction at present,' Benedict said, wiping the stains of tears from Aelred's cheeks. 'Remember your responsibility when you speak to the Abbot. You have already been rash with what you've said to Father Justin. Now is not the time for us to sort all this through. I understand your feelings for Edward. I understand his for you. Have I not myself wanted all this? Have I not wanted you in this way? I will pray for you to come through, to regain the aim of your ideal, the demands of our vocation. Pray that you can deepen these desires.'

Aelred saw the Abbot that afternoon. Father Justin brought him a message that the Abbot would see him after None.

Aelred felt that the effects of the tranquilliser were wearing off. The artificial suppressor of his anger dwindled in the hot afternoon, which rumbled with thunder and sudden flashes of lightning. He could feel that anger which he had discovered while waiting for his interview with Father Justin that morning rising again. It was taking hold of him, so that he wanted to tear apart the institutions, rearrange the past which held the untruth. He was so quickly realising so much that he was frightened by the extent of the ruins and how he was to rebuild himself. He felt that his self was running out of his hands like some river he could not stop. Where would the reservoir be? Where could he regain himself?

He was not well enough to go to choir and he sat in the window seat of his cell, hoping the rain would break. Then he went and stood at the window of the common room, and looked out on to the fields and saw the monks beginning to go out to the afternoon's work.

The Abbot was to see him at two thirty. Edward passed him on his way to work. He came and stood close to him. At first he said nothing. Then he spoke gently. 'For us, don't ruin it for us.' Aelred felt removed. He had taken a strength from Benedict which contact with Edward could make weak again.

'No. And remember you have your meeting with Basil. Listen to him. He will tell you that this is a gift. This love is a gift. But it is also a fire. He will tell you that the rewards are sweet.'

'Yes.'

'Go now. I need to be on my own, get my thoughts together.' They held hands. Then Edward left the common room.

He was now alone on his own mission. He was determined to hold on to everything. He wanted his love for Benedict, his love for Edward and this life he had given up so much for. He knew no other life, had never imagined anything any different since Ted and he had been so forcibly torn apart. How would all that be possible?

Aelred let the heavy door knocker fall against the dark oak door and wished it were Aelred of Rievaulx he was entering to see. He heard the Abbot's 'Ave.' He found himself at the end of the long room with the Abbot rising at his desk at the other end; behind him the life-size crucifix hung the length of the wall.

'Come in, brother.' Aelred walked to the desk and stood next to the leather upholstered chair opposite the Abbot. 'Sit, brother.'

This man was his father, his spiritual director, Christ on earth, God's representative. It all seemed too much for Aelred to obey, and too much for this small man to carry, dwarfed by the crucified Jesus behind him.

A hagiographic portrait of St Benedict hung above the fireplace to the right of Aelred. St Benedict was kneeling in the cave of Subiaco and the devil as an imp prodded his ankle with a tridon.

Aelred tried to smile. This was his second main meeting. He had left frustrated after the last. The spiritual direction of the novices was left to the novice master. The Abbot was remote from the novices, closer to the senior monks. He was a figure of authority to the novices or, when he visited them at Sunday tea, a beneficent or daunting presence. It should not be like this, Aelred remembered thinking last time.

'Father Justin says there's been a problem.' The Abbot spoke, tugging on his abbatial cross as usual, which hung from a gold chain about his neck.

'No,' Aelred said. He did not want this to be the

starting point. He did not wish to allow the Abbot the pretence that they didn't know exactly what had occurred. Why not start right in at the centre of the fire?

'It's a question of love, father.' Aelred realised it was a spirit that had entered him that morning which spoke, but he could feel in himself the language of Benedict. He could feel the clarity of his mentor. He would take responsibility for this - though he also felt that what Benedict meant by responsibility was caution.

'Indeed, brother. This is the symbol of that love which has saved us, and an example of that love which we must live: the love which Christ had, by which he died so that our sins might be forgiven and we might enter the kingdom of heaven.' The Abbot turned to point to the life-size crucifix behind him - as if it needed any more of an introduction than the one it gave itself with its overpowering presence, Aelred thought irreverently, already impatient with the Abbot's sermonising before he had even begun.

Aelred looked at the crucifix, then again at the Abbot. 'It's the love of mothers and fathers, the love of brothers and sisters, the love of friends, the love that exists between us as brothers.' He felt he was giving a sermon himself and that he should stop and let the Abbot continue his sermon. 'It's the love of home and country. All these loves which I have had to give up, deny myself, or so it seemed. Now I find that I want to claim them all back. I want all that human love and I also want my life here, and yes, that is a problem if you say so.' He found that he could add that bit about the problem and not seem impertinent to the Abbot.

He wished the Abbot did not remind him of his father.

He remembered the rows he used to have with his father, about nothing, just about the strengths of their wills. That in itself made him want to resist his authority.

'You have been asked to leave mother and father, brother and sister, and land, and come follow me: that is the call of Jesus to those who would be perfect.'

Aelred did love the word 'perfect'. The life of perfection fired him; the Little Flower, St Thérèse of Lisieux, doing each small act perfectly. He wished to be perfect. He wished to be an angel, as he used to say, of whom the monks at school reminded him. He still wanted perfection.

'Carnal love has no place in our life, brother' The Abbot and his novice looked at each other. Aelred didn't like the word carnal. It meant meat. It meant dog, because dog was *canis* and it sounded the same. He remembered seeing two dogs on the promenade near his primary school stuck together. It made him sick to look at, but it also fascinated him, and he found he got excited sexually. Carnal. The Abbot was referring to Father Justin's rightly held suspicions, the ones he hadn't wanted to voice to Edward, giving them the authority and reality, the meaning words confer on things. Aelred still saw the dogs backing, a word used on Les Deux Isles, one humped on the other. The Abbot was speaking about rooting out carnal lust.

Then he heard the word buller, which was used on Les Deux Isles for what men did with each other. It was wrong to be a buller man. Carnal meant dogs and bulls, what he saw the cows doing in the fields, backing, bulling each other. Then he saw Edward, his white smooth body lying on the hay. He stroked his arms and legs in his imagination and entered his body, backing him, bulling him. That's what they called it. But he was not an animal. This was pure. And, anyway, what animals did was good. It felt good. They had said that to each other, lying in each other's arms, their kisses wet on their lips and cheeks. It was good. Edward entered him. That was good.

'God made this love and he saw it was good,' Aelred said to the Abbot, mimicking Genesis. He felt like being provocative and saying, 'And on the eighth day God made the love which men have for each other and he said this is good and he saw that it was good.' But what he had said was provocative enough.

The Abbot cut immediately to the quick of this exchange and said, 'Brother, I will have to ask you to leave Ashton Park. What you are advocating is wrong on all counts within and without the monastery, and I cannot afford the scandal you will create among the innocent and impressionistic young novices.'

Aelred suddenly felt a wild thought tear at his heart, and he stood up over the Abbot. Facing the life-size crucifix, he said, 'You can't make that decision. This is my decision, my vocation, my call from God to be here, to enter here, and no one comes between me and God.' Then he sat down trembling, hardly knowing or hearing what he had said.

The Abbot rose and then sat again and composed himself, putting his arms beneath his scapular. 'I want you to go to your cell, brother, and quieten yourself, and return to see me tomorrow.' He showed the novice to the door.

Aelred left the Abbot's room, desperate for the open air. When he entered the cloister, he felt the first signs that the skies were going to open, and the rain, which had been threatening for days, was going to fall at last. And just as suddenly as he thought that, he saw the fine drizzle making the walls of stone grey. There was a wild clap of thunder and then lightning and more thunder, and he thought of rain back home, drenching rain which made the hot pitch steam and smell of tar. Heavy drops of rain began to come down slowly, and then faster and thicker, until it was crashing around the abbey and splattering the floor of the cloister where it was open to the enclosed garden at the centre.

Aelred walked into the rain, putting on his hood, and went through the gate at the end of the path that lead down to the drive with the poplars, leading to the open fields. He was running now, running, hooded, and wildly pulling up his habit above his knees so as not to trip and fall. He reached the fields where the large horse chestnuts and copper beeches grew. They gave him some shelter and he stood near the trunk of a copper beech, looking up into its branches black with the rain - more and more branches spreading black and no longer the red-purple they had been in late summer.

There was no shelter from this rain. It crashed through the black branches and drenched him where he stood hooded, his habit getting more and more soaked. He heard nothing and saw nothing but the black rain crashing around him. Then there was more lightning, and Ashton Park, the Ashton Park he knew, was transformed. The electric sky lit up the fields with wild gashes of light. The thunder rumbled, and he thought of the Abbot pulling his heavy chair across the floor of his room. The sky seemed to want to rip itself open and give him a revelation. The woods, the interior of the woods, were suddenly shown to him, opening up hallucinated groves. Aelred made himself the trunk of the tree and, standing there, he thought of the real danger he was in of being killed by a stroke of lightning, of a tree falling on him. He left his black shelter for the open fields and the drenching rain.

The storm seemed to be moving away from directly over Ashton Park, and Aelred could behold the wonder of a new creation over the valleys like a gigantic *son et lumière* specially put on for him alone: a private revelation, a storm, a flood. The oppression of the last few days drained out of him with the falling rain, loud in his ears like the rain of his childhood drumming on the galvanised roofs.

As the thunder and lightning moved away into the distance, opening up horizons he could hardly imagine, horizons with new mountains and valleys and open flat plains, he became exhilarated by his visions. His anger turned to elation as he raised his face to the sky, which had cleared and was now a luminous blue as evening came early, the sun banished by the storm.

The rain continued to fall as a fine drizzle as he strode through the long grass of the fields. He was now some distance from the abbey. His instinct still instructed him to avoid trees, the copse on the knoll, the spinney near the pond. He came to a field, where the grass was like a lawn, wet and newly cut. He realised it was the field where he had been yesterday during haymaking. He sat on the ground in the rain and looked back at the abbey rising out of the valley. Against the hill, on top of which were the graves, the stone abbey stood out in relief. A trick of light made the hill part of the encroaching darkness and allowed the abbey to stand out, pricked with orange lights coming on in the windows, glowing like embers.

The rain was not so heavy now, and Aelred, accustomed to its fall, now heard other sounds. He could hear the heavy dripping in the woods, and the freshness of the rain had awakened an unaccustomed chorus of birds for this time of day. He could hear runnels of water flowing down the fields, meeting up with the streams which fed the pond. Then the bells for Vespers began to ring, echoing and echoing around the valley of his visions with the storm racing away in the distance, as if illustrating the perils of the future that lay ahead for Aelred.

He began to walk aimlessly away from the abbey, circling without direction, losing sight of it and then regaining sight of its lit-up windows. The ringing of the bells had ended. He thought of the lit-up church and other windows as a great ship on the sea. He had felt so safe there. It was the safety he had wanted as a boy at school. What it looked like from the outside was safety. He used to think, When I become a monk I will be different. I will be good. I will be perfect. The fear and guilt which grew out of a vision of Ted in his coffin would be absolved. He would be new. Ensnaring desire would be replaced by a perfect love. Once on that ship, he realised the truth of Thomas à Kempis's words in *The Imitation of Christ* that 'a change of place did not change a man.' He had brought his nature here on to the ship. But then he had grown in Benedict's love. Benedict had taken the responsibility of holding it all together and offered him Aelred of Rievaulx.

This reassessment continued as the darkness became

more complete around Aelred, so that he hardly knew where he was. He began to sing to himself: not his favourite chants, but songs he knew as a boy, wild romantic songs of love. 'Just Walking in the Rain', then Paul Anka's, 'O Diana, I'm So Young and You're So Old'. He put his own words to the tunes he remembered. He heard the house bell for supper. He ignored the life of the ship. His elation grew with his singing as he strode through the long wet grass in the darkness. The storm in the distance had waned: only now and then there was a faint glimmer of sheet lightning lighting up some very distant land for hardly a second, and then there was darkness again.

Aelred thought of Edward, and then of the future and what would happen if the Abbot really expelled him. It was an unthinkable thought. He had no other life, had never had any other future. He knew boys who wanted to be all sorts of things. But he had only ever wanted to be a monk as he and Ted were swirled around the school yard in the cotton folds of Father Maurus's habit and he smelt the incense of his armpits, the wine of the blood of Christ on his lips and the smell of the wafer breads of holy communion. Then he saw the blood in his veins, the blue of Quink ink, like the blue in the veins of the marble of the high altar.

He had made his way aimlessly to where the small streams that came through the watercress beds fed the ponds where the winter birds migrated. A faint mist was rising off the water. It was silent at this time of the year, with only the ducks which lived there all the year round. He sat on a log near where the streams ran into the brown water of the pond. The water slid over blue-grey stones streaked

with red. He sat and stared into the water running over
the blue stones streaked with red. He lost himself in that
vision.

As Aelred stared into the stream flowing over the blue
stone, he saw his own face beneath the running water. His
face was black. It was blue-black and it stared back at him.
It altered its stare, its look. His face was the face of Ted. It
was the face of Jordan.

A breeze shook the branches and drew a curtain, as a
cloud covers the moon.

In the darkness, Aelred heard the bark of a dog. His
vision returned.

The bark of the dog became the scampering of many
feet in the grass. He heard the yelps of hunting hounds. A
hunt was gathering in the shadows around the great
house of Ashton Park.

Master Walter was to have his way.

A figure with a flaming torch cut across the field from a
hayrick towards the house. Suddenly, behind the hunt,
the house was ablaze. The figure cut behind the hedges
for the fields, a burning torch still in its hand. Then the
burning torch was extinguished in a pool of water. Soon
every hedgerow, copse and spinney, holly and laurel
bush, every bit of long grass, every reed in the shallows of
the pond, was alive with the sniffing and yelping for the
stink of fox, for the stink of a nigger.

Ashton Park was on fire.

The instinct of the running figure was escape, to run
away. Its horizon was freedom. It ran to maroon itself in
darkness.

The figure, only a shadow, crouched so that it might

be mistaken for a mound on the fields, for a tumulus on a knoll, for a stone or a grazing sheep, a cow chewing its cud in the night air. It sought to inhabit animal or plant so that it might live freely in this world of men. It sought to be nothing but a shadow, part of the air, an illusion of the light. It was learning to prefer this element to the light of the world that had enslaved it to a life of cruelty and pain, had enslaved it as a part of commerce, as a chattel, as a crop: coffee, tobacco, sugar, cocoa, molasses, rum.

Aelred felt the shadow, as soft as cotton on a cotton bush, brush against his face.

It made an effort to fly, but it was too heavy to fly.

Aelred heard a hymn, which was the song of a field-hand singing in a sugar-cane field. He heard Toinette: 'The River Jordan is mighty and cold, halleluia, chills the body and not the soul.' He heard the clapping and the singing of the women in the chapel down the hill in the village of Felicity below Malgretoute.

The moon spilt its calabash of white light.

Jordan sought the secret tunnel.

He turned, bent down, picked up a stone and threw it. Then he bolted.

Aelred saw the boy fall into the stream, and the stream ran blue and red. The yelps of the hounds hung in the branches of the trees. The tongues of the hounds lapped, red and blue.

The next morning, two farmhands lifted Aelred's vision from the stream. As they lifted Jordan's head from the stream, Aelred bent and stroked his face, kissed his lips: a forbidden love, the love of Aelred's sin. He kissed the lips of Ted's brown face. The body was taken from

him and taken to a hole against the chapel in the cemetery. He followed and saw on a Christian cross the name,
Jordan. As they lowered the body into the wet grave, he
saw that Jordan was indeed Ted and then that face was the
face of all those friends whom he had left behind:
Redhead, Espinet, Ramnarine and Mackensie. Now it
seemed as if they had all died with Jordan and Ted.

As the men filled in the grave and stuck the cross in the
mound of earth, Aelred noticed that they too were black
and that they had the faces of men who worked on his
father's estate at Malgretoute: in spite of everything.

His vision faded.

Aelred felt that he had walked miles as he rested against
the wall of the medieval chapel. The community would
be finishing supper. He was beginning to feel cold. His
habit was soaked and muddy. He felt he belonged here
with the rain, grass and mud. He felt calm, as if his head
had been washed out. The tranquilliser had lost its effect,
and the walk through the rain had released all the tension
of the morning and the afternoon and the happenings of
the night before.

He lay down near Jordan's grave.

The next morning, he was awakened by the bells for
Matins. He was cold. As he descended to the abbey, he
saw the dawn beginning already to burn over Ashton on
the horizon.

He would go and see the Abbot and find a way to mend
his life, to stitch together what seemed against all odds an
impossible task to mend, stitch together what seemed
impossible loves. In his heart he felt that he had the
courage of one who had made unimaginable journeys.

The boy would see him through. Jordan!

After the night of the rain, the atmosphere had cleared and the already verdant park seemed almost tropical. The Abbot allowed a few days to lapse before asking to see Brother Aelred. He stopped him himself after Prime. 'Let us talk this afternoon brother.' The Abbot smiled. Aelred felt that a huge pressure had been lifted off him. It was almost as if getting everything out into the open, but not quite, had released a lifetime of tension. It was as if everyone, including Father Abbot and Father Justin, had benefited from this, once they were assured that no major scandal had been caused for the other novices. Aelred felt that he had been heard. Benedict, Edward and he went through their monastic routine with a greater calm. They did not seek each other out. They observed the boundaries set by the rules. There was a way in which the community, sensing a danger which could threaten it at its heart, rallied a support which allowed the offending brother to feel integrated once more.

When Aelred arrived at the Abbot's study for his talk, the Abbot met him at the door and suggested that they stroll outside and go and sit in the sunken garden. He had asked Brother Julius in the kitchen to bring some tea and cake out on a tray. Together the Abbot and his novice talked under the wisteria arbour.

'There's colour in your face again, brother. You were so pale the other afternoon.'

'Yes, I feel much better, father, much better. I ...'

'Yes, you are much better.'

'I'm sorry for all this trouble I've caused everyone,' Aelred said apologetically.

'Now, now. We've all learnt something valuable here. I'm sure. Let's have some tea. And have a large slice of Brother Julius's fruit cake. I certainly will.' The Abbot, usually a very abstemious person, surprised Aelred with his enthusiasm for Brother Julius's cake. Aelred had not seen this side of the Abbot. He felt sure, though, he would say something wrong and spoil this newly found peace and accord. He cut the Abbot a slice of cake and took a mug of tea from him.

'In the lead up to your profession, brother, there is someone I would like you to see. Now, this is only a suggestion. I want you to have an interview, and if you feel this is what you would like, I'm going to offer you a chance to explore some of these - let's call them emotional problems.'

'Who do you want me to see, father?'

'Well, he is a man I've known for some time and comes very well recommended. He has helped us in the past. He is a good man, a great admirer of our life. Strangely, you know, he's not one of us, not a Catholic, but a man of great human insight, I think. I feel sure you would like Dr Graveson .'

'He's a doctor? What kind of doctor? 'Aelred began to be nervous. 'You don't think I'm mentally unstable, do you, father?

'Oh, nothing of the sort. Get that right out of your mind. Dr Graveson will explain it all. There's nothing further from the truth. It's entirely up to you.'

'Why do you think I need any kind of doctor?'

'Now, now. I won't suggest this if it's going to worry you. Dr Graveson is coming down from Bristol and will stay a couple days. You can see him initially, and if you wish to see him again we can arrange it.'

'What have you said to him about me?'

'Now, brother. I think it is right that we talk about our friend Aelred of Rievaulx.'

'Yes. I did find Aelred of Rievaulx helpful.'

'Yes, without doubt a very extraordinary man, a saint of the church. But the writings of the fathers have to be interpreted. In the wrong hands the scriptures can even be the instrument of the devil.'

'Yes, but -'

'What is absolutely clear is that Aelred of Rievaulx thought that carnal love was the road to damnation. That is certain. Now the other things he says are right and proper. Carnal love must be denied.'

'Doesn't he talk of transforming it?'

'Yes, but you can't transform it, brother. You have to pray that God in his mercy will. You have to avoid the occasion of sin. You see, if that had been followed in the first place, and I'm sure Father Justin advised correctly, a lot of our present trouble would have been avoided.'

'What about the things he says about holding hands and recognising attraction?'

'Yes, brother, things exist. St Aelred tried to deal with this abnormality in himself. I think you have to see that. He's very unique. Now this is where I think Dr Graveson can come in. He can do something about changing that.'

'Changing me?'

'Now, I don't want to go into it. Dr Graveson will be better at describing his work. The medievals had their way but we have ours. I think I want to try and use Dr Graveson's way to help us with using God's Grace. Because we must help ourselves if we want God to help us.'

Aelred felt that he could hardly swallow the fruit cake. He was to be changed.

'I think that this has been a good talk,' the Abbot said. 'Now I want you to try and return to monastic life, the normal routine. It is our routine, without distractions, which is our way. If we look after the little things the more difficult things will look after themselves.'

Aelred carried the tea tray back to the kitchen.

Edward looked worried and said, 'I think he's what you call a psychoanalyst. You talk to him and it helps you. He'll have to explain.' They stood in the library and Edward folded his hand over Aelred's.

'He wants to change me.'

'I saw Basil. He's been really inspiring. He says that we must use our love in our monastic life. There's no question of changing ourselves, as the Abbot suggests.'

Benedict was a little more alarmed. 'Well, you'll have to see. But when you talk to Dr Graveson, think carefully if you want to embark on this. My feeling is that we can cope. Look at Basil and Sebastian. There's nothing wrong with you.'

'The Abbot said that Aelred of Rievaulx was abnormal and what he did was to deal with his abnormality, for his time.'

'I've got permission to fast.'

'Also, I see that you are using the discipline.' Aelred was referring to the five-strand whip which he had seen on Benedict's bed.

'Yes I've had permission for a limited time.'

'Is this what I should do. Beat myself?'

'No. I don't think it would be appropriate for a novice. Basil has allowed me, though reluctantly.'

'I remember the monks at school doing this. We used to eavesdrop on Friday nights in the corridor of Mount Saint Maur, Ted and I, huddled in the dark giggling. We thought they used to beat their pillows.'

'Brother. This is serious.'

'Don't you think it's a bit extreme. Aelred of Rievaulx killed himself.'

'It's unusual, but it can help, with guidance. This will be a part of my retreat before my final vows. You must pray for me. You must help me.'

'I will. I won't be an occasion of sin.'

'Oh Aelred. You aren't. My love is strong. You will see. This gift, as Basil calls it, will help us.'

'Dr Graveson will change me, so that I can't love you.'

'He can't change you.'

'Then why am I going? I don't want to be changed.'

They stood silently, looking out of the library window over the park. Aelred said to himself, Jordan! He rose from a previous time, from an ancestral past of pain.

Not before have I experienced a love like this! There are the events of this place and the events on the island. There have been great omissions. Sins of omission. I have found them hard to describe. And believe me, at this time, I am in the throes of something my experience has not known before: the meaning of this love. My education, my social and political class have not prepared me for this. I must prepare myself. His life is preparing me.

Joe prepares me. Miriam prepares me.

I'm witness. This is a testament, a testimony. Witness for the prosecution. Witness for the defence. For I fear they will always be prosecuted.

As Joe says, We're still prosecuted.

Benedict took up what he later described to me as the responsibility he felt he had had for both Edward and Aelred, and in becoming the counsellor of their love - no easy task - he was himself stepping beyond any boundary he had known before. He was in fact finding a way to sanction a love the world as yet had no name for, except names of hate, ridicule and disowning. This is where I echo the early journals and Benedict's thought.

Joe says, The history has been obliterated. We have to rewrite it.

He gives me histories. At least what they show is that nothing is simple. There's never been one simple view of any of this. There are also a lot of conflicting views.

But, as Joe says, there has been more tolerance and understanding than we give history credit for. This must be the basis of our change.

Yes, Benedict retreated, then advanced, then retreated. I can understand. I have returned for this moment. And it is this which makes his sudden death such a loss, because I had hoped to go over a life with him and to bring all these meanings together with him, into one tapestry. I remain with fragments. I'm weary with reconstruction, with paraphrase. Tampering? Have I tampered? Tempered?

Joe says, That's all you can do.

Miriam says, That's what my work is. If I have a fragment I'm lucky; mostly I have dust in my hands and it tells me nothing, she says. You have more than dust. You have living memory, she says.

Fire is a metaphor. Blood is a metaphor. That is his poetry of pain.

Where does it leave me? Missing them all, his guides, now my guides. I meet them in words, in history.

Would I have kissed Benedict on the mouth? Funny how I keep considering this now. Like when I'm with Joe sometimes. We touch. It's in my culture to put my hand on his shoulder, to reach out and pull his shirt in the heat of discussion. He smiles. He says it reminds him of J. M.

You're so alike, Joe says. Then he says, No, you're not him.

Then I wonder. I mean, I could I do some of these things. Why am I not impelled in this way?

Why am I not impelled to feel these things for a woman? Joe asks. They are much more common, if we take statistics. But I might, I could, he says.

I have made myself J. M.'s scribe. Inscriber. What of me? What of my life? It's been changed.

I wake from a dream in which I am back at Malgretoute and an old black man tells me he remembers his father's father telling him that they hanged a black man from the silk cotton tree in the gully. They used to do that, he said. I wake to the darkness of the copper beeches outside my window. So red, they are purple, so purple, they are black, J. M. used to say. They rattle their empty branches. I wake worrying about Malgretoute. Krishna was on the phone yesterday. I have to go back home.

There is flame on the horizon.

From the window of the upper lodge room I saw it all again: the abbey, the valley, the spinney with the pond, the copse, the holly and laurel bushes, the copper beeches, the horse chestnuts. This is where I first learnt these names. Other words, other echoes. Ash. Ashton. Ashtown. Ashes. I have heard it said that they burnt down the first house at Malgretoute.

They burn it down, yes, the same man from my dream said.

I see the walk at the edge of Ashton Park. The one which leads to the quarry, that excavation. Time has altered things.

His name is not Aelred. J. M., my brother. But he grows in my mind, his pain and his visions, his love. So, that friend of his, that man, Benedict, we buried this week. So, so Ted, so those spirits from the past. So Aelred of Rievaulx, so Jordan, the letter J as clear as light carved in the moss on the Christian cross. So Edward. Time and memory. Memory and time.

Now these letters which tell their tale. I place them side by side. I sort them out, the ones I find here, the ones I had back from Benedict. For a conclusion. How to reach a conclusion to this *roman*, this romance, this sad love story of our time.

Abbaye de St Bernard
St Severin
Toulouse 29
France

15 September 1964

My dearest Aelred,
In order to avoid any danger of censorship, which would only exacerbate the situation at home and give Father Abbot more to deal with than he can understand and cope with at the moment, I am writing to you, *poste restante*, as you suggested. I regret we have to do this, but at the moment I think it is for the best. That is what I want for both of us. I too wish that we lived in a world where these feelings could be expressed and understood, where our love could shine. But it is not so, and maybe it has been given to us and our time to make that happen, as so much is changing, so much understood anew.
My dear friend, I want to say at once how much I miss you. But I also want to say that I think that this separation is for the good. When Father Abbot put it to me, I agreed to it for us. Yes, it fitted in with the plans for my study, and I must say the school

here is very good. There is a great group of monks from different abbeys in different parts of the world, and you would so enjoy the discussions about the different interpretations of monastic life which are being talked about and experimented with. The monks from America are particularly interesting and there are some Protestant monks from a new abbey in France. This school of theology is truly trying to be ecumenical.

But don't let me go off the point. The reason for writing is to draw close to you. This separation, these words, these letters are our new way, a truly good way to continue our original ideal of chastity and love. I feel I love you now more than ever. I feel a tremendous freedom in that love, and in being able to say it here, so openly, and knowing that you can read it, and reflect on it, and have it by you to help you through the difficult time you are having.

I am so happy that you have come to an accommodation with Father Abbot, and that things have continued to be peaceful since I left you. I am so happy to hear that Father Abbot has agreed to your profession in December. I know your vocation is secure and you must nurture it.

These have been the pains of growing, of finding ourselves. I feel I have grown tremendously in an understanding of myself and our love. It is you who have been so brave in expressing your feelings and risking yourself. Many others keep things hidden all their life and do not grow, and then, I agree with you, those repressed feelings manifest themselves in destructive ways. To know who one is is a tremendous freedom. The philosopher's injunction: know thyself.

Oh, I am so happy writing to you, talking to you, and I long for your next letter. With these words I look into your eyes, I touch you, I kiss you, my love. Yes, a year is a long time, but it will fly by when our lives are so full of new discoveries. And, as I said before, this separation is God's way of helping us to strengthen our chastity. That dangerous chastity which we embarked upon.

I think of Edward too, and know the danger for you. I plead with you to keep your eyes on your goal, December and your profession. For Edward I hope that he will complete his novitiate and eventually join you in professing his vows.

You must try to see things from the Abbot's point of view, understand how difficult it must be for him - all these changes in the church and in the world. I think he has shown great insight in soliciting the help of an analyst, now that I think about it from here. I've been talking to other monks about this and they think there is much to be gained in self-knowledge of this kind. This will be good for you and I look forward to hearing all about it, as much as you feel able to share.

Dear friend, I must leave you now, and in doing so, I embrace you with love and offer you peace in Christ.

Your dear friend,
Benedict

Poste Restante
Bristol
22 September 1964

Benedict, my dearest,
So excited to get your letter. Could not believe it
was there when the clerk went and looked in the
poste restante pigeon-hole. I feel like a naughty
schoolboy. I read it and read it just to feel you
near. Ashton Park is desolate without you. I miss
you terribly all the time. Yes, there is Edward. But
we have no comfort or peace in each other. We
have to avoid each other and see each other with
others, and the pain of that is not worth thinking
of. I am going along with Father Abbot. He is
kind and he has helped. I will try the analysis,
which is why I am here today and able to get your
letter - the best part of this whole thing. I feel so
depressed at the moment. Dr Graveson says that
it is to be expected. I am exhausted. I am exhausted
all day. I can hardly get up for Matins and miss it
very often and have to go and see the Abbot. It is
not him but the other senior monks in the council
who will not like that in the lead up to my profession
which I am excited about, yet I do wonder about
it and about carrying on. The Abbot and Dr
Graveson say I must not make any decisions at
the moment. Sometimes I feel so cruel to Edward,
so cruel. We are very careful though. Nothing
has happened again - not that I don't feel all
those feelings still, and I know this can pain you.
I don't want to cause you any pain, any more

than I already have, dearest. I love it that I can write and say what I want and unburden myself to you. You must let me do that because there is no one else. I am so happy for you, but it was cruel for the Abbot to move you so soon, so soon when I needed you so much. But you are better off without me. I hope this analysis will help. At the moment it makes me feel so terrible. I spend the whole day in the city just roaming around till my appointment, and then I go to bookshops after. I know so little of England, so little of this is known to me, cloistered at Ashton Park. I like to go to the port and I have found a cemetery that I like to go and sit in. Excuse me babbling on. Not a paragraph even. I want to finish this in the cemetery where I am sitting now and post it before I rush for the train.

I read your words over and over. I kiss you with this dearest, dearest friend, the only one I have in the whole world.

Aelred

Benedict,

I hasten to write again to say I am sorry I wrote such an emotional letter. Not saying anything. What is there to say? I think one thing one day and another day something quite different. I want to be calm. This is supposed to be calm. I am either very excited or very depressed. Dr

Graveson says that is normal. I am not sure about anything any more. I am not sure about my parents, about my faith, about monastic life, about who I am or what I should do. Dr Graveson has his own interpretation, and he tells me I must not read any theory. I do find it interesting reading Freud and Jung. He says that if I fill my head with theory I will read things into my situation. I have found a good library, and that's another place I visit if it's raining and I can't sit in the cemetery or go to the port. Dr Graveson talks of neurosis. I must say he is trying hard to get me to sort things out so that I can continue at Ashton Park, but I think this sorting out will eventually pose the question whether I should stay here or go on. He says that I am a classical example of an Oedipal situation, an over-loving mother and an absent father. I say fine, that fits the description. Understanding it does not make me feel differently. Either I feel happy when I come out of his office, or I feel angry, or depressed, or flat. I know what I feel because I feel it. I understand more. If this is understanding. What isn't happening yet is the meshing, I suppose: understanding and feeling. Dr Graveson says he wants me to get to the point where I can choose and choose for the right reasons. Dearest, here I am again just going on about myself and not a thought about you. None of this understanding makes me feel differently for you. Or Edward. Dr Graveson does not listen too carefully about what I say about you and Edward. He says things

will fall into place. I must go. Keep well and
write to me and tell me you love me. Still no
paragraphs.

Love, love, love,
Aelred

> Abbaye de Saint Bernard
> St Severin
> Toulouse 29
> France

2 October 1964

My dear Aelred,
I look forward to your letters so much. You sound
as if you are making a great deal of progress. It is
hard. Any self-examination will be hard. I too am
making a kind of analysis. I don't think I need it
formally; anyway, it is so expensive.
But I am looking at all that has happened again. I
am certain of my vocation, I am certain of my
affection for you, but I do want it to be lived out
within the vows of chastity. Those needs I have for
sexual love I will accept, but I want to sublimate
them into my contemplative vocation and my
ministry when I become a priest. I am beginning
to look forward to my ordination. I wonder what
Dr Graveson thinks about sublimation - taking
that sexual energy and utilising it for a greater task.
My theology lectures and seminars are very

interesting, and I am working very hard. Father Abbot would like me to come back home for Christmas and your profession. He was so good in thinking that I would like to be there. He is a good man really. But I don't think I should, as it is such a short break and I will lose ground gained in settling down here. So, much as I would love to see you, I am going to decide against the offer. I also think it is too soon for us to meet again. We must see this separation in a creative way, as a creative chastity. In the summer I am sure things will be quite different.

I don't mind you unburdening yourself to me. That is what friendship is about. Write to me and tell me all that you are doing and thinking.

Your dearest
Benedict

Abbaye de St Bernard
12 December 1964

Dear Aelred,
I have not heard from you for weeks. Father Abbot wrote for Christmas and mentioned that he found you so mature. He thought you were benefiting enormously from the analysis. He mentioned your profession. Congratulations and greetings in Christ. But I am worried you have not written. I hope all is well. This will also be my

wishes for Christmas. I hope that Christ will be reborn in you and bring you to that clarity of thought you seek so earnestly. Do write soon.

Your dear friend
Benedict

12 January 1965

Oh Benedict,
Life has been so awful. I am sorry I did not write before Christmas, or write about my profession, a beautiful ceremony, but I felt flat. I think I wanted it to transform me and it hasn't. The singing and the liturgy were beautiful, but I wonder for how long it will continue to mean something for me.
I have a lot to say but find it so hard to express it all. I don't know how to start to tell you what has been happening. It is so sad, so terrible, so - so that I can't imagine how my life has become like this. Father Abbot does not know half of what goes on in me or in his monastery. Yes, I am doing fine. Yes, I am mature. I wanted to make my profession, so of course I behaved myself as much as I could, but I wonder what I am doing. But I will go along with the analysis till, as I hope I will, I feel better and can make a clearer decision. It is Edward. I feel so terrible for him. I have deserted him. That is how it seems to him. Of course we are kept apart. We have to be very

careful in our meetings. I am getting help but I don't feel that he is. He needs help too and I don't know how to help.

Such terrible things happen sometimes that I feel so distressed. I feel so heartbroken. I wish you were here. This will hurt you, but what can I do? I don't feel it would be proper to talk to Dr Graveson about it. Though I might. Then he will sound so calm and dismiss it as immaturity. Immaturity is very hurtful, I can tell you. If it is immaturity.

One of the things I do with Dr Graveson when I have run out of dreams, is interpret pictures which he gives me or to paint pictures. Yes, I have paints and I just paint whatever comes into my head. I can't really paint like an artist, but that does not matter. Then we interpret what I paint. It brings up a lot of things. Now, Edward is quite a good artist. He was very good at school, so I thought, why does he not do the same? He wants to talk to me. He wants to show his love for me sexually. It is so strange: that was the last thing in his mind at the beginning, and now it is foremost. I wish he could have analysis too, but Father Justin says the monastery can't afford it and Edward would have to be nearer to making his profession, and that is not certain as yet.

I feel so drawn to him, yet I can't let myself respond. This is terrible. Sometimes when I enter the library and no one is there, Edward is there and he is standing there naked, looking at me. This happens at night or in the early morning. It happens when we are alone in the dormitory. It distresses me so much that I can't even speak to him about it. But now I have: I have told him it must stop. We can't carry on like this and I asked him to do some drawings about his feelings. Oh, Benedict, this will hurt you, but who else can I tell? He drew the most beautiful sketches of two men. They were of him and me making love, doing those things which we did in the barn. He says that he cannot draw us as chaste. I cry when I think of his pain, when I think of how there is not a world for us to live in and love each other like this. For if there were I would choose it. I think so. But I will not make any decisions now. Since the pictures, which reminded me of Ted, but above all of that night when we existed in another world in the barn, since then, I talk to Edward regularly now; I must. I must take the risk. I have elected with him that dangerous chastity which we had. I must give him this. I must give myself this, and I have reintroduced him to Aelred of Rievaulx and the theology of spiritual friendship. We find it hard but we are keeping our vows, or those vows I must keep. Please don't be jealous. This is real charity. I think Edward will leave. He talks like this. I try. I don't know what will happen. In a way the monastery, the community, cannot help when this kind of thing occurs. Either you're in or you're out. It's sad. I wonder what the world is like?

All my love,
Aelred.

St Bernard
14 February 1966

Dear Aelred,
Please be careful with your vocation. If Edward decides to leave, you must know that you have done all you can to help. But you must take care of your own commitment, your vows. For psychological reasons you found your profession flat, but nevertheless there is a reality and meaning to those vows and they must be taken seriously. I know you know this. I trust you. I am not jealous but I fear for that dangerous chastity. I feel that when I return to the abbey and we are together again it will not be a dangerous chastity but an achieved one. We will have achieved it.
You ask about the world. The world is a hard place. I go into the city here and I see things which make a life of virtue difficult, many temptations, many occasions for sin, but some people are called to live in the world, and endanger themselves. Please, my love.

Your dear friend,
Benedict.

18 June 1966

Dear Benedict,
Edward left Ashton Park this morning. It is a day

of terrible sadness for me. I think he has made the right decision; that is the only consolation. I feel desolate for myself and I am so fearful of the world for him; and part of me has left following him into the city. We have arranged to meet when I go to see Dr Graveson. He will try to look for a job in Bristol, so that he can live there and we can continue to meet. I know you will say this is so dangerous, but I must. I see no alternative. I have never seen anyone suffer such mental anguish in trying to contain his feelings for me, and trying with all sincerity to make a decision about his vocation. He was so good. He does not want me to leave and yet I know nothing would give him more joy than for me to join him. That which can give the most joy can give the most guilt and he says that he would feel so guilty if I left. He would feel responsible. Of course he would not be. I have talked to Dr Graveson and I know I must make the final decision about my vows quite apart from Edward. Yet I can't get him out of my mind and all he has to face in the world.

Yes, I do wonder about the world that I left so young and did not know. I wish you were here and I wished you could have been here to talk to Edward. Anyway, that is the end of a chapter. Things are more peaceful in a way because I found it so difficult helping Edward in the last two months.

I am sorry I did not write, but that is the reason, as you will understand.

Dr Graveson thinks I can start coming to him only once a month, which of course is good, but also horrible as it will affect how much I see Edward and how much I write to you. I won't be able to write to Edward from here.
Pray for me. I have such doubts.

Love,
Aelred

I place their letters side by side. They tell a story. A little story, a big story. A personal life. An era.

They put your brother through the wringer, didn't they? Joe says. This analysis! This attempt to change the poor boy. Psychological claptrap.

Joe! Miriam exclaims. I think J. M. thought he got something from the analysis, Miriam adds.

Yes, but you know all the usual clichés. Distant father, over-possessive mother, et cetera! Joe says with a flourish.

I know what J. M. thought, Miriam says.

We're not discussing dear J. M. We're discussing this poor nineteen-year-old, shipped off to a monastery because his teenage lover kills himself, probably.

Joe, Miriam says, annoyed. Think of Robert's feelings.

Robert knows how I feel. Joe looks knowingly at me. Then he has to suffer the insufferable Father Justin and that patronising abbot, before he's sent off to Graveson to shrink his young passion.

Joe is angry now.

Yes, but there was the lovely Basil. Doesn't he sound a

real sweetie? Miriam tries to lighten things. J. M. said he
was astonishingly nice and caring. Miriam smiles at me.

I let you construct the story that follows. Yes, I've selected
the material. I have placed it in a certain order. I've
paraphrased, and passion has spoken. But I can no longer
reconstruct, interpret and reinterpret. They had kept
each other's letters. Now, I, as archivist, as Miriam calls
me, receive them back again, receive what they gave to
each other, testimonies of their love. Confessions.

As I read I hear them in the flat. Laughter, crying,
tears. There is pain, loss. Talk, late into the night. Friends
come and go. A life of coming and going. Now I'm here,
bereft.

·

19 St John's Way

Bristol 8

Somerset

9 September 1967

My dearest Benedict,
I'm writing right away because there is so much
to say, and when I start to think it all out, I can't
put it down, so I must just start writing to you and
hope that what I say is what is in my heart, and
will be clear to you.
I know that somewhere I have hurt you, and for
that I'm sorry, though I know I can't erase it. And
I know that is so, because for you, as it is for me, it
is a moral question. It is almost metaphysical, the

difference between us. Yet we were one, the love
we had, questing after an ideal so perfect. That's
it! I came to see it not as my ideal, but as one
given to me, which masked my true nature. hat
ideal was what lay before me since I was very
small, and now,without it, I'm like a duck out
of water - or is it a fish - I never get English
expressions accurately. Perhaps they're both
awkward, out of the swim. I am.

I keep wanting the routine of the bell and the
office, my meals and my brothers around me,
and you. I miss you. And like last night, when
Edward came back from his job. God, it sounds
so strange. We both said that we missed the
community. It is so strange, me in this room
with Edward, he going out to a job, me still
here, waiting to know if I'm going to be able to
study or if I will have to return to Les Deux
Isles. That, of course, is another question. My
return.

As you know, there is a part of myself that must
return. There is unfinished business. How else
could it be? I left so young, not knowing anything.
But Dr Graveson says I must continue with him
for at least another year. You know he was
disappointed by my decision to leave Ashton
Park. He had wanted me to work towards an
integration which was within the monastic life.
Now I think he's scared of the enlarged dimensions
within which I must integrate. He doesn't really
accept Edward as a part of my real life. He sees it
all as a fantasy which will diminish in time. He's

not censorious, but neither is he approving. I've had this series of dreams in which a small black boy is climbing in through my bedroom window in my childhood home at Malgretoute and when I wake up I am terrified - in the dream, and also literally. He says it is my dark self, which I am fearful of confronting. I tell him that it was a childhood fear of mine, and that I lived in a country with black people whom I was taught to fear, not to love. Had he not heard of the slave trade, the plantation society? A tropical collective unconscious. I was talking as if I were an expert. Yet, I was so conscious of how little I know. So much I need to return to, in order to understand. He cut short the session. He dismisses this. A huge chunk of my life dismissed by one of the most brilliant men in the psychoanalytical world. Can you imagine it? I've told him about Jordan too! Because I still see him, talk to him, and of course I feel I have betrayed him, by leaving his grave untended, by leaving his portrait unvisited, and I may never walk again in Ashton Park where he was killed. Murdered. I know you think all this sounds fanciful, but there are these disjunctions in my life which I must yoke together if I am to survive. Aelred's sin, I call it.

Near here, near the port, there is a cemetery and there are other graves. I visit there and think of him. I have found the names of many others, many, many, so many without names. Buried at the end of a journey. So many buried at sea on that fatal triangle.

I go off at a tangent, and I really want to talk to you. I will this letter to get through the abbot's censor.

Yes, it is a moral question, and I hope that in time we will respect each other in this, in order to regain some of the old belief and love. It is not, as I've said before, that I could not continue to love you, but that I could not continue to pretend to be living as one who has taken the vow of chastity. Your ordination was a sign of a final separation.

I know that at the moment the church does not recognise anything which my love for Edward represents. It is indeed the love that has no name, the love that must not be spoken. For me it has a name. It is brotherly love. It is my need for a brother. Some need a sister, a wife, a mother, a father, and I need my brother. My friend. I admit that I myself don't fully understand it. I am not clear about any of it. I was certain enough to know that I had to leave Ashton Park to be with Edward and that I do want to express my love physically and sexually in a full way. That was not possible for either of us at Ashton Park. It was never possible for me as young boy to conceive of my love for Ted as really legitimate. It was a sin. I call it Aelred's sin.

I hope you will be able to come and see us. We both need to talk to you.

I will write again soon and I hope to hear from you.

My love,
Aelred (I still use the name, for how long? I don't know)

Then the letters got fewer and fewer. Or I have not found them; what about that lay brother's cleaning out of the cell. Incineration. The journeys. Time. Odd that Edward should've continued to live in the same flat all these years.

19 St John's Way
Bristol 8
Avon

26 September 1983

Dear Benedict,
It has been a long time and I hope you are still there. It is like old times and there is no one else for me to write to.
Edward died this summer.
He wrote to me in Les Deux Isles (you knew I had returned, as I put it then, following my Jordan story and looking again for my memory of Ted - so strange that he was the diminutive of Edward) - telling me of his illness. He was seriously ill and they had no idea what the matter was.
Benedict, I could have written back and hoped for his recovery. You know a little of how Edward and I eventually parted, how that love we risked so much for could not hold, had little to hold it up at first, no community to give it recognition, no traditions, no laws, no rules. They allowed us nothing but secrecy and anonymity. You know how I lost him and he lost me in the quest for our

desire, thinking it was a kind of freedom. How it seemed that if we were made into criminals we acted that way. It seemed that the one thing, the pleasure that men can have together in each other's bodies, being so denied, so outlawed by church and state, made it the narrow quest of so many of us. There are those who have reached in and reached out from our prisons. A way to say: this is who we are. They allowed us places outside the city, those places where those who died of the plague are buried. They allowed us dark places in the city. Alleyways, dives, seedy cinemas, public lavatories where we scratch our messages of desire. Their law for consenting adults in private, a protection for the rich and powerful against blackmail. There were some of us who luckily found in a wider freedom both love and desire. We need those men so much now. We need the work that so many are doing to unearth the writings, the history, the poetry, the stories of the long and arduous quest to give this love, a legitimacy, a name, as we see it happening, and now again so cruelly threatened and misunderstood. We need the freedom of the law, our own emancipation. Fortunately, there seems to be a determination which is stronger than death.

I came back to him, Benedict. I thought to write to you then and ask for your support. I came back to him. I nursed him to the end. Allow me this, Benedict, this outpouring. A more quiet truth must be written some time.

There was little the doctors could do; nothing

seemed to work. They didn't know what to do. They allowed me to take him back to his home. I met some courageous men who helped, friends of Edward's. Now friends of mine. Men like these labour now for other sick they keep reporting.

This was at the end of the summer. Then it seemed a long journey to the end. He hung on through bouts of pneumonia. I was so frightened by his suffering and his wasting away. He became so thin. Then he developed what the doctors called a rare cancer. The sarcomas appeared like purple blotches all over his body. Oh, Benedict, I had loved that body. He had been so beautiful. So known to me and yet so unknown. We drove each other away with our desire for and against each other and others.

We came and went from each other. I'm so grateful for the last months, weeks, days.

There had been great days! It was a good love.

In the last days it seemed as if he had become transparent, so thin and white he had become. Night sweats. Fevers. Raging. Frightening. His eyes so wide and staring in his head, his sarcomas like purple roses blooming on his skin. He was so thirsty. Always by his bed a bowl of ice, and I held the cubes to his dry thin lips. Between the drugs and encephalitis, I think Edward saw the world he left as an hallucination.

I only hope that his visions were good ones. I know that some were bad ones. I knew his nightmares. I hope he realised somewhere the love for each other which we recovered.

I want to come and see you and talk about these times. I only hope you are there. What will I do if you are not?
Write soon.

All my love as usual,
Jean Marc (Aelred)

I don't know if they ever met. Benedict did not talk of that meeting, he talked only of earlier ones. The one referred to here, he must have kept a secret.

'I want to come and see you and talk about these things. I only hope you are there. What will I do if you are not?

Write soon.

all my love to mama,
Jean Marc (Aelred)

I didn't know it then, ever since that morning, he talked only of earlier ones. The one referred to here, he must have kept absent.

Epilogue

It was my last evening in the flat in Bristol, and Joe and Miriam prepared dinner. I got a bottle of rum. Real rum.

None of that Navy stuff, Joe said.

Miriam excelled herself with recipes she had found in a West Indian cookery book: chicken fricassee and curried shrimp. These are prawns, she said. Rice and peas, melangen grantin.

My favourite, pumpkin, she made into a soup. I got the avocados for the salad. These are zaboca, I said.

We were all doing the washing up, standing in the kitchen. A favourite place for English parties, I've discovered, leaning up on the fridge and sink, drinking and joking. It felt like we were avoiding something. Joe had been avoiding it for months now.

In the corridor outside J. M.'s old room, Joe and I stood up and talked. Like we couldn't sit down.

You must take it all, if you want to. You should take his academic papers, that one called 'Atlantic Junction: Toxteth, Brixton, St Paul's'. I think we'll take the rest to Oxfam. Miriam and I have chosen our mementoes. Small things, like this photograph. Have I shown you this one? 1967! The year of consenting adults! Joe said cynically. On the steps of the student union in Bristol. That's where we all met. Edward read History, J. M. English and History, and me, Sociology and Politics. We were educated for the sixties: '68 was Paris and Prague! We went through everything together. That story you've been piecing together, Joe said, is a horror show as far as I'm concerned.

But there were ironies. Here is another photo I've kept. Polonecks and jeans. Their hair is already getting long. Barmouth in Wales. We'd speeded up to Shropshire in an old mini to visit Ed's parents. I remember them loving Tintern Abbey. J. M. quoted Benedict quoting Wordsworth as we drove along the Wye. 'O sylvan Wye! thou wanderer thro the woods,/ How often has my spirit turned to thee!' He leant over from the back and put his arms around Ed's neck. He was always doing things like that.

They got cold feet in Shropshire. Ed couldn't face his father. He wanted to 'come out' in '68. Imagine! I had an aunt in Barmouth with a guest house, so we went off there. It was hot. The hillsides near the estuary were purple with wild rhododendrons and shimmering with yellow gorse. High mountains sheer to the Irish Sea. In the distance mountains in haze.

Reminds me of islands, J. M. said.

It blew our minds. I think we were high anyway. Look at how young and lovely they are. I'll make you some copies of these and send them out to you. All the way in the car we sang along to 'Are you going to San Francisco, be sure to wear some flowers in your hair.' I had some hash and we got high, falling about on the grass where we stopped for a picnic. 'There's a strange vibration, people in motion.' We giggled so much.

I remember, when were were sorting out the sleeping arrangements at my aunt's, J. M. saying, It's not much different out here, is it? We can't hold hands in the street. We worry about being caught sleeping together. It's

worse, he said, in some ways. I saw 'QUEER' written up on
the wall on the seafront.

I remember that time vividly. It was odd being with
them, lovers who had been lovers in a monastery. There
was a kind of other-worldliness about them. Don't get me
wrong. They loved having sex. In the evening, we walked
on the front. 'Under the boardwalk, down by the sea ...'
we sang along with The Drifters.

Near a funfair, J. M. suddenly ran off in the direction of
the square. Right there, standing all alone was a black guy
playing a steel tenor pan.

J. M. said, God that music! I've not heard it in years. I
would know it anywhere.

Ed said, Ask him where he's from. J. M. was shy. Ed said
teasingly, which I didn't understand at first, Bet his name
is Jordan.

J. M. was absorbed. Then he turned and poked Ed in
the ribs playfully. The metallic notes bounced off the steel
basin. We tapped our feet, moved our hips. J. M. said,
Calypso, man! Hear that calypso music!

Joe couldn't stop talking. He was circling in the small
space of the corridor playing with the photographs in his
hands all the while he was talking.

I've never told you, have I?

I knew what he was talking about and I said, No. You
want to, so tell me. I want to hear. We sat on the bed in
J.M.'s empty room. I pictured it as Joe talked. Ed's dying
was bad enough. It was I who wrote and told J. M. to come
back. I knew he would. I couldn't cope on my own. You
should've seen your brother: he was not that indulgent
romantic of the story you piece together. No, I loved him,
really, in '67! Don't mind me. He was a practical, caring

man who sat by Ed's bed and nursed him. We took it in shifts. A year ago we didn't know as much as we know now. I expect we took a lot of risks. He had the works, that rare cancer with horrid sarcomas. The sweating was the thing, having to repeatedly change him through the night, high temperatures, raging, frightening. My memory of J. M. at that time is him sitting by the bed in the other room, the one Miriam now uses. Sitting there putting ice cubes to Ed's mouth. His mouth was a grey line. He hallucinated about his mother a lot. You know he sort of lost his mother when he was young. He used to see her at the door to his room. She had been ill and had to be away from home. His father did come and visit him when he was in hospital. He didn't want to come to the flat.

But with J. M. it was different. It was very gradual at first. It was an ordinary cold and cough which just wouldn't go away. I would hear him coughing at night. I still hear that cough in the flat sometimes when I'm in on my own. But he had the fevers, the night sweats. There was an early bout of pneumonia which miraculously he recovered from. It left him wasted. His breathing became difficult. He needed oxygen. As you see, we've never taken back the cylinder. He had terrible pain, which they gave him morphine for, so we would lose him for days. It became too much and we had to take him to casualty. Then bring him home again when he was recovered, for more often than not they needed the bed.

Miriam was brilliant. She came to live here. She had always been fond of J. M. since that time I took him back home as a student. What shocked her was the cancer. He used to call them his sunspots. It was extraordinary how handsome he remained despite his gauntness and the grey pallor.

Joe twirled the photographs in his hands.

He had nightmares. He would call out in the night. Sometimes I or Miriam had fallen asleep. It was very tiring. He often dreamt of Les Deux Isles. He would describe these lurid dreams, always full of tropical ferns and lilies and heavy rain. He would describe the house at Malgretoute and the cocoa hills. I think these were caused by the morphine. He dreamt of Ted, the waterfall. The whole Ted thing came back, all that awful teenage stuff. It was as if his whole life was being played back as a Spielberg film. The past returned as a terror. He mentioned you. He tried to talk about you.

He said, I have a younger brother whom I don't know. I haven't been able to get to know him.

The names of your sisters popped up: Chantal, Giselle.

He recalled your mother's death. Her dresses, he said. I remember her dresses hanging in her press. I went and smelt them. And Dad... then his voice faded.

But he wouldn't let me write. He once said that despite all the work he had done on himself he could not bring himself actually to say to any member of his family that he was gay. Somehow, that very deep sense of sin, shame, never left him. Catholicism, a pernicious religion! Joe said, characteristically. Miriam wasn't there to moderate him.

Joe's voice goes on in my head. The two photographs arrived today. Krishna brought them up in the post. I've propped them up on my desk on the verandah where I do the estate work.

J. M. and Edward.

Joe's voice is under the rain which is falling in the cocoa. Like an English summer's rain. Now I make the comparisons.

He asked me to plant some hyacinth bulbs and put them in the dark, Joe continued. He said that I must bring them out in in February or March and put them on the windowsill. I saw him look as far as the window and stop. I thought he must've wondered how far his future stretched. Always, from his student days he had hyacinths in the spring. What did he say the smell brought back? The pomme arac! There were geraniums in the summer. Always red, in terracotta pots. Funnily, though, he would often say of the plants, I've got to clear these out and get some other fragrances in my life. There was always a hankering for a monastic cell.

Miriam was out. I was there alone with him. Miriam promised she would get back early, but there was some hold-up at her work. He was in and out of consciousness. He wouldn't go into hospital. He begged me not to put him into hospital. He said, Let me leave from here, Joe. The effort to breathe was intense, but he didn't always want the mask on.

He called for Benedict. Is that you, Benedict? Benedict, my love, he said. After all these years! He called for Edward to come and get him. I think he's coming, Joe, he said, and turned his head towards me. It was a real effort to turn his head. His eyes were crossed. The doctor had said something was going in the optic nerve.

I was standing looking out of the window watching the bulbs grow. I heard something different, like a gurgle. I turned around to look at him. He was gone.

When I took his hand there might have been some

consciousness there. I was alone with his body for half an hour before Miriam got back.

Thank you Joe, I said.

Now, again, Thank you.

I wanted to tell you, he said. The rest you know: his ashes sprinkled in the cemetery with the African heads where he had sprinkled Ed's.

Yes, yes.

The rain was coming in at the window, Joe said.

I hear the drip of the rain in the cocoa. The scent of pomme aracs rise from the garden below the window at Malgretoute.